The Case of Emily V.

by the same author

Brain Mechanisms and Mind
Perceptions and Representations
Selves in Relation
Best Laid Schemes

Keith Oatley

The Case of Emily V.

First published in Great Britain in 1993
by Martin Secker & Warburg Limited,
an imprint of Reed Consumer Books Limited,
Michelin House, 81 Fulham Road, London SW3 6RB
and Auckland, Melbourne, Singapore and Toronto

Reprinted 1994 (three times)

ISBN 0 436 32602 7

A CIP catalogue record for this book
is available from the British Library

Phototypeset in 12/15 Perpetua by Wilmaset Ltd, Birkenhead, Wirral
Printed in Great Britain by
Mackays of Chatham plc

for Jennifer

Preface

There can have been few previous occasions on which lost writings by two celebrated authors have been discovered simultaneously. I was fortunate enough to make just such a discovery. Some manuscripts came into my possession through the will of a relative. One was a case history by the founder of psychoanalysis, Professor Sigmund Freud. Another was an account by Dr John H. Watson describing a case of the famous detective Mr Sherlock Holmes. There is little doubt that the manuscripts are genuine, since I have had them authenticated by experts who have agreed not to discuss the matter until this book is published.

As if it were not enough to come upon these two manuscripts, a third was with them, and it throws new light on the work of the two investigators. It was written by my relative. It is in the form of a diary which becomes a narrative. Had this account been published when it was written it would have shocked its readership. It may be considered shocking even now, but from the distance of nearly a century we may contemplate what is described with a degree of detachment.

Because their methods were in some ways similar, there has been speculation as to whether Sigmund Freud, whose work started later than that of Sherlock Holmes, was influenced by

Holmes. The novelist Mr Nicholas Meyer has written a story in which Freud and Holmes met.* Mr Meyer's work is of course fiction, and very excellent it is too. By contrast this book is an account of events that did actually happen – the two men did meet, but rather than Holmes having influenced Freud's development it is clear that until this meeting they had proceeded independently. The case recorded here was one of the last to be written by Dr Watson, and so we are not well placed to trace Freud's influence on Holmes subsequently. How much influence Holmes had on Freud as a result of the meeting will be a subject for scholarly debate.

Freud and Holmes met because they were both investigating the same person, my relative. In the summer of 1904, while she was receiving treatment from Freud, Holmes began to suspect her of being involved in the death of her guardian, who was a British diplomat. For Freud the case was intended to provide evidence that sexual molestation during early life, sometimes described by his women patients, was fantasy rather than reality. For Holmes it marked a transition from his usual practice as a consulting detective to employment on secret commissions of the British government.

I have edited these materials lightly. I have translated Freud's manuscript into English, preserved the pseudonym chosen by Freud, 'Emily V', and expanded her name to Emily Vincent elsewhere in the account. I have also arranged the material in three books, and given titles to the chapters. To allow the reader to follow the flow of events I have interspersed segments of Emily's journal and narrative with the other two accounts. All the footnotes in the text are mine; I have provided them to clarify some technical concepts and to give references to works that are mentioned, where these might be obscure.

*In *The Seven Per-Cent Solution*.

Readers of Freud's works and of Watson's may notice that their writing here contains reflections that may be considered injudicious. No doubt this is due to the manuscripts being drafts: neither was brought fully to a conclusion, and neither had been subject to the usual preparations for publication. It seems that neither author saw fit to write anything further on this case.

In this book, however, the ending of the story is revealed. The conclusion is given by Emily Vincent, as also are the reasons why neither Freud nor Watson published the manuscripts on which they were working and which later came into my hands.

Enough of these introductions: the principals can, I think, speak for themselves.

Book 1   Confession

Confession. **1**. A making known or acknow-
ledging of one's fault, wrong, crime, weakness, etc.

Shorter Oxford English Dictionary

1

Emily's Journal

Thursday 12 May 1904

Sara has insisted that I consult a physician. I lie all day in bed but am unable to sleep. If I do I am pursued by evil dreams. Is it the dreams that are evil, or is it I myself? I pass my time thinking of how I might die. I cannot live with what I have done. He was an unspeakable man, but God will not forgive me. I think of poison, of drowning, of fires. I fear to be so much alone. Waking and sleeping I dwell upon his death, then upon my own.

Sara has brought me to her house, and her cook makes me soup, but I become nauseous if I should smell it or even see it. I try to be polite but I cannot eat it. Sara wants me to consult a physician who was known to her family. Her father visited me to explain that this man helped people who were troubled. They think that I am troubled for no reason. I know that I cannot eat or sleep or even live because I killed Charles S.

There it is. Written on paper. I killed a man.

Here I am writing this down. Perhaps I will write in Greek, then no one will understand it, should I be careless. No, I will write in English. Then it can just blurt out, as it seems to wish, of its own accord. Few people here can read English.

Sara brought me to her house since she says I am certainly ill, and must be attended. It is true. I am ill. I have a sickness of the soul.

Friday

I went to see the physician today: Dr Freud, or rather Professor Freud. His rooms are in the Berggasse, which is only about five minutes' walk from my lodgings, but a much longer journey from Sara's house. There is a wide entrance next to a butcher's shop. One goes under an archway, and before one reaches the courtyard at the back of the house one turns to mount a few steps on the right-hand side. Then the door of his consulting rooms is facing. The Professor has busts and other antiquities in his rooms, which seem friendly to me. I have to lie on a sort of *chaise-longue*. It is by no means comfortable. He sits behind me while I am required to talk. He says his treatment is a talking cure.

The whole procedure smacks of the most outright char-latanry, but I caught myself thinking when I was with him that maybe he could help me. There seems to be something serious and reliable about him. He has helped others. Maybe they also have been wicked. This is an irrational thought. I grasp at a straw. How can he or any person help me, since I have done what I have?

He asked me to speak of my past, of my parents, of their death, of my guardian, of my godmother. I told him what I could, but why do I speak to him at all? The worst of it is that he insists that he is unable to treat me in just one visit. I must see him again tomorrow, and the next day, and the next. The treatment he prescribes lasts for weeks or months. He recommends that I go every day at least until the middle of July, when he takes his holidays.

His treatment requires that I tell him everything that is on my mind: 'Candidly,' he said, 'and with no attempt to censor it for my benefit.' It is impossisble to imagine anything more utterly absurd: 'Please, Professor Freud, I am a murderess and I am tormented by thoughts of what I have done. No, I have not given myself up to the police. I am a coward. I feel too frightened of what will befall, and I do not wish my friend Sara to think badly of me.'

Why do I spend what little money I have on this? I could use it to escape to South America, to the other side of the world. His fees are quite expensive, and it is folly to become responsible for a large bill that will mount each day. Perhaps, if I am not going to live for much longer, that need not be a concern. He says I should come each day except Saturdays and Sundays. I think he wanted me to attend on Saturdays too, except that he did not have a time that was free.

I have agreed to see him. I go because of Sara, because she wishes it. Not to go, after her kindness, would be cruel, ungrateful. Without her I know I would simply kill myself, perhaps throw myself from a high place. It is the distress it would cause her that keeps me from it.

I think about him continually. Him, him. Charles S, yet more inescapable now he is dead than when he was alive. What can I call him as I write this. Mr S? Or perhaps just S, a cipher; but signifying what? A serpent?

Really, why am I writing this? I began yesterday evening because Sara had arranged the appointment with Professor Freud.

There has been nothing in the newspaper about a body being found. Sara brings me a newspaper each day. I have tried to appear nonchalant, but yesterday I was unable to restrain myself from perusing it while she was with me. She must have wondered why, when I take so little interest in anything else. How can his body not have been discovered? It is six days since it

9

happened. The body may not be visible from places that people go, but by now someone might have found it. Perhaps it has lodged somewhere that is impossible to see, or impossible to reach. Perhaps, even, he did not fall far. Perhaps he was just stunned for a short time and recovered. Then he will pursue me again, with my guilt at pushing him away in such a dangerous place a further means of persecuting me.

People must be looking for him. Perhaps Mrs S is worried. I think she is not a bad woman. Perhaps in English newspapers there are reports that he is missing. I bought an English newspaper today after I had been to see the Professor, but there is nothing in it. When each day has passed and nothing has happened, I even feel reassured. If the body were not found then I would only have to live with myself, would not need to disgrace others, not disgrace Sara.

I am guilty. Why do I not simply give myself up?

A small movement passes through my mind that maybe I dreamt that he followed me. When I think about this, it cannot be so. The recollection is too real. I can almost convince myself that it was a dream, like one of the daydreams I used to have, when I wanted only to escape. Is this a germ of hope? Perhaps I have already picked up some idea of the Professor's, that the mind may be deceiving me. But I remember the clothes that I wore. My dress was torn. Tomorrow I will go to my rooms, to see that torn dress.

2

Address to the
Psychological Wednesday Society
by Professor Sigmund Freud
A Case in Progress

Gentlemen, I wish to set before you this evening some preliminary reflections upon a case which is as yet unfinished, and in which I have made notes of the exchanges that have occurred while they were fresh in my memory immediately following each session. These relatively confined surroundings offer me an opportunity to discuss with you the unpolished product of a work in progress, or perhaps more correctly something like the initial stage of an archaeological excavation where the upper layers have now been uncovered. You will see in places some pieces of rough terrain not yet properly explored, and occasionally you may hear a sharp sound as the spade inadvertently hits the marble of a valuable monument when perhaps a more delicate clearing of the earth might have seemed appropriate. I do not apologise for these imperfections. They are part of the process of discovery. Already we will be able to see outlines of the site, with some of its main structures visible, though we suspect that at the next stage further structures will emerge, as yet barely suspected, which will contribute to our understanding of what we now see.

The subject of this case is twenty-five years of age. She is a young Englishwoman of unusual accomplishments. I shall call her Miss Emily V. At the age of eighteen she journeyed to America.

She has translated two books of German philosophy and aesthetic theory, as well as having rendered versions of Sophocles' classic dramas into English. She had been working for two years as a teacher, by which means she had supported herself. More lately one of her translations has, I understand, begun to achieve some popularity in the United States and has started to earn royalties which, although they are not large, enable her to supplement her small income.

The patient had been referred to me by a friend in our city, a man I greatly respect. His daughter, a young widow, who was my patient's colleague at the school at which they both taught, had become alarmed at her behaviour. Miss Emily, a normally responsible person, had taken to her bed when she had been expected to give an address to parents on the subject of moral virtue, at the Founder's Day at her school.

Barely an hour before the ceremony was due to begin, Miss Emily was discovered by her friend, not yet risen from her bed, and declaring herself quite unable to speak in public on moral virtue or any other subject. She was, she said, unworthy of any influence over the young, and she was therefore unable to fulfil her duties. She was of course dismissed from her post, though I rather suspect that the parents at the school were pleasantly surprised not to have to endure a learned disquisition from an earnest young woman. Since then, Miss Emily became anorexic, having virtually ceased to take nourishment. What concerned her friend most of all was that she had constantly spoken of suicide, and hinted at crimes she said she had committed that were too heinous even to imagine. It would be better, she had said, if she simply ceased to exist.

This young woman interested me because by her own efforts she had achieved some success. Although her literary work could not be considered creative or original, it nevertheless indicated a level of accomplishment uncommon in members of her sex. At the same time, her symptoms, as they were described to me at third hand by her friend's father, were of a kind that are all too commonplace, and typical of women whose education was far inferior to Miss Emily's.

It was this discrepancy between the attainments of this young woman, and her distressing but banal complaints of anorexia and melancholia with a tendency to suicide, that interested me. The task, as it appeared to me, was to discover why this discrepancy existed.

In the manner in which I now treat these cases, I started by explaining to Miss Emily that she should first give me an account of her life up to the present time, as it occurred to her, without withholding anything even if she might deem it irrelevant. Then during our consultations she was to say whatever came to mind without trying to censor it.*

I have enough experience in this method now to expect that the key to the mystery in this case, as in others, would be found not in what the patient deliberately says, which too easily allows of artifice, but that it would come into my hands from those productions of the patient that are unconscious. Dreams and unconsidered manners of speech would provide the clues I sought.† I was confident that we would encounter such phenomena soon enough.

Before I come to them I shall give the story she told me, abbreviated in the interests of this presentation, but in outline and details, essentially as it was related.

Miss Emily is the only child of a diplomat. The family had lived abroad when she was young, and she reported that they had been happy. Her mother had been a cheerful and even-tempered

*These are the instructions for 'free association' which around this time became the main method of Freud's psychoanalysis.
†Freud is evidently wishing to use the methods laid out in his *Interpretation of Dreams*, and in *The Psychopathology of Everyday Life* in this case.

woman. She had been sociable and did not tire of contributing to the round of diplomatic life, making calls on wives of other diplomats, particularly those whom she thought found the life irksome. She had been a Quaker. Her husband had been brought up a Catholic, though Miss Emily thought her father had not been scrupulous in observing the requirements of his church. She told me that there had been no tensions between her parents because of these differences, though her mother's strong religious beliefs had had a considerable influence on her own upbringing.

The young Emily's father would amuse his wife and daughter with imitations of people he met, and he would describe events in the world of diplomacy in humorous ways. Most unusually for a man of his rank, he took an interest in his daughter's education. He himself tutored her from an early age in Latin and Greek. This may have indicated that the father had wished that she were a boy; this in turn could have had effects on the child's development. Emily could not discover any corroboration of this conjecture, though she said that many of her fondest memories were of discussing with her father the adventures of Odysseus, or the life of ancient Athens. On family holidays the three of them would visit sites of classical antiquity, and Miss Emily had vivid memories of Delphi, of the Caryatids who hold up the roof of the Erechtheion on the Acropolis, and of the island of Delos, on which she had been fascinated to learn that nobody was allowed either to be born or to die.

When Emily was but thirteen years old, tragedy befell her family. They were living at the time in London, but her parents had been for a few days in Paris on diplomatic business, whilst she had remained in London with her governess. The building in which her parents were staying caught fire one night. The occupants of the upper rooms perished, and they included Emily's father and mother.

Emily's grief was exacerbated by a considerable change in her circumstances. Because she had no close relatives, her father's will had specified that she be cared for by her godparents, another diplomatic family. She said her guardian and his wife treated her with some consideration, but she found that her life with them became less and less easy for her to bear. Her father's will had stipulated that at the age of eighteen she could choose how to employ her modest inheritance, though I understand she believed that her guardian maintained some legal jurisdiction. She used some of her inheritance to attend a recently established university for women in Pennsylvania. She had a little money left over, though barely enough to allow her to live comfortably without either marriage or some gainful occupation.

It was at the American university that she completed her education, becoming proficient in Greek, Latin, French – and German, which she speaks as well as we do. In America too she started translating and achieved her first published works.

I asked why it was that she had determined to pursue an education in America. Her answer was haughty: 'Do you think then that only the male members of our species should be allowed an education?'

I replied, 'If your guardian and his wife had been considerate to you, why should you wish to interpose three thousand miles between them and yourself?'

'There is consideration and consideration,' she remarked, and would say no more on the subject. Since the end of our hour together had arrived, since also it was a Friday and I was not to see her again until the following Monday, I said we too should need to allow some distance between us, and that I would see her again after the weekend. I forbore from remarking what she knew as well as I, that she was determined to conceal more than she revealed.

None of what I have told you so far may seem to warrant your attention. Nor does it seem remarkable that Miss Emily was for the most part dejected and preoccupied as she described her life to me. She would enter with her eyes downcast as if ashamed, and although polite in every respect she seemed agitated, and was eager to leave when her consultation finished.

None the less, I exhort you to bear with me. To my experienced eye her demeanour sounded a false note. She was acting as if some great evil had befallen her. She was moody, reluctant to speak, and I had to prompt her often. At times she would sob, and beg me to pardon her for doing so. At other times she would describe how she found it difficult to think of anything but suicide, and that the world would be better without her. This manner, of course, would be consistent with a diagnosis of melancholia, were it not for occasional outbursts of a quite different kind, when she would speak with a sharp intelligence that was sometimes directed at myself.

She said that she would be unable to obtain another teaching post now that she had been dismissed, even if she were competent to care for young people, which she was not. She said she had enough money to pay my fees for a limited period, but her small income would not be enough to live on. Seeing me, she said, seemed her only hope, her only possibility of regaining an equilibrium which she felt she had previously achieved, but which was now quite lost. She stressed the word 'equilibrium', a distinctive term I thought. I asked her about it and she said that it derived from physics, which she had studied with her friend Sara.

Now that teaching in this city was ruled out, it was not easy, she told me, for a woman in her position to earn a living if one excluded prostitution and the giving of seances. This was again said in a disconcerting manner that contrasted markedly with the rest of her comportment.

I asked why she felt it necessary to speak to me so sharply. I said it seemed odd that she should imply that if one excepted teaching posts the only occupations open to women depended on taking advantage of either moral weakness or spiritual gullibility. Miss Emily's fire was then directed squarely at me. Indeed, whenever I made any observations touching on the occupations of women or their place in society she would immediately take the opportunity to give me a stern rebuke.

One such was earned by my enquiry about whether a young woman in her circumstances might not achieve a more secure livelihood by marriage.

'Exactly,' she observed. 'The only respectable occupation for a woman is to take care of a man. Is that how you see your own life, Professor, as one to be lived in subservience to someone of the opposite sex?' I could only suppose that it was in America that Miss Emily had acquired such views. I was not able to refrain from asking whether her opinion was a result of education in a women's university.

I now regret having asked this question, and I had occasion to apologise for it at our next meeting. It is important at this point to explain why. I have discussed in my cases with Breuer* that often in treatment a patient is reminded by the physician of some person in his past, often a parent. A false connection is sometimes made and I have called this transference. When it occurs the patient is unable to avoid acting towards the physician as he has towards some figure from the past. Here was Miss Emily speaking to me with considerable acerbity, while shortly beforehand she had been saying that treatment by myself was perhaps her only salvation in her perplexity. In such contradictions the key to cases of this kind will be found.

The physician may not always find it easy to recognise such manifestations for what they are, and I have to confess that I myself was not quick enough to recognise the signs. Instead I

*Freud and Breuer, *Studies on Hysteria*.

17

allowed myself to be provoked. In retrospect I have no doubt that, rather than responding in the way that I did to Miss Emily's remarks on what she distastefully called 'feminism',* I should have taken the opportunity to observe that it seemed that someone in her earlier life, perhaps her father or her guardian, had given her a very poor opinion of men.

This, indeed, is what I did later say, when the next day I made my apology to her. As I did so, I observed that she was struck by this suggestion, saying: 'No, not my father, he was a kind man: I loved him dearly. I respected him, and I miss him more than I can say.'

'Your guardian, then?'

'In that,' she said, 'you might be right. No doubt he had many qualities, but the ability to inspire respect in me was not one of them.'

'You say he had many qualities. Does he not still have them?'

After a long pause Miss Emily said, very slowly, and deliberately: 'I have not seen him for a considerable period. I do not know what qualities he may now have.'

She went on to describe how her guardian had substantial presence. He was an urbane man, though not a warm one. His preoccupation seemed to be his collection of paintings. He had been taken with the works of the French Impressionists. Miss Emily said that collecting had become a passion more important, she thought, than his diplomatic career.

'Mostly,' she observed, 'the paintings were of unclothed women of ample proportions, and they occupied the walls of his house.'

In her guardian's manner towards his wife Miss Emily told me that he alternated between disdain and condescension. Before

*This term, in its meaning of advocacy of women's rights, was in use as early as 1895. It seems that Freud may have been hearing it for the first time.

she had left for America her godmother had confided in her that she had been disappointed in their marriage, though she could see no remedy other than to bear her situation. Miss Emily described how she found herself taking her godmother's part as she listened to her. In their relations with each other her godparents made the atmosphere tense and uncomfortable. This contrasted markedly with the harmonious atmosphere of home that the child had enjoyed when her parents were alive.

It did not escape my attention that as Miss Emily spoke the atmosphere between us changed perceptibly from time to time. I have described the alternations between melancholia and spirited hostility. Occasionally these moods, neither of which is at all suited to making rapid progress with analysis, were supplemented with a calmer attentiveness, when I had glimpses of an engaging young woman of considerable warmth who would be able to benefit from what I had to offer her.

It was also impossible to avoid noticing that areas of ordinary concern were not touched upon. As well as the subject of her guardian, about whom she attempted to do no more than speak in monosyllables in answer to questions I might put, she was also unusually reticent on that subject usually so close to the hearts of young women, namely young men. It was, therefore, after she had been describing to me her life at university in America, that I remarked: 'It seems from the way you speak that the syllabus of women's universities entirely excludes discourse with the opposite sex.'

She smiled, and said, 'No, that's not quite right. I am not a harridan, Professor Freud. I do rather avoid some of the usual preoccupations of my sex, but while I was in America a young man whom I liked and admired wished to marry me. He was at Princeton, and was to become a lawyer. No doubt he has achieved this aim by now. We formed a friendship during my third year there. He liked the way in which, even though I was a girl, we could both talk about everything we were interested in. His family was welcoming to me. I stayed with them during one of the vacations. They would have liked us to get married I think. Although he was a good man, he was unable to escape from the preconceptions of his sex and his upbringing. I knew that, however well we might have started off together, and whatever protestations he made, if I married him I would soon become just another wife. I told him that I wanted to follow a career, and that he had much better pay his attentions to some other person, not because I did not like him, but because I would not be able to be what he would wish in a wife. I am sure, by now,' she said, glancing round at me wanly, 'that you know my views well enough to be able to guess that I wanted something different than that in my life.'

'So you broke off your friendship?'

'Yes, I am afraid I did. About a year later he married someone else.' There was a long silence, and then she added: 'Now I think that I was quite wrong. I could have made him happy. That would not have been an unworthy occupation. I could have been happy with him. I could have been safe and lived a life of contentment. With what has happened it seems impossible that I will be happy.'

'With what has happened?'

'Yes.'

'Is what has happened sufficient to destroy all possibility of future happiness?'

'So it now appears to me,' she said, and again relapsed into a silence, from which I did nothing to disturb her until the time came for us to end our work for the day.

3

Emily's Journal continued

Seduction Disclosed

Saturday 14 May

Today I started to think more clearly about whether it would be possible for the police to identify me as his murderer. If his body were found they would want to know why he was in Austria. He told me that he had business here, but he took special pains to find me. Even if there were no reason for him to be here other than to visit me, the police would not know who I was, or that I was connected with him, or even that I live here. Mrs S must think I am still in America. He told me that he went to my address in America and asked for me, pretending to be a lawyer. When Caroline was out he burglarised her apartment, and found her book of addresses, in which was my address here in Vienna. When I think of this I know why I hated him so much. It was his utter absorption in what he wanted, his disregard of others, and his amoral propensity to stop at nothing. As much as anything that is what has terrified me. Other people are restrained by certain things, but not he.

Would he have told Mrs S that I was not in America? I hardly suppose so, but I do not know. Our names are different so none of my acquaintances in Vienna will link us when his body is found. How sordid to be thinking these things, like a criminal trying to evade arrest. Which of course I am.

What of his arrival at my rooms? I keep reliving the horror of seeing him there. I had thought that I was free of him. He seems to have travelled from England to America and then to Vienna just to find me. Can he only have been here to find me? Could that be so, or did he have some other reason as well? And what a thing to say to me, that I was like a sickness for him, so that he could think of nothing but me these last seven years, and that he must see me or he would die. I could have told him what a sickness was: a return of that horror and revulsion at the sight of him, of the creeping, humiliating, enveloping dread of him. That is sickness. Then sprang to my mind the certainty that having found me it would all begin again, that I would never be safe, never escape from his hands feeling me and his eyes touching me. He must see me or he would die, he said. Well, now he has died. Why did I write that? I am become as callous as he – perhaps worse, since I believe that I once knew better.

He pleaded with me to love him, if only a little. He said he would arrange things as I wished, that he had money and that I would be able to do whatever I liked. Would I not give him the opportunity to prove himself? I thanked God for that small opportunity. Now I curse myself for it. I said he must grant me three days to think the matter over with the utmost care, but I could only do so if he would desist from approaching me. We would meet at the Griensteidl coffee house at six o'clock in the evening on Monday, in three days' time. I gave him directions to find it. I would give him an answer then. He protested, but I insisted. 'How,' I asked, 'would you ever know that I loved you, if there were not some element of choice on my part?' I have never said anything so hypocritical. I also said I would make a great commotion which would surely be heard if he did not leave. I do not know how or where I found the courage to say that.

Eventually he was persuaded. He did depart, leaving me in a shaking fit of terror, clutching in my hand, of all things, the address of his hotel. I break into perspiration and tremble now as I think of it.

Perhaps I should try to estimate how likely it is that anyone would link me to his disappearance. He could have been seen entering my rooms. Frau König in the opposite apartment is usually at home during the afternoon. Even if she saw him coming in, could a visit to me mean that I had killed him?

The next day I had taken the train southwards to where the mountains begin. That is the irony of it. I was going there to make doubly sure that I avoided him and any impromptu visits that he might decide to make, so that I could think calmly about how I might leave Vienna and escape from him. I went to the mountains especially because I know he hated them. Unaccountably, he was terrified of heights. Mrs S had said that they could never travel in the mountains because he was seized by panic when he was high up.

Though I left early on Saturday, there were people at the Sudbahnhof. I was not remarkable. Perhaps nobody noticed me. I must have been an obsession for him. Imagine him lying in wait for me to emerge into the street, then following me from the city to the station, then taking the train to G— and up that mountain path.

He must have trailed me for two hours beyond the village before overtaking me. He was careful that I should be utterly alone when he made his presence known. For once that worked in my favour. I do not think that anyone could have seen our struggle or heard us, although how can I be certain? It was a remote spot. Once I had seen him fall I waited for some time there. I could not believe what I had done. It was as if it had happened without my will, as if I had been some spectator at the theatre. I could not see where he had fallen. Just beside the path the mountain was sheer, and I could not see anything from the edge. No one came anywhere near while I was there. I descended the mountain without coming upon anyone. I should have gone straight to find a search party in G——, or to the police. But I did not. I did not and I have not. I spoke to no one, and I do not think that I would have been noticed. My shawl covered my torn bodice. I probably even looked composed, because I remember thinking that I must not attract attention. What a hypocrite. Why did I not go directly to send out a party to search for him? He may have been lying there injured. Should I go now? 'Please sir, will you arrest me? I pushed a man who was my seducer over a cliff. He may even now be lying injured and dying.' That is my moral weakness. I am unable to face the fact of being known as someone who killed a man, even though I am just such a person.

Yesterday, to try the idea that it had not happened, I went to my rooms. I braved the reminders of his appearance there. I looked for the dress I had been wearing. As I had remembered, it was torn. And there on my shoes was mud, from my walk in the open. It was no dream. It is plain fact that I, who had tried to be good since I escaped to America, am irredeemably wicked.

Perhaps the chance of linking me to his murder is slight. He may never be found. Or the police might think that he fell accidentally. Is this not more proof of my wickedness, should more be needed? Here I sit and scheme like the criminal I am.

Sunday

I read what I have written here. It seems unbelievable. I can scarcely even put words together now. Just a few days ago my notebooks were filled with translations of sublime poetry. Now here is this: sordid, self-absorbed, depraved. I know I have been wicked to have allowed the unspeakable things that he did with me in the past, but now I am of more mature years. I did not know I was such a thoroughly base person as to be a murderess. Perhaps that is what all murderers feel. The plays I translate are full of passionate killings, but this was not passion. It was panic and revulsion. It was not tragedy, just weakness. If I am not careful such a confused mass of words and feelings will rush out on to the page, inarticulate and vulgar. I must be calm. How have I come to this?

Tuesday

I was puzzled by something Professor Freud said today. This talking cure cannot, of course, be efficacious for me (if it works for anybody), but he said today that everyone has things they do not allow themselves to talk about, that they hide even from themselves. He fully expects this 'resistance'. I do not follow his reasoning. Can the treatment succeed despite the resistance? Or would the reistance make it fail? I do not understand. I used to be able to think. That was my one accomplishment. My mind now is in tatters. How can a talking treatment possibly succeed? In my case how can it do anything other than make me betray myself? If I do blurt out what I did, what could the Professor do then? Would he inform the police? Or would our talks really be confidential, like confession for the Catholics? Could Professor Freud be an ally? Would he stand up in court for me, and give testimony to my character? If so, what could he say?

Thursday

I should be tried and hanged. Perhaps when I am arrested I can just go to prison, and not speak to anyone ever again, until all is finished. Then I will simply walk to the scaffold, and just not speak at all. That will be best. Then justice will have been done. I need not kill myself. I need not explain myself. Society will properly have shown its revulsion against murder. I shall be no more.

Sara sits and talks to me each day. She thinks I am calmer. She wants to believe that my consultations with Professor Freud have a beneficial effect. Maybe I do feel calmer. My calmness is because in the newspapers there is still no mention of the body.

I look forward to Sara returning home in the evenings and coming to sit with me. Without her I would already be dead. She is capable. She always seems to know what to do. She is a thoroughly capable person. Is it because she is older than me, or because she once was married? She always seems to know how everything should be done. Since I have been feeling somewhat better, yesterday we even laughed together. What an extraordinary thing to do, to laugh.

I have known Sara now two years, since starting at the school. I have often thought about my first meeting with her. She was warm and friendly to me from the start and quite unaffectedly she invited me to visit her at home, evidently on an impulse. We spent that first afternoon talking about colleagues and my first impressions of the school. Her observations were percipient and witty. I was shocked when she said that she was a widow, although she was barely thirty. Now she lives in her own house. She has her own servants, her own means, and she arranges her own life. Even with all this she devotes herself to teaching. I left her house on that first day feeling cheerful, enlivened. Sara's interests are in science and the biology of all animals including, as she often tells me, 'us human animals'. What she knows is quite different from what I know, but somehow we were able to share our understandings. Now I too have become interested in such matters as the theory of evolution. Not a proper subject for a young woman, let alone two young women.

Whatever is happening? Here am I thinking of Sara, and suddenly writing a light-hearted comment.

Sara's parents held the belief that girls should be brought up to have a profession. Her education, like mine, had been more like a boy's. Perhaps that is what drew us together. She is such a good person too. She is much better than me in every possible respect. Not content to devote herself to the girls at school during the day, she started the Evening Educational Association to teach young women who are servants, shopgirls and the like. She says that it is important for women to be educated so that we can take our proper place in the world. She thinks that we have a proper place as the equal of men. There will be women who will be doctors, who will run great concerns, who will even be national leaders. Of course I agree. A thousand times over, I agree, but my interests in such things seemed, beside hers, so abstract. When moved by an idea she does something about it, like starting the Educational Association. She just thinks something like: It is right that all women take their proper place in society. To do this they must be educated. Therefore I will start an Educational Association for women. She creates a syllogism that leads not just to something that is true, but to action, just like that. Hers is a life that is worth something, unlike mine. Every thought tends back to this.

For a while I have been thinking about Sara. It relieves me to do so. Perhaps if I could think fully of some person other than myself I could somehow redeem myself. I could make restitution. I do not believe he was a good man. Perhaps he deserved to die, but it was not for me to decide. I did not decide, it was all too quick. Instead of being hanged perhaps I could instead live unselfishly, for someone who is good, like Sara.

I think that in truth such thoughts are just fear of my own humiliation.

Perhaps to think about Sara might mean I am not totally absorbed in the mire of my wickedness. Sara and I were the youngest women at the school. We were thrown much together.

We took such delight in how we would help one another to plan lessons. My learning in science was quite rudimentary and Sara's in Latin and Greek was limited. The idea of tutoring one another in our own subjects and meeting to do this transformed my existence, so that I no longer felt so much on my own. She was a lively and quick pupil for me. After a year we were able to read the *Odyssey* aloud to one another. We would argue about it long into the evening. At the same time I read Darwin's *The Origin of Species*, and we discussed these momentous ideas. She invited me to help in the Educational Association. The classics are not much use to the women we teach, but languages are. So that is my department, or rather it was. I am no longer fit to teach any person upon any subject whatsoever.

We would talk of aspirations, and of how she might want to train in medicine. She says also that she may marry again. I think she loved her husband very much. I imagine them happy together. I do not know how she has resisted other suitors these six years, but she says she will not marry again before she has properly achieved something. When the time comes she will look for a man. When she is no longer good enough for anything else she will become a companion to some deserving soul. She says such things and then laughs. She has given up thought of children of her own. She and her husband conceived none. She believes herself to be barren. 'I cannot have children. My pupils are my children. I sometimes am lonely, but that emotion I have overcome. Why married should I wish to be?'

That is the kind of thing she says, speaking with that irresistible Austrian accent, when we talk in English, and she laughs. She had a tragedy in her life, but she can laugh. Her tragedy just befell her. She did not bring it upon herself. If only I could laugh like that with her as we used to.

I have often wanted to tell Sara about my experiences with him. If anyone would understand, she would. I have sometimes felt that I would tell her, but I have always drawn back. She is too important to me. She could not think of me in the same way if she knew how tainted I am. Now the taint has come to this.

Friday

Another day, and the body has not been discovered. Professor Freud keeps insisting I must censor nothing. That is his term: 'censor'. It is not the right metaphor. For myself I am in pieces. One piece is here in this journal. Another is with Sara. Another lies in bed at night, unable to sleep, shaking with fear. Another is with Professor Freud. It is not so much a matter of censorship as of keeping these pieces separate. I must avoid one part leaking into the other where it should not be. Strangely, I looked forward to my consultation today. What is he doing to me? Am I under some spell? Is this how charlatans work, by entrancing people? I must be careful, keep these parts of myself separate. The murderess must remain here in this notebook, the friend with Sara, the patient with the doctor.

Monday

Now I have spoken it. Not the killing, the other matter. It indicates what I have known all along: that I should not be consulting Professor Freud at all. His technique is to listen minutely to everthing I say, and then to pounce like a tiger on peculiarities and inconsistencies. I made the mistake of thinking that if we discussed something as harmless as a dream we would be off the track, and I could be safe. Instead it was there that I gave myself away. I have told him now about the hateful attentions of Mr S, of his wretched actions upon myself since I was fourteen.

I own that I feel relieved at doing so, but the main issue

remains. If I can give myself away in this, then I can also in the other matter. It is madness to be making these consultations. I must find an excuse to stop. Yet, in part he seems right. I feel better for having told him. I cannot understand why. I cannot understand it. He was not especially sympathetic.

How can I have told him of that shameful, sordid thing? I know not what to think. Now he knows that I hated Mr S. When the body is found, he will guess, will he not? He will deduce that Mr S came here to follow me, and that somehow . . . Somehow what? Why would he think that? I do not believe I have told him Mr S's proper name. My mind is too panicky to realise. I think I have always just said 'my guardian'. My secrecy, without really thinking about it, has served me well on this occasion. Everywhere I see suspicious things. I feel discovery imminent. I can no longer think. My mind is in a hopeless tangle. I must guard at least from mentioning Mr S's name. I must remember not to do that.

4

Freud's Lecture continued

Trauma or Phantasy?

At the beginning of the next session, since it was clear that Miss Emily had told me all that she cared to of her life and since, as it appeared, there were matters in which she was determined to be less than candid, I said that in cases of her kind one usually found that conflicts hidden from consciousness were at the root of the difficulties. If she were serious about her treatment with me, as well as telling me the more ordinary events of her life she should relate also any thoughts that occurred to her when we were together, even if these seemed untoward. I mentioned too that she might tell me any dreams she had had since we had begun to meet.

After a considerable interval she said she had experienced a dream that had occurred several times. Her account of it was as follows.

'I am sitting in my room in the house at B—, at my desk, writing with my fountain pen. I notice a man looking through the window. Then my pen is nowhere to be found. I call out, I think to my godmother, but my hands are tied, and no sound will come out of my mouth. I go half-way downstairs and stand there. I can hear two people shouting at each other behind a closed door.'

I explained to Miss Emily that dreams did not reveal much as they stood. Rather, I explained, they were like hieroglyphic inscriptions. To try and see a meaning directly would be like looking at Egyptian pictograms and saying something like: 'A tall man in a loincloth regards a stork standing close to the water's edge.' Instead each pictogram has to be translated into its proper meaning in a modern tongue, then from these translations the meaning of the whole becomes clear. So it is with dreams. I pointed out for instance that in her own dream she first observed someone looking in through a window, and then found herself going downstairs, presumably from an upper floor. She agreed that this would scarcely be possible if the dream were depicting a direct sequence of events. I further explained to her that analysis requires that she take each image of her dream in turn, and tell me what came immediately to mind as she thought of it. These mental associations would point to the meanings we sought.

'Take the first image,' I said, 'of yourself at your desk at B——. What occurs to you? What do you see in your mind's eye when you think of it?'

'I am at my desk,' she replied. 'It is the place that I can go to be on my own, without interruption. I can write, and think, and make something of my own. Elsewhere in the house I am in an alien place. It is not my house. It is my guardian's, where he comes and goes as he pleases.'

'Being at your desk makes you invulnerable from intrusions?'

'If only that were true.' She smiled a wan and ironic smile. I had the sense that, in my brief discussion of Eygptian hiero-glyphs, the atmosphere between us had become reminiscent of herself as she had been with a father whom she had loved, and I was reminded of her describing how she and her father had discussed the life of ancient Greece. Now, as I had explained how translating dreams was like translating ancient hieroglyphic inscriptions, we were also talking about antiquity, about her own past, and she was speaking openly without her usual defensiveness.

'Very well,' I continued, 'what about the man's face at the window?'

'I suppose the face is that of my guardian.'

'Was there an occasion on which you saw him looking in at you like that?'

There was a pause, and I noticed some considerable agitation.

'What comes to mind,' she said after a pause, 'is a time, about a year after my parents had died, when I was in the large drawing room. He startled me by appearing at the window. It was during the school holidays. He had come home unexpectedly, but without my godmother. I thought they were both on the Continent. He just appeared. For some reason, instead of coming in through the front door, or speaking to any of the servants, he had walked round to the back of the house, and was looking through the window. I was discomfited, as I was in the drawing room where I had been only rarely on my own. I had been feeling aimless, and had been looking at the paintings, and then behind them. I was aware that these paintings were by well-known artists. I wondered whether anything might be written on the back of them, and thought about what grown-up people do by collecting such things. Then when he appeared I felt guilty, as if I had been caught at something I should not have been doing.'

'What next?' I asked. She had become somewhat calmer as she spoke.

'I think that is all,' she replied.

'I scarcely think so. The scene that you describe would hardly be enough to cause the agitation I witnessed as you began to speak. I am struck also by the phrase you used: "wondering what grown-up people do". It is sufficient to make me conjecture that there was soemthing else about this occasion on which your guardian returned to find you alone in his drawing room, that was connected with what a fourteen-year-old girl might think about what grown-up people do.'

At this point Miss Emily's composure vanished utterly, and she sobbed bitterly for several minutes.

Finally she said: 'I do not know why I have come to see you. I should have known it was not safe to let myself be put into the position of having to talk about what is in my mind. I have too many awful things in my mind. I cannot see how you could possibly help me.'

'I have the strong sense that something important happened on this occasion when your guardian returned unexpectedly. Possibly he made some kind of sexual overture to you,' I persisted.

There was a silence of many minutes. 'How could you know that? I cannot bear to think of it, let alone relate it to you.'

'Perhaps if you were to do so, the reasons for your recent great distress would become clearer, and we would be well on the way to restoring you to health.'

With some difficulty and further agitation she related the following.

'My guardian said we should have dinner together in the dining room. During those holidays I had been eating with my governess, and we had become close companions. She had gone out on the evening of which I speak, and my guardian had said that on this occasion I should get dressed and as a treat I would have dinner with him.

'I must have been excited about this prospect, though looking back this thought appals me. But as well as still feeling bereft, my life at that time had been little enlivened by events of any kind. So I planned what I would wear and thought about what grown-up people talked about so that I should not bore him. When I came down for dinner he gave me sherry to drink and told me that I was becoming a lovely girl. He took my arm when we went in to dinner and I sat in my godmother's chair. He was kind to me that evening. The candles were lit and he smiled at me through dinner

34

with his handsome face. We talked about my school and about what I had been doing since he had been away. I went up to bed after dinner. It took me a long time to fall asleep. My guardian was always busy and had not previously paid more than slight attention to me. I had thought that he had not wanted me living with them, and that having to fulfil his duties of guardianship was a burden. I remember thinking for the first time that perhaps I was not unwelcome in his home.'

She became very distressed. I gave her time to recollect herself, and asked: 'And then?'

After another hesitation she said that she was woken up by someone stroking her hair. Her guardian was sitting on the side of her bed. 'He held his finger to his lips, told me to make no sound, and said he had some important things to say to me. That when one was grown-up, as I was now, one became open to new sensations that are kept secret from children.

'I guessed what he meant. I was not as naïve as he thought. My governess had spoken to me of the man with whom she had been conducting a love affair. I have to admit too that ideas of love had occupied me of late. Perhaps I was interested in the adventures of my governess, I do not know. All the same I felt terrified at my guardian sitting on my bed. My ideas of love between men and women had been quite different from this. There seemed nothing I could do. If I screamed, it was unlikely that the servants would hear. My governess, who slept in the room next to mine, was, as I have said, absent that night on an assignation with her lover. My guardian was much stronger than I, and there was nothing to do but to lie there silently, as still as I could, and listen to what he said. He told me that this must be our secret, and I should never tell my godmother. I was turned to stone, and he must have seen that I could offer no resistance. His stroking of my hair gave way to other attentions as he spoke to me, explaining the practices of love.

'I am sure you can guess what followed. I was horrified by it, and I still feel revulsion if I think of it. It was not at all as I had imagined when I had discussed such matters with my governess. My situation had become a nightmare. For the next four years these scenes were repeated. An arrangement had been made for me to attend a boarding school. Now my guardian suggested that I should continue being educated at home, but I succeeded in persuading him that I should attend the school. Though it was in some ways a dreary place, it was also a haven, and I dreaded the holidays. Several times during each school holiday the despicable events occurred again.'

At this point the girl broke down again, and wept copiously. 'I do not know how I have been able to live with the shame of it,' she said. 'I had to believe that my parents had made the most unspeakable mistake in arranging that this man should be my guardian in case of any accident to them. He had deceived them. He was a wicked man. They cannot have known him. I spent much of my time planning how I would escape and make myself entirely free of his influence.'

'That is why you went to America as soon as you were able?'

'Yes, of course.' At this she wept again, without relief, for a considerable period.

Had I been hearing such a story as this for the first time, I would no doubt have accepted her account more or less at face value. In fact accounts of this character, of seduction by a male relative, are not unfamiliar to me. Moreover, weeping is an invariable accompaniment of such accounts.

The reason I was hesitant to assume that what I heard had actually taken place was that I have recently had occasion to revise my previous hypotheses about sexual traumata. I gave a lecture on the subject to one of our learned societies, and I know some of you were there. In that lecture I said that I had treated eighteen cases in which young women with hysterical symptoms

36

complained about sexual molestation during childhood, usually by an older male relative.

It is with some considerable mortification that I have now to announce that I was too hasty in my judgement of these cases. My original hypothesis was not necessarily completely mistaken, but it was certainly incomplete.*

I had been, so to speak, taken in by the convincing renditions of these women. My convictions were at that time strengthened by the fact that enabling them to give their accounts of such sexual events allowed their symptoms to abate. Subsequently, however, new considerations have come to light. They are as follows. In the first place, I have become aware that the relief from their symptoms that my patients gained by relating these incidents was temporary. Whatever provoked their hysteria was still at work, like an infection or a foreign body, below the surface and still able to cause further symptoms. Secondly, I have now seen that in many ways my early theory, that the trauma of sexual seduction in childhood causes hysteria, was too simple. I began to realise this when I commenced the painful task of analysing my own dreams, and was horrified to realise that dark forces lurk in the breasts of us all. It is too easy to blame some other person for traumata which we imagine have scarred us. As in Sophocles' great tragedy, the detective, if I may use that anachronistic term for the action of a classical drama, discovers that he himself is the man he seeks. Oedipus discovers that it was he who killed his father, and it behoves anyone seeking some other to blame for his own misfortunes to consider first whether they have stemmed from his own heart. Thirdly, the idea that hysteria is occasioned by purely accidental and external events is also, I believe, too simple. We must make allowance for the normal development of sexuality within each individual, and for strong forces that this

*This sentence was scored out in the manuscript.

37

can release, which are by no means mere accidents of circumstance. These forces can often lead a young person into paths that seem unexpected or strange.

So, with Miss Emily, I am not saying that a seduction could not have taken place. The position we ought to adopt, if we are to penetrate such a case as this, is to bear in mind the processes of sexual development, and to reserve judgement on the issue of seduction for the time being. On this latter issue, we must, as in a law court, first listen carefully to the evidence on both sides. The final court in this case will be Miss Emily herself. Unless what we find allows her consciously to recognise the inner sources of her perturbations, and unless her symptoms are permanently relieved, the case would remain, as in the law of Scotland, not proven.

The symptoms that brought Miss Emily to me were most likely to be due to her being caught in a maelstrom of her own developing sexual libido opposed by equally strong forces with which society necessarily keeps such motives in check. To put the matter plainly, the recitation of this puritan girl could well have been an account of an elaborate sexual phantasy. For such a girl to admit that these ideas came from herself would be unthinkable to her. So she herself would be unconscious of the origins of the events that she retold to me with such vividness and emotion.

I have, of course, neither the power nor the desire to negate either of the great forces of developing libido or of societal prohibition, but my experience is that if the consequences of libidinal development have been forced into unconsciousness, as I suspect was here the case, then allowing them once more into consciousness will enable the symptomatic eruptions to abate.

5

Emily's Journal continued

Sara Becomes a Confidante

Tuesday 24 May

I have come back to my own rooms. I could not remain to be waited on by Sara's cook and maid. I feel too much under scrutiny there. Coming here is no better. It has the taint of him still here, and I feel less able to sustain myself. I have made the decision, however, and I will abide by it. Sara did not want me to return here, but I insisted. Now that I am not in her house, I just await her visits.

Professor Freud today said something that reached straight into my soul. He said I was longing for my mother. He is right. He is right. But why should it come as such a revelation? Why should his saying that make me feel that I am lovable in some way, not a wicked person? I feel now, for the first time, that I can trust him. Perhaps he is not after all a fraud. I do not know why. It is all so irrational. Why should I feel so moved by him saying such a thing? Today I wept for my mother, and for my father too, for both of them. I am somehow left here to defend myself from dangers to which I do not feel equal, like a child who does not know enough to be able to care for herself. None of this would have happened had they been alive. I would have been able to feel loved and to love.

I have made another mistake. I have bought Professor Freud's *Interpretation of Dreams*, and also another book, recently published, that I found with it in the medical bookshop: *The Psychopathology of Everyday Life*. Now I am reading again. It keeps my mind from other matters, at least for some of the time. I think Professor Freud believes that his book on dreams will be the means of fame, but that as yet it is not yet properly recognised.

My mistake is that I see an active mind at work. As usual, I am excited by it and I shall start admiring him. Perhaps already I am doing so. It will make me more frank than I should be. Except for being with Sara, which is the only comfort I have found in the last weeks, this is the first thing that has distracted me.

It is becoming clearer to me what his objectives are. He wants me to talk about dreams and incidents in my life. Then he will work out how these point to other meanings that have some-how become unconscious. These meanings, when they are unconscious, produce hysterical sicknesses of the mind, but if one discovers them consciously, then the sickness is cured. It is a strange idea, a bold idea. He keeps speaking as if analysis is like an archaeological excavation, an excavation of a person's psyche. Of course such talk very much attracts me. I must be careful. If this puts him in the position of being able to guess unspoken thoughts, he is the last person on earth I should talk to, but I cannot help feeling fascinated.

I have been quite active today. I went to see Bertha, who works with us in our Educational Association. She has a position as an assistant librarian at the Medical School of the University. I have asked her to trace any other works of Professor Freud that she can find on his methods of treating patients, and to see if she can borrow them for me. If I can understand better how he works, then I will be able to arm myself against giving myself away.

All this is having effects I cannot properly control. I start by telling him what should never have been told. Now I have told Sara too. She is interested in this psychoanalysis. She wants me to talk about it. She said it seemed to be having a beneficial effect on me. She wants to know how it works.

She too is now fascinated by the idea of dream analysis. She too likes the idea of layers on layers of meaning, like an archaeological site. She gets passions for intellectual ideas. When I first knew her she was absorbed in experiments on the habits of woodlice that she later published in a learned journal. She thinks deeply about biology, and says that dream analysis is like reconstructing fossils from a few fragments of bone. She has not yet read any of Professor Freud's works, but my talking about them has made her want to. She has borrowed the dream book. She asked me about the dream I recounted to Professor Freud, and then I had to go through each of the images and tell her what my associations had been, and what I had said. At one point I demurred and said that it meant revealing things about my experiences that I had never talked to anyone about.

That is how it came out. She became angry with me. I would never dare be angry at her in case she might cease to like me, but she is better at such things. She said that she had treated me for a long time as her closest confidante, that she had felt closer to me than to anyone. She had spoken even on matters she would not have spoken about to her husband when he was alive. But I was not open with her. I preferred to remain private, or to talk to a man whom I had known for a couple of weeks, whom I paid to listen to me, rather than speaking to her.

She threw back at me all our discussions of how as a woman one could feel perhaps closer to other women than to men. She reminded me of my arguments about how it was important to put concern for women before concerns for men. I am theoretical as usual. What I think and what I do are not at one. She was furious. I found myself shaking, with fear that she would hate me. I begged her forgiveness. I said that if it had been any ordinary thing I would of course have told her. In my heart I know that this is not true. She is open, and whatever she is thinking can just come straight out. I am always more secretive. I feel that I have to be. I did not say that. I just said that it was something worse than she could ever imagine. She had never done wicked things, and so did not need to be secretive. I could not bear that she would think of me badly.

I had to compose myself. I had lost the first shock of talking about it when I had told Professor Freud. At last I told her. I wept more tears than I knew the body could contain. I found myself describing how frightened I had been when it was time to go home from the school for the holidays. I told Sara about those times when I felt sick from anxiety thinking about how he would come to me. Sometimes I would vomit and usually be unable to eat for days. I felt dirty all over, no matter how often I bathed. Sara looked astonished when I told her. She kept asking how a man responsible for my welfare could do such a thing. Not for a moment did she disbelieve me. She cried as I cried. Then, as the despicable story continued, she became more and more angry. Not with me, as I thought she might be, as she should be, but with Mr S. She started striding about the room, expostulating and saying: 'How could he? How could he? The beast. He was your guardian.'

She was baffled about how and why I had kept this secret for so long. Why had I not told my godmother or my governess? Why had I not told someone at school? I said I did not know. I

42

think it was because I was ashamed, and felt wicked. I thought that in some way I must have been bad. I still think so. I hoped all the time that my godmother would somehow prevent it or let me stay at school. I hoped for that before every holiday.

Sara was filled with the indignation that I had not been able to feel. 'How could the man force himself upon you in such manner? That is a bad and unforgivable thing. Why does not your godmother see what happens and protect you?' All this I should have felt. For a moment I could look at if from Sara's viewpoint. Instead of the mire of shame, for the first time I felt perhaps I had been misused. Maybe it had not been my fault. Maybe it was his. Perhaps he had been wicked, not me. I had some moments of relief last night.

Tuesday

Perhaps I am grasping at a straw. Then again, and I had not realised this, perhaps I have been made sick by the experiences with Mr S. That is what Sara said, and this is why I should continue consulting Professor Freud. He had been right to think that I laboured under some dreadful secret which had made me ill.

Wednesday 1 June

I know, of course, from literature that sexual relations between men and women are not always furtive and sordid, but I thought it was the usual thing for men to feel sexual desire that they cannot control. I thought that because this is so contrary to everything else in society, everyone keeps it a secret. That is why, in some fashion, I had been the subject of Mr S's attentions. Sex is the secret of our society. I had to keep it secret too. Sex of this kind is one of those things that women just bear. It is also one of those things that some women, such as myself, bring upon themselves, by inflaming a man's desire. Then we suffer its consequences.

To try and gain some perspective I read that book, *Sex and Character*, which caused such a commotion last year.* It says that woman always has something of the prostitute in her, that her life is taken up entirely with sex, that she is incapable of logical thought and is unconscious whereas man is logical and conscious. Until I was able to see that this book was not scientific as it purported to be, but was mere ranting, it made me despair that I should ever be capable of understanding.

I had read the male poets writing of their desire. My own conclusion had been that men could be inflamed by desire when they saw certain women, or saw women in a certain way. Then they are unable to help themselves. That is why the trade of women working as prostitutes continues. 'Prostitute' means standing in the stead of some other person, in the stead of respectable women. Prostitutes are necessary in society so that men, inflamed by their sexual desire for respectable women whom they meet, can satisfy this desire. It is sordid but it keeps respectable women safe. Is there another explanation? What ordinary women must do is to keep men at a distance. They must avoid all occasions for inflaming that desire. That is what respectable society achieves to a large extent. On the one hand, only carefully controlled meeting between the sexes occurs,

---

*This book, *Geschlecht und Charakter* by Otto Weininger, was published in Vienna in 1903. It struck a chord, was widely reviewed, hailed by some as a masterpiece, and became a best-seller. Weininger had shown a draft to Freud, who advised him not to publish. At the time of Emily's analysis Freud's former mentor and confidant, Wilhelm Fliess, read the book and accused Freud of having broken confidentiality by passing Fliess's theory of human bisexuality to Weininger, who then stole it.

except in marriage. On the other hand, the trade continues of poor degraded creatures who receive the attentions diverted from respectable women who have excited desire, perhaps unknowingly.

Since I came to Vienna I know just how shockingly numerous prostitutes are because two of these poor creatures, whom I feel for terribly, come to lectures at our Association. Sara found out their real profession, I do not know how. I expect she just asked them. She advised them to keep it from the other women, who might be scandalised. They have spoken frankly to Sara and myself about their lives and the conditions in which they and their fellows live.

I am not entirely sure about these ideas of mine, but at any event this is the kind of theory I have formulated. Because I was orphaned, ordinary social arrangements had not achieved a safe haven for me. My mother would have had my welfare at heart. She would have known what to guard against. None of this would have come about. The flaw in my theory is that I cannot believe that all men are so easily inflamed. Do some achieve a greater moral sense? My father, for instance? I think perhaps some of them can master themselves, do master themselves. I feel very unsure about this part of my theory.

Somehow my appearance, perhaps my manner, had inflamed Mr S. I had some streak of wickedness inside me, or perhaps as Weininger says some aspect of the prostitute. If I could have avoided inflaming him, it would not have happened. Or if I could have known about men's proclivities earlier then I could have been forearmed. I could have been more demure, more drab. Perhaps it is women who are bad like me who inflame men, then descend to the depths and actually become prostitutes.

Now it seems maybe my theory is not correct at all. Perhaps this is not the pattern of relations between men and women. Sara says not. She says my ideas have become dreadfully distorted by my experience. She says that men are like us at heart. They yearn to be close to another person. She and her husband had found comfort in each other. Men do not assault women unless they are wicked. Such an action would stem from wickedness, not sexual desire. They might just as well be burglars or murderers, she says.

Yes. There we have it. I am wicked. I assaulted Mr S, and murdered him. I pushed him away when I should have thought how dangerous that place was. Are we all, men and women, subject to such impulses? Are we all wicked within? Is this what is meant by original sin? Sara does not seem like that. Is it just some, such as myself, who are wicked? I do not know. Everything is confused.

Friday

Today we received two volumes from the Medical Library in which some of Professor Freud's previous work had been published. They confirm what Sara has been saying. I have been made sick by being seduced when I was a child. Professor Freud talks about this quite explicitly in the case of a patient called Katharina.* She had suffered from hysteria, and Professor Freud thought that the reason was that her uncle had got into bed with her one night and that she had felt his body. The Professor wanted her to say which part of his body she felt. She was shy, of course, and would not tell him. But it is clear that it must have been the male organ. Then this uncle had continued to pursue her. It all seemed so familiar. Poor woman. I know that wretched male organ, pushed against one, and into one. So there we have

*'Katharina' is the name given to one of Freud's brief cases in his publication of 1895, Freud and Breuer, *Studies on Hysteria*.

46

it. It can cause hysteria. The shock and shame of it somehow makes one suffer symptoms. Perhaps I too suffer hysterical symptoms.

I am not clear from the Professor's writings what all the symptoms may be. They seem to include many mental and physical states. Maybe they include being unable to act properly in certain situations. I now wonder whether it was part of my sickness to push Mr S away even when we were in so dangerous a spot. Perhaps I am not wholly to blame. Perhaps the Professor can cure at least some of the sickness. Perhaps Sara can adopt his methods. I can trust her. Then I shall know how sick I have been, and perhaps start towards a cure.

Perhaps if I can understand all this properly I may be able to think better about what to do. Maybe I will feel morally stronger. Maybe I will be able to go the police and say, 'I have not come forward before now because I have been ill, but I have now had treatment. I now admit I killed Mr S, but I believe it to have been an accident. I had not intended his death. I was suffering from hysteria. I was frightened that he would take advantage of me again, as he had previously. I just tried to repel him, but at that moment I did not think how dangerous it was for me to do so in that spot.'

This seems so unconvincing. Would the police accept this? It is still too much of a muddle, a skein of tangled thoughts and fears. Still the danger is that I myself threaten my disclosure. Still there is no news of a body being found.

What if I were to allow Sara to begin treating me following the Professor's methods; could I help but tell her of my crime? She does not allow me to be evasive. Though I can be vigilant, I cannot be sure that I would not give myself away. I do not know what I should do. In part the tangle is unravelled. In part the knot just becomes tighter.

Wednesday

I must think of how to earn my living. Perhaps I will look for a position as a governess. That does not seem right to me. I should not have an influence on the young. Also I can provide no letters of reference. I think of writing articles for a newspaper, but I do not know how to begin. I think too that only men have such positions. I must apply my mind to the problem, as I have so little money. If I were just to give myself up, then having a position need not concern me.

Friday

Though Sara comes to visit each day, I feel unbearably lonely here. Without a position I am aimless.

I finished *The Interpretation of Dreams* today. It is long, and in some ways rambling, so I have not read it straight through. It is none the less an impressive work. In other circumstances I would be proud to have the opportunity to know the man who wrote it. I have also finished reading Professor Freud's other works, on hysteria. His whole theory now seems clearer, and I feel excited by the new world that he is exploring. I do not understand it at all fully, and much needs to be explained. I must talk about it with Sara. Her scientific mind is better than mine on such things. Perhaps I can ask the Professor also, during our consultations, about matters on which I am unsure.

I think the Professor now believes that there are two reasons for falling ill of hysteria. On the one hand something can happen, like an intruding sexual experience as occurred to Katharina, or to myself. Then in the book on dreams, and the one on the psychopathology of everyday life, the Professor writes about a second kind of cause – of conflicts from within. Miss Lucy, who like me was English or perhaps Scottish, suffered from melancholy and other symptoms which were not due to a degrading experience, but to the fact that she had fallen in love with her employer.* She had tried to put this from her mind. She was caught between wishing for her employer's love and not being able to admit this to herself. So I believe the Professor thinks that warring thoughts within the person can appear in dreams and also cause hysterical illness. Especially when some of the thoughts have to be kept secret.

How well I know these fearful guilty secrets and their suppression in myself: I, whose life had to become a guilty secret and is now doubly so. The idea seizes me that others may suffer in this same way. Could I be free of this, and of its harmful effects? I think I could perhaps have been cured of that other thing, of the effects of Mr S when I was young. But my situation now is quite, quite different. On the mountain it was I who performed the guilty act, and the Professor says nothing about therapy for the effects of such acts. They are merely crimes, meriting punishment. But what if I acted while ill? Would that make a difference? Would it make me less guilty? I cannot think my way through to what is best for me to do.

Sunday

I think I will admit to the Professor that I have been reading his book on dreams and the one on the psychopathology of everyday life. I had better not say that I have read his articles on hysteria, because they are only available in medical libraries. See how easily being secretive immediately occurs to me. I believe that would be best, none the less. He would not approve of my finding his medical articles.

*Emily refers here to another of Freud's cases, reported in Freud and Breuer, *Studies on Hysteria*.

49

If it were just the matter of Mr S's sexual conduct with me – notice how I now say 'just' to this horror that has blighted my life – if it were just for that, I would feel confident that his method would have great benefit for myself. I now believe he is right. Because of that, my mind had been terribly torn. I have not been well. I may have been more ill than I realised.

6

Freud's Lecture continued

The Dream Unfolds

In my publication with Breuer,* I had occasion to remark that my case histories read like short stories, and seemed to lack the stamp of serious science. I have struggled against this tendency, but in the case I set before you it has been more than usually difficult since, as you will agree, Miss Emily's account has a melodramatic quality which is impossible to ignore. Our task, however, is not simply to believe what the patient says, any more than we should do so if we were a detective interviewing someone suspected of a crime. Instead we must persevere, gathering evidence where we may, until we can solve the mystery entirely. What I am telling you has some of the marks of a story of detection, but with a difference, because very near the beginning we already seem to know the crime. A description has been given by a witness of seduction of herself as a minor by her guardian. What is missing are the motives. Let me point out to you, gentlemen, that without these the case is incomprehensible. So it is motives that we seek.

At the meeting next following her revelations, Miss Emily declared herself to have felt relieved by recounting to me the

---

*Studies on Hysteria.

story of her relations with Mr S. She had, she said, lived all this time with a sense of guilt, foreboding and confusion about this period in her life. It still seemed to her a kind of fog, in which she groped darkly. She still lapsed into periods of silent brooding when she was with me, and it was clear that in giving this account we had not arrived at the bottom of the matter.

It was several days after I had first heard the story of the evening dinner and bedroom seduction when I interrupted one of her periods of quiet brooding, to remind her that we had scarcely begun our analysis of the dream of herself at her desk and the face at the window. She still remembered the dream so I encouraged some further associations to its images.

'What about this fountain pen?' I asked. 'What comes to mind when you think of that?'

'I had a fountain pen that I valued very much,' she replied. 'It had a gold nib, and the lid had two thin gold bands round it. I thought the pen just wonderful for writing. It was given to me by Sara, my friend, whose father approached you to ask if you would see me. Recently I have lost it. Though I have searched I cannot find it. You will think it sentimental to be affected by the loss of such a utilitarian article, but I was attached to it, and I sometimes used to clip it to a gold chain that I wore around my neck. I have lost this chain as well. Perhaps it broke, but the chain is of no importance. I suppose you will say that my dreaming about losing the pen is significant in some way.'

'I am sure you know,' I said to her, 'that, in the period of ancient Greece in which you are interested, symbols of the male phallus were worshipped quite openly. In Delos, for instance, two sculptured penises stood in the *agora*. I believe they were nearly twice as tall as a man. In more modern times, of course, such manifestations would be considered tasteless in the extreme, but I wonder whether the symbolism does not live on in elongated objects of recent design, fountain pens for instance. It does not escape my attention either, that in your native language "pen" and "penis" have the same Latin root, which I imagine you must know. Could it be that in the life that you have chosen for yourself you have lost this male organ?'

Somewhat to my surprise, Miss Emily – who had, as I say, been sunk in gloomy contemplation – chuckled at this suggestion of mine, and said: 'What a wonderful idea. Yes, I have lost something like that. Looking into what is known of the rituals that surrounded the worship of the phallus in ancient times, I have very much the sense that it represented male influence, which of course the men of those times were happy to celebrate. The coarse sexual implication obviously catches one's attention, as it is meant to do, but it is the more or less complete power that men had in ancient Greece that was the key, and I am sad to say I do not think things have changed very much. I almost like the idea of the pen as a kind of phallus. Mine was not so much a male thing, but it did allow me a place in a man's world. It allowed me some special influence. And yes I have lost it now. Not only can I not teach, I can no longer write to earn my living. And yes, that is a matter of very considerable distress, since as you point out the only alternative to not living at all is to give up the idea of any kind of independent existence and become a wife.'

'The loss of that more sexual element, you say, means nothing?'

'Well, if you mean the loss of the attentions of my guardian, it means a great deal. I am heartily glad to be rid of them. If you mean the young man in America, I have more mixed emotions, but I assure you it is not his male organ that I miss. I was not troubled by that when I was in America, and I therefore do not miss it now.'

'One thing strikes me,' I said. 'You are vehement in your protestations about the male sex, yet you say that for four years you had sexual relations with a man. For all this time did you derive nothing from this save the contempt that you now express verbally towards men?'

'I scarcely know how to talk about it. I did not ever enjoy my guardian's embraces, though I know that women can enjoy the sexual act. I felt ashamed, and very often it was painful. I think I just waited for it to be finished, which I have to admit never took long. I remember often feeling nauseous as he was doing it, and several times, I vomited after he had left, though more usually I just cried. He never stayed with me after the act, I am glad to say. When he had departed, and I had washed the repellent residues of his activity from my person, I would just lie as still as I could, trying to think of nothing whatever, until at last I fell asleep.

'Perhaps what you are asking about is that from the time it began, he was much kinder to me. He paid attention to me, gave me presents, would concede to requests I made. Whereas I had felt that he resented having the responsibility of my care, I felt more welcome in his house. It was even a little as he had said, that I now felt special, and knew something that I had not known as a child. Looking back I think I was very wicked. I knew I could influence him, and wanted some influence, after feeling completely on sufferance in that place. Influence again, you see? But now, if I think about it in that kind of way, it seems hateful. Like a courtesan, being allowed special status in return for . . . what do they call it? My favours?'

Again she lapsed into silence, and at last said: 'I suppose you are right, it has been better to talk about all this. I had tried to banish it from my mind, since I escaped to America, and until recently I believed I had succeeded, but I suppose it had not ever really disappeared. Do you think it will, now that I have told you about it? Sara thinks that it has been good for me to unburden myself to you.'

I thought it imprudent to reply. At my suggestion Miss Emily had described a certain satisfaction in a status associated with her relations with her guardian, but her account still seemed far from transparent. I was struck by her description of her reactions to sexual stimulation. Let us consider the possibilities. Suppose first that a normal young woman had submitted to sexual penetration. She would have experienced sensations in the genital region, but in her account of sexual penetration, Miss Emily described a very different reaction, taking place in a different region, in the alimentary tract, where nausea and vomiting were sometimes induced. Here, described in convincing detail, is a reaction which is purely and completely hysterical.

Let me here reiterate that such phenomena occur when, unable to contemplate the existence of the genital organs, a hysterical woman displaces sensations to parts of the body that may more acceptably be acknowledged, in this case the stomach. Nausea, moreover, is among the symptoms of anorexia, a condition of which Miss Emily now complained. Pointing out to her the connection of her present anorexia to the nausea that she had felt more than ten years previously had its therapeutic effect, as was confirmed in her response to an enquiry I made a few days later, in which she agreed that she had begun to eat more normally than at any time since her recent collapse.

Thus Miss Emily recounted an event that included the symptom of nausea. Then at my interpretation a connection was made, and brought into consciousness, and the symptom disappeared. In clearing up this symptom it may seem that the mystery of whether the seduction had taken place is also settled. I would beg that our judgement be suspended a little longer. Recall the story of the candle-light dinner and the visitation to the bedroom of the sleeping maiden, and ask yourselves whether any other account could more perfectly correspond to that of an episode derived from the imagination of an active girl just past puberty who read widely and whose mind was inflamed by the amorous adventures of her governess. Although the description of hysterical displacement of sensation is genuine beyond all reasonable doubt, it is possible that what I heard from Miss Emily was an account of masturbation with its accompanying phantasies. The hysterical reactions of nausea may have occurred in response to her own acts, which were then vigorously denied, to be replaced by the conviction that the powerfully imagined scene of seduction had indeed taken place.

In our next consultation I reverted to the question of the fountain pen and its meaning, as well as to the question of what may have been behind her calling out to her godmother in her dream. She said that nothing whatever came to mind with this latter image. It just seemed like one of those occasions in dreams when one is trying to act but is somehow paralysed.

'I wonder what you felt about your godmother, following the scenes you described.'

'I wished I could speak to her but I could not do so.'

'Just as in the dream?'

'I had not thought of it like that.'

'And . . .? You seemed as if you were about to say something else.'

'Yes. I think now that perhaps it was not my godmother in my dream, but my own mother. I do not know. It seems indistinct. The image seemed to change, and I cannot now recapture it exactly when I think about it.'

'Is there anything else?'

'When I think of her, the word "godmother" seems to fall apart in two halves, "god" and "mother".'

'You mean perhaps that your mother is with God?'

'Perhaps.'

'And that you long for her now, since being with God she could protect you. She is the person who would know how to protect you from the danger you are in.'

'Yes. That is right. Completely. I used to pray to her often after she had died. You may think it childish. I know I have had to look after myself. But you are correct.'

'Perhaps you feel that now I could protect you as your mother or your father had.'

'Yes, I suppose I do. I did not want to consult you, but I do look forward to coming.'

'In the dream, you feel that your godmother should have protected you as your own mother would have done?'

'I can remember thinking that if only she would somehow just know, and protect me. Or at least if she could have avoided being away from the house the problem would have been solved, because that was always when Mr S would find opportunities to visit me.'

You may find it strange that behind the self-assured façade of an independent woman there lived on the childlike wish that her mother, alive in heaven, would rescue her. I think we must understand that often the child and the adult live side by side. Nor was I surprised when Miss Emily said she thought perhaps I might now be standing in the stead of her parents.

Miss Emily next spoke about how, after her parents' death, she had often spoken to them in her imagination. She still did, though less frequently. As time passed, their voices had become fainter. She realised, she said, that really she was alone. She had become accustomed to this. She had decided that to preserve the memory of her parents she must strive to be what they would have wished. So she worked hard at school, and on her own at Latin and Greek, the subjects she had studied with her father. Her aspirations seemed spoilt, she said, by the shame of her relations with Mr S. This occurred particularly if she thought about it in the wrong sort of way. She said that, although she wanted to be good, she felt herself to be very wicked.

She said that feeling alone had also spurred her on to escape. She had imagined herself in daydreams as having been captured by her guardian, and kept in his castle. Sometimes she imagined herself as an envoy of a foreign government, such as her father had sometimes described. She had been captured and had to make use of the sexual influence she had acquired to forward her plan of escape. Usually, she said, this idea seemed unconvincing to her after she imagined it for a while. She knew really she was a disgraced creature. The best thing, she had thought, was to work hard at school, where her guardian could not intrude, and to read all she could so that her father would be proud of her. She said she kept all that in a separate compartment of her mind, so that she could be what he would have wished, in at least one way. This was how the idea first came to her of translating ancient texts, and of living by her pen. She had felt proud of this, and said it was one thing she had salvaged from the wreckage, though all this was now lost.

Although at first Miss Emily had spoken of the loss of a fountain pen, she now spoke of being no longer firmly in possession of her ability to write. I remarked that, although it was in some ways premature, I would venture a tentative interpretation of the first part of her dream, in which she sat at her desk with her pen, and called out to her godmother. It seemed abundantly clear that behind her godmother in her dream there was the figure of her mother. The cry to her mother might have been something like: 'Look, Mama, now see I have this penis which gives me influence.' I added: 'I think you might prefer the term "phallus" to "penis" at this point.' I also added that, although I did not dispute that her guardian and her father were very different, it seemed likely that behind the scene of Mr S and herself was a longing for the love of her father. This in turn might then imply that she was calling for her mother to be witness that she had gained her father's love, that she had been able to substitute herself for her mother in his affections.

'So the meaning of the first part of the dream,' I said, 'may include something like the following: "As I sit alone at my desk, I fear to be penetrated, but at the same time I am excited. I want my father's love, and I want the influence it can give me." '

'Oh, Professor Freud,' said Miss Emily, 'you do try so tremendously hard, and I am touched by some of what you say. Of course I loved my father. Along with my mother I loved him more than anyone I ever have or ever will. Tears come to my eyes just to think of him. I have no recollection of wanting to have sexual relations with him, though I have often imagined being comforted by him, or rescued by him from Bluebeard's castle. He would come along, see how wicked Mr S had been, take me away and tell me that it had not been my fault. I would not even think it so tremendously wrong if in some way I did want everything about him. But you must see that it is quite different from anything connected with my guardian, who never was a substitute for my father; never in any way. Perhaps I wished to entice my father away with me on my own; sometimes he would come away for the day, exploring, just him and me; and that was away from my mother. Maybe I even harboured such dark wishes. Is that what you would call them? But that does not mean that I ever really would want to take him from my mother, or that my life was ruled by desires to do such things. I am not shocked at these suggestions you have made. You forget that I have myself translated the plays of Sophocles from the Greek, and thought long and hard about their significance for ourselves. I have also read the theories of Feuerbach about gods being transformations of our own human desires,* and these make much sense of the Greek myths. I have to say also that, although you probably will disapprove, I have recently been reading your new book on dreams, and I was very impressed by it. So you see, I think some of what you are saying is right. I also do not dispute

---

*Emily is perhaps here referring to Feuerbach's *Essence of Christianity*.

that my mind is in the most terrible muddle, but I do not think I have been moved by a desire to have a sexual relation with my father masquerading as my guardian.'

I was taken aback by this. In anyone less earnest than Miss Emily, it might have been considered pert. I said, 'Do you not think it possible that the scenes with your guardian were your imagination, manufactured from your grief and loneliness, and from your own nascent sexuality, inflamed by accounts of your governess?'

'No, Professor Freud. You see before you a woman who was deflowered, is that the right word?, by a man whose duty it was to protect her. I do not even dispute that I must have done something to encourage what happened to me, though I do not know what it was. I can imagine that I longed for love from either my guardian or his wife. It is indeed a source of the most bitter shame that somehow in my manner I must thereby have encouraged my guardian's attentions. I was close to my father, and I kissed him often, and sat on his lap as he read to me. I have puzzled long and in anguish about whether I did unknowingly provoke my guardian by signs of affection I might have held out towards him. He certainly told me that women have men in their power, and once captured by their beauty there is little they can do to resist, but I still feel very confused about all this. I remember myself as a sad waif, a child who had become an orphan, not an enticing prospect for a man. I can certainly tell you that the events I described did take place. They were not my imagination.'

Once again we had reached an impasse. There are two inescapable facts. The first is that Miss Emily had fallen ill. The second is that since she had begun treatment with me her severe symptoms of anorexia had abated. Her nervous collapse could scarcely have occurred if all were as it appeared. I communicated this conclusion to her, and she received it in silence.

That day she left me with the words 'I don't really want to be so cantankerous, Professor Freud. You are right, I have been ill, very ill, and I have improved considerably under your care. Please forgive me.'

7

Emily's Journal continued

Sara Learns All

Friday 17 June

Last evening, when Sara had left my rooms, and after I had deliberately refrained from reading the newspaper all day, I read that the body had been found. Although not prominent, and on an inner page, it was there for all to see.

> The body of a man, identified as Mr C. S. of the British Diplomatic Service, was found on a mountainside yesterday afternoon in the region of G——. He appears to have fallen accidentally whilst walking. The police have invited any who know about the circumstances of his presence in Austria to come forward with whatever information they may have, etc., etc.

I sank into a chair and I think I let out a sound in horror when I read it. Last night I lay in my bed, alternately hot and cold, in such a bath of perspiration that I had to rise and change my bedclothes.

I did not visit Professor Freud today. I cannot face anybody. Sara came this evening. I said I was sorry to have fallen ill again, but I could hardly even speak to her. I begged her to leave, which she did with reluctance, saying she would return first thing on the morrow. I cannot eat. I shall vomit again. I am as bad as I was before I started to see Professor Freud, or even worse. It is not even worth speaking about. There is no mystery about what has befallen me. The truth is that I am filled with panic about being found out. Found out!

Saturday morning

I am too wicked to repent of my sin. I think merely of what will become of me. I could not sleep. Instead I waited for the police to arrive. This morning I disposed of the clothes I was wearing, and the shoes. I went out before dawn with my clothes in a bag that was not conspicuous and walked to the Danube, which took nearly an hour. I thought that dropping them into the canal near where I live would not be sufficient, that somehow they might be recovered from there. I found some heavy stones to weigh them down, and dropped them from the bridge into the river. People were beginning to move around the city, but it was still dark and I think no one saw me drop the bag. A fear grips me that something I have overlooked will tie me to the murder. I behave furtively, like the murderer I am. In trying to cover my tracks I may give myself away. I was terrified that someone would stop me on my way to the river, or see me picking up stones, or dropping my clothes from the bridge. I think about it obsessively. Like Raskolnikov, except that he had planned his crime, and had thought logically about it.* I seem to have been marked out for an evil fate. Why, I ask. Why? I think perhaps it was to test my moral courage, and I have failed. I have tried to be good, but failed the test. I hide this journal whenever I am not writing so

*Here Emily refers to the central character in Dostoyevsky's *Crime and Punishment*.

63

that it will not incriminate me. Incriminate! As if it would make me into a criminal.

Sunday

Sara has insisted that I move to her house again, where she can look after me. She accepted no argument. She said I should bring what I needed immediately. Then she arranged for my books and possessions to be brought. She says I will not be going back there. I feel she is imprisoning me. She says she will tomorrow give notice on my behalf that my tenancy here is ending. She will make sure all my financial obligations are met. That is what she is like. When she gets an idea, she just arranges things. If I wish to live on my own when I am better, she will help me find new rooms. She thought my rooms were in any case too gloomy for me.

Monday

I have done little but lie in bed. Sara's family doctor came to leave me draughts that I might sleep. He says I am suffering from some nervous strain or excitement. Sara told him that I am consulting Professor Freud, which seemed to make him uncomfortable on some ethical ground, as if he might be trespassing on the Professor's province, but Sara seems to know him well, and was able to reassure him. She said that I merely needed some temporary relief. Whatever he prescribed, it worked. I have slept, and it kept my panic at bay. Though now I am feeling better, it takes almost nothing for the panic to return. I wait hourly for the maid to announce the arrival of the police.

Sara insists that I go back to see Professor Freud. She said that I had been getting much better and whatever has now made me worse again will just have to be faced. I will be more able to do that with Professor Freud's help than without. I will write him a note tomorrow. Perhaps I will go again after the weekend.

Tuesday

Here I sit, gazing out of the window. I have a lovely bright room in Sara's house, two rooms in fact, a bedroom and a sitting room. One opens into the other. There is a small dressing room too. I may regard them as my own, she says. Sara has rather a grand family house, the kind of thing that a family with children and half a dozen servants live in. There is no want of space. My rooms are on the floor next to the top one, just below the servants' attic rooms. I have this whole floor more or less to myself. I must admit I am glad to be out of my own rooms. They have felt oppressive since he visited me there.

Sara held me in her arms last night, like a mother with her child. She just held me for many minutes and stroked my hair gently. I could do nothing but sob. I wanted just to let myself be in her arms, let myself be. But I could not. I feel too bad, and should not be held like that.

After a while I found a way of freeing myself. It is too close. We spoke instead, which was easier. Sara spoke of the school and our colleagues. She hopes that the Headmistress will give me my job back when I am better. I know that she will not. She should not. I wish that I could explain everything to Sara, or to someone, but I can explain only to this diary. It was difficult to bring it from its hiding place when I was coming here. Now I have nowhere to hide it. I keep it in my leather bag, in a wardrobe. I will seal it with sealing wax to know if it has been opened by anyone.

Morbid fears are never far from me, that something I have overlooked will tie me to the murder. The police are even now

65

putting the pieces together and soon they will arrive. I can do nothing but wait. Then it will be over.

Wednesday

A dream that I dread has come for a second time. It is not the dream I recounted to the Professor but another, yet more terrifying. Perhaps the thought of writing to the Professor provoked it. My dreams betray my own evil within me. I imagine talking to the Professor about this dream, and of him being able to understand in the fatherly way that he sometimes has, but that would be fatal. I have been thinking of telling Sara everything. I must to speak to someone. I cannot get anything straight in my mind now. It is all in a terrifying whirl, and I feel I may truly go mad. I think perhaps I have already gone mad. I cannot think.

Thursday

I will ask Sara to help me analyse this dream. There, see: that in itself is mad. It is a provocation to discovery. Why do I feel compelled to do that? I do not know what else to do. Now I have another reason for not sleeping, for fear of having that dream again. So I tried to read late into the night, though I cannot concentrate. I am seized by feelings of dread. I tremble without being the least able to control myself, though I am not cold. Indeed the weather is rather too warm at present in Vienna. When I finally fell asleep I had the dream once again. Professor Freud has mentioned to me the idea that if a dream is analysed then one will not be haunted by what it means. Perhaps I could analyse the dream myself, though I do not think I could. It seems to need another person to see things that one cannot oneself. I can trust Sara and I need someone to talk to. It is not really the dream that haunts me; it is my guilt. I am mad. I have gone mad. I am a lost soul, still for a few days wandering in this world, but soon to join those souls in the *Inferno*.*

Friday

Sara and I talked some more about interpreting dreams yesterday. Professor Freud's technique which we have read about and discussed is to get me to recall incidents or thoughts associated with each dream image in turn. Then he tries to understand the whole dream like a story, linking these associations. A wish motivates the whole. He also pays attention to inconsistencies, or gaps in the story, which are little signs that prompt him to ferret out more information to fill the gaps.

Sara laughed at my description of the Professor ferreting out information. His method seemed to her an excuse for him to indulge his curiosity. She said that she too had always wanted to know more about me. It provoked her, because one of my faults is to be secretive. She teases me about this, but it is not something to be laughed about. So she thought she would like the same excuse as the Professor. She will help me analyse my dream and also have the right to ferret things out. I both want her to know and feel panic-stricken.

By now Sara has read the whole of the dream book, and the *Psychopathology of Everyday Life*, as well as the Professor's works on hysteria. We have discussed them and she says she thinks she will now be able to do very well as an analyst.

'Maybe I give Herr Professor's earlier treatment, I give hypnosis,' she says. 'He was not so capable with this method. I think with a practice I shall be better. Or I give you baths every

*Emily's use of the Italian *Inferno* no doubt refers to Dante's work in which the pilgrim meets various souls who wander there, in torments that suit their own sins.

day. I shall massage your whole body, as he describes with Frau Emmy von N.* Then all your sad memories would come flooding out, and you would be cleaned.' And she laughs joyfully.

'Don't talk of the Professor massaging that lady. It is too much like Mr S,' I said.

Sometimes when Sara laughs I feel that this is all that is important in the world. If I could just hear her laughter I would not hear the horrible thoughts that plague me.

So I did recount my dream to her. Why did I do it? Now I have told her the worst. Yes, the very worst. I am calmer. Calm enough to write these pages, not just a few scraps of words. Professor Freud would say it was because I really had wished to confess to her. I knew I risked talking about what has happened.

In the dream I am walking through Vienna. I feel a perfect happiness as I walk along. Someone calls my name, and I know at that moment my happiness is shattered, completely turned into its most bleak and grinding opposite. When I look round it is someone with a horrifying huge face which somehow expands, and crushes me downwards into the ground. I feel terrified and wake up screaming.

Sara asked me first what I associated with feeling happy in Vienna. I said that often in the last year I had felt happy. I would walk home from the school thinking how fortunate I was. During that year I started the habit of evaluating the things that happened each day, and their relation to my life as a whole. I had been thinking that, though my parents' death and what followed had been a cruel reverse, now I had recovered and was making progress. I had my work, which I enjoyed. Everyone had said I

---

*Sara refers to Freud's implication that he found hypnosis unsatisfactory; and to one of his cases, Frau Emmy von N, described in Freud and Breuer's *Studies on Hysteria*, in which he visited the patient every day and gave her baths and massage.

was doing well at the school. I was pleased that my translations had been successful.

As Sara started to turn over the dream in her mind, I told her that my happiness came from being with her, and that I always looked forward to us being together. Was that part of the excuse that I wanted, to tell her my dream? No, I think not, for I did not quite tell her the truth. It is my secretiveness again. The truth was that I felt overwhelmed by affection for her. I do not know how to say it. I do not know much about love, but I think perhaps that I had come to love her. For the first time I had a friend to share so much with. Sara's existence had transformed how I felt. *Had* transformed? All seemed lost now, turned into its opposite. For a short time, the first interval since childhood, I had felt truly happy. I know it was because of her, because of her friendship. Of course I could not say all that to her.

So I just said that her friendship made me happy, and that I valued it very much. Also I was pleased that I could live contentedly on my own and work, and that I had not fallen into despair or entered into marriage through being lonely or frightened.

Next she said, 'What about the next thing you spoke? Someone calls your name.'

I thought about this for a while but nothing came to mind. Nothing. It truly did not.

There, see? One could not have plainer evidence of Professor Freud's theory of the unconscious. My mind had repressed something. It had kept it out of consciousness. It was only when Sara said, 'Can you think of a time when someone calls your name and you are surprised?' Then there flooded into my mind the day at my apartment when Mr S came to my door, and said my name.

I started to cry then. I said something like: 'I am not sure I can bear to think about this, Sara. I try to keep myself from thinking about it. If I talk about it, things will become much worse, infinitely worse. You do not know what you are asking.'

She said that she thought I probably was not right, and that maybe I should face whatever it was. I should not try to avoid it. Then the dream would go away, and, with it, whatever had been troubling me.

In the end I could resist no longer. I told her. I told her about how I had been working at home one evening. I was preparing my speech to the parents that I was to give the following Monday. There came a knock at the door and I told Sara that I thought it was her. I was a little surprised because I did not expect her at that time, but I went to the door and opened it. I almost died of fright. There was Mr S at my door. He just said my name: 'Emily. Emily.' I could not speak and motioned him to come in. What else could I do? It was appalling. He sat down and remonstrated with me. Why had I lied to him about where I was? He was, after all, still my guardian. (I do not know whether that is correct. I am twenty-five now.) He went on speaking. He said he had been worried when I was not at the address I had given him in America.

Then I told Sara what I had not told her before. How secretive I am. I said that when I decided to return to Europe after finishing at the university, I did not tell my guardian. I felt that if I was too near he would insist that I live with them again. I could not bear that thought. So I said I was teaching at a school in Philadelphia. I arranged with a friend who lived there that she would send on letters from my guardian and his wife. When I wrote to them I sent the letter to my friend in America and she posted it from there. There were delays, of course, but they did not expect frequent correspondence. So it worked. I had not imagined that he would arrive in Philadelphia, unannounced. He had said that he did not like America, and would refuse another posting there if he were offered one. Nevertheless a month before he came here he had gone to Philadelphia and had called at the address of my friend, to find me. Then, by entering her apartment as a thief, he had found my address. Thus he came here to Vienna.

'It shows how determined he is,' I said. 'He would stop at nothing, nothing at all.'

I told Sara how he tried to insist that I return to England with him. I did not think he could insist, but I do not know. I am not very practical about legal matters, and I did not know if I could prevent him taking me away. I told her he said that his wife had not been in good health for some time. She spent much of the summer at the spas and her doctor had advised warmer climates. So she had wintered in Italy. He said she needed me, that they both needed me. It was my duty, and so on and so on. How could I? If his wife were away there would be nothing to stop him harassing me again. I could look forward to a life of his awful attentions.

I told Sara how I was filled with terror, and of course said no. I said I had made my life here now, and did not need a guardian. Then came the worst part. He started pleading. He said he loved me and could not live without me. I had become an obsession for him. Would I but consider him kindly, he would do whatever I wished. He had money, and it would allow me to do whatever I liked. He felt sure that I could grow to love him, just a little. Or even if I could not, he would be satisfied. He would not bother me if only he could be with me sometimes.

'It was madness, but I was terrified that you might arrive,' I said to Sara. 'I could not bear the thought of anyone seeing him there, especially you.'

I told Sara how I promised to consider what he was asking, if only he would give me three days to think about it. I told her how I had to kiss him, and how finally I managed to get him to leave.

Sara insisted that I tell her what happened after that. I spoke about going on the train to G— that next day. I found it very difficult to talk. While I was telling her of the train journey and walking on my own she came and held me. I was feeling more and more terrified as I was speaking. I was shaking uncontrollably again. I recounted how after two hours I heard footsteps coming up behind me. Suddenly he was there, again calling, 'Emily.' I had been preoccupied with the occurrences of the day before. When I heard the sound behind me I stopped to look round. There he was. We were some way from the houses we had passed coming up from the valley. I felt deathly cold, and sick. I had a presentiment of evil.

The memory of it is vivid. It keeps returning. As always I think about it piece by piece, wondering what I could have done. I know now I should have run, of course, further up the mountain path, until I came to an Alpine house, where the farmer would shelter me. That is what I should have done. I am nimbler than he. I doubt whether he would have been able to catch me. Instead I just stood there. I seemed rooted to that spot. He came as if to embrace me, with his arms held out. The path was narrow. To pass on it, one person would have had to stand close to the rockface that jutted out on to the path, while the other carefully went past on the outer side. He clasped me to him and started saying things about how he loved me. He said he was desperate to feel my body again. He said it had been impossible to live without me. He was rough with me, ripping at my dress, clumsily caressing my bosom, trying to kiss me. I felt an overwhelming revulsion and horror.

'Please get away. Please. Take your hands from me. Please,' I said, or something like that.

It was then that I pushed him. At least I think I must have pushed him. I do not properly know. I just wanted him away from me. I pushed and scrambled backwards, back to the rockface at the side of the path. I held on to the cliff. As I did so, I saw him losing his footing, slipping first sideways and then towards the edge of the path as it rounded the side of the mountain. He must have realised in that moment what was happening. He tumbled, and then he was over the edge. I could not have helped him. I was too shocked to react but it was also so quick. Then he was out of sight. I do not remember whether he cried out. I only remember the sound of small rocks falling down, then nothing. After a few seconds or minutes, I do not know, I went to look over the edge. It was impossible to see down for more than a few yards, to where he might have fallen. One could not get down from the path. Perhaps one could approach the place from lower down. I do not know.

I write it again here. This is as I remember it, as accurately as I can. It is as I told it to Sara. It is my memory of it without censoring anything. It is the plainest I can do. Soon the police will come to imprison me. I shall be hanged as a murderess. It will be finished.

Sara held me while I wept. I do not know why, but my feeling of wrongness as she held me, of somehow needing to pull away, did not occur. Can I trust her? She said that it was not my fault. It was at least partly an accident. Anyone would have done the same in my position. We sat together for several hours. She soothed me as I talked sporadically over the crime that I had committed. Sara was calming. Not once did she make me feel that she was shocked, or that I was wicked for what I had done. She did not make me feel like a murderer. She did not make me feel that she wished not to associate with me. She insisted on staying with me that night in the bedroom she has given me.

I was grateful not to be alone. She lay with me and soothed me through the night. I fell asleep at some point and had my most restful sleep for a week. The dream did not come to haunt me. When I awoke Sara had risen. Some minutes later she appeared and immediately embraced me.

She said: 'It was good for you to talk about Mr S. Now we start thinking what to do.' Then she herself brought breakfast up from the kitchen, which we ate together.

'Perhaps Professor Freud could speak on my behalf in the court. Do you think he might do that?' I asked. 'Really, I think I should not see him any more.'

Sara has left me for a while now. She says she will be back later, and I write this. I am glad I told her. I feel like a child who has done something bad and found that her mother has not stopped loving her. Perhaps I can trust her. The facts, however, are these: I am wicked, I have killed somebody, and I must submit myself to justice. If I do not give myself up, they will in any case discover me.

Later

Sara returned. She has sent a servant to the school to say that she is ill and will not be there today. We have talked a great deal. She has said that I had completely misunderstood the whole incident.

'One must think scientifically and practically,' she announced with great authority. 'Incidents such as this kind are discussed in Darwin's book on expressing emotions,' she said.* She had brought the book with her, and read to me a passage about how, at the Zoological Gardens in London, Darwin had tried an experiment upon himself, with a deadly snake in a glass case. He decided to put his face up close to the glass, which he knew was very thick, and not to jump back when the snake struck at him. Even though he had determined not to jump back if the snake struck, because consciously he knew it could not reach him, he leapt back two yards. The emotion made him do so.

*Darwin's book referred to here is *The Expression of the Emotions in Man and Animals*.

She had looked up the passage when she was away. She made me listen carefully: 'Darwin insists it is the direct action of the excited nervous system. These movements are made because of the habit of escaping the thing you fear, or when you feel an emotion, simply because of excess nerve force. They occur without the will. The will is powerless to prevent them. This is what Darwin's experiment shows.

'Now observe this,' she said. She made me raise my nightdress above my knee. I am ashamed to say I was still wearing my nightdress. She made me cross my legs, and then she tapped me with the side of her her hand below my kneecap. My leg kicked forward. 'This is a reflex,' she announced. 'Now try to inhibit your leg to kick.' She hit my kneecap again, and I could not stop my leg kicking forward. 'You see, you cannot stop it? Now observe,' she said. 'I bring my hand quickly near your face. Do not close your eyes. There,' she said. 'You cannot prevent closing them. It is a nervous mechanism of protection. On the mountain such a fear reflex was a mechanism of protection. If it was not on a mountain your act will make a small space between you and the brute. For short time it will make you free. Darwin says that in an opposite way you could not act. Fear pushed Mr S away without your will. You were in fear of him. How can you then be guilty? He was guilty, following you like a hunting dog. He was a hateful man; he was also a fool.' Sara was speaking in her matter-of-fact way. 'The only thing we must decide is what to do next. I am thinking most carefully about it.

'There are two alternatives. The first is to ask a lawyer for you. You must not be concerned about money. I have more than I need. I pay the fees. You will give yourself up. The lawyer will go with you. Then you would be arrested, put in prison. There will be a trial. With this plan we cannot know that it will come out well. People should be angry for his crime against you, but one cannot say how it will come out. If we win, your name will be

75

made to sound bad. You must describe publicly everything he did to you. Your godmother, people you know, might think badly. Perhaps the judge thinks: She did something to excite him. There is never smoke without fire, and such things. Even when you are made free, you would be, how do you say?, famous. The woman who kills her seducer. We will have to escape to live in America or somewhere large where no one will know us. I cannot see that any good comes of that way.'

I listened to this. I listened to Sara's practical way of thinking about things, and marvelled at it. She is so different from the muddle I am in, so different from my usual mixture of daydreams and feeling incapable of getting anything straight, except of course if it is about people who lived thousands of years ago. Most of all I heard what she said as she finished this speech. She said, 'We will have to escape to live in America'. She said 'we', meaning herself and me.

She continued. 'The other way is we do nothing. One advantage to be Jewish is that I am not completely a member of this civilised society of ours. So I do not believe in their justice. One lives justly, of course. One must never do things against the law if possible. At the same time one must not expect justice.

'When my husband was a student, a friend, a student of physics, was dismissed from the university because he came first in an examination. An important professor said the examination paper was stolen from his desk. This was enough to allow my husband's friend to be dismissed. There was no evidence against him. There was a great scandal. On this side and that people spoke. The affair was discussed. This friend, you see, was Jewish. He had had differences with the professor, which I do not remember. I believe he had spoken on some matter, or had been critical of this professor. My husband was certain that his friend was honest. My husband had gentile friends who also hated what happened. They knew this friend was dismissed because he was

Jewish. The only evidence was that this friend in the examination had done well. The professor said that he had inserted a question in the examination, just to challenge the class, that was far too difficult for them. Only the Jewish boy could answer it, he said. The professor said, on grounds of his reputation, that dishonesty was involved. He said that the examination paper was missing. Then there was a story of his rooms unlocked because the lock does not work. Everyone knows he is a man of untidy habits. He does not know if his room was locked or not, or if he had kept the paper in his desk or not. Everyone says he is a person also who makes plots, but makes himself to be right. Because he is from a good family, he continues to this day in his position in the university, able to say such things. My husband's friend grinds glass to make lenses. I do not know if you realise, Emily, the way the world works. The error of my husband's friend was to draw attention, to stand out, to do well in the examination. We Jews learn not to do this.

'I have thought often that all women are in much the same position as all Jews. We must make ourselves not noticed. If we are too much noticed, then severe consequences come. You see, Emily, although you are more clever than I, in many ways you are more innocent. In a world of ideas you live. You manage with your American Quaker friends to be with honest people, and to think about high ideals. Despite the fearful things that happened to you, you have kept yourself pure. In some way it did not touch you. You think you should confess. You must give yourself up for justice. How unlikely will be justice you do not understand.

'True justice will be to speak of how a man like that can break his trust, and how then to make your life miserable he follows you. True justice would know the suffering he made. Justice means that the judge and other men who hear the case would say that he was the criminal, and those who do such things should be punished. You do not understand that only men will speak on the matter. No woman's voice is heard, to ask if men will be able to judge truly, or if they understand the pain you were in. The judge and other men are not scientists. They will not understand the scientific evidence that a person in fear will push away. Most of all, many men do not think women are serious. They would not believe anything that you say. How also do we know that among them are not those who have themselves made approaches to women in their care, to servants, or to other women who have for fear been unable to resist?'

Sara was in full flood. I do not know what it is in her, but injustice makes her full of determination. Somehow she sees through all the talk, and the usual habits of the world, which I seem just to accept. She was right that I lived in a world of ideas. I feel pale and insubstantial beside her. Her world was of acting to make something better. Not in a general way. She seems to get into these states only for people she knows, I think. I had realised as I came to know her that she was quite wealthy and that she used a great part of her money to help people. The Educational Association for women depended completely on her. She started the two prostitutes with a dressmaker's shop in a fashionable part of the city.

'Even if they become tired of dressmaking, they will be able to attract a better kind of gentleman there,' she said, and laughed gaily, as if to think nothing of it, though I knew that she cared about them a great deal.

Now here was I. The thought came to me that I did not know whether I wanted to be one of her causes. I should keep that thought quiet.

'I do not want to become one of your causes,' I said. 'We used to be friends . . .'

'Do not be ridiculous,' she said. 'I love you very much. I am sorry I was excited. You are not a cause. You need to be cared for, and to do that I will. I understand perfectly what happened. I wish I had been there. I would give him a greater push. You are not guilty. He has done wrong. It was wicked for him to follow you when he was alive. It would not be justice for you to be punished for what he did now he is dead. If you pushed him away from you by the reflex, or if he slipped, it is not different. He had no right to be there. That is an end. I wish I could take some of the load of it for you. I know I cannot do that fully. To live with what has happened, you must be brave. I will be by your side.'

Now instead of thoughts of the unspeakable Mr S there goes around in my mind what she could possibly mean when she said she loved me very much, and that she cared for me. What can she mean? I feel confused.

Sara says she thinks I should see Professor Freud again after the weekend. I have written to say that I will be there. How will I face him? I do not know.

If I see him I must be alert to the danger that I will let something slip that will let him guess about the murder. He is quite cunning with his dream analysis. He gets things out of me that I thought were locked up tight. His mind tends to dwell on anything that has a connection with sex. That may be the chink in his armour. It may prevent him from guessing what really happened.

No doubt he will want to know why I have missed these consultations. If I go back I must distract him from asking too much about why I did not go for several days. We have still got some of my dream of myself at my desk left to analyse. He becomes very engaged by dream analysis, and will not let it be. He rather loses himself in it. So many of the dream thoughts turn out ultimately to be sexual! I think this is what fascinates him. Perhaps the Professor is right. Sex is somehow at the bottom of things. At any event that will be safest, to talk about sex, perhaps of Mr S's sexual attentions. We will talk of the dream and we will talk of sex. The sexual acts of Mr S and myself may be shameful but at least they are not murder. I will ask him to finish the dream analysis as if I were as fascinated as he. He will, I think, be pleased by that. That will be best. I will discuss the whole thing with Sara this evening. Perhaps she will think that I need no longer go.

8

Freud's Lecture continued

A Scene of Humiliation

It was with concern and speculation that I awaited Miss Emily's arrival at our next times of appointment, but she did not appear. After the first missed appointment I wrote to her saying that if she were indisposed I would be grateful for a message to that effect. After the third, and no reply to my note, I thought of making a discreet enquiry via her friend's father, but I have learnt not to become anxious about missed appointments. Often they are reactions to a stage reached in the analysis, and can later be discussed as such. On the fourth day I received a note from her, saying that she had been unwell, and that she hoped to be able to keep her appointments after the weekend as usual. I also received a note from a colleague, a family doctor of my acquaintance, saying that he had attended Miss Emily, who was in a state of collapse and staying with a patient of his own, that he prescribed a morphine sleeping draught, and hoped that in doing so he had not breached etiquette.

When I saw Miss Emily next, she thanked me for my note, explained again that she had been unwell and apologised profusely for her absence. She seemed tense, but without her previous restlessness. She thought she might have been set back during her illness since our last meeting, but prayed that we continue as before.

'I am sorry if I was impertinent to you last time we met,' she said. 'I would regard it as a great favour if we could finish analysing the dream that we started.'

'Very well,' I replied. I would have preferred to hear the reasons for her absence, but decided that these would emerge in due time. 'In your dream an image appears of yourself with your hands bound as you try to call to your godmother.'

'Yes, that is so.'

'What comes to mind in relation to your hands being tied?'

'There was a time when my guardian threatened to tie my hands together.'

'Go on.'

'Sometimes he would trace lines with his finger on my body, several times, like this.' Miss Emily gestured towards herself with her forefinger as she lay on the couch, tracing the outline of a triangle between her genitalia and breasts. 'Once I caught hold of his wrist, to stop him. He became angry and that is when he made the threat.'

'Is there anything else? Does anything else come to mind?'

'What he said about tying my hands terrified me more than ever. I had a strong mental picture of him gazing down at me while I lay there, bound and defenceless.'

'I wonder,' I asked, 'whether you felt that your hands should be restrained because otherwise they might stray, and find themselves at some mischief.'

'What can you mean?'

'Perhaps you had sometimes found yourself touching your own genital region, masturbating, and felt ashamed of this. You may have felt that it would be better if your hands could be prevented from an action you could not yourself restrain.'

She seemed lost in confusion, but recovered herself, and seemed determined as she spoke. 'Oh Professor Freud,' she said. 'How can you say such things? I know you are a doctor, and that I am a disgraced woman, but even so. But if I must, I own it. I have done that, but not now.'

'And did you think of a liaison with your guardian when you masturbated?'

'No, I did not think of that liaison . . . No, that is not what I meant.' She seemed again covered in confusion. Finally she said: 'I have admitted to shameful acts, is that not enough? I did not do it while thinking of him. Or rather, I stopped because when I did so, sometimes, I could not help the idea of him coming into my mind. So I just stopped altogether. It is too shameful . . .' Again she was in tears.

You may think my questioning heartless, but you will appreciate that we were led directly to this point by the patient's own dream image of her hands being tied. Invariably in cases such as these, matters of sexual conduct must be discussed. In my experience it is best to do so frankly. Without doing so we will never reach the seat of a neurosis, and would therefore have nothing whatever to offer our patients.

Her confession and admission, while not entirely satisfactory, are, I think you will agree, grounds for taking seriously the theory that a seduction by her guardian had not in fact taken place. The evidence so far is consistent with Miss Emily imagining scenes of seduction as a masturbatory phantasy, and her being disgusted at herself for indulging in this activity. It was the moral horror of a girl of puritan upbringing at acts that she found herself secretly performing. This in turn had precipitated the symptoms of nausea and anorexia, from which she was to suffer intermittently. Symptoms arose because of contemplation of a sexual act in which she felt disgusted at herself. It would not surprise me if this association between nausea and her sexual feelings were not also founded upon some earlier episode; perhaps a sight of sexual activity that she had witnessed when she was a child. We will have to wait patiently until we may come to that.

It is not sufficiently understood that the production of phantasies of this kind is common if not invariable in hysteria. Such phantasies correspond to the intense daydreams of early adolescence. We know that Miss Emily was prone to such daydreams. She had recounted her dreams of escape from Bluebeard's castle, and of being an envoy of a foreign power. In this case, I believe that her phantasies of defloration by her guardian served a double role. First, as befits mental products of a daydream, they excited her, and formed a focus for her developing sexual feelings. Secondly, since they stimulated masturbation, they brought alive a sense of guilt about that activity. This guilt was then transformed into disdain for members of the opposite sex. This is another kind of displacement, accompanying the displacement of genital stimulation into sensations of the alimentary tract. Displacement is the hallmark of the hysterical reaction. Her guilt and disgust at herself becomes disdain towards her guardian and other men, heightened by the depravity of the acts she imagined her guardian performing upon her.

While considering this explanation, I should point out the similarity of hysterical phantasies to paranoid delusions. We all accept that if a paranoid patient tells us how he is being influenced, let us say by a mysterious machine which puts thoughts and voices into his mind unbidden, then we know he is deluded. He may sound convincing, but we know him to be in the grip of a phantasy because there are no machines capable of such effects. Hysterical phantasies can also sound convincing, but of course we have not the same sense that what is recounted could not have happened. Bearing paranoid delusions in mind, you will grant me that mere convincingness of the account will not help us to determine whether the description is based upon actual events or upon phantasies.

I have to say that, in Miss Emily's most recent remarks about what she said took place with her guardian, one indication especially made me veer more strongly towards the view that this was a phantasy. It was her account of the threat of being bound. I have not enough evidence to convince you yet, but this is not the first case of the kind to have come to my attention. Its significance I believe is this. Hysterical phantasies are themselves often a joint product of both homosexual and heterosexual wishes coexisting in the same person. I hope in a few months' time to bring you a more fully articulated theory of bisexuality in human development. For the present I will sketch this idea baldly. Miss Emily's phantasy served a number of purposes simultaneously. It expressed the idea that her hands should be restrained. It allowed her to imagine herself being penetrated by the male organ, with the additional meanings of being punished and of not being able to resist this penetration. Tracing the triangle is a ritual act, no doubt functioning, like all such acts, to relieve anxiety. In addition, I draw your attention to Miss Emily's words: 'I had a strong mental picture of him gazing down at me while I lay there bound and defenceless.' Here, if I am not mistaken, Miss Emily imagines herself in the position of the active male gazing upon the body of the passive female. I am unable to corroborate this for the present, but I lay it before you at this stage, in case we may have an opportunity for corroboration as the analysis proceeds to deeper layers.

When she had composed herself, I asked Miss Emily whether what she had told me had contributed to her disdain for men. She agreed that it had.

'Indeed,' she asked, 'would you not feel the same about men if you had been treated in this way?' Notice now that she addressed me as a woman confidante, asking me about how I would feel as a woman in the position she had described. So far so good; but when I suggested that her disgust at the image of her being bound and subjected to sexual penetration was a way of fending off her

85

guilt about masturbation and her own sexual desires, she would not follow me.

Her defensive wall was still too strongly in place. We would need to return to this at a time when this wall had been weakened, or circumvented, and when she was more able to accept such ideas. The structures of illness often take much time to be elaborated. Correspondingly they are seldom removed easily. I had no doubt that if the pathogenic formation continued to work within her, as seemed to be the case, she would offer me other opportunities for recurring to this issue.

9

Emily's Journal continued

Whatever Comes to Mind

Saturday 25 June

I held to my plan of trying to keep the conversation with the Professor upon sex yesterday. I succeeded, but with a terrible vengeance. Not only did he manage to get me to recount degrading scenes when Mr S threatened to tie me up, but he made me admit to masturbation when I was younger. Had it not been for my resolve, I would have been quite unable to say anything whatsoever. I would have been been appalled. I would have been mute.

He seems to guess also that I want to discontinue my consultations. Perhaps I can continue for another week.

It was a relief telling Sara. I feel now that, even if I am hanged, she at least will understand. Now she just arranges everything, including the decision about what to do. It is as if a heavy burden has fallen from me. She is capable, where I am not.

We have decided to do nothing, not to give myself up. Sara thinks that probably nothing will happen. Then all I will have to do is to live with the memory of what I did, and to put behind me the attentions of Mr S. I will continue to see Professor Freud, at least for the next week.

Yesterday evening and this one were spent discussing plans. Now Sara has gone to bed, and I find again I cannot sleep. So I write.

Sara told me that she had known that there must have been some great suffering in my life, and had longed to help me be relieved of it. Now, she said, she would be able to do just that.

Coming from anyone else the suggestion that I should do nothing, not give myself up but be looked after, would have seemed wicked, even though it is what I longed for. Coming from Sara it appears different. She is an honest person. I do not think she would act in an immoral way. She is able, quite mysteriously, to know not the expedient course, but the right one. I trust her.

'I will make restitution,' I said to her. 'I will. I will try and do something to atone for the wrong I have done.'

'I know you will,' she said. 'That is how you Christians think. It will be good for you psychologically. I approve your plan.' She laughed gaily. 'You will find perhaps many who are persecuted by wicked men. You can be a comfort to them.'

I seem not to want to write much here now. Everything seems so uncertain. Or is it that I now talk to Sara instead? I go for an hour to see Professor Freud. Then I walk around the city. Then, rather than the compulsion to write, I find that I do nothing much. I am in a kind of daze. Yesterday, I waited in a suspended state for Sara to come home. Today there were times of comfort when I was with her – I was not wanting her to keep at a distance. Then there were times of waiting to be with her again. One such is now. If I can sleep it will be shorter.

Sunday night

We have spent the day together talking.

In all the turmoil of the last weeks I have used this journal as a confessional, just like the Catholics. Perhaps it has helped me think more clearly. Not clearly – I no longer think clearly – but it has helped me think. Now I need it more than ever. It is three o'clock in the morning. I am wide awake. Sara lies sleeping in the big bed in the next room. My head is awhirl. We have talked all evening and half the night. And we have done more than talk. Much more.

I do not feel ashamed. I experience no insistent desire to wash myself. I feel aglow.

We have had sexual congress. That sounds strange, but how should I write of it? I have no words to describe it. I am wide awake. I do not know what to do except write something here, in the hope that it will become clearer by doing so. I did not feel disgust, or want to hide. Is this the next in a line of steps towards my utter perdition? It may be so, but it does not feel so. It feels a step towards my salvation.

How should I speak of it? Let me just try to record it. Sara had held me sometimes during the last few days. She had comforted me like a mother. I had stopped resisting it. I allowed myself to be held by her.

Then this evening, as we were talking, she said, 'You must go to bed now. You need some rest, you dear.'

Something like that. I undressed, and she folded my clothes. Even that seemed no longer strange. It felt as if I was happy for her to be there. When I got into bed I think I said, 'Do not go yet. Lie here with me a little while.' I do not know where my words came from. They came from me unawares.

She removed her shoes and came beside me under the covers. We lay there together, looking at each other, holding each other's hands, just beneath our chins.

I said: 'Sara, I do not know how I would have lived, had it not been for you.'

She said, 'I like to receive appreciation.'

'If only you were a man. Or I were a man. It would not matter which,' I said; 'we could think about becoming engaged, getting married.' How did I speak so unguardedly with her? Some unknown part of me spoke despite myself. I knew that she would not mind such talk, but I did not know what made me speak.

'I do not think my father would approve,' she said. 'They would find it hard to accept someone who was not Jewish, though of course you could be converted.' I could not tell until she had finished speaking that she was teasing. I knew she meant that she too had thought of this. She was not just looking after me like an invalid. Our friendship had become like one which normally draws men and women together. How can one speak of it? She had said, two days before, 'I love you very much.' I asked myself whether she had meant that, and then out it burst.

'Do you know, the day before yesterday you said you loved me? Did you mean it in that way? Or just that you care about what happens to me?'

'You know what I meant. Why otherwise should it in your mind remain?'

'Yes,' I said. 'I think I know. Being with you made me happy before that fearful event, and even now with you I can feel happy once more. I can remember being a child again. I believe Mr S had made it hard for me to feel I was good enough to be loved. I am a very base person. I could never have loved Thornton, but you remind me of before all that, of when I was once happy, of being with my mother and father. That must sound so foolish, but it is the only way I have of expressing it.'

'You have made my life happy too, for the first time since my husband died,' she said, quite simply.

'What was it like being married?' I asked. 'I cannot imagine it.'

'I found it – how can I say – the closest I can imagine to being perfect,' she said. 'We were very happy. I was proud of him, and loved him. He loved me. I feel sad we did not have a child, but apart from that, it was everything. I was devastated when he died. I thought I would never be able to live. For a year, or even more, every day I thought I would not be able to get through that day. But, you can see, I did. Here now I am. And you make me happy again. It is you, not just one of my causes. Why do you say this? How could you think this?'

'Tell me what it was like being married.'

'I do not know how to describe it. Whatever you ask, I tell.'

'What is it like having, you understand, sexual relations, with a man? No I do not mean that; I mean with a man you love. I have only the experience of Mr S, and I fear he has poisoned my idea of it.'

'Yes, I fear he has. Do not think me shameless, or you may if you will. I found it wonderful. At first it seemed strange, because I knew only the little my mother had said. I was not prepared at all really. I did not understand anything. He had told me before he asked me to marry him that he had had an affair of love before he knew me, with a woman older than himself. I was pained at first. He begged my forgiveness. I do not think there was harm done. Later, when I spoke to other married women, they gave hints that they found the passionate side of marriage very difficult. I thought perhaps I should be grateful to that older woman. He told me that she had explained many things to him that he otherwise would not have known. I felt very awkward, embarrassed and nervous. We are taught to be ashamed, but he knew how to hold me. And I felt, I do not know how to say it, just – well, perfect. I was with the person I felt I would spend my life with, to whom I already felt devoted, and then this, quite unexpected, this whole private, wonderful thing, together. So I felt safe, but then more excited than I can say. Some days my mind would be full of him, and of it. I felt unable to wait until we would be able to be together again. Warm and glowing, but liable to tremble as if I were shivering. Does that describe? I do not know how to describe this. He taught me really what happens between a man and a woman. I was very ignorant. Then I just marvelled at it. Do you think me depraved? Yes, you must do.'

'No. I am astonished. I had no idea. I do not know what I thought. But not that. It sounds as if that is how it should be.'

'Yes. I believe this.'

I was transfixed by what she had told me. I believe I said, 'It sounds glorious. Like the poets describe. I had not properly believed in the possibility of any such thing, or maybe I had thought it was just for men, because nearly all the poets are men.'

'Not only men feel sexual desire,' Sara said, as if sensing my thoughts. 'Although one must not speak such things, I miss this most painfully. I think one would not know, until one had experienced it, how much one can miss it. I have sometimes thought I would allow a man to tempt me, I think just for that, but it has never felt right, and something inside speaks that it would not be the same unless one loved that person.'

Then it happened between us quite suddenly. She said something like 'But now I love you.' She unclasped our hands, which we were holding together between us. She put my arms around her, put her hands at the back of my neck, and kissed me. Not just a friendly kiss, but a passionate one, like that of a man kissing a woman to whom he is engaged. Like the way in which Thornton had kissed me.

I do not think that I protested. I did not wish to protest. I do not know whether it was because I felt excited by what she had said about married love. At any event, I kissed her too. I held her to me. Soon she jumped quickly out of bed, removed her outer garments, and returned to burrow beneath the bedclothes again. Then we stroked each other, her me, and me her. Not in that maternal way in which she had before, but in a soft exciting way, which I cannot describe.

Then she said, 'Take off your nightgown.'

I felt frightened for a moment. It was as if again I was to be the victim of something I would find painful and humiliating. Then a word of Professor Freud's came into my mind: 'What about your own sexual desire?' he had asked. I knew in that moment, for the first time, that I had my own sexual desire, and it was for Sara. Why should this take me by surprise? How could it be there without my knowing?

In a moment she jumped out of bed again, extinguished the lamp, and returned. We hugged and hugged. We just lay there. Kissing. I felt more close to her than I had felt to anyone. In the dark. 'Do you feel all right?' she asked.

'Yes, I do,' I heard myself say. 'I feel very close to perfect.' We both laughed.

'Just do as I say,' she said. 'If there is anything you do not like, anything at all, then tell me, and I stop. This is the only test. Otherwise you need do nothing.'

I could not say I did not like it. I longed for what she was doing, longed for her to continue. I did not want her to stop. I wanted her to go on. I wanted her not just to go on, I wanted it somehow to become more, and it did. She knew what to do to make it become more. She knew exactly. Our faces were close together. I could not stop trembling. I thought I would burst. Then it was as if my body were not my own. It was as if I had burst. No, not burst, that is all wrong. I just blossomed, more like a bud bursting into flower, but taking seconds not days. Then I was in tears. Tears of happiness I think they must have been. Then, peace. I lay with my head on her shoulder.

So that is what the sexual act should be, I kept thinking. I never knew. I never knew. These words kept returning. In between, my mind just allowed thoughts to enter it, unbidden. Without my having to guard myself against them.

'It is strange,' she said. 'You feel like me and not me. Both at once. I feel I know you exactly.'

'I think perhaps you do. Is that what a woman is supposed to feel? It must be. I never knew. Why does one not know these things?'

Then I lay there for a while, thinking, wondering if I should have the courage, the skill, to caress my friend. Then it was if she read my thought.

'Will you mind?' she asked.

'No, I want to, but I do not know if I will know how.'

'You will know,' she said. 'Just be with me. Just be with me here.'

I found that I felt a little of what she had said to me, that she was both the same and different from myself. My actions felt strange. I did know what to do. I felt excited all over again. She trembled, then sighed. I felt afraid the servants might hear. 'I'm sorry,' she said, 'I should not make this noise.' She laughed, and then she too started weeping, quietly and peacefully. 'Just lie here with me. Stay close to me.'

I think I have never been so moved in my life, as by her asking that. Just saying that: to be with her in that moment. Then I knew that she did not just want to take care of me. She needed me too, in some important way. Perhaps she even loved me. I knew too that I could love her. Though we were not at all the same, we were in some way equals. Though this was something that God seemed to have meant only for men and women, I felt too that somehow there could be a bond like that between me and Sara.

'Emily,' she said in a little while. 'You do not know how happy this makes me.'

'You mean being in bed together. Doing this?'

'I mean being close so that we can be in bed together, doing this.'

We talked and talked, of this, of what physical love is, of a hundred things. I have to say there was also more kissing, more

94

holding close to each other. 'Just think,' she said. 'I used to have to do this on my own.' She laughed again. I was not even shocked at this shameless statement. Simply, I have absolutely no idea how she can talk with such frankness. Perhaps now I feel close to her I shall be able to talk in the same way, completely open. Shall I have no more shameful secrets?

'Do you think what we are doing is wrong?' I had asked.

'I do not believe so,' said Sara. 'The only thing I have to compare is with my husband. I am sure that was not wrong. It is an important part of marriage, a very important part that helps to make grow the love between two people when they are married. It renews that love even when strains appear in other parts of life. So for me it is not wrong. It cannot be wrong. I think my love for you is like this. It is different in some ways, but that same quality it has.

'I pity you poor gentiles,' she said. 'I have read some of our Jewish mystics. They say that we have characteristics of male and female, both. So why should not female and female love each other. I feel very much that we should love each other in that way.'

'Is that what God intended?' I asked.

She laughed again. That laugh which lights my life. 'You are too theoretical,' she said. 'Why should God not have intended it? If God had not intended it, then it should not be possible.'

I was writing these last words, in the sitting room that Sara has given me, while she slept in the big bed which we have been in together. Just now, Sara has risen, come into the room, and said, 'I missed you. I was frightened you had gone, or that you were angry or had regrets. What are you doing?'

'I have no regrets, but I am wide awake. I am writing in my journal. I need to write things there to try and keep them straight. Soon I may not need it. I will stop being secretive. I will just tell you everything instead.'

'You should keep writing in your journal if you want. It is probably very important. I will buy you a desk with a drawer in which you can lock it, so that no one can see it. Then your secrets can have a special place.'

'Tomorrow, I would like you to read my journal, so that you can see what has been going through my mind, which I may have been unable to tell even you properly. I am not yet very good at being able to speak just what comes into my mind.'

'Very well. I will read it tomorrow, I mean later today. Now come back to bed. I miss you.'

'Let me just write this down and I will be with you immediately.'

Now I go to her.

Monday

It is morning now. My appointment with the Professor is at four o'clock this afternoon. I promised Sara I would return to see him, so I shall. Though maybe now, after what has happened, she will agree that there is little point. To her at least the causes of my sickness have become clear. To me now there seems at last the hope of recovery, though I do not know whether I shall be able to do what Sara suggests, and put what I have done behind me, out of my mind. I think that with her help I may be able to. Perhaps if I could become generous, like her. Perhaps, as she said, help people whose lives have been spoilt by some unhappy experience.

Later

I have been to see the Professor, and when I returned a desk had arrived. Even though she is supposed to be at school, Sara has somehow found me this most beautiful desk, which was delivered while I was out. It has a top that rolls up, and a drawer beneath. Then under that there are cupboards with shelves for books or whatever I may wish. Within the desk are all sorts of little pigeonholes and places to put things. But the best part, written in a note, left in a sealed envelope by those who delivered it, is that there are two secret drawers. These I have now found.

Sara has come home from school now and says that the desk is like me, with many compartments, some of them secret. She says she will never intrude on it or me. In return I must learn to say to her what is in my mind – that is the Professor's prescription, and now it is hers. There can be no excuses, and no censorship for thoughts that are in any way about her or about us. Otherwise, she says, we will not be able to be properly close. My secretiveness will maintain a distance.

'Do you promise?' she asked, seeming unusually serious. 'It is important.'

'I promise.'

'Very well. There must be no lapse, is that what the Catholics say?'

I can use the desk, she says, to hide things in that I need no longer really keep secret from her, just to know that I could if I wished. I will keep this journal locked up. The servants might find it and, although it is in English, I cannot take risks.

Then there was the Professor. I felt in a calmer mood with him today, and will continue to see him, perhaps until the end of the week. There is something he could do – to help me remember my mother and my father. Being with Sara seems to make it possible to think of such things, to contemplate my life with something other than horror.

10

Freud's Lecture concluded

A Rosetta Stone of Psychology

We came to speak of another image of Miss Emily's dream. I asked: 'Do you recall anything that might be associated with the image of your coming downstairs, and hearing raised voices behind a closed door?'

'Yes, I do. There was an incident when I stood half-way down the stairs, and I heard my godparents arguing about me in the drawing room. I will tell you how it happened.'

Miss Emily's way of speaking indicated that she had prepared herself for this part of her narrative. I wondered again why, after her absence, she had been eager to revert to her dream. She spoke in a matter-of-fact way. Now I realised why she wanted to finish her dream. It was a literary sense of completion. I could not avoid the impression that she was finishing her narrative for my benefit, as if to close the case.

She said, 'When I was eighteen my guardian's behaviour began to alarm me considerably. Though I am ashamed to say it, I suppose I had become used to his embraces. I had thought that since occasions for them were not too frequent, and that since I hoped I might soon be able to escape, it was just a matter of time until my release. By then I had heard that other women had to suffer attentions of men that were not welcome. I had come to wonder, indeed, whether my experience of the sexual act was not common, even though usually the women who suffered it were married.

'Then I noticed a change in him. I began to realise that rather than treating me as if he had some kind of right over me, he was becoming obsessed with me. I would catch him staring at me. He wished to walk with me in the garden when my godmother was in the house. Worst of all, instead of relatively brief encounters on the nights when he visited me, he now wished for tête-à-têtes, which were prolonged. He said he was abjectly sorry for having taken advantage of me when I was young, but he had not been able to stop himself. He said I must understand that I had power over him. He had fallen desperately in love with me. Could I not learn to love him just a little, perhaps unbend and regard him kindly? He spoke incessantly about how, as he put it, he got nothing from his wife, but that he knew he could make me happy if only I would allow him to.

'This made my situation even worse than before. I had previously asked my godparents to allow me to go to university in America. I knew I had some money of my own that would enable me to do this, but I was unsure what the legal situation was, and whether I needed their permission. I was still a minor and I imagined that they could have me restrained if I tried to leave the country, and perhaps be able to interfere with my inheritance if I did succeed in escaping. For some reason I did not think of obtaining legal advice; perhaps my shame prevented me. Instead I had appealed to them, asked them for their permission to go to America. My godmother was sympathetic, but my guardian, whose will prevailed in most things, was adamant in opposing any such move.

'Now his obsession with me created a further obstacle, in fact several new obstacles. Not only did I have to endure an increase in his ardour, but whereas previously he had been discreet in

99

arranging his assignations now he became careless. Previously he had only come to me in my room when his wife was away. Now he would come upon me at other times, and I became terrified that we should be discovered.

'Do you see how this kind of thing takes one over?' Miss Emily addressed me directly. 'I was terrified that *we* should be discovered. Not that he would be discovered, or that he might then be stopped from his wretched activities, but that I would be implicated, and that my disgrace, which had already poisoned my life, would become public. It was one of these other times that the last image of my dream brings to mind. My guardian had come upon me during an afternoon. I heard him return to the house unexpectedly. Then with an awful inevitability he came upstairs as I sat at my desk, in my room, writing. He had his way as usual, and I listened to his entreaties, about how lovely I was. I heard his words about how, if only I would let myself love him, he would do anything for me. He went on and on: how cruel I was to have bewitched him, and so forth. He had required me to remove all my clothes, and I had complied. It was when he was on top of me that I thought I heard a sound. I must have been startled, for I said, "What was that?" He had told me that he had sent the servants out for the afternoon. I was not sure whether the sound came from outside my door or from elsewhere, but I wondered if it were possible that I could have been seen in that degrading position through the keyhole. I afterwards ascertained that had there been someone looking through the keyhole they could indeed have caught a glimpse of my indecorous posture. He too was alarmed by the noise. He composed his dress and went downstairs.

'Some minutes later I was dressed. I had followed him half-way down the large staircase. This must be the origin of the image from my dream, because I heard from the drawing room the raised voices of my godparents. I missed the first part of their quarrel but my godmother was saying that he must allow me to go to America as I had wanted, otherwise he could imagine what the consequences would be.

'I cannot remember everything they said, but I know I felt confused and ashamed, wondering whether my godmother had indeed seen us through the keyhole, or merely heard her husband's voice in my room, or whether perhaps she only knew he had been there by his coming downstairs. Perhaps he had become confused when she had asked him what he had been doing upstairs, since it would have been unusual for him to be there at that time of the day. His study, where he usually worked when at home, was on the ground floor. Its interior was visible from the front of the house.

'I returned to my room and wondered about all this. I was not able to separate it from my own horror and shame. In the end I concluded that perhaps my godmother may not have seen or heard us. The staircase creaked quite loudly, although I myself had discovered a way of ascending and descending without making it creak. But the creak that it usually made had always been a comfort to me, and I had been used to hearing this as a signal when I was upstairs on my own. I had not heard that sound, either before or after Mr S and I were disturbed. Although it was clear that the quarrel was about me, I could not be sure that my godmother knew anything specific.

'My guardian was absent from the house for the next two weeks. At the end of that period, just before I was due to return to school after the Easter holidays, my godmother told me that he had consented to my leaving for America.

'Although I knew that she was not a happy woman, she had always been considerate to me, and, as I said before, she had confided in me. She now told me that she was sorry for what she had now to tell me, but that she had realised that her husband had become attracted to me, and that he had gone to stay in

101

London until the school holidays were over. She said she hoped that his attentions had not become too obvious to me because she was sure that if they had they been, they would have embarrassed me, and deeply upset me. She said he was not a bad man. She said that sometimes men just found themselves quite involuntarily being attracted to young women, especially beautiful young women like myself.

'Now, Professor Freud, you can see I am not especially beautiful. I knew that what my godmother was doing was trying to apologise, as tactfully as she could, for her husband. Without being specific she spoke in a way that would embarrass us both as little as possible, while letting me know that she forgave my part in what had happened. I still do not know if she realised whether her husband had actually had sexual relations with me. It would of course have been mortifying for us both even to admit the possibility, but at that moment I was immensely grateful for her way both of putting my mind at rest with regard to her feelings towards me, and of avoiding any occasion for either of us having to make specific admissions.

'I also do not know how she persuaded my guardian to give up his aspirations towards myself. Perhaps she had threatened to denounce him in some way to his superiors. If so it was a very brave act on her part, since my guardian was a powerful man. All I know is that she is a generous and kindly woman.'

Miss Emily composed herself. She had spoken as if this brought the matter to a close.

'You speak to me as if this is a conclusion,' I said. 'As if, having started on the story of yourself and your guardian, you think you should not deprive me of hearing the end of that story before you take your leave.'

'It is true,' she replied. 'I wish I were not so transparent to you. I have been thinking of leaving, and I thought I should give you the opportunity to complete the analysis of my dream. I have read your book on dreams, and thought you might wish to reach the end of its analysis.'

'Perhaps too you want my permission to leave, just as you wanted the permission of your godparents to leave for America, otherwise you need not have come back to see me after your absence last week.'

'Perhaps so.' She was visibly taken aback by my suggestion, which indicated to her that she was not so much in conscious control of the situation as she had supposed.

'I must confess,' I continued, 'that what strikes me most forcibly is that, although what you have said makes sense of some of your distress, it does nothing to explain why you suffered a collapse when you were to give a speech at your school. Your account of your relations with your guardian is coherent, but was it really to tell me this story that you came to see me in the first place? Or was there something that pressed you more closely at that time? I wonder what it is you want from me.'

'I have wondered that myself. I am not at all sure. Nevertheless, I thank you,' she said. She seemed flustered, unsure of what to say, and rose to leave. 'I will not be absent from our next appointment. I believe there is something.'

At our next meeting Miss Emily began thus: 'My friend Sara persuades me to keep seeing you. She thinks that I have been much better since I started consulting you.'

I ended the silence that ensued by asking, 'I wonder what it was you were intending to say in the speech that you failed to give at your school Founder's Day, and why you were unable to speak. You mentioned that your speech was to be on the topic of moral goodness. Was it that, having prepared to speak on that topic, you felt it hypocritical to do so because of thoughts of yourself with your guardian?'

Miss Emily was again silent. Finally she said, 'I had prepared a speech based on Aristotle's *Ethics*. I had discussed the idea with

Sara, and I had thought there might be something there that would have been worthwhile both for the girls and their parents. I had reread many of Aristotle's works in the previous weeks, to get myself into his frame of mind. Did you know, Professor Freud, that Aristotle thought the way we are conceived is that the male seed carries the male form, and that at conception it tries to overwhelm female matter?* Aristotle thought that form, or function if you will, was the essence of things. If the male form succeeds, a male child is conceived. Aristotle would think of this as like a piece of clay taking on the shape and characteristics of a man. If the male form does not prevail, then the female matter is not affected, and a female results as an imperfect being. Aristotle makes it clear that women were somewhat better than slaves. These were, in turn, superior in their faculties to animals, but we women are nowhere near men. We do not have the souls of men, of proper people. Maybe we do not have souls at all.'

'Is this what you were to vouchsafe in your speech?'

'No, of course not, but it occurs to me that few women have been in a position to read the classics until now. What do you think we should make of such passages?'

I was unsure whether she was testing me, or asking whether, as is indeed the case, women have a specific susceptibility to neuropathic conditions. I replied, 'It seems less important, for the purposes we have agreed, what I may make of it than what you make of it. You appear to believe that, as in your relations with your guardian, the women's share has been inequitable.'

'Perhaps we people without proper souls should consort with each other. It must be very trying for you men to be concerned with such creatures.'

'You mean, of course, that it is trying for you women to be concerned with us men.'

*Aristotle, *Generation of Animals*.

'Yes, I do, in a way,' she replied. I was struck that at this point she blushed. She added, as if by way of explanation or excuse, 'How would we then be able to live, when you men seem to be responsible even for the food we eat, for the clothes we wear, for almost everything?'

Again here was the spirit of defiance, of accusation even, but behind that, in her blushing as she had spoken, there was something else. As well as evading my question about why she had been uanble to give her speech, I had noticed also that Miss Emily's references to her friend Sara had become more frequent. It is often the case that, however deeply run those currents whose presence becomes clear early in an analysis, there are often deeper currents yet. This indication implied, I think, that one such deep current in Miss Emily's nature might be a forbidden homosexual desire. Both masculine and feminine drives exist in all of us, as I hope shortly to make clear in a forthcoming publication.* Normally we take on the proper characteristics of our sex, that is to say of being attracted to people of the opposite sex, but even so both heterosexual and homosexual potentialities live alongside each other in all of us. If development is arrested, earlier forms of affectionate attachment can remain and become predominant. For instance, an attachment between a young girl and her mother can become recast as an attachment between a young woman and another woman who takes on some of the characteristics of the mother.

It was becoming clear to me that, in Miss Emily's case, her development had been fixated at some earlier stage. What relation this might have had to her parents' death, or to the story she had told of her relations with her guardian, was still obscure. Some weeks previously I had observed to her that she seemed to be longing for her mother. What was important for my

---

*Three Essays on the Theory of Sexuality.

investigations was to be especially sensitive to the possibilities of a fixation in a homosexual phase of development, and the possibility therefore that what I had heard had origins in layers that were deeper than those uncovered thus far.

Scientifically the facts are these. Homosexuality in men is not uncommon, and unless I am mistaken it is almost as common in women. I do not mean to say that Miss Emily was odd in manner, or unfeminine in demeanour. Indeed, although somewhat thin, she was an attractive young woman, who would pass anywhere as suitable object for a young man's attentions, so long as she were not exhibiting either her dejected mien or her intellectual bent. Such considerations, however, are conventional rather than scientific. What we must be concerned with here is the direction into which the currents of this young woman's libido had flowed. We have seen that she had adopted the entirely male pursuits of a classical education, and that at the same time she was for the most part disdainful of men.

The question I put to you is this: How we are to understand these phenomena? The answer I offer is that her libido was displaced, from auto-erotic activities and from her narcissistic engagement with her self, to become cathected to a member of her own sex. Like many cases in which such inversion occurs, this had occurred partly because of opportunity. Perhaps the absence of her father, and her later education at institutions entirely populated by women, had worked their effect.

Such a fixation in the homosexual phase of development provides the link with the school for girls at which she had taught; to the speech on morality to the parents of these girls which she felt herself unable to give; to her disdain for all of the male sex save her father, who being dead could safely be idealised; to her shame at the auto-erotic activities in which the image of her godfather predominated; and to her frequent references, and if I was not mistaken her deference, to her friend

Sara. These at least were the impressions that I had gathered and only partly resolved at this stage. If I was not mistaken, however, further indications of this tendency were now becoming visible. These I think will allow us to perceive the outlines of the mental structures that we have sought to uncover.

Miss Emily had told me that she thought that part of what she wanted from me was to be able to remember her mother and father more clearly. She asked whether my methods would allow this. I did not dissent from the general aim of uncovering some of the events of childhood, but I had not been encouraged by the immediate results. Her account of her childhood was that it had been happy. Beyond her longing for her mother, and beyond the possibility that her father may have preferred a son to a daughter, which I had already inferred, and the possible effects of sitting upon her father's lap, which she said had occurred from as far back as she could remember and which could have led to stimulation, there was little I could uncover that indicated the causes of her illness. This however did not surprise me. One must think again of analysis as an archaeological excavation. One cannot reach the deeper layers without first passing through intermediate levels, and indeed one reaches these only by dint of much spadework, which may seem in itself fruitless, and which may produce only the indication of where there is nothing of interest. When we stand back, however, we can see in broader outline that the vacant areas make sense. Though they may not themselves contain treasures, they appear as the spaces between monuments where layout is highly significant, or the centres of rooms which appear as such when the walls become visible. Without these blank areas, we may neither know where to look further, nor be able to understand the significance of the broken shards of the deeper levels.

Pursuing this idea I prompted Miss Emily to speak of her father and his encouragement of her interests, and I took the opportunity of asking her then what he would have made of Thornton, the young man who had offered his hand in America. 'I think he would probably have approved,' she replied.

I asked, 'As for you yourself, do you think you might have married him, had it not been for the years you spent in the care of your guardian?' I was careful not to indicate to her in any way that I took her account of relations with that person as having attained its final form.

'I do not know,' she said. 'I have sometimes thought about things like that. My life would have been so different . . .' Then, after a pause, which I thought might indicate that she had remembered that she must be careful to maintain the story of her seduction: 'Oh, you mean would I have found the prospect of marriage to him more attractive had I not received the attentions of my guardian? I have wondered about that too. I did feel apprehensive that marriage would include sexual relations, sexual intercourse, between man and wife. In the end I do not believe it was that. Thornton was a gentle and kind person. He might have been able to . . . I do not quite know, but all might have been well.'

'Your own sexual feelings towards him? Were they as you would expect from a young woman to whom an offer of marriage was made?'

'I think so. It's hard to know what other people feel on such occasions. I am sure, with people recounting the intimate details of their lives, you must know better than I what is normal to such states.'

'Maybe so, but for yourself?'

'Thornton was affectionate towards me, and not the least like my guardian. I do not know if it was immodest but we would sometimes kiss each other.'

'Did you never have sexual intercourse with him?'

'No, Professor Freud; I have only ever performed coitus, that

108

is the word you doctors use, is it not, with my guardian.' Again she spoke sharply, using a technical word in a disdainful manner.

I knew from this that a resistance was at work and I that must persist. 'Perhaps there were other kinds of embrace, perhaps some other contact with his male organ?'

'No, no, no: only with my guardian. I see you strive for completeness. The only male organ I have ever seen, or been touched by, or have myself ever touched, is that repellant appendage of my guardian. Yes, I touched it too. There, I admit it. I have been depraved. Is that what you want to hear? Now I think that I was a child when he seduced me. I did not know how to escape his abominable clutches.'

I noticed how she now spoke very differently about her relations with her guardian than when she had first described them. At first she had been uncertain, shameful and confused. Now she seemed to speak with some heat, as if she were elaborating the story. She was reinforcing the view that she had been a victim, and her guardian a wicked assailant. I regarded this development with interest, and inferred that it could have a role in shoring up her defences against the ideas of her own, evidently strong, sexual desires.

I have to say also that I had been inclined to believe her assertion that she had not had sexual intercourse with Thornton. Why, you may ask, should we believe this part of her story, when we suspend judgement about the other part? You would of course be quite right, if we had no other evidence that might bear on the matter, but other evidence we do have. The next day there occurred the breakthrough for which I had been hoping. I had occasion to ask her about her periods of anorexia. Was there disinclination to eat when she was in America? She replied that she had eaten normally when she had first arrived, but that there was a period when she had found eating exceedingly difficult, in about the third year of her stay there.

'That, if I remember, was when your relation with Thornton occurred,' I remarked.

'Yes it was.'

'And did your anorexia subside when you had told him that you could not marry him, and broke off your relations with him?'

'Yes.'

I was able to explain to her that her nausea and anorexia had originated with her thoughts about her guardian. Just as with the Rosetta Stone, there is a translation, as it were, between different languages.* Psychologically, one language is of symptoms – nausea and anorexic disinclination to eat. The other is the language of human emotion, in this case Miss Emily's disgust at her own libidinal feelings. The rejection of normal sexual impulses had become translated into a rejection of eating, and of any possibility of enjoying food.

Miss Emily seemed interested in this idea of this translation: 'Yes,' she said, 'I believe you may be right. I did find it very difficult to eat, and was often nauseated during that period when Thornton was courting me. I had not felt easy about eating, or free from feelings of nausea, from about the age of fourteen, which I suppose was when my guardian began his attentions, except for a year or so after I had become settled in America and began to feel happy in the university there. Eating did become difficult for me again soon after I met Thornton. I believe you are right.'

Her active mind had become engaged in this question, which now interested her, and she was free of the resistance she so often displayed in her sharpness of manner.

'You say,' she continued, 'that the thought that if we were

---

*The Rosetta Stone, discovered during Napoleon's military expedition to Egypt of 1798, contained a decree of Ptolomy in three languages, hieroglyphic, demotic and Greek. Greek was a known language, so the stone's discovery provided the first clues to deciphering Egyptian hieroglyphs.

married Thornton would want to have sexual intercourse with me made me feel disgust? Then this appeared as a symptom of disinclination to eat? I had not realised that connection. It is an interesting idea. I think you are right. Why did I not realise that myself?'

So you see, gentlemen, it was not the denial of any specifically sexual activity with Thornton that is of principal significance. We have Miss Emily's clear description that her relationship was accompanied by nausea and anorexia. We have her own statement of how this connection had been unconscious to her. As we also know, her anorexic symptoms arose in her, as they arise in many hysterical patients, as manifestations of disgust in contemplation of sexual activity.

In considering this case as I prepared this account for you, gentlemen, I have to report that I now regret that I did not follow up the advantage I had gained at this point, while Miss Emily was in that mood of co-operative engagement with the issue. It is significant, however, that symptoms of anorexia had reappeared accompanying her recent illness following her failure to give her speech at her school.

Despite the imperfections, we were at last closer to seeing the outlines of Miss Emily's mental territory, and another opportunity to return to this matter was to occur quite soon, when I asked her to speak once more on how she thought her attitude to her guardian had affected her courtship by Thornton. 'Your nausea indicates that you felt unable to contemplate the sexual activity that would be likely to follow an engagement and marriage. Is that so?'

'I had not given Thornton any hint of what had happened with my guardian,' she said. 'As I have told you, I have wondered sometimes whether that held me back from marriage. I own that I was apprehensive. I had never told anyone before you, but I think I would not have liked to be married and to hold such a horrible secret from someone I loved. This was in part why I had determined to be independent, and to earn my own living. I have thought that I would have to tell her, I mean him . . . Thornton, because my degradation had made some kind of awful knot in my life. I was worried that something might happen to reveal the secret. I do not know; but against that I also did not know whether it would have been right to tell him. It might have made him think so badly of me that it would destroy anything good between us, change his opinion of me irrevocably, so that he would never be able to master it mentally, even if he had wanted to. So when I thought about it like that, I feared I would never be able to speak to him. Then I also wondered whether he would have found out on our marriage night that I had been violated. I have read that men can tell if their wife is not a virgin. So, you see, it was a hopeless tangle.'

'Is part of the tangle that you made a small mistake just now, and said "her" instead of "him"?'

'I noticed that I did so.'

'Do you think that might mean anything?'

'You mean unconsciously?'

'Exactly. I was wondering who the "she" might be.'

'Since I told you about my guardian I have also spoken to my friend Sara about him. I suppose Sara may be the "she".'

'Are your relations with her as close as with someone to whom you were married?'

The pause before she next spoke indicated to me that her answer was considered. 'It may be that they are closer than any relation I could now have with a man.'

'You indicate that there are some things that you would not be able to tell me.'

'No, not necessarily . . . I don't know. Yes. Probably you might be right.'

Miss Emily was silent. I said that I thought I was beginning to see more clearly the difficulty in which she found herself.

'As sometimes occurs,' I said, 'it seems that in you the current of sexual attraction towards women may be stronger than that towards men. This had partly accounted for the feelings of nausea that you experienced as you dwelt upon the idea of embraces from your guardian, perhaps also for your reluctance towards the man who wished to marry you, and now also perhaps for your reluctance to be fully frank with me. Is there perhaps some connection between this current and the fact that you felt yourself unable to address the parents of your schoolgirl charges on the subject of morality?'

'No,' she said. 'I do not know. I do not believe so.'

A patient saying 'I have never thought of it like that before', or some such phrase, regularly indicates that an interpretation I have made is correct. Also, with material that has been deeply repressed, and against which the patient had defended herself, correctly identifying it elicits a negative response, as was here the case: 'No' or 'I do not know.' This is the voice of the repressing agency speaking. It is an indication that the unconscious process that first made the material unconscious is still at work. It speaks here, in protest as it were, though perhaps ineffectively, since by speaking so it makes it clear that we are nearing an understanding of its significance.

At our next meeting Miss Emily came in wearing a becoming outfit that I had not seen before. She looked on this day a slim and engaging young woman. She seemed taller than the impression she had given before, no doubt because she held herself with poise. I wondered whether this change had been due to my interpretation of her disgust at ideas of sexual intercourse with men, and that this had allowed some of her symptoms of melancholia to abate.

I was surprised that she began by asking, 'Last time you said

113

that my conflicts and my nervous collapse might have been because I somehow have turned away from men in my feelings. Do you think my guardian turned me against men generally?'

'I cannot avoid remarking your low opinion of men, and that this often extends to myself, even though I have been acting purely as a physician.'

I thought it important to take this opportunity, which as I said before is important, to point out to the patient such indications of transference, in this case the frequent sense given to me by Miss Emily that she regarded me in something of the same way that she regarded her guardian.

'Until now,' I said, 'your wishes for intimacy with someone of your own sex have principally been expressed in the form of their obverse, namely a strong antipathy to men other than your father, whom you idealise.'

'Why do you say "until now"?' she asked.

I thought this a striking question, since she had been but recently recounting to me the closeness she felt to her friend Sara. This apparently innocent question finally gave me the indication I had been waiting for, and which made sense of what had gone before. I was able to remark, 'Your question prompts me to think that something important has happened recently, just "now": something more than just verbal intimacy between yourself and Sara.'

She turned her face away and said very quietly, 'Is it so obvious, then? I wish you had not guessed this.' After a pause: 'I do not wish to say any more about it, simply that, although you may think me more than ever depraved, I feel that now there is at last something that blots out the memory of my guardian. Not blots out, that would be too strong, but there is something good. I cannot say more.'

'You speak again as if you draw towards a conclusion.'

'Perhaps I do. I do not know. I must tell you that I have benefited both from your analysis and from your writings.'

'You feel you have no more to learn about yourself?'

'I think that I have much to learn. I am grateful to you for not condemning me, either for what happened with my guardian or for my present feelings. I do think I could learn more, much more, but I think that perhaps for now this is enough.'

'Let us say this,' I proposed. 'My experience leads me to believe that you are as yet only at the beginning of uncovering in yourself structures that have been laid down earlier in your life. We are in the early stages of our excavation. I would be surprised if we were not able together to uncover much more, in a way that could be of considerable benefit to yourself and to your health. Of course, I am powerless to work on your behalf if you do not wish to come. I am due to leave on my summer holiday very soon. You may be interested to know that this year I am to visit Greece for the first time. I can tell you that it is with some envy that I have heard your accounts of your several visits. I am now about to repair this omission in my own life. If you wish to do so, we may take up your analysis again after the holidays.'

'Thank you, Professor. I am most grateful to you for your help in a time of deep despair, and for your very kind offer of continuing. May I wish you every pleasure in your visit to Greece. May I write to you about the possibility of my resuming our consultations when you return?'

Her thanks were warm and sincere. We ended our session early, and shook hands as we parted, without either of us knowing, I think, whether we should meet again.

Gentlemen, we are now in a position to take stock of this case, at least provisionally. Now we can perceive its outlines. Our next task, if the patient would allow it, would be to search for where the fixation in the homosexual phase of love for her mother in childhood might have come about. It was possible that she had kept this from herself by her idealisation of her father.

Her homosexual wishes, which previously had been expressed in a more or less acceptable way by her denigration of men, and perhaps by the phantasy of scurrilous scenes of degradation by her guardian, had now taken on a new form. This had been begun by her confiding to a woman this matter that had previously been kept closely secret and excluded from every other discussion. Of course we do not know the terms of her confidence to Sara, whether she described a seduction by her guardian or whether she had confided to Sara what she had not yet been able to bring herself to say to me: that she had found herself helplessly caught up in passionate auto-erotic phantasies which both excited and disgusted her. I rather think that she might have been able to admit as much to Sara, though not to me.

It is incontrovertible that there had been some event, of which I had not yet heard, when the two young women worked together at the school for girls, and which then gave rise to such intense anxiety that the prospect of giving a speech on morality contributed to her collapse. Could this perhaps have been a kiss or an intimate gesture between the two young women, which she only now was able to contemplate with equanimity?

Now, gentlemen, we must conclude, at least for the present. Although Miss Emily had still not been fully frank with me, so that there was doubt as to whether her guardian's nocturnal visits had or had not occurred, and although the event that had precipitated her collapse were still inexplicit, and although also there had been resistance to the admission into consciousness of her strong homosexual desires, it seemed to me at last that the case was now well on its way to solution. Now, I believe, it would require only patience on my part, and the will towards health on the part of the patient, for these final elements of the puzzle to fit into place.

11

Emily's Journal concludes

Tuesday 28 June

For the first time in what seems like an infinity, I feel a sense of equilibrium, an absence of that sense of dread. For an interval that imminent doom, waiting in the background to engulf me, has been absent. It had been with me continuously, even if I were not thinking about it directly. For the first time I can allow my mind to run unconstrained for periods without knowing that some vision of Mr S, or of my own wickedness, or of imprisonment, would break upon me.

If now I allow my mind to think what it will, just let it go, Sara comes to fill my mind. Not that I have stopped thinking about Mr S. Rather I am no longer taken over by him. Not that I have stopped feeling frightened about what will happen to me; I still have periods of the utmost apprehension, and of guilt. I had a time of being overcome with trembling and dread earlier today, but the period was shorter. Perhaps I know I can speak to Sara about it if necessary. I still feel I have been guilty and wicked. It is completely and utterly wrong to kill another human being for whatever reason, in whatever way. I have done that, even though I do not know if I willed Mr S to be dead. I think too that I must have provoked Mr S's attentions in the first place. Without that none of the rest would have occurred.

I have some hope today that I may be able to spend my life in making amends, that I can undertake a regeneration of my life, perhaps by loving Sara, or by doing something good in the world that is not purely selfish. I do not know. I often think that I should hand myself over to the authorities. Perhaps I shall. I now know that, if I did, one person would not condemn me. That would allow me to face the ordeals to which I would have to submit.

Last night Sara said: 'Tell me something. Tell me truthfully. Did you want to do what we did together? I was fearful today at a thought that came. I thought I might have seduced you. I might have repeated what Mr S did to you. Because of my own weakness, and my own sexual desire, which I was not able to control, I took advantage of you when you were vulnerable, when you were in my care.'

Sara wept bitter tears. The poor dear. I had not known she had that side to her. She seemed to me always strong and capable. Now she was admitting her weakness. I cannot say how relieved I was, that she was not always strong. I felt very tender love for her at that moment. That she might need me, not just that I needed her.

'Oh, Sara,' I said. 'You silly. You must not misunderstand me, but I am glad you feel doubt, because this gives me an opporunity to lecture you, and for me to see that you are not complete in yourself. I like you to need me, even a little, because otherwise we would be too hoplelessly unequal. So just you listen,' I continued. 'I was not able to speak of what I felt for you, not even to myself. Still less would I have been able to take any action. I would not have known how. I would not have had the first idea, but when you did, and I am so completely thankful to you for doing it, I knew that it was right. It is what I would have longed

118

to do if I had known. I am, as you have told me, too theoretical. I have put my life into compartments in my mind. It seemed the only way to keep things from running into each other, from allowing things that were not safe to occur. For myself, I now know that what we did together was absolutely right. It is what my whole soul had been longing for, although I did not know how to express it. You did not seduce me, or intrude upon me. I am only sorry I had to leave the initiative to you. If we are bad in what we did, then we are bad in it together.'

Sara's eyes were still wet with tears. 'So you think we are bad?' she asked.

'No, I do not. I should not have said that. I know what it is to do evil. I have done it with Mr S, and now I have done it *to* Mr S. What we did was not that. Forgive me, my mind is still in a muddle. It is simply so unexpected. It all seems so unusual, but it does not seem wicked. It is something which has so few points of reference. I am thinking now of reading the works of Sappho.' I seemed to be lecturing to Sara. 'There are some fragments of her poems. They may help us — at least they may help me to think about what is happening to us. Perhaps also I will write to a woman who was at the university where I studied. She was not a close friend. I felt rather in awe of her. She would hold discussions in her rooms about love between women, and indeed between men, which she always wanted to point out was a feature of life in classical Greece. I found it interesting, but I suppose in what you would call a theoretical way. It occurred to me today that it was not theoretical for her. She wanted to be a writer and I think she went to live in Paris. I could perhaps find out where. Perhaps I could go to visit her.'

Sara was not so much asking me whether what we were doing was bad, but whether I felt bad about it. I had become somewhat accustomed to such subtleties since I had consulted with Professor Freud. I reiterated, 'I do not in any way feel bad myself.

Quite the contrary. It is the best thing to have happened to me in my entire life.'

She smiled at me, a little wanly I thought. She said, 'I am glad. I am pleased I ask you. I do not wish to take advantage of you, after what you suffered.'

I said, 'You have not done that. You have rescued me. If I were a man, or if you were a man, we could talk about getting married, and make all sorts of plans to spend our lives together.'

'Why then do not we do this? I do not mean that either must be a man, though if you wanted I would be that for you. I mean why do not we think about spending our lives together? It is just an accident of biology that we are both women. We could promise to each other in that same way.'

'I could not imagine anything more perfect.' It shows how far I have come from my struggling secretiveness that I can now say that to her.

Wednesday

Perhaps I could in some way renew my life, start again. When I was thinking about this, I was reminded of William James's new book on religion,* which I read last year because I was interested in the part that religion played in classical Greece. Once I heard Professor James lecture when I was in America. He is a wise and perceptive man. He writes about religious conversion in his book, and about the possibilities of regeneration that it brings. I must talk to Professor Freud about this, to see what he thinks.

William James writes a great deal about the Methodists, and the Quakers, my own religious denomination. He writes of how conversion is a liberation from sin – and for me this is just what I long for. I know I have been sinful to have encouraged Mr S and

* *Varieties of Religious Experience.*

allowed all those things, even to have done them myself. Now doubly, much more than doubly, I am sinful. Can there be a worse sin than to kill someone? If only – that phrase again – if only my life could be regenerated. If I am not careful I can become apprehensive that with Sara I may have fallen into yet more sin. It does not feel so to me, but these things can be most deceptive, and I know that almost everyone would regard what we do as depraved. They would say that I have taken yet one more step towards perdition.

Thursday

Sara says that pushing Mr S was a gesture of fear, of revulsion from his embrace, not with murder in my heart, but how is it possible to know? I have not told her this, but I had sometimes imagined Mr S dead. I had wished his ship lost in a storm when he went abroad. I had imagined him falling from his horse to become an invalid who could not walk. Professor Freud would say that these thoughts show that I wished him to be dead or maimed: the Professor's whole system is based on the idea that wishes get translated into thoughts such as these, which seem innocent but are not. They may become actions that seem to be one thing but are another. If he is right, and I cannot deny that I had imagined Mr S dead, then I may have wished him to fall off the mountain on that day. If he is right, I am guilty, as I feel myself to be. I do not think about this so often now, but I still think about it a great deal. If I do not give myself up, and if I am not apprehended, I think that I shall always have it there. Always I shall know that I have done that wicked thing.

With the Professor today I was able to talk and think about my mother and father. I wept a good deal, but strangely that felt comforting, as if their loss were a simple human tragedy, not made horrible by the hateful Mr S and my own degradation. I cannot recapture what I said to the Professor, but he helped me feel that they did love me, though now they are lost. Now as I write I am in tears again.

Friday

I have finally managed to escape from the Professor. Is that the right term? It feels as if it is, since he has an uncanny knack of getting me to say things I should not. Every day I put myself in danger of self-betrayal. As it is, I have betrayed my feelings for Sara. He has guessed that our relation is more than the usual one between friends. This is, however, a lesser price than branding myself a murderess. In the end we have managed to part amicably I think.

Professor Freud thinks I am abnormal. He does not say this directly, and he is careful not to seem disapproving, but he also wishes keenly that I return after the holidays. This makes it obvious that he thinks there is something dreadfully wrong with me that must be cured. He thinks that what he calls my homosexual tendencies have been at the root of my problem, and he regards these as abnormal. He says such tendencies are part of the development of us all, but he also says that he thinks that in my life the course of my development has been stopped short.

My symptoms of feeling nauseous and disinclined to eat, in which he was so interested, now seem to have lost their interest for him. He assumes they are cured. He has explained to me how my difficulties with food have been a result of what he calls repression about sexual matters. Now I have been able to recognise these repressions in myself I will be free of the difficulties. It does not seem to me as simple as that. I had become abstinent about food partly I because I felt disgusted about the way in which some people indulge themselves, and are so gluttonous. It is possible to see very capacious people in restaurants eating and eating, evidently quite without any ability to control themselves. I used to find it impossible to eat some kinds of food, particularly those that are very rich. I am aware too that I have avoided as much as possible having to eat with other people, but living in Sara's house has taken me by surprise. I feel happy to eat meals with her, and even to eat whatever she is eating. I even eat quite a lot without worrying about it. Being Jewish, she has certain dietary habits, but these are quite acceptable to me. With her at least I feel much more at ease, not tense when I eat. She says that I must have started to be abstinent with my godparents because I did not want them to think that I was taking part enthusiastically with them in their life. Sharing food, she says, is a mark of feeling warmly towards someone. I expect she is right.

Professor Freud thinks that it is all sexual. If only it were not so painful, and if only it were not all muddled up with the dreadful thing I have done, I would find all these matters of the utmost interest. I feel it has greatly helped clarify all kinds of matters for me, and I could try and work out more exactly what has been going on, what fits together with what. I am not cured, however. My melancholy has not fully left me as I had hoped. It returns in waves during the day, as I wait for Sara to return. I still find myself thinking, If only, if only.

If only when I was fourteen I had not in some way encouraged Mr S's attentions. If I had been drab and insignificant. I had thought I was drab and insignificant. I felt like a waif, but obviously I was not enough so. If I had not gone to the mountains that day. If I had left earlier, before he had time to keep watch outside my apartment.

Here I am again caught up in that spiral of hateful, torturing thoughts. Probably I will never be free of them. Probably I will go back to Professor Freud after the holidays, having driven myself mad with them, with an inescapable urge to confess, like

Raskolnikov . . . That is what crime does. It drives one mad, and destroys the culprit, expanding the seed of evil from which the crime sprang into a huge tangled tree of self-destruction. I will drive myself to confess. I shall be punished by deserved death, and be cast into perdition. Now I have multiplied my sin by involving Sara too. Have I made her love me in a way that is itself wicked? At very least I made her love me so that when I am hanged she will suffer yet another loss.

Is there no end to this circle of damnation? No, how can there be?

———————

There. I have drawn a line. It is to show where this diary changes. When I began writing here it was a confession. A place to write about my guilt, because I did not know what else to do with hateful thoughts. It was a kind of compulsion to try and get them out of my mind.

I have just read my last outburst, and having written it down can see how self-obsessed these awful thoughts are. I could perhaps redeem myself by loving Sara, by helping women who have been the victims of seduction.

Now I no longer need to write in a solitary way. I will remain a guilty person, but I do not have to use this diary to try and keep my thoughts from torturing me. I am not Raskolnikov, who murdered only out of his own egotism. I can be converted to a new life. Murderers can repent, start anew. Christ forgave murderers on the cross. Am I not compounding my crime with a new one of perversion, which makes me happy when I have no right to be? If I could be sure that was not so, I might be able to repent fully. Again my thoughts draw me downwards. Why do I not talk to Sara, rather than wallow in them here? It would be unfair to her. She will not want constantly to be reminded . . . I must be strong. This writing must change. A new project.

———————

There is a another line under all that. Here is another new start.

Now, instead, this journal will become about Sara and me, about our life together. Perhaps it will be just as perplexing, because I am just as unprepared for it. I understand so little about it, but it is as if the strength of my feelings for her is stronger than the fear and guilt with which I had struggled before. It does not abolish the guilt, but it makes it possible to contemplate life with a sense of hope, or possibility. Does that make sense? It is something like that.

There, that is better, but not much. I said I had drawn a line to indicate where the diary of my wicked thoughts ended, and where the story of Sara and me started. Once again I am still talking about my fear and guilt as before. So here is yet another line. Then I will need a heading, perhaps *The Story of Sara and Emily*, to make a new start, properly.

———————

12

What Freud did not Say

What follows here is not part of my lecture for the Wednesday Society. I have even had doubts as to whether I should discuss the case with the Society. I have had neither time nor opportunity to gather sufficient evidence or to think it through at all fully. Moreover, I feel obscurely that in this case I have overlooked something, something central to the whole problem. I have reread my draft, hoping there for the clue I am missing, but I do not find it. I have dredged my memory with no more fortunate result. I write these notes to remind myself of the outstanding problems.

The central piece of the puzzle that is still missing may concern Miss Emily's guardian. My only indication of this is that whereas patients refer to people in their lives in many ways, and sometimes even as if I myself knew the people, Miss Emily has only ever referred to him as 'my guardian' or occasionally as 'my godfather'. He remains a shadowy figure. At present I cannot guess at the significance of this. Who is this man? I even feel tempted to make enquiries, though since Miss Emily is English this is more difficult than if she had grown up here in Vienna.

Another matter is that though my understanding of Miss Emily's hysteria is clearer, and although I now have little doubt about some of the outlines of her case, much remains to be done, more than has been accomplished so far. It is possible even that the optimistic tone with which I drew my lecture to a close may be exaggerated.

To allow a sense of completion in the work, and also to bring my lecture to a close, I have transposed the exchange about my holiday in Greece. In fact I continued to see Miss Emily for a few days following the point at which it became clear that she was engaged in a homosexual liaison. We parted two weeks before I was due to leave Vienna for the summer. During the last few occasions on which we met one thing became clear, that her symptoms had much abated. She was largely restored to health. Talk of her guardian no longer played such a prominent part, except in one respect that I will indicate shortly. She was mainly concerned with the longing and grief she had experienced for her mother, and to a lesser extent for her father, since their deaths. Her mourning for them had been incomplete. Now her entry into a period of freer emotional relations with her friend Sara had reawakened her feelings of loss for her parents.

The longing for her father was less, I believe, because she had been successful in identifying with him by adopting his interests in the classics and antiquity. At any event, much of what we spoke of in our later meetings was her feelings for her mother, her sadness at her loss and her desire to be able to remember her more clearly.

Miss Emily was also exercised about her homosexual affair. This was not unrelated, I believe, to the longing for her mother, because her friend Sara had been able to occupy her mother's place, at least in part. To that extent her loss had been repaired. The concern with her homosexual liaison was, for Miss Emily, whether there was anything abnormal in it. She wanted me as a doctor to reassure her on this point. I preferred to draw attention to what was happening in her psychological life, rather than being either approving or disapproving.

This brings me to another unresolved issue. Here again the flaw in the fabric of the case seems to me now almost irreparable, but perhaps some months away from Vienna, away from being too close to such matters, may make it possible to think differently about it. My quandary is this. On the one hand Miss Emily has provided me not only with an example of a dream, analysed with therapeutic result in the actual treatment of hysterical illness,* but with evidence of a fundamental and invaluable kind for the theory of developing sexuality on which I am working, particularly as to the nature of sexual aberrations and their relation to the existence of human bisexuality, of infantile sexuality and the occurrence of fixations during earlier phases of the normal development of the libido, and of the occurrences that appear in puberty.† She also confirmed what has been repeatedly borne in upon me, that neurosis is frequently if not invariably associated with strong desires for perverted sexual expression. On the other hand I could hardly say that Miss Emily is now ill.

Nor is this in itself unusual. Homosexual acts must be

*One of Freud's purposes in treating Emily had been to analyse her dreams, since in his book *The Interpretation of Dreams* the argument is incomplete because examples are drawn from miscellaneous sources, and no example is offered of how dream analysis may be instrumental in the cure of hysteria. In the event, since Freud never published Emily's case, this purpose was fulfilled by another one, his *Fragment of an Analysis of a Case of Hysteria (Dora)*.

†Freud is again referring here, as he does in his lecture, to a work which was occupying him at this time, the *Three Essays on the Theory of Sexuality*. The idea of human bisexuality was originally proposed by Wilhelm Fliess, Freud's mentor. It was this same idea that had been stolen by Otto Weininger (see note on p. 44), and the question of Freud's use of it was one of the causes of the final break-up of Freud's and Fliess' friendship. Some of the phrases Freud uses here, referring to aberrations, to infantile sexuality and to puberty, are later to become titles of the three essays. This indicates that Freud was already well advanced with this work at the time he was seeing Emily. The three essays were published a year later.

regarded as perversions, in the sense that they substitute for the normal aim and object of adult sexuality an aim and object which are abnormal. Nevertheless it is often the case that inverts display no other abnormalities. Though it seems unlikely, at least for the present, that she will contemplate a normal marriage with its usual prospect of motherhood, Miss Emily seemed in other respects moderately well. She had been suffering from symptoms of anxiety, melancholia and anorexia when she first consulted me. Whether because of my therapy, or the developments with the woman Sara, or most likely for a combination of these reasons, these symptoms have now largely abated. Though there is some residual anxiety, if I am not mistaken the symptoms will not return, at least as long as her liaison with Sara lasts.

Neurosis is the converse of perversion. If on the one hand a person recoils in moral horror against his own desires to masturbate, to indulge homosexual wishes or to perform other perverse acts, he is liable to fall ill of a neurosis – this is what happened to Miss Emily. If on the other hand he indulges such wishes, we can say he becomes actively perverted. This is especially the case, I think, should the form of sexual activity that is chosen, and the erotogenic zones by which the libido is satisfied, be the exclusive means of sexual satisfaction. Such a person may not be ill in the sense of suffering from symptoms. Rather he will be fixated at some early stage in development. Therein lies the perversion. This is what Miss Emily seems now to have come to, having chosen an exclusive interest in Sara as a love object, and perhaps, though we do not know at this stage, having chosen a particular form of sexual satisfaction, probably with the aim of stimulating the oral membranes in kissing, and no doubt mutual masturbation as is usual in such cases.

As a result of analysis Miss Emily's repressions have been lifted. But the result has been to allow the satisfaction of aberrant desires, now unconstrained by countervailing forces that had held them in check. Some might argue indeed that rather than progress towards health, this is retrogression. It might be held against me that if it were a general result of my therapy to turn people whose improper desires were inhibited into perverts, then on this ground alone psychoanalysis should be afforded general disapprobation, if indeed it were not made a matter for the police.

I am hopeful that if we were able to continue after the summer much of this would become a very great deal clearer. We might even find that, in response to further analysis, Miss Emily's sexual development, having been arrested, would be able to move forward again towards its normal heterosexual culmination. Again, however, there are difficulties. What do we say about Miss Emily's ally Sara? Are we, moreover, to work towards severance of this liaison? If the liaison serves an abnormal aim, and if the patient progresses, severance would occur without encouragement from myself.

Perhaps even more decisive is this: patients tend to consult me when they are in distress; with no distress there is no consultation. As a physician I can, in one sense, scarcely complain, but if I as a scientist am concerned with completing the analysis, and not just with abatement of symptoms, the situation is insufferable. Even if as a physician I am concerned with restoring the patient to normality, this situation is hardly satisfactory.

Such conclusions cannot be other than frustrating. I hope that Miss Emily will feel enough curiosity about her own personal prehistory to wish to return at the end of the summer. Until that time, I am left merely with these few notes indicating the directions of our last few sessions, but with many conclusions as yet undrawn.

One further area of Miss Emily's concern was about whether the kind of therapy that psychoanalysis offers might allow one to be spiritually reborn. She said she had read William James's book *The Varieties of Religious Experience* when it appeared two years ago. During analysis and during the reading of my works, she said it had occurred to her that psychoanalysis was like the process of religious conversion which James has discussed. Following such a conversion a person is often able to lead a new life. It is as if his personality were transformed. The metaphor, she said, is that of regeneration. The idea that came to her own mind, she said, was rebirth. It seemed more fundamental than a metaphor. Following a religious experience a man may experience a metamorphosis, she told me, like a butterfly emerging from a pupa, in which after the experience he is able to put behind him the habits, preoccupations and structures that religious writers call sins, that had constrained him. He is able to put aside whatever great sin he had committed, and to start again.

She felt strongly, she said, that in a secular way what I was saying was comparable to this religious sense of conversion, of regeneration. She now felt a strong yearning for this in herself, to put behind her the train of events that had started with the death of her parents, and to start completely fresh, all over again. She said, 'James explains that in psychological terms, conversion is like being supported by a whole different set of mental associations. The process of moving from one state to the other appears as a revelation, James says. One emerges from unconsciousness, or from only subliminal consciousness, and this sets one free. Indeed,' she continued, 'I have looked this up again, and James specifically mentions your work in this connection in his book.'

I had not known that my work had been noticed by the great William James, and I had not read this book, though it is clear that I must do so. Moreover, as I have said before, for her sex Miss Emily was unusually accomplished and thoughtful. I could not but find this view challenging. Indeed I could only wish that

131

some of my immediate circle in the Wednesday Society were able to think as boldly as she does.

More personally for her, however, Miss Emily felt that the period of her adolescence had been as if she lived like a partially blinded larva. The outlines of this period seemed to her foggy and obscure. She felt as if she had been groping in the dark, constrained, unable to understand very much. Now she felt the possibility of emerging from the chrysalis into which she had retreated, of being reborn as another kind of being, freer, less self-concerned. Was this, she asked me, the kind of thing that I meant by psychotherapy? 'If so,' she said, 'and if circumstances permit,' she thought she might like to continue after the holidays. She felt it important to rebuild her life in a quite different way than before, with less self-absorption.

In one way this all seemed both to her and to myself fascinating and apt, were it not for the teasing way in which Miss Emily kept referring to a sin, as if she means not just her masturbatory practices with phantasies of her guardian during puberty, nor even her homosexual liaison now, but some more specific action. Again I revert to the problem that in the whole case I have have missed something fundamental, some clue that I do not yet have, or have overlooked.

I hope that her interest in regeneration will bring her back in the autumn, though I have to admit that it is not the usual basis on which patients devote their time to analysis, or their (in her case relatively meagre) financial resources.

I mentioned that her guardian no longer figured so saliently in Miss Emily's speech to me. He did, however, appear in one way. As part of what she described as the fogginess of those years, Miss Emily said she was unable to know whether in some way she had provoked his attentions, had invited his sexual interest. Again, this intelligent woman was able, as the English expression has it, 'to place me upon the spot'. She said, 'Professor Freud, during our consultations you have spoken of your theory of transference, of how a patient transfers to the physician attitudes and intentions that are derived, inappropriately, from earlier ones, from those that had been directed to some person earlier in life. You regard the transference as material for analysis, just like dreams and inadvertencies. Can you tell, from the way in which I act towards you, whether I might have provoked my guardian sexually?'

I was taken aback, though of course this was an extremely pertinent question. I answered that since she had been seeing me she appeared in three, possibly four different kinds of way, that I thought might be transferential. First there had been my first acquaintance with her when she was melancholic, shy, apparently ashamed. Secondly there had been her disdainful and rather sharp attitude to men, among whom I was included. Thirdly, there were the discussions of antiquity, in which her intellectual accomplishments were able to flourish, and there was a sense of trusting companionship. Fourthly, and possibly separate from this latter, there had been the times when she had confided in me, often tearfully.

'I take it,' I said, 'that the second of these, your disdain for men, was related to your attitude to your guardian, and the third to your warm relations with your father. I am able to say,' I continued, and here I think I may have said too much, 'that there has seemed nothing explicitly sexual in your disdain, except in so far as it is the opposite of affection. Inappropriately, however, it is sometimes experienced as a challenge, and as such can awake an interest. And as for your attitude of engaged interest, it has seemed to me warm and positive but not erotic.'

In retrospect, I believe that this response was not the proper one. I had once more been drawn by her down an avenue which, in the interests of scientific enquiry, I should not have taken. Instead of entering into a discussion of transference, I should have interpreted her act of questioning me as itself transferential. By asking it she had wanted to put herself into the position of an intellectual equal with myself, and to assume in fact that she was not a patient. Perhaps she had been able to accomplish something similar with her father by developing her intellectual interests. Perhaps she had been able to put herself on to terms with him that were not just those of a child, not just those of a dependent; rather an intellectual equal, a close companion, not at all a suitable position for a daughter.

I leave these fragmentary notes, with all their lack of organisation, not as conclusions but as reminders of what may perhaps may be clarified if we resume. I have to say that the whole case teases me more than somewhat, and I would give a good deal to be able to make the further progress I believe I need for things to fall into place. In the mean time I shall turn these matters over in my mind, since I have previously found that a period of relaxation allows me to discern some unrecognised hint, or some connection I had not previously made.

13

Beginning the Narrative of Sara and Emily

This is the chronicle of two women who have committed themselves to each other in the way that a man and a woman do in marriage. To begin with we know rather little about the right way to proceed. This will be the story of how we approach the uncertainties of this new life, a narration of what we do and think.

That sounds all right. Should we write this in German, to make it easier for Sara to write parts of it? No – she says no. She would prefer it to be written in English. That is her new language which she speaks with me, she says because she wants to practise as much as possible. She does not always, of course. Quite often we speak in German, but she has improved her English very much since we have known each other. I find it confusing, because each language has its own meanings. I prefer writing in English, so I will do that. I do not know whether she will want to write much, but she says she may do. This will be our journal.

Sara will think this too theoretical, but one of the first things I must do is to find a point of reference for what is taking place between us, some bearings. I have no access to a university library here, but I have found in one of my notebooks a fragment of a poem of Sappho about how she looks at one she loves, a woman, sitting in the company of a man. I cannot do it justice. It goes something like this.

Your exciting laughter has made my heart beat wildly in my breast.
When I see you, even for an instant, I cannot speak.

My tongue becomes silent, and a fine flame runs beneath my skin.
My eyes are unable to see, and my ears start drumming.

Sweat covers my whole body, and trembling shakes me.
I turn more pale than dry grass. I am not far from death.

So if Sappho did love other women as is alleged, and if this poem speaks of her reaction to one she loved, this must be what she felt. I marvel at it. In Greek it seems so pure, her diction so precise, her words at the same time so evocative, so descriptive. There is nothing mawkish about it – it appears to me now completely honest and direct, without a word that is excessive or for show. How I wish I could have written that. It seems exactly, just exactly what I have now myself felt. The trembling, the fire beneath the skin, the loss of voice, even sweating, which of course women are not supposed to do. She had words, whereas I have none. I do not know how to put it into words.

When I was at university, I had thought that Sappho exaggerated, that she like so many others wrote things for effect. Now I see that she was not doing that. It is extraordinary, that unless one has had the experience then words are just shadows. I know that thought must itself be old – but to me it seems vital, now this new sense of life has occurred. The only exaggeration perhaps in Sappho's words, I think now, is in her saying that she felt this while just looking at and hearing the laughter of her friend. Though perhaps if this sight and this sound reminded her, then this too was not an exaggeration, more a kind of involuntary reliving the agitation of what was between them. I can almost understand that too, though I think I am too careful in myself to feel it in that way. Even that image of laughter, Sara's laughter, is right, exactly right. That is how I think of Sara.

So perhaps we are not abnormal. Perhaps in ancient times it was quite ordinary for a woman to love another woman. Certainly in classical times there seems to have been love between men. They wrote about it quite openly. I will show this to Sara, to see what she thinks.

Sara and I have started to discuss what we shall do together. We are wondering whether to leave Vienna. I would find it hard to secure another position here as a teacher. So we have spoken about going to America, or to Italy, or to Paris or Berlin. Sara is reluctant because her father and mother are here, and also because of the Evening Educational Association. Everything she knows, of course, is here.

She says she would support me financially, and I could do translations, or write other things, do whatever I wished. We nearly had a contretemps, but I was pleased that I was able to be open with her about what I was thinking. It was that her offer of support reminded me of the things Thornton had said, out of affection I know. I think Sara did not see that offering this would place me in a position like being a wife, dependent upon her. It has become important to me to be independent. I do not think that our relations with each other, even if they are like marriage in some ways, need to be like marriage in matters of money.

Then there is the question of how we should live. We have been able to keep from the servants, I think, anything unusual that could be observed between us. I have been ill, and this is why Sara has had to keep close by my side. Now we can no longer continue in this way. The servants would know if, for instance, Sara's bed had not been slept in. It seems sad for her to have to get up very early, before they rise, to go to her own bed. Yet we could not have them gossiping. We will have to live in a quite different way. It is not unusual for women to live together, but we would have to live elsewhere. It does not, I think, arouse comment in itself. Many women have other women who are companions, but we would need to live in a different way than in this house.

I went to see the Professor for what will probably be the last time today. I have said that I will visit or write to him in September when he has returned from his holiday. Although these weeks have been a turmoil, and although I feel in some ways in even more of a muddle, I am glad that I consulted him. What he is doing is very exciting, and quite different from what I had expected. Even if it had been simply that I have now spoken of what happened when I was younger with Mr S, then that has clarified so many things for me. Had I known, I would have consulted the Professor before. I might have been able to have my sickness cured, and thus not have felt compelled to push the hateful Mr S away. My mind goes off in that direction again. I must stop it.

My emotions seem to be playing now the top notes, now the bottom notes of the scale. I feel to be an instrument acted upon by haphazard forces. If only it were not for my impulsive act in pushing him away, I can imagine I would now be perfectly happy.

Then, if I had not consulted Professor Freud, probably these other things, these things that have become so precious, would not have happened with Sara, either. Although they may be wrong in the eyes of society, they are sacred to me. Perhaps I owe them to him. It seems to me that the Professor might with advantage be much more candid about what he is thinking, and in this he has not departed very far from other doctors, however innovative his methods may be in other ways. Like myself, he is secretive. As far as I can tell though, and I have to piece this

138

together partly from what he says to me, and partly from his writings, I have suffered from repression. This made me ill, particularly in the feelings of nausea and disinclination to eat which I have suffered for many years. He was able to lift these repressions, digging out these upper layers of the archaeological site as he would say, and in so doing we started to reveal the next layer. This is of my having been stopped in my development in a phase of being attracted to people of my own sex. The Professor thinks this may be traced back to my longing for my mother, which again I can recognise. I am grateful to him that I can recall my mother more clearly.

Professor Freud seems convincing in some respects, but not entirely so. He implies that had my repressions not been removed then the lower layers would not have been revealed, and this tendency of mine towards homosexuality would not have occurred. I can see, however, that I have felt very warmly towards Sara for some time, since quite soon after I had met her. I felt that she was a person with whom I could be intimate. So the Professor's story seems inexact. I cannot claim lack of interest, however. Perhaps his therapy did allow me to move beyond mere thoughts. In truth, moreover, I have found being with him fascinating, when I was not in anguish, and reading his works has opened a new world.

Here I write yet again of my own thoughts. This was to be the story of Sara and myself. Is there no end to being absorbed in my own self?

Nothing else has appeared in the newspapers, either Austrian or English, so perhaps the danger is passing. If only I can master myself.

Book 2   Investigation

Investigation. 1. The action of investigating; search, inquiry; systematic examination; minute and careful research. **2.** The tracking of (a beast).

Shorter Oxford English Dictionary

14

An Excursion into Psychopathology

(from a manuscript entitled *The Viennese Affair* by John H. Watson MD)

Mr Sherlock Holmes, although pre-eminent in the investigation of crime as I have often recounted, was occasionally unable to master aspects of his own exceptional character. Not to put too fine a point on it, he suffered from fits of morbid dejection. I have to admit now that these were sometimes considerably more severe than I have previously intimated. Medically I was defeated by these lapses, both in therapeutics and in any diagnosis that was more exact or informative than the vague term 'melancholia'. At the same time Holmes's lapses left me in a state of pressing concern. Since at the time of which I write I was married, and Holmes lived alone in the rooms that we had once occupied together in Baker Street, I was concerned that I would be unable to be of any service to him whatsoever. Not that during such passages I had been of much service when I was there. People in such states, however, have occasionally made away with themselves. This outcome is generally said to be more likely among those who devote themselves to intellectual pursuits, especially among those who live much in their own company, and this knowledge naturally exacerbated my concern for my friend.

In 1903 I therefore committed myself to learn more about these nervous afflictions, with the purpose of being of some assistance to the man whose companionship has done so much to enhance the life of a lowly doctor, and whose accomplishments have been of unique service to innocent victims of crime in three continents. It even occurred to me that should I achieve some synthesis of the medical literature on the subject, and perhaps supplement it with observations of my own, then I might write a small monograph on the subject.

My early career as an army surgeon in India had been interrupted by a Jezail bullet. Perhaps I should thank the man who fired that rifle, for indirectly it led to my meeting one of the most remarkable men of our age. When later I set up in practice in London it was rarely that I had found my medical cases as absorbing as the cases of detection that my friend pursued. Now, however, I renewed my medical determination in this one direction. I was resolved to learn all I could about the condition of melancholia, into whatever paths this might lead me, and despite the difficulties I might encounter.

I knew I had not the acumen of some of my medical colleagues, but I thought I would compensate for this by applying myself unstintingly. I had before me in Holmes the embodiment of single-mindedness; and this example, combined with my gratitude to him, would, as I believed, prevail. If anything were known, or could be discovered that would be of assistance to my friend, I now resolved to seek it out. I began studying psychopathology in earnest, reading all the medical literature there was on the subject, and where possible attending such scientific meetings as I could discover that had any bearing on the matter. Somewhat to my surprise, although the problem was not well understood and was clouded in those who wrote on the subject by thinking of a distressingly inexact kind, I found myself much taken up in my new pursuit, flexing mental muscles that had long since become flaccid.

I visited Holmes, of course, regularly in the lodgings in Baker

Street. I was more than glad to be of service in any small way I could. He was able to think aloud in my presence, I believe, using me as a kind of foil to his own mental agility. Often I did little more than reply rather obtusely to lines of enquiry that he was following, marvelling as usual at his feats of mind. I believe my presence helped his mental processes, and for that I was grateful. At the time of which I now write, however, on many of the occasions when I visited him there was little enough to indicate that he was one of the most astute thinkers of our time. As often as not, after greeting me without enthusiasm, he would sit in silence while I would leaf through a newspaper, selecting articles that I thought might interest him. I must have let slip in some way that my own concerns had taken a new turn. It was not long before my friend realised that something was afoot.

'What is this new pursuit of yours, Watson?' he asked. 'It is a medical interest, is it not? It is perhaps a psychological interest? It seems to be uncommonly absorbing. It must be all the more remarkable in that, since I have known you, medical matters have not been the guiding star in your firmament.'

'I am studying psychopathology,' I said with as much unconcern as I could muster. 'Those ailments that may cast even the most noble minds into desolation.'

'Indeed: and what has prompted this interest?'

I could see he was teasing me, but nevertheless I was embarrassed, and found it difficult to reply. 'It is important in the cases that we investigate to be able to recognise people who might be afflicted in some way. I was hoping some small expertise of my own might be of assistance in any new investigations that you might undertake.'

'Ah. You mean you are once more agitating yourself on my behalf. You fear for me in my spells of melancholy. I trust that your studies will be improving to you, but you need not be concerned on my account. You need not be concerned in the slightest. I do not believe my faculties are impaired. It is inactivity that is destructive, inactivity such as this present spell, that lays me waste, that makes my life a desert.'

I was relieved that I no longer had to conceal my motives, but I was not, of course, relieved as to the main problem, or at his last words comparing his life metaphorically to a desert. I had now learnt that such sentiments were symptomatic of that melancholy strain which again had taken its sinister hold on him.

'So you say, Holmes,' I declared. 'I admit that your powers of insight into the nature of crime and its methods of detection increase rather than the reverse. I own too that when you are working on a case that absorbs you, no one could be more alert. Nevertheless I am worried about you, professionally I mean. If there were a medical cure for your fits of black despair, it is the least I could do to offer it to you.'

'It is very good of you to consider the problem,' said Holmes, indicating by his tone that he did not think it at all good, and that he wished to drop the subject.

During that year my friend's condition seemed generally to deteriorate. There were interludes, however, and he undertook several cases – one of them, 'The Blanched Soldier', was written up by himself at my suggestion. I had thought that turning his hand to literary production might provide the mental exercise that his mind craved, although I own that in some ways I found this hard, since the excellent result that Holmes achieved also made me wonder whether he really needed me as his biographer. He declared, however, that although he might write up a case from time to time, it was not his forte, and it became clear to me also that it was no answer to the problem of his melancholia. Other attempts of mine to distract him were similarly of no avail. What was worse was that he was beginning to say that he thought he had become bored with detecting the perpetrators of common crimes.

'The police can now do as well as I,' he remarked. 'My work has become unnecessary.'

Unhopeful as the prospect of any easy cure had become, I knew enough from my studies to be considerably alarmed at such a statement. In the normal course of events Holmes believed, with good reason, that he was the superior of any in the world when it came to detection. The self-denigratory content of his remark, the idea that he now considered himself no better than an ordinary policeman, was most perturbing. It confirmed, if any confirmation were necessary, that Holmes's melancholia was of the most morbid kind.

Then something yet more disquieting supervened than I had witnessed hitherto. He began to talk of retirement, of nearing the end of his career. He even spoke of going to live in Sussex, in a cottage, and studying bees! For one who had no feeling whatever for the countryside, for one whose very life depended on his being at the hub of the Empire's mightiest city, drawing towards himself information of the minutest currents of criminal activity that were occurring there, this talk of taking to the country and studying bees seemed preposterous. In someone else I could even have imagined that he might have been indulging in whimsy, letting his mind play on fancies that he had no intention of carrying through. I knew, however, that no one was less capable than he of undirected or haphazard mental activity.

Physically neither of us was as strong as we had been when we started our association more than twenty years previously; but, as far as I could see, there had been no diminution either in Holmes's mental acuity, nor in his mental energy once he was working on a case. The combination of Holmes's assertion that he must be mentally engaged to avoid falling into torpor and his statements about retirement multiplied my concerns considerably.

It was when I had been absorbed in my studies of psychopathology for almost a year that a medical colleague, newly returned from the Continent, mentioned to me that he had come across the work of a Viennese physician, one Dr Sigmund Freud. This Dr Freud had, it seemed, proposed both a theory about illnesses that he called 'neurotic', and methods of curing them. My interest was aroused. Dr Freud had given lectures at the University of Vienna, and had lately been appointed to a professorship. His reputation was not extensive, but my friend had evidently been struck by his acumen. Since I had resolved to leave no stone unturned, I thought I should pursue the matter.

Despite my enthusiasm, despite my months of reading, and even despite the fact that the problems discussed in the literature of psychopathology had whetted rather than dulled my interest, I had become disappointed in the concrete results of what I perused. I had not lit upon anything so far that seemed unequivocally to be capable of helping my friend. What I had found were some notable descriptions of melancholia, but also a good many unsubstantiated opinions as to its cause and treatment, many of them flatly contradicting one another. Often the methods of thought of men who wrote on the subject were the very antithesis of the crystalline logic that so fascinated me in the scientific detection practised by my friend. I had of course become thoroughly familiar with Holmes's methods, and though I had long since abandoned the attempt to emulate my companion in his feats of cerebration, I flatter myself that I had become something of a connoisseur of his techniques. Thus my association with Holmes may have spoilt me, not just in the excitement of the chase which his cases sometimes occasioned, but in giving me a taste for a kind of thinking which seemed so distressingly rare in my own profession.

I had determined, however, to pursue all possible leads. Therefore I sought out Dr Freud's publications in the learned journals that my colleague had indicated. Fortunately I am moderately fluent in German and was able to read these publications without resorting to assistance in translation. The disappointment I had previously experienced in my researches on psychopathology was initially increased as I encountered the Professor's writing. First I found that his most notable work had been on dreams. What could be less helpful to my pursuits? I resolved to pass over this material, and continue. Then as I came to the journals of diseases of the nervous system in which the Professor had published, I found at first that the cases of neurosis which he described were unlike that of my friend in every respect. Their subject was hysterical young women, the unsavoury nature of whose lives was only matched, as it seemed to me, by the prurience of the said Professor Freud in his reports.

Determined to leave no stone unturned, I continued to read. Before long I found a set of case histories that the Professor had written with a colleague, one Dr Josef Breuer. The studies were again of cases of hysteria, and it happened that the first of these to which I turned concerned a young Scottish woman, who was acting as a governess to a wealthy widower in Vienna.* I started with this case, since on leafing through the pages I had noticed that this young woman had some melancholic symptoms. Then, as I read more carfully, I was suddenly overcome by something akin to *déjà vu*.

'My heavens,' I burst out, while reading in the library of one of our august teaching hospitals, thus causing some heads to be turned towards me in astonishment. What I had discovered was that Professor Freud had come upon methods very similar to those of my friend Sherlock Holmes. He worked by attending to small clues that went unnoticed by more common minds, and by making deductions of a remarkable kind. In the case of the Professor's patients, he began by finding out what had happened

*The case of Miss Lucy R, reported in *Studies on Hysteria*.

as a detective might, and his discoveries were an essential part of the cure for their condition. Obviously this was quite different from discovering the perpetrators of some devilish crime, but nevertheless I found the parallel compelling, and I was unable to banish it from my mind. The Professor's way of thinking struck me with a force that was both uncanny and irresistible. His writing clearly sprang from a mind in active and acute observation, driven to make brilliant inferences. It contrasted sharply with the lax quality of much of the other material I had read in the area of psychopathology.

I did not speak to my friend of this, since I still hoped to be of some medical help to him, and, although the young governess about whom I had been reading had indeed been in a state of melancholia, the circumstances seemed very different than any that could be affecting my friend. I concluded, however, from my further reading of Freud's work on hysteria that what had to be detected in the case of patients suffering from mental disease, perhaps including melancholia, was that certain events in their past had, like crimes, become hidden. I began to turn over in my mind the question of my friend's reserve about his own life: we had been intimate for several years before he even mentioned his family, or the fact that he had a brother!* Could it be that such a noble mind as his had suffered in some way in the past, and his predisposition to melancholia was related to this suffering? I was sure that the trauma could not be anything comparable to the degradations suffered by some of the young women about whom I read in Freud's work, but nevertheless, the idea began to take on a certain fascination for me. I determined that should an opportunity arise I would make the acquaintance of this Professor Freud, to ask whether he might have some clue as to the origin of my friend's affliction. Without being at all sure of

*See 'The Greek Interpreter', included in *The Memoirs of Sherlock Holmes*.

how it might be managed, I conceived the idea of arranging for Holmes to meet Freud, who might then be able to suggest some course of therapeutics.

I hope that an opportunity for Holmes to meet Professor Freud may indeed arise, since as luck would have it the case that I now describe, which concerns the mysterious death of a diplomat, has brought us to Vienna, where I now pen these words. I occupy myself by writing up this case as it has unfolded so far, while Holmes busies himself about the city conducting his researches; and I look forward to a meeting that I have arranged, in which I myself will make the acquaintance of the Professor.

I run ahead of myself: the case of which I now write became known to us during an interval in which my friend had been in lower spirits than any time since I had known him.

15

The Viennese Affair

A Commission from the Foreign Office

I had virtually given up hope of a new case catching Holmes's imagination when I called on him early in the summer of this year of 1904. He had asked me to call that morning, and for the first time in several weeks I fancied that he was pleased to see me. He gestured to me to take a seat. He had been pacing the room as I entered.

'Watson, how good of you to come. You have been concerned about my health. You will be relieved to learn that yesterday I had a communication from the Foreign Office. I have told them that if I am to work for them they must be prepared for you to accompany me – should you wish to do so, of course. You will be pleased to know that now I have something with which to occupy myself, and you may be confident that this is the tonic that I need. I expect a representative from the Foreign Office to call in about twenty minutes. In the mean time you might be interested in this. It is a report of the death of a diplomat, and I am told that the commission that we may expect from our government concerns this man. I had thought that there was little that could now awake my imagination, since I thirst for something fresh. It is possible that this may indeed be something out of the ordinary, not only in that will take me out of the arena of petty crime and mundane domestic mysteries into a wider world, but because already, even though I know nothing yet beyond the fact that I am to discover the circumstances surrounding this man's death, the case has set me cogitating.

'Have a look for yourself,' he continued. 'This is the report which appears to be the starting point for the commission that I understand I am to undertake.' Holmes passed me a newspaper several days old. I read as follows.

The body of a man, since identified at Mr Charles S of His Majesty's Diplomatic Service, was found on an Austrian mountainside yesterday afternoon. He appears to have fallen whilst walking, and it seems possible that the body lay undiscovered for several weeks. Mr S's career had taken him to France, Switzerland, South Africa and the United States of America. He played a prominent part in the negotiations at Vereeniging which led to peace in the Transvaal. A widow and one adopted daughter survive him.

I said that I couldn't see much mystery in the fellow's death. He had probably met with an accident of the kind that sometimes befalls people who walk in the mountains alone.

'No doubt you expect me to draw your attention to some minute detail of this report that you have overlooked,' said my companion. 'For once, however, I agree with you. There is nothing of note in this newspaper report as such, beyond an error of the kind that is commonplace in newspapers. Mr S did not have an adopted daughter, he had a ward. No, Watson, there is nothing unusual about the newspaper report at all, but I have made a few enquiries among people who knew him, just in case such information might be of use in advance of the arrival of His Majesty's representative. One small matter caught my attention. I was able to learn from one of his colleagues that there was something unusual about the circumstances of the man's death.'

'Well, my dear fellow, tell me what it is,' I expostulated, more pleased than I wished to admit that now my friend's mind was at work again.

'The colleague told me that Mr S had a profound fear of heights, which was particularly severely exercised by mountains. This fact evidently had been confided by Mr S's wife to the colleague's wife, and she had remarked to her husband on this unusual feature when the newspaper report appeared.'

'It seems rather a slight matter. It may not be of any significance,' I said, knowing by now that such remarks on my part would often elicit further information from my friend.

'You may be right, Watson. You may be right.'

'No doubt the visitor from the Foreign Office will inform us that he was there on some particular business,' I persisted.

'It is possible that you are right,' replied my friend. At this point he sat down rather stiffly in a chair, and I could see that no more conversation would occur until the arrival of our visitor.

So began the case in which my companion was once again to demonstrate his prowess to the highest degree, but which marks, if I am not mistaken, a turning point in his career. I say this as I write, not at the conclusion of the affair, as is usual with me, but *in medias res*. I began to think that my companion would not only solve the immediate problem, but that cases of this kind might elevate the employment of his talents from the realm of private practice to the service of His Majesty. A solution to the problem of his melancholia had presented itself. I would not have had the gall to suggest any such idea myself. Working for our country, rather than on such cases as came haphazardly to his notice, would give my friend a sense of higher purpose, the absence of which may not have been unconnected with the increasing severity of his melancholic mood.

To recur to the story as it unfolded: I found it hard to restrain my delight when Holmes told me of his 'commission', as he called it. At last something had attracted his attention, and if the matter were a minor one, as it seemed to me at first, who was I to protest? The circumstances such as they appeared at the outset indeed seemed meagre enough, and I was surprised too that a commission from a Civil Service department should have caught his imagination, when my friend's taste was for the freelance, untrammelled by officialdom in any form. The Civil Service stood for everything that he was not, but I bided my time, reflecting on this new and remarkable turn of events.

As the clock struck, the redoubtable Mrs Hudson showed a Mr Jones up to the rooms on the first floor of 221B Baker Street. He was of middle height, clean-shaven, with shortish brown hair and dressed soberly, as if he were a caricature of a city gentleman, looking like a hundred others, almost as if he had intended his appearance to be as undistinguished as possible.

'Mr Jones?' asked my companion. 'Please come in and sit down, and allow me to introduce my colleague: Dr Watson.'

'How do you do,' the man intoned.

'You may speak freely in front of Dr Watson,' Holmes continued. 'No doubt your superior will have told you that he will be working with me.'

'Indeed. Very well, I shall come straight to the point. You will know that on the 4th of April this year His Majesty's government brought about a remarkable coup, which may contribute to peace in Europe, in northern Africa and indeed further afield.'

'Our signature of the Entente Cordiale,' I said.

'You are correct, sir,' our visitor replied, glancing towards me. 'It brings to an end once and for all any potential quarrelling between us and France over imperial claims, and it guarantees mutual support, but abroad it has its detractors.'

'You mean the Prussians and Admiral Tirpitz with his

155

diabolical battle fleet!' I interjected. The mixture of Britain's triumphs in lands far away, the immense riches that we derived from our colonies, and tensions in Europe have engendered public excitement and apprehension which in recent years have become almost palpable. It is clear to any who think about the matter at all that the Germans envy us our position, and are now setting about doing whatever is necessary to dislodge us from our pre-eminent position in the world. No patriotic Englishman could remain indifferent to such issues.

'Exactly,' said Mr Jones. 'The Germans interpret the treaty as anti-German, and our information is to the effect that even now weighty forces in the German government are redoubling their efforts to build a navy that will challenge our own. Indeed, we believe that they will even be prepared to attack us knowing that we will win, since an engagement would leave us seriously weakened, and our overseas lines of communication would then be no longer secure. Hence we would be vulnerable in a number of quarters.

'I have to tell you that what I have just said, and what I am about to say, is to be regarded as utterly confidential. Mr S had been charged to make contact with a member of the German government, one Herr G, in order to conduct delicate negotiations regarding the implications of the Entente Cordiale for our relations with Germany, to reassure the Germans, and to reach some *rapprochement* with them, if possible laying foundations for an alliance that would forestall the challenge that they are preparing to our naval supremacy. I am not in a position to tell you the exact nature of the negotiations that were to take place, but I can say that our government gave the matter the very highest priority.'

'We quite understand,' I said. Inwardly I gasped. Could it be that even now the Germans were preparing to attack our navy, and the government urgently needed to parley with them? Or was some plan afoot to sign a treaty with them, that would maintain our overseas possessions while diverting the envious gaze of the Prussian?

'The reason why Mr S's charge in this regard was so delicate is this,' continued the representative of His Britannic Majesty's Government: 'First, Mr S had known Herr G well, and was thus one of the few people who might exert a personal influence in a sober case. Secondly, Herr G represented something of a minority view in the German government. So, although he might have some effect within the government, if it were to leak out that he had been talking to one of our officials he could be discredited, and perhaps forced to resign. Thirdly, I have to say the Germans now employ methods which are less gentlemanly than mere encouragement to resign.'

'Less gentlemanly?' I enquired.

'Both Mr S's and Herr G's lives were in danger should the purpose of their meeting have been discovered. We cannot be certain that the death of Mr S is to be regarded as an accident. It is of considerable importance to our government to learn whether the plan, known only to a very few, for Mr S to meet Herr G was betrayed, because if so the implications for us all could be very serious indeed.'

'If he had been assassinated, do we have any information as to who is likely to have been responsible?' I asked.

'Indeed we do.' Mr Jones for the first time looked eager. 'There is a small group of agents trained in the latest techniques of espionage who use assassination among their methods, and whom we believe are employed by the German government. If the moves of which I have informed you had leaked out, it is very likely that this group or some member of it would have been called in. Here are such names and details of its members as we have available. I would be grateful if, after you have made yourself familiar with them, you would destroy these papers.'

So saying Mr Jones drew from his pocket an envelope and handed it to my companion. 'Other information relevant to the matter is in the envelope, as are the terms of the enquiries we wish to make. Also enclosed are details of a bank account on which you may draw, which will provide ample funds for your expenses. Perhaps you could call in to the bank and give them a specimen of your signature and so forth.'

'I take it,' said Holmes, interrogating our visitor for the first time, 'that you wish me to discover whether Mr S did indeed meet Herr G before he died, and whether that death was a political assassination?'

'That, sir, is precisely the commission we wish to charge you with. For reasons that need not concern you, although the matter is of extreme importance, sufficient time is available for you to complete your report. We would like it within three weeks.' The man produced a small pocket diary and made a note. 'That is, on or before the 12th of July.'

'Very well,' said Holmes, 'I accept the commission. I shall make a full report before 12th July.'

'Thank you,' said our visitor. 'One further matter. Also in the envelope is a system of passwords, a code for telegrams and details of how to contact me or an associate by telephone. Please use the telephone if there is anything that you want, co-operation from any official quarter, or anything that you need to know. Please memorise the passwords, and destroy the paper on which they are written. May I suggest also that you have a telephone installed here. It will obviate unnecessary delays if we should need to exchange messages. I have already made an arrangement on your behalf, and if you agree, the apparatus will be installed this afternoon.'

'Really!' said Holmes. 'Well, sir, I agree, and thank you.'

'I am much obliged to you,' said our visitor. 'Is there anything else you need to know? If not I will bid you good-day.'

'Yes,' said Holmes, 'there are two further matters. Can you please furnish me with an account of Mr S's movements since the signing of this treaty? Secondly, can you tell me what the exact terms of Mr S's instructions were?'

'At the time of the treaty's signature Mr S was in New York,' replied Mr Jones. 'He did not have any connection with the affair until he returned to this country, which was on 25 April. On the day following this he was given his task of meeting Herr G. Everything relevant, including Mr S's movements as they are known to us and the exact terms of his instructions, are included with the other material in the envelope you now have in your possession.'

'You have been most thorough,' said my friend. 'I thank you. There is but one further matter. Do you know, by any chance, whether my brother, Mr Mycroft Holmes, is concerned in this matter?'

'Yes sir, he is. Mr Holmes had a memorandum conveyed to me, intimating that should you wish to discuss the matter at all he would be happy to see you in the Strangers' Room at the Diogenes Club at six o'clock this evening.'

'Thank you, Mr Jones. There is nothing else, then, for the present. Allow me to show you out.'

Holmes accompanied the gentleman from the room and down the stairs. When he returned he said, 'As I thought. Mycroft is behind this. All in the envelope, indeed? If everything were in the envelope, they would hardly be likely to be engaging my services. What do you think, Watson? Why do you think Mycroft wants me involved? Why did he not raise the matter with me himself? It seems that by sending Mr Jones, he has been arranging for me to be recruited by the Service. He knows I would happily undertake a case for him, behind the scenes. Why these documents, why this Jones?'

'It is certainly a new departure for you, my dear fellow,' said I.

'Before that man arrived I had thought that being employed by a department of the Civil Service would not suit you at all, but perhaps I was quite wrong. My word, Holmes. Telephones, passwords, codes, bank accounts. It adds a quite new dimension to your activities.'

'It does, Watson, it does,' my friend agreed. 'What would you say if I suggested that I take you to lunch?'

'I should accept with alacrity,' I replied.

I was of course delighted that Holmes had this commission, not just that he had work to do. I knew by the invitation to lunch that he could scarcely be more pleased, though of course he would not say this in so many words. Informed by my voluminous reading on the subject of melancholia, I reflected that the change in my companion since I had last seen him was of some considerable moment. Then he was lethargic and morose. Now he was positively talkative. As we walked down Baker Street he described the changes that had been occurring in what he called 'intelligence' services attached to national governments, and how he thought that, without of course giving up his status as a private consulting detective, a new realm of possibilities might open.

I listened to him, having to walk fast to keep up with my companion's eager stride. 'It begins to look as if the man may have been assassinated,' I opined. 'Do you think he was lured there? Or could his body have been taken there and left in a place where it was unlikely to be quickly discovered?'

'Really, Watson, you know my methods. It is futile, indeed deleterious, in any enquiry to speculate. First we gather evidence, then the facts will lead us infallibly to the conclusion. Before evidence, however, we need sustenance, eh Watson?' This was as close as my friend got to making a joke. 'Is this restaurant to your taste?'

'By all means, Holmes. By all means. It looks capital,' I replied as we came upon a small but agreeable-looking establishment in St Marylebone High Streeet.

'They are quite right of course to consult me,' said Holmes as we entered. 'I can say without conceit that in all the country there is no one better that they should have on their books for occasional commissions of an international nature. It is not logical to assume this, I admit, but I have a strong supposition that other commissions of the kind will follow, and they may even come to form the major part of my practice.'

How very different, I reflected, than the Holmes of recent days, who had thought himself to be no better than the average policeman. How thoroughly encouraging was this new turn of events.

16

The Viennese Affair

At the Diogenes Club

Holmes had asked me to accompany him to the strange Diogenes Club in Pall Mall, where the rules are that no member may take notice of any other by conversing or even nodding in greeting. Only in England, land of eccentrics, could such a place exist, to cater for men who wish to have the facilities of civilised society without being obliged in any way to take part in conversation with their fellows. The Strangers' Room is the only one in the club where the rule of silence does not obtain. As I knew from a previous visit, this would be the most deserted part of the establishment. As we entered through the imposing pillared porch with its huge doors, a uniformed footman showed us the way, and I glanced as we passed them into rooms that were not crowded, but contained a good number of very well-dressed men, making use of the excellent facilities. The club is not only furnished with every comfort but it has the best collection of periodicals in London.

I reflected that Mycroft Holmes must have thought the matter important if he first arranged the visit of Mr Jones, and now arranged to discuss it in more detail with his brother. I recalled the occasion when, nearly ten years previously, he had engaged my friend in the case where the greed-driven Hugo Oberstein had stolen the plans for the highly secret Bruce-

Partington submarine.* For his troubles the villain was even now languishing in one of His Majesty's prisons. In that case Holmes had deduced that the body of the young clerk Cadogan West, who was suspected of the theft, must have been placed on the top of a Metropolitan Line train as it passed on its way behind the Kensington houses of Caulfield Gardens. Privately I had thought that this was one of Sherlock Holmes's most astounding strokes of genius. More publicly the case had a less satisfactory end, because rather than the submarine having led to the virtual elimination of warfare at sea, as had been thought at the time of its invention, we now faced a period in history in which the possibilities of warfare at sea were multiplying with the preparations that were being made by the German Imperial Fleet.

At the time of the Bruce-Partington case, Holmes had said that his brother was entirely unambitious, that he provided merely a kind of consultation service for Whitehall departments. He was invaluable not only because of his unique intelligence but because of his incessant appetite for reading matter of every type, and his apparently unlimited capacity to store facts in his mind in an orderly manner. So if some minister might want to know, for instance, what bearing the recent changes in mining operations in South Africa and French policy on the Suez Canal could have for a particular technical development in metallurgy in Glasgow, Mycroft would be consulted in order to give an opinion, which typically turned out to come closer to the truth than the slow sifting of specialist departments and expert consultations. Sherlock Holmes had described his brother to me as someone who was even more fully blessed with the gifts that he himself possessed, but who was a creature of habit who seldom left his armchair. Having made an inference, or seen a connection, he

*In 'The adventure of the Bruce-Partington Plans', included in *His Last Bow*.

was content, and did not feel any inclination to pursue the matter further. It was my companion who used a similar, though he insisted a lesser, mental ability, but with the desire to verify conclusions that were reached. At any event Mycroft Holmes, with his encyclopaedic knowledge, his methodical approach and his ability to connect fact with fact, was invaluable to the government and was often influential in policy. Nevertheless, his younger brother had protested, he held no reins of power. As the Bruce-Partington case turned out, however, I received some indications to the contrary. Undertakings that the full resources of the state would be deployed were indications of a man with more than just a subordinate influence behind the scenes. I could not help wondering if Mycroft Holmes, in some clandestine way which it was not in the public interest to disclose, did not hold a position that was a great deal more important than his brother had indicated to me.

I was shocked as I saw Mycroft, sitting in a capacious armchair, reading a journal in a corner of the small but tastefully furnished room with its exquisitely moulded ceiling. He was only seven years older than my friend, but since our last meeting, which admittedly had been some years previously, he had aged considerably. His massive frame, once so imposing, now looked to be a burden to the man. His brow was as masterful as ever, and his steel-grey eyes had not lost an iota of their penetrating force, but his jowls had become fleshy, his jaw, once so resolute, had lost its force. One saw the face of a man of immense intelligence and subtlety, but one was simultaneously reminded, by his sagging frame and folds of facial flesh, of that end to which all earthly existence tends. I reflected that had Mycroft Holmes been under my care I would first have tried to persuade him that his sedentary habits should be supplemented by some exercise, and secondly that he might be less indulgent in his diet.

'Ah,' he said as he saw us. 'Sherlock, and your good friend the doctor. Forgive me if I do not rise. I fear the effort would take more out of me than formality warrants.'

'Not at all, not at all, my dear Mycroft,' said my companion. 'Watson does not stand on ceremony, and neither, as you know, do I.' Holmes evidently had seen his brother more recently than I, and was therefore not taken aback by his appearance. At least no sign of such an effect was visible on my friend's brow as we took armchairs around a low table and were offered drinks by the butler.

'So you have had the visit from Mr Jones. I knew I could trust you to enquire of him whether I was behind this. Well, of course I am behind it. How do you like Mr Jones?' he asked. 'I thought you might like him. Supremely ordinary, is he not? Completely unmemorable in every way. I now have several of these gentlemen working for me. They are invaluable.'

At this point Mycroft Holmes turned to me. 'I can, of course, rely on my brother, but I shall take you also into my confidence, doctor, at least to some extent,' he said. 'I know from Sherlock that you are completely trustworthy, and unreservedly patriotic. No, there is no need to speak.' He motioned to me to refrain from any utterance. 'I know this to be true. I must explain to you both that since . . . well, I will not say when, but recently, the government has instituted a service for the co-ordination of information, of which I have been appointed the head. I have a certain talent for retaining information and connecting one thing with another. I do not know whether you realise it but our world is changing. Until now, peacetime has been peacetime, and wartime has been wartime. When we have been at war we have gathered military intelligence even if it were not easily available, and even though our generals did not always use it. In peacetime all that ceased. Our armies returned home and our diplomats became merely diplomatic. They continued to send, of course, reports of publicly available information about what was going on in the countries where they were posted. Now, I am afraid, all that has changed, and I must remind you of the confidentiality of this little chat. These two kinds of function, of what we might call military and diplomatic intelligence, have become intertwined. We are now obliged at all times, whether in peace or war, to gather secret information about all countries, especially those with interests that might conflict with our own. Occasionally we must even intervene in certain matters abroad, in pursuit of our own national purposes. Fortunately we live in a country where our interest and what is right usually coincide, otherwise I can tell you this might become a very unpleasant business indeed. I imagine you catch my drift,' and with this the sharp grey eyes in that ponderous head turned to glance first at myself and then at my companion.

'Recently we have been badly shaken by a number of developments, all of them, I have to say, instigated by Germany. You may have seen published last year the so-called novel, *The Riddle of the Sands*, written by Robert Erskine Childers, who is a clerk at the House of Commons. It is about German plans for an invasion of our shores, under the cover of the Friesian Islands, from the shallow waters that lie behind them. The plan was a daring one, but if Germany had implemented the arrangements she was making we would have been in grave danger indeed. I say the book is a so-called novel, because, except for some of the names of characters and some details of the cruise that the yacht took which were fabricated, much of what Childers wrote about is stark literal truth. The shock was that the invasion plan was uncovered by Childers, as an amateur yachtsman pottering about in a small boat among the sandbanks of the German coast. He became appalled at what he saw as our national complacency, and the inability in certain official quarters to do anything about it. So he wrote the book to scotch this particular method of invasion, and to wake the country up to how the Germans were thinking. In both of these matters he succeeded very substantially. It requires no more than a moment's reflection to realise that if there were one plan, which Childers discovered by the merest accident, there might be a dozen more such, in various states of preparation, of which we know nothing. So this is partly why my department has been brought into being. In the event, it turns out that there are indeed other preparations that we are beginning to discover, any one of which, if it were fully comprehended by members of the British public, would cause them to sleep less easily at night. I shall say no more about this.'

I listened with growing horror to Mycroft's disclosures, though I determined to make no sign of my consternation. I realised, however, that much more was at stake at this moment than in any of the cases that had previously occupied my friend.

'The second development,' continued Mycroft, 'is that the Germans have formed an intelligence department. In their usual way they have several years start on us. With German thoroughness, their "squad", for that is the term by which I think of it, is both highly trained and prepared to use the most ruthless methods. It is possible that our chap Mr S, who had been seconded to my department, fell victim to their methods.'

'You mean that a civilised nation in time of peace is resorting to assassination of an official of the British government?' I asked.

'We do not as yet know whether this group was responsible for Mr S's death. That is where my brother comes in.' At this Mycroft glanced at my companion, who had the while been sitting imperturbably listening to this speech. 'We do know that they assassinated a French government official earlier this year. Their department is a little different from ours. It is attached to their admiralty and headed by a man of considerable cunning and determination, a first-rate officer who reached the rank of rear-admiral. His name is Oberlander. Jones will have given you the bare outlines of his organisation, but we have a certain amount of less formal information about it. Since our own organisation is, let us say, in an early stage of development, I regret that not all the information we have is systematically arranged. I suggest, Sherlock, that you visit one of our establishments tomorrow, look through what we have and talk to some of our chaps. Could you make a consultation with Dr Humphrey de Vere of 138 Harley Street? You will find that you have an appointment for nine-thirty in the forenoon. This is one of the houses I have set up to allow visitors of all kinds to come and go without exciting suspicion. Dr de Vere, as it happens, also sees bona fide patients, but he is invaluable to us in a number of respects. On the fourth floor you will find Jones – well, several Joneses actually – and material that may be helpful to you.'

'So,' asked Holmes, 'may I take it that you are recruiting me to your organisation?'

'My dear brother, I am well enough acquainted with you to know that you would not in any way like to be constrained. I am a sedentary creature, and to work from an office, where information reaches me of its own accord, is my *métier*. You are more suited to action, and to gleaning for yourself the evidence vital to whatever case you are working on. It would be to the nation's advantage if you were to lend your shoulder to this wheel while ensuring that the fact were not generally known. Let us put it like this. If you would consider undertaking a commission for us from time to time, no one would be more delighted than I. To be frank, my dear fellow, I think the pursuit of criminals whose intelligence is no match for your own must occasionally become a trifle dull.'

'I have to admit that things have become a little stale of late,' remarked the younger brother. 'So I am not averse to striking out into new territory. It might be the kind of challenge that would suit me. You would have to assure me though, Mycroft, that I would not have to attend meetings, or receive official communications, or sit in an office even for an instant. If I am to be fettered in any way then no arrangement is possible.'

'I understand,' replied our ample host. 'You have my undertaking that officialdom will not extend a single tentacle towards you. Allow me also to clarify the arrangement from our side, and this suits the purposes of us both, I believe: this commission and any others you undertake will be kept entirely secret. There shall be no communications with police or any other civil authority, unless we have specifically arranged them for you. Is that acceptable to you?'

'Perfectly,' said Sherlock. 'It suits me admirably. One further thing: I shall continue to act as a private consultant, entirely free to pursue my criminal work, and as in that work I shall be free to accept or decline any case of yours as I see fit.'

'Of course, of course, my dear fellow. That will also be in our interest.'

'Very well, we will use this case to see how the arrangement works. First tell me exactly about this meeting of Mr S with Herr G. Were the two of them to meet face to face? Would not some other form of communication have sufficed?'

'It was thought essential that the two of them actually meet, perhaps several times. There were many details to discuss, nuances to both convey and perceive. Only direct meeting would suffice, and it was S's commission to accomplish this.'

'Very well; that is an essential piece of information. Tell me what is known about this fellow S.'

'You can look through what we have on him when you visit Harley Street tomorrow. Though I have been able to choose some of my own people, others have been passed on from elsewhere. You may guess that the people departments pass on are those whose services they can most easily dispense with. S was lent by the Diplomatic Service in this way. He was able enough, but I did not like the fellow much. I cannot put my finger on why, and he has done distinguished work. You will think I am going soft in the head, Sherlock. Usually I am able to tell exactly by what minutiae I form my judgements. In this case I had nothing more than an intuition. There had been some talk that he spent more time than was appropriate increasing the size and value of his art collection, but that kind of thing is nothing out of the ordinary, and it was useful to us because it gave an excuse for him to be travelling around more than might be considered usual. To me there seemed, if I may put it like this, something a little too carefully contrived about him, as if he were striving for a particular kind of public conduct in all things. He was scrupulously correct in his bearing and demeanour. Apart from that, a matter that caught my attention as being of potential use to us concerned his ward.'

'His ward?'

'Yes,' said Mycroft. 'She was the daughter of a diplomat who died in a fire in Paris some years ago. S became her guardian when she was not much more than a child. She caught my attention because she speaks four modern languages and two ancient ones perfectly, and has been educated in an American university. There may come a time when a woman would be invaluable on some special assignment, and there can be few with her pedigree, her familiarity with foreign countries, her proficiency in languages and her intelligence. I had made a mental note of this, in case at some future date she might be useful to us. I wondered perhaps if you might also want to make her acquaintance in your investigations. I have not met her. I would value your opinion.'

'Hm,' muttered the younger brother. I saw that Mycroft's practical pigeonholing of possibilities had run up against my friend's enmity towards members of the fairer sex, and that we would proceed no further in that direction, at least for the moment.

'I shall not interrupt your reading any longer,' said Sherlock Holmes to his brother. 'I shall of course keep you fully informed of my progress.'

'You need merely communicate with Jones,' replied Mycroft. 'Pray regard him as one of my additional sensory organs. I bid you good-evening.'

We walked along Pall Mall, each sunk in our own thoughts. Twice I stopped myself from remarking on Mycroft's appearance, and more than twice from asking Holmes for his opinion of the new web of intelligence-gathering at the centre of which his brother sat waiting like a giant spider.

As we came in sight of the statue of Eros, that peculiar memorial to Lord Shaftesbury, Holmes said: 'I shall leave you here, my good fellow. We shall meet at the station at two o'clock as we have arranged, and go to meet the widow.'

'Yes, indeed. Good-night, Holmes,' I replied, a little chagrined that I had not been included in the visit to Harley Street. 'I shall be at the station.'

17

The Viennese Affair

A Visit to the House at B—

The next day was fine. We sat in the train as it puffed peacefully past the last houses of the great city and through the green English countryside. The miracle of modern transport soon brought us to the little town of B—, and before long we found ourselves approaching an elegant and quiet house, set in its own leafy grounds. A maid opened the door to us. We entered and I found myself gazing up towards the ornate roof light, then noticing the balconied upper landing which ran around the house on the first floor with doors leading off it, and the grand staircase which descended sedately to the hall where we stood. We were shown into the drawing room, which was at the back of the house, with an aspect on to a luxuriant and pleasant garden. A woman of middle years, with stately bearing, entered the hall to greet us. Her grey hair was carefully arranged. It was evident that she had once been a consierable beauty, and even now her finely formed bones gave her face an aristocratic appearance. She had a subdued demeanour, and I had the impression this was not entirely due to her recent bereavement.

'Mr Holmes and Dr Watson,' the maid announced.

'Please come in, and make yourselves comfortable in the drawing room here,' said Mrs S, opening the door of that room for us. 'I shall join you in just a moment.'

I looked around the large room, which was furnished with quiet good taste. For many years I had tried to emulate my friend and notice any clues that might present themselves. Though things which seemed significant to him merely passed me by, I continued to practise the art of observation on all occasions. The room was light and airy, and showed every appearance of more than adequate financial circumstances. This was the comfortable home of a diplomat, with all the advantages of the peaceful countryside yet within easy distance of London. The only thing I saw that was out of the ordinary was a large number of paintings in the French Impressionist style, arranged on the three walls other than that of the fireplace. For the most part the paintings depicted women in various states of undress. I reflected how far public taste had advanced to make this kind of thing now acceptable even in polite drawing rooms, and as we awaited the return of Mrs S I counted the paintings. There were twenty-seven of them. Holmes too had looked about the room and, having satisfied himself, sat in an easy chair gazing fixedly at the ceiling. I wondered what his practised eye had gleaned.

Mrs S returned, and as we rose at her entry she asked us to be seated once more, and apologised for keeping us waiting. I surmised that our arrival had interrupted some urgent household task that she had needed to complete.

'I am sorry to impose upon you on the occasion of your bereavement,' began my companion, 'but the Foreign Office is concerned about the circumstances of your husband's death and the fact that his body had lain undiscovered for some weeks. They have asked me to look into the matter, in a routine way of course, because I have certain skills in tracing people's move-ments, but I would be most grateful if you could regard my interest in the matter as confidential. Evidently,' he continued without further ceremony, 'after Mr S left his office on the 2nd of May, planning to leave for the Continent on the 3rd of May, they know nothing of his movements until his body was discovered on 16th June. It is important to discover where he was between the time of his departure from England and the time that he met with his death. I would be most grateful if you could tell me anything that might throw any light on the matter.'

'I will tell you anything I can,' replied the woman with a composure which indicated that the interview would not distress her, 'though I fear it will not be very much.'

'It would be most helpful if you could tell me of his movements from April onwards.'

'Of late, Mr Holmes, I have not always known of my husband's movements. The work on which he had been engaged had obliged him to be abroad a good deal, and he said he did not always know where his work would take him. Some of it, he said, was of a clandestine nature. Sometimes he would be away for a week, or a month.'

'He did not tell you where he was going, or for how long?'

'Usually only in vague terms,' replied Mrs S. 'He would say, "I shall be on the Continent for a couple of weeks," or something like that. I have to tell you, Mr Holmes, that except when my husband's work has required us to put on a show of connubial solidarity, as when we have been living in an embassy abroad, I have had as little to do with my husband's work as possible. I may as well tell you also, since it will now do no harm, that we were not close. We lived, as far as possible, separate lives. I have made my life here. I love the garden which you see there. It is a haven of tranquillity.' She motioned towards the window. 'With the help of an excellent gardener, I cultivate it myself. I sit on the parish council, and have a few charitable occupations that I pursue.'

'So you were not particularly concerned when your husband disappeared?'

'I did not know that he had disappeared,' she said, 'until I was informed by the Foreign Office that his body had been found in Austria.'

'Perhaps then you could just tell me when your husband had been at the house here, since the beginning of April.'

'Well, he returned after an absence of three or four weeks. That must have been towards the end of April. He was here for a few days, went to his office in town, stayed at his club I think for a couple of nights, spent a weekend here, then he was off to London, back here for a night or two and then off to the Continent again. I think that was it. That was the last time I saw him.'

'You do not know the exact dates?' Holmes enquired.

'I can check them for you. I do keep an engagement book, and that usually includes a note of when my husband is here.'

She left the room, and returned presently with the book. 'Yes,' she said. 'I was right, he returned from abroad on the evening of the 25th of April. He said he had been on the Continent, but I rather think he had been in America. He had returned with a new tie, which I happened to notice was from Brooks Brothers. I think he went to town just for the day on the 26th, and he was here that night and the 27th. He said he was at his club on 28th and 29th and 30th, then here on Sunday and Monday night. Then on Tuesday 3 May he left again, as you yourself know. He said he was going to Paris.'

'That is very useful information,' remarked Holmes, making rapid notes. 'The office had not known that he was bound for Paris. That was the last time you saw him?'

'Yes.'

'Thank you,' said Holmes, once more. 'That is most helpful.'

'Not very helpful, I am afraid,' our hostess replied.

'Did it surprise you that he was found on an Austrian mountainside?'

'It did not particularly surprise me that he had been in Austria, just as it would not have surprised me if he had been in Belgium or Cyprus, but it surprised me considerably that he had been on a mountainside. He hated mountains, and this had been a source of some regret to me when we first were married, since I love the open air and walking in wild places. We were not able to take walking holidays, since my husband had a fear of mountains which amounted, I believe, to a medical condition.'

'A phobia!' I exclaimed. 'People can have phobias of heights and suffer severe vertigo. They are quite unable by any effort of the will to overcome their fear of falling.'

'In my husband's case it was a fear that he would be unable to resist an impulse to hurl himself from the high place,' replied our hostess. I had read about this variation of the phobia. As always, confrontation with the actual brings a shock when one has only had the matter outlined on the printed page.

'I was surprised that he had been found in such a place,' Mrs S continued, 'but I suppose that in the course of duty even medical conditions have to be set aside.'

'One thing that would be most helpful,' said my companion, 'would be if you had a photograph of him that you would not mind my borrowing. You have some studio portraits here? Is this Mr S?' Holmes had risen and crossed to a mahogany side table set against a wall, on which stood a set of framed photographs. He lifted one of them.

'Yes,' replied Mrs S. 'That is he. You may take the picture if you wish. Please remove it from its frame. You need not trouble to return it.'

'And this?' enquired Holmes, picking up a photograph of a young woman with fair hair and a strikingly slim face with refined features, wearing what seemed to be academical dress, carrying beneath one arm a mortar board and holding in the other a scroll. 'Is this your adopted daughter?' Holmes had evidently wished to conceal from Mrs S the fact that he had been told about the ward.

'That is Emily. She is not adopted. The newspaper made an error. My husband was her guardian.'

'She lives here too?' enquired Holmes.

'No, she used to live here, but now she lives in America, in Philadelphia. We have not seen her for several years, though she writes dutifully, once every couple of months or so. She is making her own life in America. You are looking at a photograph taken on the day of her graduation from university there, where she studied the classics.'

'So she will not attend the funeral?'

'I hardly think she can cross the Atlantic Ocean in time,' replied Mrs S. 'I understand my husband's body has been returned to London. The undertakers are collecting it, and I have arranged the funeral for the day after tomorrow in the parish church. I have wired to Emily with the news of my husband's death, but told her that she should on no account attempt to return for the funeral.'

'Is this by any chance a letter from her — I see it has a postage stamp of the United States?' I was rather shocked at Holmes's behaviour. Being observant is one thing, but nosing about in the drawing room of a bereaved woman struck me as quite another.

'Yes,' replied Mrs S, without rancour. 'It arrived just the other day.'

'I hope you will forgive my impertinence,' said Holmes. 'I have recently become most interested in philately. I have started to collect postage stamps, and have acquired a particular interest in issues from the New World. Would you mind if I took this specimen over to the window to examine it more closely?'

'Not at all, Mr Holmes. If stamps interest you, you may have the whole envelope. I believe you collectors like to preserve the postmark too. Here.' She rose from her seat, took the letter from

Holmes, removed from it the folded sheet of writing paper which had been within and handed him the empty envelope.

'Thank you very much indeed,' he said, pocketing the envelope. 'You are most kind. I have another request, if I may. I imagine that your husband's effects, including the clothes he was wearing when he suffered his accident, will be returned to you shortly. Would you object to my examining them? What would be easiest for me would be to take them away for a short interval, where I can subject them to a microscopic examination. It may for instance be possible to find some mud on his boots which I can match with specimens from the vicinity of his fall, and this will help us to trace his movements up to the time of his death.'

'Extraordinary!' exclaimed Mrs S. 'Quite extraordinary. What will people think of next? Very well. I have no objection whatever to your having my husband's effects for as long as you need them. I believe the Foreign Office has them at the moment. Here, I will write you a note giving you permission to take charge of them. You will no doubt be able to intercept them before they are sent on here.' With this, Mrs S opened a handsome bureau. She sat down and penned a note, which she gave to Holmes.

'There is one further question I should like to ask,' Holmes continued. 'When Mr S travelled, did he regularly take with him any particular pieces of luggage or clothing, or had he any noticeable habits of any kind? Did he for instance ordinarily send you a letter when he was away?'

'It is quite some time now since I have received letters from him,' said Mrs S, rather tartly, I thought, 'but he did have the habit of always packing his things himself. He had a special suitcase in which many of the contents were already packed, so that he could be ready to leave at a moment's notice. In it for instance, as well as clothing, was his leather case with his toilet articles, and also a leather writing case. I had given him these cases early in our marriage, and he found them useful on his travels.'

'Thank you, madam. I need trouble you no further,' said Holmes. 'You have been most helpful. I shall see you on Saturday, at the funeral, if I may. In the meanwhile thank you for your forbearance, also for the photograph and the postage stamp.'

'Think nothing of it, Mr Holmes. I hope your enquiries, routine as they may be, are successful.'

'Well, Holmes,' I said as we made our way towards the railway station. 'Whatever do you mean by taking up philately? Is this something else you plan for your retirement, when the weather is too inclement for you to attend to your bees?'

'Bees could become an absorbing interest, Watson. Do not speak scornfully of them.'

Then, after a period of silence, he announced: 'As yet we have little to go on. We are simply faced with an expanse of a month or so of time. We must seek to ascertain how Mr S had filled it in his latter days. We may also find something germane in his effects, which I shall collect from the Foreign Office tomorrow. Until then, we must simply keep our eyes and ears open for any signs that might help us. What did you make of Mrs S and our interview with her?'

'I was struck by the detachment with which she wrote you a note for Mr S's effects. No doubt she had become used to offical procedures in her life, but her coolness at a time of bereavement was remarkable. Her sad demeanour, I believe, is not because she is in mourning. I think it is a more permanent disposition.'

'Good, Watson, very good indeed. You are coming on wonderfully,' said my companion. 'I agree with you. I am unable to make any observations about Mrs S that go an inch further than those you have mentioned. We will make a mental note that Mr and Mrs S were distant. This fact may assume some significance later on.'

I was not a little gratified. Perhaps, I thought, at last I had learnt by my apprenticeship to my friend to be as observant as he. My satisfaction was short-lived.

'Did anything else strike you from our visit?' he asked me.

'I was surprised by the quantity of Impressionist paintings,' I observed hopefully.

'Their significance being?'

'I don't know whether they have significance. We knew from your brother that he was an art collector.'

'Quite. The one thing I thought might be of some interest is this envelope that I have in my pocket.' Holmes produced the envelope, with its American stamp. 'The stamp itself has not the slightest importance,' he said, 'beyond allowing me to question Mrs S as to whether the letter might be from her ward, but what do you think of the envelope, my dear Watson?'

'It looks to me very much like an ordinary envelope, such as might enclose an ordinary letter,' I replied.

'In one sense you are right,' my friend agreed. 'The question is: for whom is this envelope so ordinary? It is only ordinary in an entirely localised manner. I would hazard that there is nowhere in Philadelphia that such an envelope could be purchased, indeed I doubt that you could buy this anywhere in America. I am sorry, Watson, that I have allowed you believe that I might be interested in postage stamps. Envelopes, though, are another matter. There is a proper subject for study. You may think that an envelope is simply an envelope. In reality, it allows infinite variety of manufacture. It is one of those items that is invariably made locally. Thus in one country or even city the paper will be of some particular quality. Even if it is white, it will be of some particular shade of white, and envelopes will be of a particular size and construction. Even different batches of envelopes from the same manufacturer are different. What struck me, when I saw the envelope in question, is that it is certainly not American, despite its postage stamp. I believe it is Austrian. I do not have a collection of postage stamps, Watson, you may be assured of that. Stamps are produced in a uniform way, and it would be difficult to imagine anything that held less interest for a student of crime. I do however have something much more valuable – a collection of envelopes and samples of writing paper from all the main manufactories in Europe and America, also from some other places, though outside the area I have mentioned my collection is patchy. Let us see if we can be exact.' Here Holmes produced the envelope from his pocket, and held it up to the light. 'No, we cannot be exact for the moment: there is no watermark. This would have made its provenance evident even to your eyes, but I shall match it with samples in my collection. It is certainly of Germanic manufacture, probably Austrian. I think it was probably made in Vienna, and if so I believe I may have a match for it.

'The possibility of any connection to our case is by no means certain,' he continued, 'and if there is a connection we cannot yet guess at what it may be. At present, as I mentioned, we have very little to go on. Like you, beyond the estrangement of Mr and Mrs S, and the dates, which will be useful, I could derive little of note from what Mrs S told us. The envelope caught my eye. It was the only thing that seemed out of register with what Mrs S herself told us.'

'By Jove, Holmes, you never cease to amaze me,' I gasped.

'It was a simple observation, Watson. It indicates that the sender probably resides in Austria, although she wishes it to be thought that she lives in America.'

'You have often said, Holmes, that your methods are founded on the observation of trifles. This may prove to be significant. Mr S tells his wife he is on the Continent, and is in fact in America, while his ward says she is in America, but is in fact in

Vienna near where our man met his death. Can that be a coincidence?'

'It could be, Watson. We shall wait and see. One additional piece of information from the envelope is the full name of Mr S's ward: Miss Emily Vincent. No doubt we could easily have discovered it in a number of ways, but the American habit of the sender writing his name and address on the envelope has served us well. I doubt whether we will visit this address in Philadelphia, but we may pay Miss Vincent a visit when we are in Austria, if only to see what she knew of the movements of her guardian.'

18

The Viennese Affair

Mr S's Effects

The next evening I visited Holmes again in the rooms we had occupied together in Baker Street, and was agreeably surprised to find him engaged in activity. Gone was the torpor, gone the lassitude. There were no further remarks about how he might leave the profession that he had single-handedly created. On the floor was a leather suitcase and several piles of clothing. On the table was a range of articles and labelled envelopes. In his hand he had a sheaf of papers clipped on to a thin panel of wood, which he held while he made notes.

'That is a good idea, Holmes,' I said as I came in and sat down, 'that board you have to support your note-taking.'

'It is an elementary idea, Watson,' he said amiably, 'but serviceable. Pray content yourself with the newspaper until I finish my inventory, there's a good fellow.'

It must have been half an hour later when he exclaimed: 'There, my inventory is complete. These, Watson, you see are the effects of the late Mr S, which I obtained this morning from Great George Street.'

'Great George Street?' I asked.

'There is a kind of tradesman's entrance to the Foreign Office, to the parts where they transact their less ceremonial business,' he explained. 'Following the custom of offices, I had to wait for a considerable interval, and sign papers. Here you see before you the effects sent back from Vienna. As well as what he was wearing when he met his death, we have Mr S's suitcase and the other things left in his hotel. In this case the police were meticulous and identified his hotel. His possessions were in the care of the proprietors. The problem set for the police was not exacting. A key bearing the name of the hotel was on his person when he was found. Perhaps inadvertently, or perhaps because they have begun to adopt a scientific approach to detection, the Austrian police did not return it to the hotel but have sent it on here.

'Can you prepare yourself for a journey, Watson?' my friend continued. 'A trip to the Continent. I trust your good lady wife and your patients could spare you for an interval. I anticipate that we will be away for a little more than a week, leaving in a few days' time. Could you manage that? I would be grateful if you could accompany me.'

'We will perhaps be going to Vienna?'

'Certainly to Vienna,' my friend replied, 'and perhaps elsewhere, though as yet I am not sure. I have not been idle today. I have sent wires to several associates. The replies may contribute to determining the course of our journey.'

'I would very much like to accompany you,' I said. 'Consider the arrangement made. I shall be ready to leave at twelve hours' notice.'

'Twelve?' asked Holmes, looking at me quizzically. 'You are very exact.'

'It will allow me to arrange with my locum tenens to take up my medical duties.'

'So be it. These,' he said, gesturing towards them, 'the suitcase, clothes and this case with toilet articles, each carefully placed in its own little compartment, that Mrs S mentioned, I will ask Mrs Hudson to pack up and return to the Foreign Office to be sent on to Mrs S. I have taken samples of material from the outer clothing he was wearing at the time of his death. We may use these in our investigations. I am more hopeful that we may make use of the samples here of mud that I have recovered from his boots. These other things,' and here he indicated a pocket book with a Morocco cover, a handsome gold pocket-watch, a fountain pen, two slips of paper, three sale-room catalogues and some other small items, 'these may be of use to us. From what Mrs S told us, she will not miss them for the duration of our investigations.'

'Is this all there was, Holmes?' I asked. 'Are these all his belongings?'

'These are all that have been sent,' he replied.

'Nothing to read,' I observed. 'With the estrangement from his wife, these commissions to travel abroad involving little contact with others of his own kind, and he carried not so much as a novel. He must have led a lonely life.'

'Hmphh,' was the only reply I received. He began to pack up the smaller articles. 'This,' he said, holding up a small slip of paper when he had finished putting the other items into a bag, 'has already been of use. It was in his breast pocket. It bears a letter E and an address, Clusius Gasse 20. I have confirmed that it is Mr S's handwriting by comparing it with a sample provided to me by the Foreign Office. One thing is odd, however, that I do not understand.'

'Pray tell, me, Holmes. What is it?'

'See here how the E is written. It is a capital letter, but not written in the way Mr S usually forms his capital Es.'

'It is a Greek E,' I suggested. 'Like the figure three backwards.'

'Yes Watson, it is,' he said, 'and I have no idea what significance there might be to it. Perhaps there is none. I have purchased a Baedeker. There may be a Clusius Gasse elsewhere, but there is a street of this name on the map, here.' He indicated the place, near the Donau Kanal, not far outside the Ringstrasse that circles the centre of Vienna. 'The fact that this slip of paper has simply this address and a peculiar Greek E indicates someone with whom Mr S was on intimate terms, so that he does not bother with the full name. There may be another person than his ward with this initial, but for the time being we will entertain the hypothesis that this is the address of Emily Vincent in Vienna. I confirmed that the envelope of the letter sent by Miss Vincent was indeed made in Vienna. At any event we can pay a visit to this address when we are there. If I am correct, then Mr S either visited her or intended to visit her.'

'By Jove, Holmes, do you think that Mr S had somehow got the girl involved in his activities? It seems very unsuitable. Not at all the kind of thing that I would want a young girl I was responsible for to be mixed up in. Foreign agents, people in the pay of the German government undertaking assassinations, that sort of thing. I know your brother had this same idea, but these are not matters for women.'

'Come now, Watson, the possibility that Mr S met his ward in Vienna, and that she had taken some pains to conceal her address from Mrs S, does not compel us to the conclusion that she was involved in Mr S's clandestine transactions. As yet we know nothing of why Mr S had a paper with this address on his person. I am proceeding on a broad front. These items of evidence will be given their proper weight as we progress.'

'You may be right, Holmes, but it all seems deuced suspicious to me. I think there is more to this case than meets the eye. Why would the girl be sending letters to her guardian and his wife as if from America, when really she lives in Vienna, if she were not engaged in some secret activity? Mr S is involved in some deep things on behalf of our government, we know that. As your brother said, we are entering a new age. More than we know goes on behind the scenes. First we find that a member of the diplomatic service is charged with secret assignments, of which one faction of a foreign government might take such a poor view as to have him assassinated. Now we find, or at least it may be the case, that he has recruited his ward to assist him, no doubt taking advantage of the fact that as a woman she would not be easily suspected.'

'You run ahead of the facts, Watson. By the way, do you plan to write up this case? Are you perhaps making notes?'

'You know how it is, Holmes. I do usually jot down some salient points, but by no means all of your cases are suitable for publication, for very many reasons, so I do not write them up fully until they have been brought to a conclusion.'

'Hm,' said Holmes.

I wondered why he asked me this. I could only assume that he had some special reason for wanting me to keep a record of this case that was more than usually minute. Perhaps it was because he was striking out over new country, leaving behind, as it were, the now familiar streets and turnings of domestic crime, robberies, private intrigues and murders motivated by greed or revenge, to make for a new territory as yet untrodden by us, the field of international affairs. I determined to write up the case as we went along, chronicling each new turn of events as it occurred. I was encouraged by Holmes's eagerness for me to record the course of the case to enquire whether there had been other developments during the day.

'There are no developments,' my friend replied. 'I have, however, instigated some enquiries and hope before long to receive information that will assist us. The ample funds that have been put at our disposal have allowed me to telegraph to an associate in New York, and instruct him in detail about an enquiry I should like him to pursue in Philadelphia. I have similarly wired to an acquaintance in Berlin, whom we may visit, to request some preliminary information and to ask him to ready himself to work on our behalf. I have also decided to employ Augustus Pemberton – you remember, the personable young man who applied to me recently as to whether he could become an apprentice at my trade. I have said that I will not be able to employ him on a continuous basis, but only from time to time, as work demands. Despite this, he was delighted. He will guard the fort here in London while we are away. He will stand by here so that he may use the telephone if need be. He will also visit the offices of shipping companies to consult their passenger lists and discover the recent comings and goings of Mr S. First he will find out the exact time of Mr S's return from America and then of his departure for the Continent, since it is important that from the time of being given his commission to the day of his death we can account for all his movements.'

'You mean you are going to construct an account of Mr S's whereabouts on every day since the 26th of April until the time of his death?'

'Exactly, Watson. It is a pedestrian scheme, I know, but as I said in this case we must proceed on a broad front. With the death already several weeks old, the trail is not exactly hot, so we must use other methods.'

'Have you decided when we visit Vienna?' I asked tentatively.

'Probably on the 2nd of July. You would like to inform your wife, is that so?'

I did not reply. It pains me to say that I did not wish to disabuse my friend of his assumption, though it surprised me that, although he so frequently warned me of jumping to unwarranted conclusions, now here he was doing just this. Or so it seemed. My wife, God bless her, would not object to the date or duration of my journey. Although I know Holmes better than anyone knows him, he remains private. If I were asked whether he had guessed that informing my wife was not the principal reason why I enquired about our plans, I would not be able to say with certainty. I was reluctant to tell him why I wanted to know our movements more exactly, because I wanted to make contact with Professor Freud, and if possible to gain an interview with him. I thought my friend would not thank me if he thought I was planning to have him meet the Professor, particularly now his morbid condition seemed so completely to have abated. At any event, I thought it best to telegraph to the Professor without at this stage telling Holmes, and hoping that, if *I* could meet him, some occasion might present itself for effecting an introduction.

'Until we leave, Holmes; what do we do until then?' I asked.

'Until then, Watson, I have a number of routine enquiries, as the police call them. Let us call it laying the foundations. The difference, if you like, is that whereas in my cases with a single criminal we could typically hope to look the fellow in the eye at some juncture in our enquiries, in this case I fear we have as our adversary not an individual but what might be called an organ of a national government. In this case I must first find out what I can about it, and its methods of working, and secondly, as I have indicated, I must form a picture of the movements of Mr S, so that we may approach the problem by a method of elimination.'

'Elimination?'

'Exactly so, Watson, elimination.'

I have to confess, as so often, my friend's thought processes far outstripped mine. What exactly was he going to eliminate, I wondered? As I was thus turning this question over in my mind, he continued after a pause: 'One enquiry on which you may wish to accompany me will take place on Saturday morning. I said I had not been idle. Earlier this evening I went down to Mr S's club in Pall Mall, and made some enquiries about when he has stayed there, in order to start to fill in the blanks, as it were, on his calendar of engagements. I learnt with interest that though he dined at his club on the evenings when his wife said he was there, he did not sleep at the club. The studio portrait of him that I obtained from Mrs S has been most useful. I was able to show it to the cabbies on the rank outside the club. As you know, Watson, cabbies are creatures of habit, and they tend to work from the same place. One of them recognised Mr S, and said he had often taken him from Pall Mall to a certain address. Would you like to accompany me there on Saturday morning? We could leave at eleven. I have asked the cabbie to call here at that time. Before then I shall make some discreet enquiries about the possibility of interviewing the person we wish to see on Saturday. If my enquiries indicate that our visit would be wasted, I shall let you know. We shall perhaps discover something about Mr S's excursions that were sufficiently frequent for a cab driver to remember him and his journeys with clarity.'

19

The Viennese Affair

The Woman in Black

On the next day I did not hear from my friend, and so on the day following I presented myself at 221B Baker Street a little before eleven.

'Good,' said Holmes, 'here you are. The cabbie is already waiting for us. Let us be gone. We journeyed westward, past St Marylebone railway station, turning north before we reached St Mary's Church on Paddington Green, and then to the west again, finally ending in a row of substantial though not grand houses, in Clifton Gardens. The one to which the cabbie conveyed us was well kept. Holmes knocked and the door was presently opened by a middle-aged woman, evidently a housekeeper.

'Yes?' she asked.

'I have come to see your mistress,' Holmes announced. 'Here is my card.'

'Mr Sherlock Holmes,' read the woman, becoming more accommodating than she had been with her initial abrupt greeting, and adopting the respect that my companion's card usually commanded. 'Is she expecting you?'

'I do not have an appointment,' replied Holmes, 'but I would be grateful if you would tell her that it is a matter of some urgency that touches on an acquaintance of hers.'

The woman disappeared indoors, and presently returned,

saying that her mistress would see us. As we entered the house, the street and exterior were soon forgotten. We were led into a room which though not large was furnished with taste. The occupant of the room was a slim woman with finely drawn features, dressed in an elegant black gown, which one might have thought would be more suitable to evening than to morning wear. She had a very youthful face, though I guessed from certain lines around her mouth that she was the wrong side of thirty. Her long hair was carefully arranged and was of the same raven colour as her attire. She stood to greet us. Her eyes were dark and lustrous, and she had a disturbing vitality.

'Mr Holmes,' she said. 'Please, won't you come in? Mrs Mountjoy, I expect these gentlemen will take some refreshment. Would you care for some coffee?'

'Thank you,' replied my companion. 'We would be grateful for some coffee. This is my colleague Dr Watson. I hope you do not mind us calling on you unexpectedly. It is on a matter of some importance.'

'Please be seated.' The lady in black motioned us to comfortable chairs, and sat down herself, as the housekeeper left the room.

'It is about a gentleman who I believe was an acquaintance of yours,' said Holmes. 'A Mr Charles S. I hope I am not the first to bear you the bad news, but he has been found dead in the Eastern Alps of Austria.'

'My God,' the woman replied, putting her hand to her brow, considerably shaken. 'My God.' It was clear that the woman was either a fine actress, or was hearing about Mr S's death only at that moment. She rose from her chair, shaking her head, and walked over to gaze from the window.

'I had not heard,' she said, as she turned her whitened face towards the room again some moments later. 'When was this? How did it happen?'

Holmes related to her the outline of the events as we knew them.

'You say this was announced in the newspaper?'

'Yes, last week. It was however a small entry, you may have missed it.'

'I very seldom read newspapers,' said the woman. 'Tell me, how did you know that he was an acquaintance of mine?'

Holmes begged her forgiveness, and said he had been able to trace her because of the visits Mr S made to her address when he was staying in London.

'It shows that one cannot be too careful,' she observed. 'I suppose you must have guessed that I am, or I suppose I should say I *was*, his mistress. He bought this house, and made me an allowance. You will no doubt think me a shameful woman, but I have an elderly mother to support, and her doctor's bills are substantial. My husband died young with more debts than assets, and if one does not want to take up typewriting, which itself is very meagrely rewarded, there are very few means of gainful employment open to a woman in these days. This was a convenient arrangement for both of us.' She paused, and after some seconds resumed: 'I have always dreaded that this would happen. The house was made over to me, but I have no idea what arrangement he made about the allowance. It was paid from a bank account in Switzerland. No doubt it will stop when the money in that account runs out. I will certainly not be the beneficiary of any will. He was not a man who would have wanted to admit to my existence, even in death.'

I was shocked to see that this woman's cause for concern was largely for her own financial circumstances, and it caused me to reflect on the callousness of these creatures who prey upon the weaknesses of men. Holmes, on the other hand, seemed unperturbed by this recitation. As coffee arrived, in a handsome silver pot, he was evidently keen for the housekeeper to finish serving it, in order to begin his questions.

'So Mr S would come and visit you?' he asked. 'How often would this be?'

'Once or twice a month, when he was in town, sometimes more, sometimes less. Tell me, Mr Holmes, why are you enquiring about the matter? You say the papers reported that the death was an accident. Is it suspected that there might have been foul play?'

'It is possible, madam,' replied Holmes, with some hauteur. 'At present I have been asked merely to enquire into the circumstances, which are obscure.'

'By whom are you employed?'

'I am not at liberty to disclose that, madam.'

'No, I suppose not,' she replied.

'I would indeed appreciate it, madam, if you could answer some questions. You have, I believe, nothing to lose. I will not disclose anything you tell me, and the doctor here is the soul of discretion.'

'Very well, I will tell you what I know, though none of it seems to me to have any bearing on him dying in Austria. I have to admit that, although I had dreaded such a moment as this, it is also something of a relief. There were aspects of my duties for Mr S that I found increasingly difficult to fulfil. I have thought about the possibility of his death often. I will perhaps turn this house into lodgings, or perhaps see if I can extend my clientele for dressmaking. Do you like this dress? I make my own clothes.'

At this point the lady, who had still not resumed her seat, swirled her elegant gown around her, and curtsied to us. How could she know that there were few men in London for whom such a display would be more inappropriate than my companion?

Holmes first got the woman to give him an account of Mr S's visits to her house since he touched our shores at Southampton on his return from America. It transpired that he had stayed in her house on each of the three nights that his wife had thought him to be at his club. 'Were you and he the only ones in the house on these occasions, apart from your housekeeper,' Holmes continued, 'or did Mr S meet anyone here?'

'Meet anyone?' The lady was visibly taken aback.

'Perhaps a foreign gentleman?'

At this she laughed. 'Oh no,' she replied. 'He never met gentlemen here.' But she had given herself away. She had not after all, I reflected, been acting when she heard of Mr S's death, and she was not acting now.

'He did meet somebody then, a lady?' continued Holmes relentlessly.

'He met a young woman,' replied our hostess. 'It is all over now, thank God. I am not proud of my part in it. I will tell you everything if you promise not to inform the police or other authorities. You are just investigating the circumstances of his death, is that not so? You have no interest in my obscure existence as such?'

'I have no interest in your existence as such,' said Holmes icily. 'I promised you previously, and I now repeat, I hereby solemnly undertake that whatever you tell me will go no further than the doctor and myself. We are not connected with the police and are merely interested in Mr S's movements, not in your own. Moreover, I do not foresee that anything you tell us will become a matter for the courts, so beyond this interview, you will hear nothing of this again. So pray, whom did Mr S meet?'

'Her name does not matter,' the woman in black replied. 'The names of none of us matter. Mr S was a voluptuary, Mr Holmes. I take it that you understand my meaning. When I first knew him I was barely twenty-three. I was at my wits' end. I had mourned for the death of my husband, who died when we had been married for only two years. My mother was ill, and I had been reduced to working as a barmaid in a public house in the Strand. Can you imagine the sordidness of such a life? At any rate, Mr S struck up an acquaintance with me, and I became his mistress. I have to admit that I fell in love with him, and thought he would be my salvation, that we should marry. He was not without charm. He was kind and he was considerate. I felt I had been rescued from the very brink of ruin. He set me up in this house here, and I was also able to look after my mother, who has a tiny room on the edge of the Heath which she refuses to leave. It was only later that I realised that I was providing a kind of second home for him in town, while he had another in the country, and that marriage to me was no part of his intention. It was not very long after that also that I realised his coming to stay with me here was not the end of the services he required.'

'Please continue.'

'I hope you have strong stomachs, gentlemen. Mr S had a kind of need. He was fatally attracted to young women, preferably very young women and preferably those who were without any experience of sexual relations. My job became to introduce him to such women. Before long I found myself making such arrangements on a frequent basis. I must have been mad. I believe I was still more than a little in love with him, and had somehow let him use some kind of power over me. At any rate, you remember I mentioned typewriting. I have a friend who runs an establishment for young women at which they learn typewriting and other kinds of work in offices. I am a good judge of character, and I was able to select certain women who, while they were presentable, were no better than they ought to be. I was able to enter into an arrangement with them whereby I would make them an elegant gown, and for an additional fee that was paid by Mr S they would come and spend a few evenings with him, here in my house. After two or three such evenings, Mr S would grow tired of them. Then, a few months later, he would tell me that the longing for someone new had come upon him again, and I would resume the process. The person he met when he last came to see me was one such young woman. I had not known that he would be away for so long in March and April. I had expected him sooner. On this occasion I did not have very much notice of his wishes. So it was with some difficulty that I was able, when he did return, to make the necessary arrangements for the evenings he wanted.' She paused, as if hesitating and uncertain as to whether to continue.

'There is more?' said Holmes. 'You hesitate, and I infer that you are debating with yourself as to whether to recount what else took place. I promise we will be discreet. Please continue, if you would be so kind.'

'I should not tell you this, but I will continue. I find strangely that it gives me some relief, now that it is all over. The other part of the performance,' she said, 'was that when the young woman had left, perhaps the same evening, or perhaps the next day, he would be particularly affectionate with me. He would tell me in some detail of the events of his encounter with the young woman, and he would become very passionate. I have thought about this often. I believe it is part of what bound us together.'

Again she became silent, lost in contemplation.

'Is that all?'

'No, not quite all. He would require me sometimes either to chastise him for his misdeeds, or to cajole him with protestations of excitement to recount every last detail of his encounter.'

'I suppose you agreed to these procedures?'

'There is no need to be so condescending, Mr Holmes. I am, as you see, a fallen woman, but this is the kind of world many of us women must live in. Yes, if you like: to start with I agreed willingly. I loved him. Perhaps to some extent I enjoyed these episodes. Is that what you wanted to hear? Latterly I had come to detest them, and am heartily glad there are to be no more. Shall I tell you why, Mr Holmes? Shall I tell you? It is because at first Mr S seemed to be interested in me. Yes in me, myself. If he needed extra excitements, it was as if this increased his ardour for me. I am in no position to sit in judgement. Let me tell you, as if you do not know, Mr S is not the only man in London whose tastes err beyond the marriage bed.' By now the woman was visibly angry, and had rounded upon Holmes, who continued to sit unperturbed. 'Perhaps you think I took part too readily. Perhaps I did. As time went by and the performance was repeated, it was borne in on me that the assignations, each new young woman, each new description of the encounter took on a dreadful repetitiveness. It occurred to me that none of it had anything to do with any affection for me whatsoever. I was nothing more than a paid employee. I was a servant, saying "sir" and "thank you" at the right moments. It was all like a piece of machinery. Like a huge steam engine, going round and round, meaningless but unrelenting. He had no affection for me. I was merely a part in this machine. I merely went round and round, performing my function. I thought constantly about how I could secure from him some token of real regard for me. I even asked about marriage. I promised that I would be devoted to him always, and that the other encounters need not cease. None of my entreaties had any effect. He would be polite, but distant. I felt that I ceased to have any effect on him. As this dawned on me my own feelings for him ebbed away. I still performed the service. The little cog still revolved obediently, but my resentment grew. I began to hate him. I wished this engine would be wrecked. Now at last it is. You need not wonder if I had any hand in it. I did not. I do not even know where Austria is. I have never been beyond these shores, and I know nothing of how he met his death, but you may record, if you wish, that I am heartily glad to hear the news you have brought.'

We sat and received this recitation in silence. 'Would you like some more coffee?' she asked. 'I am sorry for my outburst. I am afraid all this has caught me by surprise. I am sorry,' she repeated. 'I have no right to rail at you. I am not surprised that you disapprove, gentlemen. I disapprove myself, I had vested my hopes in him and I was disappointed. As I said, the more I think about it the more glad I feel that these performances will be no more.'

'Forgive me, madam,' said Holmes with his most studied politeness. 'I am most grateful to you for having given us these details. I do not suspect you of any implication in Mr S's death. I have almost completed what I would like to ask you, and then we will be on our way and trouble you no more.'

'Very well,' she said, now considerably calmer. 'What else do you wish to know?'

'I would like to know what I can about Mr S. Did he use this drawing room here when he stayed with you? Are there things of his in here?'

'Yes, he furnished it. He bought everything. Those statuettes, and the busts there are his.'

'May I just have a look round, madam?'

'You may, Mr Holmes. Feel free to look at whatever you like.' With this the young woman sank back in her chair, to stare though the window in a most pensive attitude.

After having made a rather long tour of the room and an examination of its contents, peering at *objets* such as the several miniature busts and statuettes arranged round the room, and at the books displayed in a handsome mahogany cabinet with a glass front, Holmes returned to his seat and indicated the photographs in frames upon a side table. They were too distant from my seat for me properly to see them. 'You have some studio photographs here,' he said. 'Of whom are these portraits?'

'If you look carefully you will see that they are all of myself.'

'In the majority of them you have fair hair, madam.'

'I was wearing a wig. Mr S liked me to appear before him like that. I believe he would have preferred me to be someone else.' The woman pursed her lips with disapproval.

'Someone else?'

'Yes, it is not uncommon. I reminded him of someone he had known, he said, a former flame, now lost to him. About two years ago he often wished me to dress like her.'

'And you did not object to this?'

'I should have preferred it to have been otherwise, but in the run of things I did not mind in any particular way. At first I demurred, and he did his best to reassure me that it was simply something he could not get out of his mind. Now that I was the object of his desire I need not concern myself with this other woman, who was just an idea, an imaginary person. More latterly, as I told you, I cared less.'

'And when you say "flame" you mean someone who was the object of a liaison . . . a former liaison . . . a liaison such as you yourself had, or of the kind you had, with Mr S?' I had not often heard Holmes lost for words, but he seemed anxious to pursue his point despite, as it seemed, embarrassing himself more than the woman to whom he spoke.

'Just such a liaison, Mr Holmes, a sexual liaison.' The woman pursed her lips again. 'I think that it what you are asking, is it not?'

'Thank you, madam, for being so frank,' Holmes replied, and then continued: 'These objects you say were Mr S's. And the books also?'

'The books in the cabinet there are ones that Mr S wanted me to study. He wished me to learn Greek and German.'

'Really? And did you do so?'

'I persevered at first, but I have no head for such things. For some considerable period the books have lain untouched. Now I shall dispose of them.'

'I thank you for your patience, madam. I shall disturb you no longer. Come, Watson, we will leave the lady in peace.'

'Thank you very much, madam,' I said as we passed out into the street, now warming from the midday sun. 'A very good day to you.'

'And to you too, gentlemen.'

We had walked up Clifton Gardens and turned right. When we reached the junction with Blomfield Road, we turned towards the tunnel through which the canal passes, before Holmes spoke. 'What despicable creatures women are, Watson.'

I was not sure whether Holmes had meant women in general, or the type of woman we had interviewed in Clifton Gardens, or perhaps just that one woman in particular. If he meant women in general, he was certainly over-generalising. He was not usually so inexact in his utterances. I felt compelled to come to the defence of the gentler sex.

'That woman is certainly a fallen wretch,' I ventured, 'but I would hesitate to include all women. You cannot pretend that you are ignorant of such matters, or that you are shocked by what she spoke of, Holmes. I know from your voluminous reading on all aspects of crime that the extent of prostitution and the exploits of these abject women in our city will not have escaped you. And, why . . .' now I warmed to my subject, 'why do you not include Mr S in your strictures? He seems to have been the instigator. If I am not mistaken he has been responsible for the downfall of that woman and others, even though I have no doubt that she encouraged him. Two days ago I felt sorry for the fellow, but now I have taken a thoroughgoing dislike to him, however important the mission for our government on which he was engaged.'

'You are right of course, Watson. Your sentiments do you

201

credit. I did not mean women in general. Not, for instance, your own good wife. I apologise profusely. Please forgive me. It is merely that I see too many good men being led astray. Pray let us speak of the matter no more.'

We had come to a halt, to allow several carriages and cabs to pass on their way along the Edgware Road. 'We can rejoin the canal a little further along, Holmes, and walk along the towpath until we come to the park. Shall we do that?'

'Very well, Watson. Lead on.' Again we walked in silence until my companion said: 'Did you see the photographs that the woman had? What did you make of them?'

'I was not able to study them with the care that you devoted to them,' I said. I was relieved that his mind had again started to run in its more usual channels, and had returned quickly from the diversion engendered by the outrage he had expressed.

'No, of course you were not. I can tell you the significant fact. They were remarkably similar to the photograph of Miss Vincent that we saw at B——. In fact, Watson, there was even one of that creature wearing academical dress, looking precisely like Miss Vincent in the photograph in Mrs S's drawing room, even down to adopting the same posture.'

'Really? That is extraordinary. So when the woman said that Mr S wished her to present herself as someone else, that person was Miss Vincent?' In a moment it dawned on me: 'Mr S had had an improper liaison with her? His own ward.'

'That is what I understood from what that person told us, Watson.'

'This case leads us into very murky waters indeed,' I remarked, glancing towards some accumulated rubbish floating in an unsightly fashion on the surface of the canal. I was flabbergasted at this turn of events.

'It seems so, Watson.' Then after several more paces he remarked, as if in parentheses, 'Miss Vincent studied the classics at the American university – now here is this woman being required both to look like her and also to study Greek.'

After another silence we turned into Regent's Park, and Holmes said: 'I must apologise to you, Watson. I believe there may after all have been some significance in the collection of Impressionist paintings we saw at the house of Mr and Mrs S. I intimated to you that I thought there was none.'

'You need not apologise, Holmes. Tell me what it is.'

'The man S was a collector of a particular kind,' Holmes announced. 'We know he collected works of art, but from what we heard in Clifton Gardens we may surmise that he also collected women. That I believe is the connection also to what Mycroft said when he mentioned that there was something odd about the fellow's closely regulated demeanour – it was devised to conceal these unsavoury traits. Collectors of this kind stop at nothing. They are seized by a passion to possess which admits of no restraint, though they can be secretive about the means by which they pursue their purposes. This information may be useful to us, though I do not know yet where it might fit in. Have you read anything, Watson, in your researches on psycho-pathology, about this condition?'

'It is called being seized by an obsession, I believe, an immutable idea, and it is as you describe. People under such an influence are driven in a way they cannot resist. They sense themselves to be controlled without the exercise of the will, and even against their will. Some authorities also aver that fury is never far away, and that they become angry if ever their desire is thwarted, or they are interrupted in one of their compulsive actions.'

'Really, Watson, you interest me. I see this study of yours has much to recommend it. Perhaps I too should adopt it.'

Again there was silence until we left the park and reached the top of Baker Street. Then Holmes said, 'With this new knowledge you have acquired, tell me this: are there other cases described which are similar to this condition of Mr S? S had an obsession for his ward, and it compelled him also to require that creature we have lately met to dress herself in wigs to look like Miss Vincent. Might I read of comparable cases?'

'That I am afraid I do not know, Holmes, or not with certainty,' I said. 'I have not had reason to seek out such cases in my own reading, but I believe there may be articles on such subjects.'

We had climbed the stairs into the familiar rooms at 221B Baker Street, and had seated ourselves before Holmes spoke again. 'Watson, that woman spoke of being closely attached for many years to Mr S and during that interval she engaged younger women on his behalf. This effect of instilling unquestioning loyalty in a woman by a man like S, is it a common thing? Do you know whether, generally speaking, a man who has taken advantage of a young woman would be able to hold her in thrall, and induce her to act on his behalf even against her will or better judgement? I am asking your medical opinion, Watson.'

'I am afraid it is beyond my purlieu. I believe there are such cases, but I have not read medical reports of any of them. Women are by nature quite properly loyal, but I do not know the circumstances in which this extends to thraldom. You think perhaps that Mr S might have also have held Miss Vincent under some such influence, just as he had held that woman, and that Miss Vincent was working with him in secret?'

'I hope not, Watson, I very much hope not, because if so it means we will have to spread our net wider than I had anticipated, and an already ticklish business may become downright difficult. It may mean that Miss Vincent is no longer an auxiliary in the case. She may have a principal part in this drama, and we must therefore afford her a corresponding portion of our attention.'

20

The Viennese Affair

Arrival in Vienna

I was taking my ease, reading in a comfortable chair in the suite of rooms we had taken in the Hotel Imperial in Vienna. Without warning the door opened and in came an elderly woman, back first.

'Excuse me madam,' I said, in some surprise. 'I believe you are in error. Perhaps you are on the wrong floor.'

'I don't think so, Watson.' The entering personage spoke with a voice I knew well. Then before my eyes, removing first a hat and then a greying wig, the stooped figure of an elderly Viennese lady was transformed into the familiar person of Holmes, as he raised himself to his full height. 'Sorry to come in like that. I needed to keep watch on the corridor, to ensure that the coast remained clear lest my hiding place should be discovered. I am glad you are here. I forgot to take my key, and I had not yet worked out how I would persuade the porter downstairs to give me one. It could have been something of a challenge to my ingenuity. Excuse me while I get this stuff off.'

I had once again been taken in by one of Holmes's disguises. Though I knew him as well as anyone, and though I knew his propensity for appearing in all manner of forms, so consummate was his art that I had often been caught off-guard.

We had arrived in Vienna the day previously, having travelled from London, and thence to Berlin. In that capital city we had met Holmes's colleague, Herr Kydorf, who had studied my friend's methods in order to apply them in his own country. Unlike Holmes, he was an amateur. He was very well connected and with an *entrée* to the best houses. He was also an Anglophile, and had come to London to work with Holmes some years previously. Holmes had told me at the time that he thought a network of allies on the Continent could only be of advantage to him.

When we met Kydorf, Holmes was able to convince him that the commission he had now undertaken did not in any way conflict with German government policy. Mycroft had convincingly argued that it is in the interests of all of us that information is available to the governments of Europe. It was when factions and cliques formed that plots could be hatched, and under cover of secrecy they could grow and become dangerous, even plunging a whole continent into war because of some injudicious action or some unregulated adventure. A military commander thinking his preparations are unknown to a potential enemy feels secure enough to inform his government that an attack will be successful. Such assurance itself can contribute to the belligerence of politicians, and to the likelihood of dangerous situations developing.

'Our best hope in Europe,' Mycroft had continued, 'is to live as good neighbours, each tending his own garden, respectful of others but also knowledgeable about what each is up to.' Was there, I wondered, a connection between the fact that Mycroft had spent his life amassing information of all kinds and the fact that he was now propounding a doctrine of relations among sovereign states based on each collecting knowledge about the others? I reflected, however, that if there were anyone to trust in such matters it was Mycroft Holmes. There seemed no reason to doubt his conclusion.

My companion managed to put the argument successfully to Kydorf, who not only appreciated it but enlarged upon it. He foresaw a time, he said, when the nations of Europe would be more closely bound together than they are now. At any event, he agreed to find out the information Holmes had requested concerning the movements of Herr G, the member of the German government whom S was to have met. He also enlarged upon the activities of the squad that had been formed by Oberlander under the direction of the German Admiralty. 'I very much disapprove,' he said. 'It is one thing to gather intelligence, but Oberlander is at heart a brigand. He has put himself above both the ordinary law and the conventions between states. He has taken to himself much wider powers. He goes as a kind of guerrilla force to other countries with whom officially we are on cordial terms. It is not right, it is provocative, and if these activities become known, it could only lead to Germany being seen in the worst possible light by other nations. It would certainly be interpreted as our whole nation having belligerent intentions. It happens because our government, despite its apparent unity, is not in fact united, and because a powerful faction has allowed Oberlander his head. I fervently hope that they will think better of it before long. He has been in St Petersburg recently, no doubt fermenting whatever disturbances he can there, because someone, or even perhaps he himself, thinks that it is in the German interest to do so. I tell you, Mr Holmes, that I am convinced that the availability of information between our governments is essential as your brother has proposed, combining, let us say, more formal diplomatic contacts and less formal ones. I am equally convinced that interference by Oberlander and his like is completely unthinkable in a civilised nation. I can only apologise on our country's behalf that we have countenanced it, and I hope that we shall not countenance it for much longer.'

He told us that Oberlander had a small secret bureau of five agents. If there had been an attempt on the life of Mr S by the principal faction in the German government; or if there had been an attempt to intercept any overtures from the British government to those members of their government friendly to Britain; if indeed there had been an assassination, it would have been by Oberlander or one of his men.

Kydorf spent the greater part of a morning discovering where Oberlander was, and what his agents had been doing from 3 May onwards. Oberlander had established a home base, with clerks and a small retinue with comfortable quarters in a country house just beyond the outskirts of Berlin. Kydorf found a pretext to gain authorisation at a high level to visit the house, and have one of the women who acted as a secretary there divulge some information. The information was, however, of the most rudimentary kind, not sufficient for Holmes's purposes. Apparently, during May, all Kydorf could discover was that Oberlander and three of his agents were in Russia, and the other two were not. One of them was believed to be in Istanbul, but no details could be obtained about the whereabouts of the other. Kydorf, however, found the name and description of this other.

He was a tall man, slim, with the build of a sportsman, clean-shaven and with exceedingly fair hair. His name was von Oldenburg, a member of a *Junker* family. He had a taste for adventure and extravagant living. In Berlin he moved in fashionable circles. I imagined my companion making mental notes of the description, and wondered how much of our quest might be taken up in trying to track the fellow down.

After leaving Berlin we came directly to Vienna, a journey for which we were able to engage a sleeping compartment, although as the train rattled, stopped and started through the night I did not obtain as much sleep as I would have desired.

We arrived at the Hotel Imperial, in which one of the Joneses had reserved accommodation for us, and Holmes busied himself immediately, running backwards and forwards on several errands. Visiting the police was among them, and there he confirmed that Mr S had several broken ribs, and had sustained other fractures consistent with dying from the fall. Then I accompanied Holmes to the address in Clusius Gasse that he had found in Mr S's effects. We learnt, from a lady who occupied an apartment opposite the one we had come to visit, that Miss Vincent had indeed lived there, but had left two months previously. She had known Miss Vincent slightly, and told us that she was a teacher at a school for young ladies in the city. The lady we interviewed had been asked to hold for Miss Vincent any items that arrived by post. She did not know Miss Vincent's new address, though a tall woman, very well dressed, came to call once a week to collect any post that had arrived. She had called yesterday, the lady said, but there had been no letters.

'One method of finding Miss Vincent that we can fall back on is to follow the tall lady,' announced Holmes. 'I think we need not wait a week. I shall visit the school, and find out what I can there.'

What Holmes discovered was something of a surprise. Miss Vincent had been dismissed two months previously, following an important occasion for the school at which she was to have given an address to the parents, and had failed to appear.

It was following his first visit to the school that Holmes had decided that closer investigation was called for, and that was when he had attired himself in the garb of the Viennese matron who had surprised me by entering our hotel room backwards. He had presented himself at the school as the wealthy aunt of a young girl, asking if he could see round the place and make some informal enquiries of the staff and pupils with a view to seeing whether it would be a suitable school for her niece. He had found out that Miss Emily Vincent had, before the incident that led to her dismissal, been a highly valued and respected member of the staff. Her knowledge and teaching skills were much remarked upon. She had been popular both with the other teachers at the school and with the girls. Holmes had also found that she had been a close companion of one Frau Sara Rosenthal, who taught the girls scientific subjects. Holmes said that he had been able to obtain a brief interview with Frau Rosenthal, who seemed guarded when the Viennese matron had touched on the subject of the English teacher.

'I discovered when lessons end for the day, Watson,' Holmes explained, 'and I shall adopt the expedient of following Frau Rosenthal when she leaves the school. She is strikingly tall for a woman, and very well dressed.'

'The woman who calls each week at the house in Clusius Gasse, to collect letters for Miss Vincent?'

'It seems possible, does it not?'

'More than possible, Holmes. It must be very probable, from what you have told me.'

'In any case I shall find out where she lives.'

'What about the movements of Mr S?' I asked. 'Have you made progress on that front?'

'I have located Mr S's hotel, the Stadt London: it is not one of the principal hotels. He may have wished to be inconspicuous. I have seen his name in the register of guests, and I have made some enquiries. He arrived at the hotel on the 5th of May, and stayed for two nights. On the morning of Sunday the 8th the chambermaid reported that his bed had not been slept in the night previously.'

'That is about two months ago, Holmes, the same time at which Miss Vincent left her rooms. Is there a connection?'

'That we cannot say as yet.'

'But you think the 7th of May was the day on which Mr S met his death?'

'Certainly we may say that he did not die before that time.'

'I see what you mean. He may have left the hotel, and gone somewhere else before meeting his end.'

'In this instance, Watson, I think your first conclusion was the correct one. The evidence implies that he did die on the Saturday.'

'So is there other evidence?'

'Merely the evidence that you have seen with your own eyes.'

'As usual, Holmes, your thought processes far outstrip mine. I do not know what evidence you mean. It must be something I did not notice.'

'I mean the suitcase and possessions of Mr S of which you saw me making an inventory at 221B Baker Street. They were the possessions of a methodical person making a journey abroad, an inventory of items such as you yourself have on this very journey.'

'Sorry, Holmes, I still do not see.'

'Unless he had a duplicate set of things secreted in some other place, they indicate, I think, that he had intended to return there on the 7th of May.'

'Yes, I see. Could there be some other place to which he went?'

'We should consider that question in the light of certain other facts: Mr S was found with the key to his hotel room in his pocket. The other keys in his possession were to his own home, to locked drawers and cupboards in his study, to a room and a desk in the Foreign Office, and to the house in Clifton Gardens where we visited that creature in black. This accounts for all his keys, and implies that he had no other places of resort that are unaccounted for. Add to these facts that he had been expected to return to the hotel, where his bill had not been paid; I think it probable that he did die on that day.'

'How do you know the other keys were to his own home and

to his room at the Foreign Office, and to the house in Clifton Gardens?'

'I took the precaution before we left of having Augustus Pemberton take these keys to B——, to the Foreign Office and to Clifton Gardens to check them.'

'You are very thorough, Holmes.'

'It is essential that I should be so. This is not a case for flair. Everything hangs upon elimination, as I told you.'

I still did not understand what my friend was hoping to eliminate, though I could see that, in the instance of the keys, if Mr S had been carrying with him keys to unknown doors this would indeed have set puzzles of the most difficult kind.

At the end of this conversation Holmes withdrew into his bedroom, to busy himself with I know not what, while I returned to my manuscript. I found, however, that my mind wandered, and I was unable to concentrate. In the end I called out to my companion that I was going to take a stroll.

'Very well,' he called back from behind a closed door. 'We will meet for dinner. Shall we say at seven o'clock, in the dining room?'

'Certainly,' I replied. 'I shall see you then.'

I took out from my papers the letter I had received from Professor Freud.

25th June 04

PROF. D$^{R.}$ FREUD   WIEN, IX. BERGGASSE 19.

Dear Dr Watson,

For your interest in my work I thank you. I think it is best if you are in Vienna for a week but if the dates you do not know, to attend a meeting of a small medical society in which we discuss matters psychoanalytic. We meet each Wednesday at my rooms, at the address above. We start at nine-thirty in the evening. If

212

your interest should extend beyond that meeting please say this to me, and we can make appointment for a personal interview.

Yours truly,

Sigm. Freud

I strolled through the streets of Vienna's Innere Stadt, reflecting to myself on the romance of this great city, at the heart of the great Habsburg empire, but conscious that, for all its charm, I would not exchange it for my own familiar streets of London. I had obtained directions, and made my way to the street from which Dr Freud had written to me. I had written to him immediately Holmes had said we would be visiting Vienna, and asked him to address his reply to the hotel in which I had persuaded Holmes that Mr Jones should reserve our accommodation. It was with a feeling of gratification that on our arrival I found his letter awaited me, and I was able to receive it without Holmes apparently remarking the fact.

I arrived in Berggasse, the street of the Professor's address. I found number 19 and saw the plate bearing the legend 'Prof. Dr. Sigm. Freud' on the right-hand side of an archway wide enough for a carriage to pass under it, and through which I thought that I myself would pass to attend the meeting on Wednesday evening.

I mused as I walked back to the hotel on the methods of the two investigators, one searching for those secrets of his patients' inner world that were hidden from themselves, and the other uncovering those matters in the outer world which the unscrupulous would like to keep hidden from others. Would I be able to bring the two of them together, I wondered? If so, what would be the result?

21

The Narrative of Sara and Emily continued

Panic

Sara was tense and taciturn when she returned from school. I finally wormed it out of her. They are on to me. All is lost. I am to be arrested, tried, found guilty, hanged. The process could not be more sure. The person who is on my trail is the one man I could never hope to evade: the cleverest detective in the world, Sherlock Holmes. It would be simpler if I just announced to him: 'Yes, I did it. I murdered Mr S. Pray arrest me, or whatever you do in these cases. I will come without commotion.'

'Tell me what happened exactly,' I asked, wanting to turn everything over in my mind, as if that would somehow help my predicament. 'Tell me everything.'

'First a man came to the school to ask for you. The Headmistress knew that you and I were friends. Therefore she sent to me, to test if I know where you are. I do not tell her that you live with me, or that we still meet. She is, how do you say, a busy person, and would not think it loyal to her if you and I as friends remain.'

'A busybody,' I said. 'Not a busy person.'

'Yes, a busybody, exactly. I arrived to her study. Here I am introduced to a severe English gentleman, Mr Sherlock Holmes. I tell him that I no longer meet you. I say that if you are not at your address then I do not know where you are. He says he was there, and you do not live now at the house. I think the Headmistress doubts what I say, but she does not betray by an expression that she doubts.'

'So then Mr Holmes left?'

'Yes, so I believe.'

'I must give myself up immediately,' I declared to Sara. 'In England one reads about Sherlock Holmes's feats of detection in the newspapers. He is like an Indian tracker who always finds his prey. There are books about the cleverness of his abilities at detection. There could not have been a worse stroke of fortune. I am done for.'

I surprised myself by not sobbing, but by becoming cold and matter-of-fact. I had anticipated my arrest a hundred times but I had not anticipated being the quarry of Sherlock Holmes. But it was all one. The imminence of my arrest did not cause a state of impossible confusion, merely a mood of cold terror, something to be endured, stoically. Only now as I sit at my desk to write this do I find myself trembling uncontrollably again, like a frail tree in a gale.

'I do not agree with you,' Sara said. 'I too have thought that the English gentleman's visit must be something like that. This Mr Holmes wished to find you. In the afternoon, my suspicions are stronger. Now you tell me that this man is a detective, it makes sense. In the afternoon we are visited by a strange lady. She came to ask about the school because of her niece. She also questions me about the teaching of science. I later found that the Headmistress had allowed her to speak with two girls. I questioned them afterwards. They spoke to me that she had talked of the events of Founder's Day, when you did not give the speech that was expected. She then asked more questions about yourself. I was very suspicious about this woman. She had an accent that was not Viennese. The manners of her speech said to

215

me that she was not German or Austrian. I believe that she must have been an associate of Mr Holmes.'

I remained immobile, and said to Sara that I must simply go now and give myself up to the police, or find where this Mr Holmes was staying in order to present myself to him. 'It will be an end to all my torment,' I said. 'I am guilty. Now my wickedness has been discovered. Rightly so. I will dress to go out. Perhaps you will accompany me.'

Sara would have none of it. She said we must wait and plan. We must discuss the situation and decide what to do. 'I too am involved now,' she said, smiling at me with affection. 'What will happen is important to me. Do not forget.'

That was the very moment when the maid entered, carrying the cards of Mr Sherlock Holmes and Dr Watson. Sara motioned to me to keep silent, and rapidly left the room to descend to the drawing room, where the maid had asked the visitors to sit.

I was by now thoroughly terror-struck, in turmoil, not knowing whether to go downstairs and say 'I am the murderer of Mr S, whom you seek,' or to stay rooted to the spot and obey my friend. In the end I simply remained motionless, for a few minutes or an hour – I do not know. I felt suspended in time, as if now my last moment had indeed come. I was to leave the life I had known. All I could think of was to ask God: 'Why now, why now that I have found Sara? Why now that I believe I could make reparation, and become good?'

When Sara returned she laughed. Yes, actually laughed, and said, 'That was a good escape. It was the same Mr Holmes, but accompanied by a doctor.'

'Dr Watson,' I said. 'That is Dr Watson. They are close companions.'

'You are right, Dr Watson it was. Only Herr Holmes spoke. He said he believed Miss Vincent lives here. Of course, he wanted to know why I had said that I do not know where you are. It is fortunate that I spoke to you and had thought on the matter in advance. An answer I had prepared. I believe I acted my part well. I told these men that you were a disgrace at the school. I said that the Headmistress was angry with you, because she regarded Founder's Day with great seriousness. All the school's parents were present, and it was the main day in the year when it was important that everything went perfectly. If the Headmistress hears that you live in my house she might find also a reason to dismiss me. Therefore I must speak as I did. I explained that to lose one's position is a very grave matter. I begged them to forgive me. I do not know whether they believed me, but that part of our conversation passed. Herr Holmes then wanted me to talk about you. I said you had been ill, but that you were now convalescent, this evening you were not at home. You are taking the waters at a spa some way from the city. If he cared to make an appointment for the day after tomorrow, I believe you are here, and he can interview you himself.

'There,' she said, and laughed that gay, delightful laugh again. 'How do I do? Do you think I am a good actress?' She curtsied, as the players do at the end of their performance. 'Or a good criminal?' She tiptoed around the room, not quite knowing, I think, how to imitate a criminal.

'Please do not joke about it,' I said. 'Whatever am I to do? In forty-eight hours I shall be discovered and disgraced, branded as a murderer. Which of course I am.'

'You are not,' Sara had said. 'I have taken the part of protecting you from unjust enquiry. Consider me to be your advocate for defence. Yes, that is what I am: *advocatus extraordinarius*. Is that correct Latin? I need to be *extraordinarius*, or you will not receive justice properly. You place complete responsibility of this to me. We have in two days everything to discuss. We make our plans. If necessary we leave Vienna. You say this Mr Holmes is a detective, but he is not the police?'

'No, he is a private citizen who has made a profession of detecting criminals. He calls himself a consulting detective. I have read some of his cases, which were written by his companion, the Dr Watson who was even now in your own drawing room. Mr Holmes has become famous for discovering insignificant clues and making deductions from them.'

'If he is not the police, he only has suspicions. If there was evidence, we would be visited by the police, not a consulting detective wanting to discover clues. You leave matters to me. I am your advocate, we agreed. In matters that require professional judgement, I decide. This is what I think we do.' Sara started to sketch our plan, like a general, thinking of this contingency and that. She thinks I should meet him when he comes to call in two days' time, and tell him everything but the events in the mountains.

One difficulty is that we do not know how he has traced me, or how he knows my connection to Mr S. In other words, we have no idea what he knows already. I suppose he could easily have found out from Mrs S that I was his ward, but she thinks I am in Philadelphia. Could Mr S have told her that he had traced me here? It seems unlikely, but I suppose that must have been what happened. At any rate, here he is, on Sara's doorstep, asking to see me.

Sara thinks I should say that Mr S did come and visit me, unexpectedly. I should say that I had tried to get away from him; that I had never wanted to see him again as long as I lived; but that he had found my address by burglarising my friend's home in Philadelphia, and then presented himself at my door in Vienna. Sara thinks that I should tell Mr Holmes about the reason I had wished to escape from Mr S. I should tell him about the foul deeds. I should say that when he materialised again I was terror-struck. I am again now. She says his arrival would explain my collapse, my inability to give my speech at Founder's Day. She

218

thinks I need say nothing else. I should say I spent the Saturday with her, and she will corroborate that. She will say that I had become ill in the morning of Saturday, that she had put me to bed. By evening we should say that I had recovered sufficiently to go home. When she came to call on me on Monday I was again ill, unable to rise and perform my duties.

We have not got the details worked out yet, but this account is possible. We think it is best if we let Mr Holmes think that I had not told Sara about Mr S's visit to my rooms until later. She says that apart from the day I went to the mountains, I should tell the truth. Nothing, she says, will be as convincing as that. This shows how Sara thinks: if Holmes does gather clues, then all, or almost all, the clues he could gather would be corroborated by the version I give; 'Just like a scientific hypothesis,' she says, 'it will account for the large part of the evidence.' I will be able to tell the truthful parts perfectly well, with all the uncertainties about trying to remember exactly what happened and all the emotion and reticence that would surround my having to tell the hateful story of my seduction to a stranger. What could be more convincing?

What she says has a hideous ring of plausibility about it. I am practised at keeping secret what I think people must not know, but I am not so practised in direct lying, so the fewer lies I tell the better. But they are lies. This evil drives me ever deeper into the mire. Sara does not see it that way. She says that if society were just it would have put Mr S on trial long ago, and not now be subjecting me to pursuit.

'You have to stand back a little,' she said. 'This is not a just society in which we live. It is arranged by men, for men's convenience. A woman who is mixed up in their actions does not receive a fair judgement.'

I think perhaps she is right, but I do not know. How can I

know? It seems best to let her take charge. She is so capable, and can think a hundred times better than I.

Mr Holmes will come and ask if Mr S had visited me while he was in Austria. I shall say yes. Then I shall tell him the awful truth about what happened when I was young. Perhaps he will be so shocked that he will leave me in peace. Or will he think that I had cause to kill Mr S? Yes, of course he will. He will. He will.

But Sara says that probably nobody saw me going off that morning or saw me at G——. It seems unlikely that anyone will remember, because many people took the train that morning and went walking in the sunshine. I was in no way different from dozens of others, except of course that I was a woman on my own. If someone remembered me then I might be done for. It needs but one person. Otherwise he will be hard pressed to connect me with Mr S's death. Mr S might just have fallen while he was out walking. Why should he not? But why, if it were thought to have been an accident as reported in the newspapers, is Sherlock Holmes investigating the matter?

Sara thinks there is a small chance that I was seen and remembered. Mr Holmes could not have found that out yet, however. He has not met me, and would therefore not be able to describe me to officials at the station. So he will have to meet me first, and only then will he be able to make his enquiries. But what if my godmother had given him a photograph of myself? This would be better than a description. My poor mind cannot keep up with the possibilities.

'I think it is best just to wait. Then when he comes you speak to him,' Sara said. 'We can ask him too, to try and find out what he knows. Then we find a way of observing on him. If he comes on our path, then we can leave. Abroad we will go. I will get everything ready in case we must do this. You must not worry. Money I have plenty. We will make three steps: first you allow him to interview you, then we keep observation on him, then if necessary we escape. Do you agree?'

'If only I did not have to think about it in the interim,' I said.

'I forbid you to think about it. Nothing will happen before he comes to visit. He must now be busybodying about, collecting clues all over Vienna. He probably suspects ten other people. If he only wanted you he will not agree to wait two days, but instead he will want the address of the spa, and travel to see you there. This he did not ask.' Sara came to clasp me in her arms with the most tender affection. Her last statement was somehow convincing, and quashed my doubts.

Somehow too she was able to be light-hearted about it, to give me the sense of not being a wicked person. She even made me feel confident that we were doing the right thing. After all the waiting, and the tension, my worst fears were now confirmed. I was discovered, but Sara's presence, and her taking charge of matters, somehow lessens the terror, at least when we are together. She can make my fear dissolve even as it forms in my mind. I had an image of myself as a very small child, and a memory of my mother. When I had felt terrified in the night, of something, I know not what, she would come, and in her arms the terror melted. Now here was Sara, able to work the same miracle. What can I do but give myself over to her care?

22

The Viennese Affair

An Interview with Miss Vincent

When we had at first visited the elegant house of Frau Rosenthal and she had asserted that Miss Vincent was not there, I was not certain that she was to be believed. She was a woman of striking good looks, although of a very un-English kind, and some six foot tall. She held herself erect, and there was a look of authority and determination in her face that I more usually associate with young men of good breeding, although in her case it was not at variance with her feminine qualities. She had spoken to us, I thought, with a certain hauteur.

When we returned two days later at the appointed hour, she met us in the same elegant drawing room, but on this occasion she was accompanied by a slim woman of middle height, with a pale complexion. She reminded me in all respects of an English rose, demure, agreeable and charming in every way, though perhaps slightly on the side of being too slim. I have to say that I found it hard to reconcile her appearance and demeanour with the slanderous stories that had been told us by the fallen woman whom we visited in Clifton Terrace, although as matters turned out these stories were true, and the only conclusion to be drawn was that this young woman had been mistreated in the most shameful way possible.

'*Guten Abend, meine Herren*,' Frau Rosenthal greeted us, and motioned us to armchairs in her spacious drawing room. She continued, as at our previous meeting, speaking in German: 'I know that you, Mr Holmes, speak excellent German, and I have no doubt the doctor does also. Since my English is not good, I hope you will not mind our conversing in German.'

With this speech she smiled winningly at me, and I found myself saying, 'Of course, madam, we are happy to speak in German. It is only right to do so in your house.'

'Emily, my dear,' she continued, 'allow me to introduce Mr Holmes and Dr Watson, who as you know wish to speak with you. Mr Holmes, Dr Watson, may I present Miss Emily Vincent.'

We exchanged greetings and handshakes with the young lady, who remained seated. Frau Rosenthal asked us also to be seated, and then turning to Holmes she said: 'I trust your stay in Vienna is proving pleasant.'

'Yes, madam. I thank you for your enquiry,' Holmes replied.

'Is your hotel comfortable? They treat English guests well, I hope.'

'Yes, thank you.'

'Which hotel is that?' she asked pleasantly, with every show of concern for our interests.

'We are at the Hotel Imperial,' I said, 'and they treat us very well. The Manager insists on addressing us in English, and on serving us tea on frequent occasions.'

'Indeed,' said Frau Rosenthal. 'I believe many English people stay there. Well, I am glad that you are made comfortable and welcome in our city. Now, gentlemen, allow me to offer you some refreshment? Perhaps I too can offer you tea? I have some excellent Darjeeling, from Jacksons, which can be obtained here in the city.'

'Nothing, madam. I thank you. We will be brief,' my companion replied. 'I have been engaged by the British Foreign Office to enquire about the movements of Mr S, an envoy of our government. He came to Vienna, and I wonder whether while he was here he might have come to visit your friend Miss Vincent, who was his ward.'

My companion spoke in an even tone, and turned to regard Miss Vincent impassively. He was the soul of politeness, but I knew that he would be unmoved by sentiment of any kind, and that his falcon-like eyes were watching for the least sign. I noticed no movement across Miss Vincent's clear brow, but since she did not respond immediately, Holmes continued.

'You must excuse me for tracing you here. My curiosity was aroused when I visited your godmother. She thought you were in Philadelphia, but I perceived by certain small indications that you were in no such place, and were in Vienna.'

'Pray, Herr Holmes, how did you reach that conclusion?' Frau Rosenthal enquired.

'Your friend was in the habit of writing to her guardian and his wife, and when I visited their house I noticed an envelope which Mrs S said contained one of these missives. Although it bore on its exterior an American postage stamp, and an address in Philadelphia, it was obvious that the envelope was not of American manufacture. It was in fact Viennese.'

'Mr Holmes, you must forgive my duplicitousness.' Miss Vincent spoke in German and with an accent that, as far as I could tell, was impeccable. 'I had my reasons, very compelling ones, for wishing to conceal my address from my guardian. Not from my godmother: for her I have every respect and affection, and it was to her that I wrote, adding my guardian's name for the sake of politeness. It had become important for me to lead a life that was independent of the influence of my guardian. I thought that in this way – by living in Austria but letting him think I was still in Philadelphia, where I had attended university – I would achieve that independence.'

'I see,' said Holmes, with some gravity. 'To recur, madam, to my original question: did Mr S visit you when he came to Vienna?'

'Yes, I am sorry to have to tell you that he did.'

'That was during the first week of May, was it not?'

'Yes, I believe it was around that time,' she said. 'He visited me a few days before our school Founder's Day, at which I was to have given a speech, a speech I did not give.'

'Mr S had discovered your hiding place then?' Holmes was evidently wanting to persist with the visit of Mr S, and was uninterested in Miss Vincent's speech.

'He had,' replied the young woman. Her voice and attitude, as she looked steadfastly towards the floor, indicated to me that she was in some distress. 'I asked him how he had found me. He had illegally entered the apartments of my friend in Philadelphia, the one who forwarded my letters to England. There he had discovered my friend's book of addresses, and that is how he found that I was in Vienna.'

'And a note of your address in Clusius Gasse was found among his possessions. He had clearly gone to some considerable trouble to trace you. We must assume that he wished to see you on a matter of some urgency.'

'Mr Holmes,' Miss Vincent replied, now looking up from the floor which she had been contemplating so fixedly, and regarding my friend with a frank gaze. 'My guardian was not the most upright of men, as you will have been able to gather from his felony in entering unbidden my friend's apartments. In fact I believe he was an unscrupulous man. I lived in fear of him. That is why I had left England for America, and that is why I had tried to avoid the possibility of his ever discovering me again.'

'Madam,' said Holmes, 'you have described an effect of Mr S upon yourself, in occasioning sufficient fear to induce you to make arrangements to avoid him, but you remain reticent about the cause.'

I noticed that Holmes's formality had, if anything, become more marked, and I was concerned lest his aversion to members of the opposite sex, which usually manifested itself in courtesy, should take a hostile turn. I interjected in a more friendly way, 'Mr Holmes merely wishes to enquire why you had gone to such lengths to avoid Mr S.'

At this point Miss Vincent had again cast her eyes downwards. After a considerable interval she said, looking up briefly: 'Mr Holmes, I know your reputation for relentless pursuit of your quarry. It is only that reputation that urges me to say what I will now tell you; and only because you, sir, are a physician,' she glanced towards me, 'that I allow myself to utter such things in your presence. Mr S had overstepped his position when I lived in his house. Do you understand me?'

'No, madam, I do not entirely. I am sorry this is painful to you, but would it be possible to be more explicit?'

'He took advantage of me when I was in his care, when I was but a child, when I was only fourteen years old. Is that sufficiently explicit? That is why I had to do everything I could to avoid him.'

'You say he took advantage of you,' said Holmes. 'What do you mean by that?'

'Come now, Holmes,' I expostulated. 'Miss Vincent's meaning is plain. The man was . . . he was . . .' I was lost for a German word suitable to Mr S. 'He was a very bad man.'

'Please, Watson, allow Miss Vincent to reply.'

'I thank you, sir, for your gallantry on my behalf,' Miss Vincent said, 'but if your friend wishes to hear further details, I shall tell him.' At this she glared at Holmes through eyes misted with tears. She was in some considerable agitation, as a young woman would necessarily be, subjected to such questioning. I had not often had occasion to doubt Holmes's judgement. Now I was convinced he had gone too far. 'If you wish to hear it spelt out in so many words, sir,' she continued, 'Mr S had subjected me between the ages of fourteen and eighteen to embraces which I had been powerless to repel or to discourage. When he again discovered me in Vienna, it was because he wished to resume these loathsome activities.'

Miss Vincent's command of the German language far outstripped mine, and I give here only the general sense.

'Were you on the occasion of his visit able to dissuade him from such a resumption?' Holmes persisted.

'He said he had become obsessed with me, that he loved me, and that he desired to make his life with me, to do whatever I wished, to live wherever I wished. He told me that I could occupy myself as I chose. To persuade him to leave my rooms, I promised to consider his offer, but said I needed time to think about it. I said I would meet him in a certain place, in a coffee house, the Griensteidl, to give him my decision.'

'How long did you request to make this decision?'

'Three days.'

'Did you keep the appointment you had made?'

At this point her friend interjected: 'No, Mr Holmes, she did not. The next day she arrived early in the morning on my doorstep in a state of extreme collapse. I put her to bed, and nursed her during the day. She was ill, and although it was Saturday I asked our family physician, Dr Woolf of Florianigasse number 35, to come to visit her. He gave her a tonic. By evening, although she would not say how her collapse had occurred, she declared herself recovered. Despite my entreaties she insisted on going back to her rooms, so I took her home in my carriage. The next day, when I went to call, she continued to assert that she was recovered. I had an appointment with relatives that day. On Monday, when I again visited her, she had relapsed. I brought her back here, and, except for a brief interval, she has been living here since. No doubt when you visited our school, you and your accomplice that strange stooped foreign woman, you discovered that Miss Vincent was to have given a speech on Founder's Day, which was that same Monday. The Headmistress dismissed her because she had written not to say that she was indisposed, but to say, without giving any reason, that she was unable to fulfil her obligations at the school.'

'Indeed,' replied Holmes. 'So the reason she did not give her speech was connected with the arrival of Mr S? Was this Monday the day when you were to deliver your decision to Mr S?'

'Yes,' said Miss Vincent. 'I don't know what I can have been thinking of to give the day of my speech as the one on which I was also to give my decision.'

'Miss Vincent suffered a nervous collapse with the arrival of her seducing guardian.' Frau Rosenthal had taken up the account again. 'His reappearance, having chased her half across the world, undermined her completely. I think it is also clear that the too-hurriedly contrived undertaking to make a decision of such magnitude, under the most appalling duress, contributed to Miss Vincent's inability to give her speech at the school. Should she submit to a life with a person whom she reviled, or should she throw up everything in an attempt to escape from this person, who would stop at nothing?

'While on the subject of that school,' Frau Rosenthal continued, during a pause in which Holmes had evidently not prepared his next question, 'perhaps, Herr Holmes, you could tell me who the woman was who visited there earlier this week on the pretext of making enquiries on behalf of a niece, but in truth to ask about Miss Vincent? It is clear that she was not genuine. What have you to say Mr Holmes?'

Holmes seemed unperturbed by this: 'She was indeed an associate of mine.'

'Her accent when speaking German, and her inflexions, were

very similar to your own, Mr Holmes. Was she perhaps more than an associate?'

'What do you mean, madam?'

'Herr Holmes, why do you not tell me who this person was? This person who spoke perhaps in a higher pitch, but in tones like yours, asking questions as you do, with an accent like yours, and with English mannerisms of speech like yours, even making the same mistakes in German as you do. Who was she?'

'Madam.' Holmes was at his most icy. 'I have made an appointment with you, and come here politely to ask your companion a few questions, not in order to be cross-examined by yourself.'

'If you expect us to answer questions it seems to me just that you too should answer questions. Otherwise I suggest we terminate the interview. I believe you have no special jurisdiction in Vienna. At present you are a guest in my home. What do you say, doctor?' She turned to me, and gave me a very winning smile. 'As an impartial observer, does it not seem equitable that Herr Holmes should tell us who his associate was, or do you think this conversation should be entirely one-sided, with the English gentlemen asking questions of the most intimate and embarrassing kind and the ladies who live here having to provide answers as if they were schoolgirls at an examination?'

'Well, madam, I am not sure.' Frau Rosenthal seemed a formidable person, and the hauteur she had displayed on our previous visit was used to withering effect. I for one, having felt embarrassed by Holmes's enquiries, was finding the whole situation deucedly uncomfortable. I did my best to calm the situation. 'It is very unusual,' I said. 'Usually people do not mind answering questions. Though I realise that those Miss Vincent was answering were of a most painful kind. I am sure my friend regrets having to ask them.'

'I did not say that either of us minded answering questions if the reason were a good one. I merely observed that it would be equitable if your friend reciprocated. He expects us to answer questions, so in this case he himself should be prepared to do so. It is very vexing to find oneself the object of enquiries by strange women, calling at one's place of employment and instigating unpleasant speculations on the part of one's colleagues.'

'Very well, madam. I do not recognise the principle you enunciate of reciprocal rights in questioning, since as you have just intimated I do not ask questions for my own amusement but because there is an issue of importance at stake,' Holmes interjected. 'Nevertheless, I will concede to your request. The woman who visited your school was myself in disguise. I congratulate you on your powers of observation.'

'Ah,' said Frau Rosenthal. 'So it was you. I thought so. Visually your disguise was convincing, but I knew something was wrong. It was not until this visit that your manner of speech gave you away. I could not understand who would be making such enquiries. Who it could possibly be, speaking like that, who would work on your behalf? I thank you for your frankness. Now, have you anything more to ask us, or have you finished your questions?'

'I have just a few more things to ask Miss Vincent,' Holmes replied. Turning to her he said, 'Did you see Mr S again after his first visit to your rooms?'

'No I did not.'

'And Frau Rosenthal has said you did not keep your appointment with him?'

'No, I did not keep the appointment. When Frau Rosenthal came home from her duties at the Founder's Day, I told her why I had collapsed, and about my guardian's visit, and its hateful significance. She thought quickly and said that I should not in any circumstances see him again, and so to prevent his finding me I have stayed here since, as Frau Rosenthal has told you, and I have as much as possible kept from going outside. I don't know whether you can imagine it, gentlemen, but the shock was a severe one. I was mortally afraid of him. I thought that my escape would be temporary, and that he would find some way of tracking me down.'

'Did you hear from him subsequently?'

'No. I learnt of his death in the newspaper. Then a day or two later my friend in America telegraphed to me saying my godmother had sent a wire. Sara had picked up the telegram from my address in Clusius Gasse. The telegraph boy had left it with Frau König who lives there, and Sara collects my post from her every few days. Fortunately we got it the day after it had arrived, so I was able to wire to my friend in Philadelphia, and she in turn wired to my godmother as if from me. I apologised that I had been away for a few days so that I had not replied immediately, and that there would not be time for me to make passage back and attend the funeral. I later had my friend send a further wire with more condolences. I had also dispatched a letter which I said had been written after I had recovered from the shock of hearing of the death, although in reality I had dispatched it to Philadelphia on the day that I received her wire. You will no doubt think me callous, but I felt much eased.' With this, Miss Vincent cast her eyes again steadfastly towards the floor, and I could see that she was shedding tears. I was not sure that Holmes had appreciated the gravity of what she had told us of her early life.

'I see,' remarked Holmes. 'You were not despondent at hearing of your guardian's death.'

'I have admitted that I was not. I was relieved.'

'So, to sum up, you saw Mr S on just one occasion in Vienna, when he visited your former rooms in Clusius Gasse, and not subsequently?'

'That is correct.'

'Do you know why he was visiting Vienna?' Holmes was still formal, but I fancied his tone had moderated.

'Other than to pursue me, I do not.'

'Did he mention any other reason, or give the name of anyone whom he was seeing, or say where he was staying?'

'He said he was staying at the Stadt London, in the Fleischmarkt.' Miss Vincent still looked far from composed, and did not look at her interlocutor. She continued, 'He mentioned nothing about any other reason for his visit than his desire for propinquity with myself. Nor did he mention anyone whom he had seen or intended to see. I am sorry I am unable to throw any light there.'

'Are you able to throw any light whatsoever on how he died?'

'The report in the newspaper indicated that it was an accident.'

'Your guardian had a considerable fear of heights, and of mountains. He can scarcely have been walking there for recreational purposes.'

I noticed Holmes regarding Miss Vincent quizzically as he made this last speech. As I glanced in the direction of Holmes's gaze I thought a shadow crossed her brow.

'I have no idea, Mr Holmes, about how he came to be there.'

'You knew he had a fear of heights?'

'Indeed I did.'

'You did not think it strange, when you read the report in the newspaper, that he had died in the mountains?'

'At first, as I said, I felt relief that an ordeal that has been the very bane of my existence was over. Later, when I reflected upon it, I thought it somewhat apt that he had met his nemesis in a manner that he had feared all his life.'

'Have you any conjecture about why he was in the mountains?'

'I thought, Mr Holmes,' Miss Vincent glanced upwards at her

interlocutor, 'that conjectures about such matters were your speciality.'

'Not conjectures, madam. I deal in facts and deductions.'

'I beg your pardon, sir. In that case neither of us has a conjecture.'

'Indeed, madam,' my companion replied. 'I thank you for your forbearance in allowing me to question you on this painful matter. I regret having had to ask you to dwell upon it again, and to recount these unpleasant details to a stranger. I shall leave you in peace. A good evening to you both, ladies.'

'Good-evening Mr Holmes, and to you too, Dr Watson,' Miss Vincent responded.

'Allow me to show you out, gentlemen,' said Frau Rosenthal, suddenly speaking now in almost perfect English. 'I wish you both a very good evening.'

23

The Viennese Affair

Mr S's Lists

'Miss Vincent has been much put upon,' I remarked as we made our way in a cab back towards our hotel, 'and her friend Frau Rosenthal is a formidable lady. She would not be intimidated, would she?' Since Holmes did not reply, I continued: 'Miss Vincent seems an uncommonly fine girl to me. Everything we know of this Mr S indicates that he was a blackguard of the most despicable kind. Miss Vincent did right to try and escape his evil influence.'

'What you say may be correct, Watson,' my companion replied. 'At the same time I have a commission to fulfil, and if Miss Vincent is implicated in this matter then I intend to discover it, be she ne'er so wronged.'

'You are very obdurate sometimes, Holmes. Very very obdurate indeed.'

'I do not say that I am without sympathy for Miss Vincent, merely that I shall not allow any sympathy I might feel to obstruct my assessment of the evidence of the case, to prevent me from making whatever logical deductions may follow. I agree we have corroboration of what the woman in black told us. I also agree that Miss Vincent was embarrassed to give us an account of her treatment at the hands of Mr S, but why, if all is as they say, do you think that Rosenthal woman was so belligerent?'

'She *was* a trifle sharp with you, Holmes. But perhaps you brought it upon yourself.'

'I disagree. It is transparently obvious that those two women are concealing something. The question is: What do they know?'

'Miss Vincent seemed to me to be alarmingly candid,' I replied.

'She was candid about one matter, in order to conceal something else.'

'What do you mean?'

'I paid a boy a small sum of money the day before yesterday to ascertain whether the fair-haired young lady was visible at all through any of the windows. She was, and thus we may conclude that Frau Rosenthal had been deliberately delaying our interview with Miss Vincent, who was not at a spa, but in that very house. Also there were several instances during our interview when it was clear that they were being less than frank. If you think back, Watson, I am sure you will recollect them.'

'Well, Holmes, I have to say that as usual the matters that you notice have escaped me. Both ladies seemed to me the soul of candour, except perhaps . . . except perhaps just before we left, when you asked whether Miss Vincent knew of Mr S's fear of heights.'

'Good, Watson. You see, your powers of observation are excellent. They merely need training and application.'

'You asked her that question deliberately, to see whether she had found anything unusual in the public account of the death being an accident?'

'Exactly, Watson. As you saw, she was surprised by my question, because she had not known that I would be acquainted with this peculiarity of Mr S's character, and therefore she had not rehearsed an answer. Unfortunately we know little more from this indication than that I surprised her. She recovered, I thought, moderately well.'

'You noticed other indications too, Holmes? You said there were several.'

'Indeed I did, but again they were all indications of the same thing, that we have been subjected to a carefully rehearsed performance. We would not have seen better had we bought seats in the front row of the theatre.'

'I would not have said so,' I replied. 'Miss Vincent was evidently in great distress when she was asked to recount matters of which she was wretchedly ashamed.'

'I do not doubt her distress, Watson; at the same time I cannot accord it my main consideration. Nor do I doubt that there had been some kind of liaison between herself and Mr S when she lived at B——, since we now have heard this from two sources. Nor, since she was a minor, do I doubt that this liaison had been instigated by S. What I do not know is what relations Miss Vincent and S have had in the intervening years. The aspect of the recitation that I most suspect is that given by the woman Rosenthal. Did you notice how she assumed the principal part at a certain point in the narrative?'

'Yes, now you draw attention to it, I do remember that. It was she who said how Miss Vincent had been ill on the day following the visit of Mr S.'

'Exactly, Watson. She took over, because she thought she would be the better able to give a plausible rendition of what the two of them had agreed to. In the event, the switch of speakers was an error. Frau Rosenthal made a mistake that Miss Vincent would not have made.'

'Really. What was that? I heard no false note.'

'She first gave the name of the physician who attended Miss Vincent on that day, and then she told us his address. Had things been as she described, she would merely have said "our family doctor" or "a doctor who was a friend of the family", or some such phrase. To give us a name and address was an invitation to

236

me to visit this physician and ask him to corroborate the story we have heard. I have no doubt that he is indeed a close friend of Frau Rosenthal, and that she has asked him to do this favour for her, should I pay a call on him. I shall of course pay him no such visit, since I have no wish to witness further theatrical performances, and since he will certainly describe how he attended Miss Vincent on that day. Even if his rendition is in some detail at odds with what we have heard, we shall be no further forward. We already know that on that day Miss Vincent was doing something that those women do not want us to know about.'

'So you think she saw S again, on the Saturday when he died?'

'I do not know, Watson. I merely know that on that day she was not doing what she and Frau Rosenthal wish us to believe. We will discover what she was doing by other means. Meanwhile the enquiry has to proceed on a broad front. Miss Vincent threatens to monopolise our interest, while in reality my commission is primarily to discover what Mr S was doing, and whether he had made contact with his man.'

By now we had regained our hotel, and we mounted by the heavily carved mahogany staircase to our rooms on the first floor. We entered, and Holmes opened the shutters, sank into an armchair and gazed out on a pleasantly leafy prospect.

'So have you made any progress in the matter of Mr S and his movements?' I enquired, anxious to prompt Holmes to continue his soliloquy while he was still in the mood to discuss the matter. I was not disappointed that I had continued to press him.

'I have discovered further signs of Mr S and his activities,' he said.

'Well, Holmes, do not keep me in suspense. Tell me what you have found.'

'You remember that Mrs S described a writing case that Mr S habitually took with him on his travels.'

'Yes, Holmes, I do remember that. Was it not in Mr S's effects when you collected them?'

'No. The case containing toilet articles was there. If you think back you will remember that the writing case was not. Nor had the Vienna police retained it. So I enquired of the chambermaid who cleans the rooms on the floor where Mr S had stayed in the Stadt London. She was a young woman of an unsavoury kind. I observed from an amulet of the type that young women wear as keepsakes that she had an association with a man. When I confronted her with an inference about this association, she pleaded with me not to reveal the fact to her employer. When I questioned her further I ascertained why she was so unwilling for this to be known. Her beau is being detained in prison. Armed with this knowledge, I confronted her with the theft of the writing case from Mr S's room. When it had been realised that Mr S was not returning, the hotel's proprietor decided to have Mr S's possessions packed up and the room was relet. The slattern had purloined the writing case, and a gold cigarette case. She said guests occasionally failed to reappear, usually when they wished to avoid payment of an account that had mounted up. On such occasions she knew that objects she appropriated would not be missed. The hotel kept the property in a cupboard for six months or so. It was not typically requested and, even if it were, by then suspicion would not fall on her.'

'So did you get the writing case back?'

'Indeed I did. I had expected a petty larceny of some such kind when Mr S's writing case failed to appear at the Foreign Office with the rest of his possessions. The fact that the young trollop's associate was in prison was a stroke of luck. He had enjoined her, on fear of severe punishment by himself, not to tamper in any way with articles she stole. She was to pass them over to him intact, and he would then dispose of them as he chose. I augmented my threat of disclosure to include delivery of her person to the police. It was not difficult to persuade her to return to me the items she had stolen. The piece of luck consists in the fact that the writing case contained papers that may be of interest, and the woman had not thrown them away, as she would certainly have done had she herself made use of the case.'

At this point Holmes left our sitting room, entered his bedroom, and returned with a handsome leather writing case. 'Here, Watson, here is the case, and here is what I think may be of interest to us.'

He handed me the case, which was not merely handsome but eminently practical. As well as a place for writing and blotting paper it had pockets for envelopes, postage stamps and notes. It also had elastic retainers which held a fountain pen, a pencil, a small bottle containing spare ink, sealing wax, a pair of scissors and other items. It seemed to contain everything one might need to hand in a bureau, and I found myself thinking how good it would be to possess a case of this kind, for travels such as I was now making.

'These are the objects of interest. They are in S's handwriting, and they were written with the pen in the case here. I believe they may provide clues to S's clandestine activities,' said Holmes, interrupting my inspection of the case. He now handed me several strips of paper, each about three inches wide by ten inches long, and each bearing a list of items written in a meticulous hand. On one the items had been ticked as if they had been reminders of actions, with the ticks indicating that they had been performed.

'There are nine of these slips in all. I can make sense only of some of them,' he said. 'Take this one: part of it is easy, but it is also enigmatic.' It was headed '6:v:04'. Then on the next line was the Greek capital letter E, like a 3 written backwards, that we had seen before on the paper with Miss Vincent's address that had been among Mr S's possessions sent back to England. Then following that, on one line each:

When?
Where?
What?

Following that was the figure of an equilateral triangle.

'This corroborates his visit to Miss Vincent: he uses the same Greek E for her initial that we saw previously, on the paper with her address,' Holmes said. 'These interrogatives I suppose are reminders of questions he was to ask, but they are perplexing. Why would one wish to write down such questions?'

'You think they are reminders to ask about spying?' I tried mentally to reconcile the account that Miss Vincent had given us with an alternative that I thought Holmes must be pursuing. Holmes did not reply, so I continued: 'What is this triangle, Holmes? Do you have any idea about it? Is this is a sign of some sort?'

'I regret that I have not the faintest conception of its significance, Watson. Here,' he continued, handing me another slip, 'try this one with items that have been ticked. This may be more informative.'

This second slip of paper was headed '5:v:04', and then on the next line, '7.30', on the next 'Zwierschütz', on the next 'von Oldenburg'. Then following this there was a list of items, each ticked. The first was 'E C', then 'Morocco', then 'Berlin-Baghdad'. Some items were places, some seemed to be the names of people. Others I could make no sense of at all.

'This is an important find, Holmes,' I said. 'Von Oldenburg was the chap attached to the German group of intelligence gatherers, or assassins, or whatever they are, but what are these other words? Are they a code?'

'I do not believe so, Watson. I think Mr S saw no particular reason for codes. I believe these are reminders to himself. This list headed 5:v:04 is I think a reminder of an appointment on that date, 5th May, with von Oldenburg at 7.30 at Zwierschütz, which I have found is the name of a restaurant, so presumably 7.30 means seven-thirty in the evening. Then there is a list of topics to be discussed or considered, an agenda.'

'So what are these topics, "E C", "Morocco" and so on?'

'It grieves me to have to say, Watson, that I am as far out of my depth on this issue as yourself. E C, I surmise, is the Entente Cordiale. Morocco is a French colony in northern Africa. Possibly the Germans have designs upon it. Berlin-Baghdad I have no idea about. These matters are my brother's department. I have not the slightest doubt that he will be aware not only of the significance of each of these items but of the connections among them all. The only other matter that I notice is that the two lists I have just shown you bear dates, but the others do not. S was methodical. The two slips with dates are appointments, whereas the others are in a different category, perhaps notes of what had already happened. Perhaps they include notes of the meeting with von Oldenburg, and on the undated slips, though some of the places mentioned are familiar, I can discern no connections among the items listed.'

'So you think they indicate political matters, perhaps of the gravest importance, that S discussed with von Oldenburg, whom we definitely know is a German spy!'

'It is possible, Watson. That is one possibility.'

'So this fellow S is not only a blackguard but a traitor?'

'I think we must now seriously consider that possibility, Watson,' said Holmes, a little unhappily I thought.

'You mean there is another possibility?'

'If you think about it, Watson, you will see the converse is also possible.'

'The converse?' I asked, feeling, as so often with my companion, that my grasp was not so strong as I had thought.

'Von Oldenburg could be a traitor to Germany, and co-operating with S. Our man S was acting partly as a spy in my brother's organisation, and he may have been making use of von Oldenburg.'

'I see, yes, that would be a possible explanation.'

'I was not told about such a possibility in my instructions. We only heard about the existence of von Oldenburg from my friend Kydorf. I have, however, sent a wire to the Joneses. I did not wire back the contents of these lists, though I said I had found them. Perhaps Mycroft may know something, and if so he will ask for details. I have also wired to young Pemberton to see whether S had inherited money, and what his sources of income were.'

'Ah,' I said, with a flash of insight. 'You mean, if he were not himself wealthy, he might have been paid by the Germans for passing over information, and that might help his expenses with his second establishment in Clifton Gardens?'

'Exactly, Watson. You follow my reasoning exactly. Collecting paintings too is an expensive taste. Here, look at these sale-room catalogues that were among S's belongings sent back to London. Each of these three lists here bears a date corresponding to the date of a sale described in each of the three catalogues. Moreover, if you look at the numbers of which these three lists are composed, each number corresponds to a lot number of a painting of the Impressionist school. I have also asked Pemberton to find out how much works of this kind fetch at auction.'

'Are any of the other lists informative, Holmes?'

'I regret that they are not informative to me.'

I paused: into my mind came the connection of the list indicating S's appointment at the restaurant with von Oldenburg, and the appointment of which Miss Vincent had told us, at the coffee house. 'I say, Holmes. There isn't one with the name of that coffee house Miss Vincent mentioned, the Griensteidl, wasn't it? I made a mental note of the name, in case we might need it.'

'No, Watson, there is no slip bearing that name. We have no corroboration of what Miss Vincent said in that respect.'

'This is becoming a complex case, Holmes,' I said.

'It is not the complexity of it that disturbs me, Watson. It is the large area of uncertainty. Though we may hear from Mycroft on the subject of these lists, and this will as always be informative, we are here without knowledge as to whether S was working exclusively for the British government or also for the German one, and similarly whether von Oldenburg was working for the German Admiralty or was collaborating with S in our government's work. I feel confident of a solution in this case, but ambiguity may be general in this kind of international work. I fear facts may become hard to discern. I am used to dealing with facts, Watson. I see that if I enter this business I may have also to deal with probabilities, and possibilities. Items of information may have to be marked as being of uncertain reliability.'

'I agree, Holmes. Perhaps this is part of the new world your brother was speaking of. Perhaps his doctrine too, of states having knowledge of each other's actions, is too sanguine, if much of that knowledge is unreliable or subject to the possibility of taint.'

'We may safely leave that to Mycroft, I believe,' said my friend. 'Meanwhile one fact we may be sure of is that S and von Oldenburg did meet. I was able to determine not only that von Oldenburg had reserved a table for two for seven-thirty on the 5th of May at the Zwierschütz, but that even now the waiter remembers the two men, one with very fair hair and the other corresponding to the photograph of S that I showed him. They ate very well at table number six, drank the most expensive wines and talked together earnestly in English.'

'Von Oldenburg might have pumped S for information and arranged to meet on Saturday in the mountains, on apparently friendly terms, to exchange information that they could not risk being overheard in a restaurant, or perhaps to pass over some papers. When he had got what he wanted, von Oldenburg pushed S over the edge!'

'You run ahead of what we know, Watson. I myself shall proceed by making some enquiries of the more fashionable hotels in Vienna. When I find where Herr von Oldenburg was staying, we may be closer to knowing whether he would have been in a position to assassinate Mr S.'

'Do you think those two ladies, Miss Vincent and Frau Rosenthal, are implicated too – they are concealing something, you said so yourself. Perhaps Mr S was here setting up a network of spies to work for him, either on our side or the other, and the women were among them, as well as von Oldenburg. Although I can scarcely believe it, Miss Vincent may have been in love with Mr S, just as the woman in black had been. Perhaps everything she said about how horrified she was to see him, and how ashamed she was of her earlier liaison, was subterfuge. She may have been having assignations with her guardian for years. When you think of it, since Mr S travelled often on the Continent such assignations could have been her reason for living in Vienna while keeping her address a secret from her godmother.'

'If ever you should tire, my dear Watson, of relating my cases of detection, I believe you could do very well with fictional stories of crime and intrigue.'

'I am sorry, Holmes. I know you have not yet gathered all the evidence, but it helps me to see the possibilities if I imagine what might have happened.'

'I hope you will not think me impolite or unfriendly, Watson, and of course I do not wish to discourage you, but I have to say it does not help *me*.'

244

Despite Holmes's protestations, I felt stung by his rebuke. None the less, I determined to press ahead with the task I had set myself, of recording events as the case progressed. 'What about the other things you recovered?' I asked. 'The cigarette case and so forth. Have they been of significance?'

'I cannot as yet see significance in the cigarette case,' Holmes replied, 'but one thing may be of use. It is the pen.'

'Well, come on, Holmes, out with it.'

'Microscopic examination of the samples of Mr S's handwriting in my possession, including the sample I collected from the Foreign Office, the address of Miss Vincent's rooms and these lists, is consistent with them having all been written with the fountain pen that was in the writing case.'

'Yes, Holmes?'

'What then are we to make of the other fountain pen, the one that was passed to us with Mr S's effects? I have been told, indeed, by the Austrian police that it was found on the mountainside near Mr S's body. By examining the wear on the nibs, I found that the nib of the pen in the writing case was worn more on the right side than the left, an indication that he held it in a slanting way as he wrote. Here, Watson, you can see for yourself, under the low-power lens of this folding microscope which I have brought along with me.' I examined the nib, as Holmes indicated. 'Now look at this other pen, the one with the two thin gold bands round the lid, which was found near the body. The pattern of wear of the nib is quite different. It was held straight when used.'

'I see,' I said, as the significance of this dawned on me. I felt that my friend had been correct to rebuke me for allowing my mind to wander off into unconstrained speculations, when his own mind was turning on such compelling evidence. 'So, this other pen, the one found near the body, had a quite different

245

pattern of use, and was not Mr S's own. It might have been lost in a struggle. It might have been the assassin's.'

'For the present, Watson, we must merely say there are just three possibilities. First, the pen may have been lost at that spot purely coincidentally. Secondly, Mr S may have acquired it for some reason. Third is the possibility that you suggest: it could be a clue to the identity of a person who was at that spot when Mr S made his final descent.'

24

The Narrative of Sara and Emily
continued

Counterpoise

The interview with Mr Sherlock Holmes and Dr Watson was concluded without undue mishap, or so at first we believed. 'I think it went well,' said Sara when they had departed. 'A convincing account of your troubles with Mr S you gave. Also, the doctor has sympathy to you.'

'That may be correct,' I replied, 'but we cannot be certain that I am not suspected. Mr Holmes works by noticing the smallest of clues.'

'I agree we must be careful. Now I think I made an error. It was better if I waited until the request before offering the name and address of Dr Woolf. This was a mistake. It is not natural to give an address without request.'

'I think that may be right. Mr Holmes also caught me off-guard with his question about why Mr S was in the mountains although he had a fear of such places. How could he have known that obscure fact? I suppose Mrs S told him that she thought it strange that he had been in the mountains. I had not anticipated such a question, and I believe I hesitated before I gathered my wits to respond.'

We were both silent for a period, musing on how we could have conducted ourselves better, and on the implications of what had occurred. 'That interview will not be the end of it,' I said.

'We may be sure of that. I think I had far better go to confess; perhaps I will go to find Dr Watson, and throw myself on his mercy. He seemed to wish to treat me kindly.'

'You do no such thing.' Sara was again being very firm with me. 'Herr Holmes is a simple detective. He can know no more than he has discovered. When he visits Dr Woolf he will be told you were in collapse on Saturday. I have made that sure. Dr Woolf is perfectly trusted. Then for Monday everyone knows that you came here, and did not leave the house for several days.'

'You may be right, but I did feel that Dr Watson was sympathetic to me, and could see that I had been wronged. He might intercede with Mr Holmes, and perhaps convince him that I had not deliberately caused Mr S's death, that my action was what you call a reflex action.' I found myself appealing to Sara: 'You could talk to the doctor biologically, and tell him that this is what happened, that it was a reflex, not an intended act. You could describe it as we have discussed it ourselves.'

'We will keep that as second choice. I do not reject it, but there are many steps to take before we reach that place. Before then I make a plan.'

'Oh Sara, not another plan. You are indefatigable.'

'What is this word?'

'It means you do not grow weary or tired.'

'For you I do not. I love you dearly, and it is best that, until this thing is complete, you do exactly as I say. You have agreed to that.'

'Very well. Tell me what your plan is. Are we to escape to another country?'

'Perhaps we may. I shall prepare everything to depart if necessary. We will travel without servants, and will live in a different way than we do here. First I am going to find out what Mr Holmes does, and what he thinks concerning you. I shall ask Dr Woolf to write a note to the school saying I am ill.'

'Then what will you do?'

'Last night, while you slept, I finished reading all the cases of Mr Holmes in that book we bought, *The Memoirs of Sherlock Holmes*. Many of them are most interesting. I also gave much time to think about his method. It is really to apply science to detection. He gathers evidence as a scientist does, but it is not a science of general principles, like evolution, but of the particular actions of people. He deduces from the evidence his conclusions about what the actions were.'

'I agree; but how does that help us?'

'I too have the habit of thinking in such a way, although I do it about other matters, about biology. I believe that if we discover what evidence he has, then we might know what conclusions he can make, and therefore how to proceed. We have talked of the events many times, and I do not think there is much that is substance that he has to work with. Now I have met the man, I do not believe he is without error. He is just a man. I think Dr Watson writes about only those cases which are successful; no doubt he writes, how do you say, with some ornament. He does not write of Herr Holmes's mistakes, or of cases that fail to make a conclusion, yet we know from science that inference is unsure: all theories, even of the greatest thinkers, are uncertain, and mistakes are frequent.'

'So what shall we do, exactly?'

'You must do nothing. I will arrange all. To me this is a challenge. It is practical science. It is not right that a man, and from another country also, should come here and pursue you as if you were guilty. It is Mr S who was guilty. So I am justified in what I do, and I begin to enjoy this challenge. Here is my idea. Dr Watson writes the cases, and no doubt rearranges things to make a good story, but the method they use is science, and in science one must always keep a record of each thing that happens as one goes on the way. Herr Holmes makes the observations and deductions, but he speaks them to Dr Watson. In the stories, Dr Watson makes himself seem simple, but I think he does this to hide his real part in their collaboration, which is, how do you say, too ordinary for an exciting story. I think Dr Watson is the keeper of the records. That is his real part. So if we visit Dr Watson's room at the Hotel Imperial, we discover his records, and know what evidence they have. Two paths then we could take. First we could follow their movements while they are in Vienna, which can be arranged since they are strangers and must ask people for things. In this way we will know whether they discover anything in addition to what they now know. Second we decide whether what they know is enough to make it necessary for us to leave Vienna.'

'Sara! You have thought all these things without telling me. That is why you asked what hotel they were staying in?'

'The good doctor kindly gave the information, but yes, that is why I asked. Please do not speak that I keep this as a secret. I am not such a one for the secrets as you are, and this you know.'

Sara made as if to reprimand me, but instead came and kissed me lightly on the brow. 'I tell you my plan soon after I have thought it,' she continued. 'I have not decided it fully until now, after I had seen this Mr Holmes and Dr Watson with my eyes.'

'How will you get into the hotel and get the notes? Will you become a burglar?'

'If necessary I will become so, or I will employ a burglar. This thing is not so difficult, but I think I know a better way. You have said that you think me too altruistic in working with the women of the city for their education, in our Association. Now you see this is not altruism but storing up for myself a thing which will be an advantage.'

'I do not believe it, but continue.'

'Well, most of the women in our association have occupations. Not so many are domestic servants. Several work in hotels, in the kitchens or as chambermaids. I am not certain, but I think that Ida – do you remember her, the woman who is slightly plump, and with dark hair with curls, who brings very delicious pastries to meetings sometimes? Well, I believe she works at the Hotel Imperial. It is one of the large hotels, and I think she may oversee the work of the chambers. Even if this is not so, then it is another hotel nearby at which she works, and she will know people who do work at the Imperial. She is a woman who has many friends, and I know she will help us if I explain that you are in the difficulty. I shall say that Mr Holmes and Dr Watson try and make you return to England against your will, and that they plan to do this by accusing you of something bad, and then threatening to lay it before the police.'

'I would sooner the women in the Association did not think I was wicked,' I replied.

'Do not worry, I will make sure they do not think so. Anyway, to see Ida I now go. Do you agree?'

'I only agree because you have already decided, and because I know you are the most stubborn person on Earth, and because I love you. If I did not I would not be able to believe in myself. I would go now to the Imperial Hotel, and wait in the shadows until I saw Mr Holmes go out, and then I would find Dr Watson and tell him everything. I would throw myself on his mercy, and trust that he would be able to dissuade the bloodhound, to call him off my tracks.'

Sara went out for a considerable period. She was marshalling her forces. Ida, who was in our association, did not, as it happened, work at the Imperial, but at another large hotel. She did however know some of the women at the Imperial, since she had been in the process of forming an association of women who work in hotels. She had thought that in future there might be a possibility of creating a kind of trade union of the kind that men have. At any event Sara and Ida had met with one of Ida's friends who worked in the Imperial. It had proper male waiters at lunchtime and for dinner, but in the morning the men had other duties. At breakfast the more respectable-looking maids waited at table, and they were supervised only by a kindly, avuncular man who would not object to a substitution among his waitresses.

The plan was this. One of the women in our association, Lotte, whom I had taught, had become very proficient in English. She would substitute for one of the maids who waited at breakfast. Hotel labour, it turns out, is somewhat casual, and members of the hotel staff quite often make substitutions if one is ill, or has to attend unexpectedly to a sick child or relative. Our spy Lotte would listen to the conversation of Mr Holmes and Dr Watson, to see if she could pick up any intelligence by that means. Meanwhile, Sara herself would act as chambermaid for the room in which the two sleuths were staying. I thought this was too risky by far, but I was overruled on the grounds that the beds were made while guests were at breakfast, and chambermaids are never seen by them. Sara was to make a preliminary reconnoitre to see if she could take a quick look at the manuscript. If she heard that the two men were to be absent for a large part of the day then she would steal it, so that she and I could study it in detail, and be able to return it before they came back. Sara even had the idea of recruiting a small group of women from the Association who work at typewriting to copy the manuscript, but I vetoed this plan. It was too elaborate, and unnecessary, since we would be able to determine by reading the manuscript, and perhaps from breakfast conversations, the stage their investigation had reached.

One of the unexpected effects of the plan was that Sara, who had always lived in a house with plentiful servants, had to receive a rapid training in the arts of bed-making and the other duties of a chambermaid. She afterwards said this had been very good for her, and the experience had helped her realise more directly the nature of the life of servant women.

The first day of operations was moderately satisfactory. Sara performed her part as chambermaid, and was even complimented by the supervisor on her bed-making. She made a full inspection of Mr Holmes's and Dr Watson's quarters while they took breakfast. They occupied a suite of rooms, a sitting room and two bedrooms. Beside a desk was an attaché case bearing the intitials J.H.W., which was locked. On the desk there were some unwritten sheets of paper, and some books, including one by Professor Freud of all people. If the doctor were keeping a record of the case it was not immediately accessible. It must be in the locked case.

At the same time, Lotte had taken up her post as breakfast spy. She was able to overhear the conversation between the two gentlemen. On the first day, Sara reported, not much conversation occurred. Dr Watson read an English newspaper of the previous day, while he munched his way through quantities of toast. He had spoken to our spy in German, giving her instructions as to the manner of preparation of his toast. He had requested butter and marmalade. The butter was forthcoming, but our spy told us that he had had to content himself with apricot preserve, since eating marmalade was an English habit not catered for in the hotel. He had drunk several large cups of coffee with milk. His companion, meanwhile, ate nothing whatever, but drank black coffee and stared intently through the window beside their table.

Ida's friend who worked permanently in the hotel, meanwhile, entering into the spirit of the enterprise, instructed other members of the staff. They were primed to keep watch and to pick up gossip about the two English gentlemen.

253

Although I had agreed to these arrangements, I had the severest misgivings. While Sara was out I had another episode of the most wracking terror, in which I found myself again alternately trembling and weeping, without being able to stop myself. It is still the trembling that is the worst. I have no influence over it, and it is accompanied by a sense of dread so intense that I believe I shall not be able to survive. This dread is yet more torturing than previously, since now I know that when I am arrested my life with Sara will end. I am painfully aware also that she has formed an equally strong attachment to me. Even though I am a wretched creature, she too will be stricken with grief when the worst occurs.

Eventually my dread and the shaking of my frame subsided. When Sara returned I was able to converse normally, and to hear of her activities at the hotel. She has started to treat the matter as a kind of game. She talks of our troops, and of the enemy.

'It is a war of minds,' she says. 'Is that how you say?'

'A battle of wits,' I replied.

'Very well, a battle of wits. Those men think they can pursue and question. They follow us as if we are animals of the hunt. Like men always, they do it without thinking, as if they have perfect right, given by God, but they do not have this right. Perhaps we surprise them. There is another side to the question which is to them so certain. There are other minds as well as their minds. We too can think, and collect evidence, and draw deductions.'

Sara continues to assert that Mr Holmes and Dr Watson are in the wrong to pursue me. She says we have every right to defend ourselves, that a proper justice would not simply consider how Mr S had fallen from a cliff, but determine that he should not have been there at all. She continues to say that it was he who was guilty, not me.

Of course I find this a great comfort. I even sometimes think that she is right, and I imagine an impartial tribunal, a bit as in a Renaissance picture in which there are saints, both men and women, who are sitting in a row. Sara, like Portia in *The Merchant of Venice*, is dressed in the robes of an advocate. She addresses the company on the matter of the case. She makes it sound very convincing that I have had wrong done to me, rather than that I have myself been the wrongdoer, but when the time comes for me to withdraw, while the company of judges or jury, or whoever they are, consider the matter, I experience that dreadful anxiety once more. I do not know what they will decide, and cannot obtain a picture of a decision being reached that would exonerate me. I can imagine very clearly the scene of a trial, but I have no image of an acquittal. In my heart I feel guilty, and underneath I think that is how I shall always feel, even if by some miracle we escape the bloodhounds.

I realised too, today, that by treating this as a game Sara can avoid thinking about the dire consequences of my being caught. By throwing herself into activity on my behalf, and speaking of it as a battle of wits in which right and wrong are not foregone conclusions, she keeps from her mind how degrading and terrifying it will be when I am hanged as a murderess. Must she think of it like this in order to love me? Will she stop loving me when I am arrested, and publicly disgraced? I do not believe so, but I cannot help wondering. Does she love me as I am, or does she love someone who needs help? Would she only love someone who has not really done a terrible evil?

I cannot resolve these questions. Am I now writing them here in order that Sara shall read them and reassure me? As I read them, these thoughts seem cruel, after Sara has been so kind. It is so hard to know. Since my consultations with Professor Freud, I have started to see things in a psychological way, in terms of the many possible reasons for actions, my own and Sara's. I must stop this incessant round of merciless, torturing thoughts.

Why does Dr Watson have a book of Professor Freud's? Is this coincidence? It seems strange. Perhaps the Professor is very well-known in England among the medical profession, and Dr Watson purchased his book because in Vienna he saw it in a medical bookshop. It contributes to making me feel the deepest unease.

25

The Viennese Affair

The Doctors' Meeting

I arrived at Professor Freud's rooms in the Berggasse at the appointed time. When I entered I was surprised to see a much smaller gathering than I had anticipated, seated around a long table. There were perhaps eight physicians there, members, if I am not mistaken, of the chosen race. I, who had served Her Majesty in places more alien than this, was not to be discomfited by such matters.

The Professor rose to greet me. He was a man of modest stature but of surprisingly commanding presence. He was soberly dressed, with a well-trimmed beard and a pair of the most penetrating eyes I have ever seen.

'You must be Dr John Watson,' said he. 'Allow me to welcome you to our meeting. We seldom have visitors from overseas. Let me introduce you to my colleagues.'

When these formalities had been completed, the Professor said, 'I hope you do not mind if I smoke. I have to confess that I am addicted to the cigar, but I believe it is preferable to the habits for which it is a substitute.'

I am of course well used to being in rooms where the air has become opaque with the smoke of the dark shag of my friend Holmes, so I was not in the least perturbed by cigar-smoking, but I was unable to understand the way in which the Professor smiled as he spoke of the habits for which smoking is a substitute, or the ripple of laughter that went round his companions at this speech. I think perhaps my German was more rusty than I had believed. At any event, this seemed to have broken the ice. Very soon all had regained their seats and the Professor began his talk. This had evidently been carefully prepared. He referred to his notes only occasionally as he spoke, but addressed us with a mixture of formality, as if we had been a much larger audience, and informality, as he would glance at us in the course of his delivery. I have to say his mastery of the material was absolutely first-rate. He held his audience, including myself, spellbound as he began to describe the case of a young Englishwoman who had recently started to consult him.

It was not long after the Professor began to speak that, to my utter astonishment, I learnt that the young Englishwoman who was the Professor's patient had suffered a nervous collapse on an occasion when she was to give a speech at her school! It could be none other than the same Miss Emily Vincent whom we had but lately interviewed. Nothing could be more natural in Vienna than to consult Professor Freud if one had suffered a nervous collapse; even so, it was astounding that on the one occasion that I attended a medical meeting in Vienna, the subject of the case being discussed would be someone Holmes was investigating. We heard how Miss Vincent's failure to give her speech had led to her dismissal from her teaching post. Holmes would, I thought, be interested in this corroboration of what she had said to us, though it occurred to me that he might think this was only partial corroboration, since both accounts would have come not independently but from the lady's own lips.

The Professor went on to describe how his patient had been the victim of unnatural practices of the most repellent kind, perpetrated upon her when she was of tender years. With the shock of realisation that the patient was none other than Miss

Vincent, I was of course prepared for some such revelation by the results of our own interviews with the woman in black and with Miss Vincent herself. But I was scarcely prepared for the degree of depravity to which S had sunk. As a medical man it would be wholly improper for me to disclose the further excesses in which S had indulged, but what the Professor achieved in his presentation was to allow me, an ordinary unimpressionable fellow, to imagine vividly the predicament of this young girl, separated by a cruel fate from her parents, and thrown unknowing into the den of a debaucher whose evil lusts knew no restraint.

Miss Vincent's own description in response to Holmes's austere questioning had been pale beside what she must have told the Professor in the intimacy of his new therapeutic method. The more I listened, the more I imagined her impossible situation, and the more it made my blood boil. Even though I had formed an unfavourable impression of Mr S from our interview with the woman in black, I now thought him to be a worse criminal than any that I had encountered in all my years at Holmes's side. It was into his care that Miss Vincent had been entrusted, and he had betrayed that trust in a despicable way that is scarcely imaginable.

Then the Professor began to expound his method of deciphering dreams and gathering clues from them. I continued to give careful attention, since I had learnt from my reading of his work that it was in unconsidered hints that he found signs of matters that were otherwise hidden. This was the method that came so close to Sherlock Holmes's discovery of the significance of unconsidered traces left at scenes of crime.

It was while thus listening that I heard the Professor describe how Miss Vincent said she had lost a fountain pen that she used to wear on a gold chain round her neck: 'A pen with a lid that had two thin gold bands around it.' At that moment a fearful realisation struck me like a thunderbolt from Jove himself. The description matched exactly that of the pen that was found with Mr S's body on the fatal mountainside, the pen I had held in my own hand just a few hours earlier! Although fountain pens are common objects, and although I knew from a hundred occasions on which Holmes had cautioned me against leaping too soon to conclusions, a mental picture arose unbidden to my mind. I saw Miss Vincent standing on a bleak mountain path as the devilish Mr S lunged at her, grasped at the clothing near her throat, was repelled, and fell.

The more I thought about this, the more mentally agitated I became, though, of course, I concealed this from my fellow auditors of the Professor's discourse, who afforded him their rapt attention. My mind raced: we could interview Miss Vincent again, I thought, and find out whether the pen we had in our possession was the one she had lost. Our interview with Miss Vincent had convinced me that, whatever had befallen her in her tragic life, she was very much a lady of the better sort. She was not a practised deceiver. If she were the culprit, our possession of her pen would surprise her and she would betray a sign of recognition, even if she did not say outright that it was hers. This pen alone would be enough to implicate her in the death of Mr S.

In all the adventures Holmes and I had shared, and in all the strange byways of life that my friend's researches had taken us, I had seldom experienced such turmoil. As Holmes's constant companion, I had become acutely aware of the part that motive plays in crime and in the detection of crime. Now here were both motive and means. I had myself heard this motive of utter repulsion from Miss Vincent's own lips. Now I was confronted with it once more, from the confessional of the Professor's consultations. I could understand all too easily how she had ordered her life to escape from her seducer. As he pursued her again, the unhappy woman had no recourse but to thrust him away from herself in that high and rocky place. Was I now to be the instrument of her accusation and certain conviction, by making known what I had heard?

Although I had often accompanied my friend Holmes on his adventures, and although I had sometimes been of some trifling service in times of danger, it was but infrequently that I had been able to contribute anything substantial towards the solution of a mystery. My friend's mind travelled too swiftly beyond my own. It was invariably his ingenuity that provided the key to unlock each case. I flatter myself that I am tolerably conversant with his methods, and even that I have become expert in describing them; I nevertheless regret that am I not able to apply them. Now, however, albeit by accident, I had come across the one thing that would provide the solution of this case.

The information divulged by the Professor meant that Miss Vincent had not been co-operating with Mr S in any way. What she said about wanting to escape from him must have been the plain unvarnished truth. The horrific fact was that the very same sentiments of repulsion from the torments to which she had been subjected, and which in my judgement would exonerate her completely, would, when Holmes brought his mind to them, cast her indubitably into the role of Mr S's slayer. Should I try to keep from Holmes the depth of Miss Vincent's repulsion from Mr S and withhold this new evidence of her lost pen, or should I vouchsafe this new information, and pin my hopes on prevailing upon Holmes's chivalry not to allow his researches to reach any conclusion that would submit her to the exigencies of the law?

Because of the whirl my mind was in, and perhaps because I overestimated how serviceable my German was for a discourse on psychopathology, or perhaps because I had become mentally exhausted by concentrating on a complex argument phrased in a foreign tongue, I did not fully understand what the Professor was saying in the later parts of his speech. I believe he was raising the question of whether we can take the evidence of a patient's account entirely at face value, or whether we should consider alternative hypotheses. He outlined one such which, if I understand it, was highly improbable. No doubt he was doing this for scientific reasons, to set off as it were the diagnosis which presumably he had made against an alternative one from which it should be differentiated. I also remember that he adumbrated a theory of development of the person in childhood. He did not describe this at all fully, and what I understood of it I found far-fetched. He concluded that Miss Vincent had been psychologically arrested at an early stage in this development, but I think that this had the character of a surmise, and I do not believe that this contradicted the evidence given clearly in the opening part of his talk, of how Miss Vincent had fallen ill because of her subjection to the most vile humiliation that it is possible to imagine.

As he finished, I observed that the Professor had spoken without interruption for well over two hours, a substantial lecture. There was then some general discussion, to which I listened but did not contribute. Other members of the Professor's audience were evidently much impressed by his discourse, and strove to apprise him of this.

The hour became late and the formal part of the meeting broke up. I had then an opportunity to speak to the Professor briefly. I made an appointment to see him the following evening. I asked if I might bring Holmes, although he was not a medical man. The Professor was courteous enough to say that he would welcome me, and any companion I might wish to bring. As I left, I told the Professor that I had been most uncommonly interested in his discussion of this case. I feared, however, that my German may have become more rusty than I had thought, and that therefore I may not have been able to follow some of the finer points of his discussion. I asked then if he would, as a great favour, be prepared to lend me the manuscript of his talk until the following evening. I could understand German when written more clearly than when spoken, and if I were able to borrow the manuscript I would apprehend his arguments with more certainty than I had so far.

'Your request is unusual,' the Professor replied, 'but since you have heard what I have to say on this subject, and since I have also a copy of my talk, I see no reason why you should not borrow this. You will appreciate, though, as a doctor, its confidential nature. I trust that you will keep it safely, and return it to me when we meet tomorrow.'

I assured him that I would take every care. I took my leave carrying the precious document, which I would be able to study carefully for whatever indications it might have about the pen, and said I would look forward to our meeting on the next day.

As I walked back through the dark streets of the centre of Vienna towards our hotel, I felt more and more outraged at the thought of the scoundrel whose death we were investigating, and the blight that he had cast upon the life of the girl who had been in his care. The more I considered the matter, the more I found it difficult to banish the scene that had sprung into my mind as I listened to the Professor, of the vile man rushing towards Miss Vincent. This same image rose again, yet more clearly. She stood with her back against a huge ruggedly outcropping rock that was dark against a pale sky, and with her fair hair stirred by a breeze. Then her tormentor leapt towards her throat, ripping her clothing and tearing her pen from her neck, missed his footing and fell helplessly, with a cry, down the sheer side of the mountain.

Of course if that had been what transpired she would want to keep all suspicion of her presence on that mountain path a secret. Her motive for wishing him dead was now transparently clear, and even if Mr S had slipped without her so much as touching him she would be unable to prove her innocence. I thought that I must do everything in my power to protect that defenceless creature whom S had victimised. My mind was in violent commotion. In the end, I decided that it would not be within my power to divert Holmes from the inexorable course of his investigation. Though he sometimes was unable to bring a case to a conclusion for quite extraneous reasons, his intellect and fortitude seemed almost superhuman. He had expressed confidence that he would, within days, have enough evidence to report conclusively to the Foreign Office on how their representative had met his end. Whenever he had expressed such confidence it had never been misplaced. If Miss Vincent had been there at Mr S's death, Homes would discover this by one means or another. There seemed no point in trying to keep from him either her loss of a pen of identical description to the one in Holmes's possession, or the confirmation of her motives.

My hope, then, was to appeal to Holmes's sense of fair play. Though sometimes he seemed abstracted, distant, beyond merely human considerations, he was not without such a sense, and so I determined that the best course for me was to lay all the new evidence I possessed before my friend, not sparing him any of the gruesome details, and to indicate to him that if indeed she had killed her guardian, she was a hundred times more the victim than the perpetrator of a crime. The world had been well rid of an unspeakably evil man. Since in that lonely spot it would have been impossible for her to provide evidence that her guardian had lost his footing and had fallen by accident, who in the world would be better than Holmes to help defend her, I thought, if he were to agree to come to her side in this matter?

I mentally rehearsed what I would say to Holmes: 'You must see that this unhappy and innocent creature, orphaned at a tender age, was subjected to the most insufferable torment by one who was responsible for her welfare. Now here she is, once more alone, though now in an alien land, ignominiously dismissed from her employment. Probably he slipped as he rushed at her. And even if some action on her part did contribute to sending the despicable fellow to his death, it could only be that, as she herself said, he had followed her once more to torment her. He is the guilty one. In dying thus he received far less than he deserved. Roasting on a spit above a slow-burning fire would have been too good for him. Miss Vincent deserves our most assiduous protection, not our condemnation.'

It was with some such words as these that I intended to address my friend, but when I reached the hotel Holmes was not to be seen, and I assumed that he had retired for the night. I reluctantly decided that the morrow must be soon enough. We had planned to go early to the mountainside on which Mr S's body had been found, and we would have ample time together on the train. Despite the lateness of the hour I arranged with a member of the hotel's staff to bring up a bottle of brandy. I thought it might help quell my mental agitation. I also wanted to write, while it was still fresh in my mind, my impression of the meeting at which Professor Freud had spoken.

I have now written this impression rapidly, and glanced again at the opening part of the Professor's manuscript. I am gratified to find that I had indeed understood him. The description of the pen was indeed as I had understood it. I had the doom-laden sense that this very pen was just a few feet away from me in Holmes's bedroom. The Professor had said at one point that we should suspend judgement as to whether the despicable betrayal that Miss Vincent ascribed to her guardian had really occurred. He was being too academic. We knew, from the evidence of the poor fallen creature in black, that she had been grievously wronged. The sordid details had fired my determination. Sipping another glass of brandy, my eyelids begin to grow heavy. Here I shall end what I have written tonight. I shall read the rest of the

Professor's manuscript on the morrow and perhaps make some further notes on our case, after we make our excursion to the mountains, and before I have to return the manuscript in the evening.

26

The Viennese Affair

A Mountainside in the Eastern Alps

The train drew away from the buildings of Vienna, and I regarded my companion as he gazed through the window of the train carriage. He looked for all the world like an ascetic English gentleman travelling through Europe, perhaps bent upon some recondite historical study. In fact I knew him to be deep in thought about a more immediate matter, and I wondered whether the countryside as it slid past made any impression whatever upon his brain.

For my part, I had been fairly itching to tell Holmes of my discoveries of the previous evening, and to lay before him my plea on Miss Vincent's behalf, but except for practical issues he had spoken not at all, and he had asked me especially to be a good fellow and allow him to think. I knew that while he was in this frame of mind it was useless to attempt any other course, and that I should have to await a later opportunity. I contented myself, therefore, by watching the succession of farms, while alternately rehearsing the speech that I would make to him and wondering what clues Holmes could possibly discover now that the trail had been cold for so long.

I suppose I must have dozed, not having slept for the accustomed interval the previous night. I found myself waking to hear my companion saying, 'Come, Watson, you have been asleep. Here is G——, our destination. Keep your eyes skinned now. Observe the layout of the place. A visit has the beneficial effect of being able to see exactly a picture of a crime as it was committed. Picture, now, Mr S alighting from the train here, walking through the village and setting off along the mountain path. Is he alone, or accompanied? Who else might be on this train? Don't speak, just observe and think.'

So again I was constrained to silence as we dismounted from the train and left the station. Holmes shouldered his pack, which I knew contained a map and diagrams that one of the Mr Joneses had arranged for him to obtain from the Vienna police, a climbing rope and pitons, as well as provisions, should our excursion extend into the afternoon.

I was surprised, though, that he did not at once set off towards the mountains. 'First we must call on the services of a young constable who works here, and who was a member of the party that searched the spot where Mr S's body was found. In many ways I would like to visit the place alone, but mountain paths can be difficult to find, even if the map I have been given is entirely trustworthy. So I prefer to have some local knowledge.'

The three of us walked in silence through the village, reached its outskirts and started to ascend the mountain path, in Indian file, led by the young constable. We had few pauses, and had walked for an hour and forty minutes by my reckoning, when after a steep piece of upward path the constable announced our arrival at the fatal spot. The path in this place wound summitwards, with the mountain on our right and with a sharp drop to our left. At the spot at which the constable stopped, a rock perhaps ten feet high jutted into the path, so that to continue on the path one had to pass this rock, with some care. The constable stood with his back to it, facing us as we came up to him, and momentarily the mental picture of the previous evening, in which Miss Vincent stood with her back to a rock, appeared to me. A small pang of disappointment occurred, that the rock in my mental picture was a great deal larger than the one behind the constable now and other details were very different also, but this disappointment was replaced by the reflection that a more exact match would have been perplexing, with its implications of some form of second sight.

'Is this the place from which it is believed he fell?' asked Holmes. The young constable assented, and motioned with his hand down the steep side of the mountain, where the path narrowed. As we looked over the edge, we could see for perhaps ten feet before the steep slope fell away into what seemed to be a sheer drop.

The constable began to speak, but Holmes motioned him to be silent. I could see that as usual he was going to conduct his own observations, untrammelled by police theories. He busied himself securing the climbing rope to pitons on the path. He eased his way down the rope, while the constable and I waited. A few minutes later, Holmes surprised me by walking down the path from higher up the mountain. 'There is a ledge below which slopes up to rejoin the path a little further on,' he announced. 'Come, Watson, you will find this way easier than descending by the rope, unless of course you desire the exercise.'

We all three walked up the mountain path a little further, and then scrambled down to stand on a rock-strewn ledge, perhaps eight feet wide. The constable indicated that it was on this ledge that the body of Mr S had been found. The spot on which the body had lain was quite obscured from above, and must have been about thirty feet below the path. The young constable pointed out the places at which Mr S's hat and the pen had been discovered. Holmes thanked him for his services, and said that although we would stay and make measurements, he might as well go back. We all returned to the path, and Holmes and I watched him descend again by the way we had come.

'Good,' exclaimed Holmes, 'now we can work properly. First we must search the area thoroughly, to see whether there is anything the police have failed to notice. We shall look in vain for signs of the actual fall itself, I think, since the police have been swarming all over this area, but there may be something. Then, we must determine by experiment the likely place from which Mr S fell.'

After Holmes had spent some time surveying the rocky ledge, and searching it thoroughly, we reascended to the path. We next attached the rope to the rock that jutted into the path. Holmes instructed me to pass a turn of the rope around my shoulder in the manner of rock climbers. Thus I was able to lower him bit by bit down the steep slope as it fell away from the path. I was to move a few feet this way and that along the path, so that he could search even the steeper parts of the area systematically. The day was hot, and the exertion was considerable. Although we both rested from time to time, and although I am no weakling, I was about to say to Holmes that we would have to stop for a while, when I heard a shout from below.

'Lower me down to the ledge, Watson,' he said, 'then I will come up. I have something here which may have made our efforts worthwhile.' He regained the path. We were both breathing heavily from our exertions, and he showed me a thin gold chain, once presumably worn round the neck but now broken. 'What do you think of this?' he asked.

'Extraordinary,' I expostulated. 'I have been itching to tell you all morning, Holmes. I learnt last evening that Miss Vincent had lost such a chain.'

'Did she indeed?' said he. 'Did she really? Very well then, you had better tell me your story. What exactly did you learn last night? Let us rest for a while and take some of these refreshments which I had the hotel restaurant pack for us.' At this Holmes produced a package from the rucksack that he had left beside the rock on the path, and we sat in the sunshine looking out over the wide and craggy expanse down towards the valley and its houses whence we had ascended.

At last I could tell Holmes about the extraordinary fact that Miss Vincent had been consulting Professor Freud and receiving his new therapeutic treatment called psychoanalysis. I had forgotten that I would have also to tell him about my interest in the Professor, and how it had started when I was reading up on psychopathology to see whether anything was to be found to help his own condition of recurrent melancholia, and that, of the many authorities I had read, it seemed likely that the Professor might be the most helpful. I now took the opportunity of apprising him of this idea.

Holmes seemed unabashed, and remarked that he had wondered what the letter was that awaited me when we arrived at our hotel, and what I had been doing last night. Then he said, 'Had this case not brought us to Vienna, I suppose you would have had to find some other pretext for inducing me to come here.'

This small embarrassment having passed, I was able to tell him in detail about the meeting, and the manuscript I had borrowed from the Professor. Of course, rather than letting me come quickly to the point, he now wanted to know exactly what I had been longing to tell him all day, the intimate details that Miss Vincent had narrated to the Professor.

When I had explained the nature of the treatment, I said: 'You see, Holmes, several things have come to light. First, and no doubt you will think this is much the most important, it seems that Miss Vincent had lost a fountain pen and a gold chain. Her pen had two thin gold bands on the lid. The pen that came with Mr S's effects has two gold bands and you said it was not Mr S's. So it occurred to me when I was listening to the Professor last night that the pen could be hers. As the Professor spoke the

271

conclusion just came flooding into my mind, much against my previous inclination, I may say. Now that you have found this chain, it must be certain that it was her pen, and that she lost both it and the chain at this very spot.'

'Yes, Watson, that is all very well.' I felt pleased at his accolade, but I was uncertain whether he was perhaps discomfited at not having made the deduction himself. 'Your assumption that the pen is Miss Vincent's is not warranted; we know merely that she lost a pen with two gold bands on the lid, and that the pen found on this spot was not Mr S's. It causes me some chagrin,' he continued, 'that I have a specimen of Miss Vincent's handwriting on the envelope that Mrs S gave me at B——. I could have determined whether it had been written with that pen or no. I am becoming dull, Watson: I should have considered that possibility. The ink in the pen that was found here was dried out, as one might expect with it being left in the glare of the summer sun for six weeks. I did not fill the pen with new ink and compare the strokes it makes with those of my sample of Miss Vincent's handwriting. No matter, Watson, I shall make the comparison when we return.'

'So you agree that Miss Vincent was here, at this spot where Mr S fell?'

'If we were to find that the pen and gold chain belong to her, she would have a weighty case to answer. If she were implicated in Mr S's death, and if we can separate her from that friend Frau Rosenthal, then by confronting her with this evidence I think it likely that we should find out from her exactly what happened.'

'Well, Holmes, I have not finished yet. For my own view of the case, I believe that I learnt something just as important. In Professor Freud's account I heard much more about what actually went on, I mean what Mr S actually did to that poor girl when she was just a child, when he started having his way with her. How can I put it? With your logical brain you may not be

272

able to understand this: I recognised, as if it were happening to my own daughter – I don't have a daughter of course, but do you see? – I recognised the full enormity of what had been done to her. She was not only devastated by it, but it drove her to the very brink of madness, Holmes, which is why she was consulting the Professor. She was not working with Mr S as a spy. Much less was she in thrall to him. She loathed and feared him, so that when he arrived at her door, and exacted the promise to consider his odious proposition, she suffered a nervous collapse. Now of course you will say, "That then completes the case, because now we also know the motive," but I have still not come to the important part, Holmes. The important part is that even if she were here when Mr S lost his footing, even if she herself in some manner assisted that fall by some action or inaction, she is not the perpetrator of a crime, Holmes, she is the victim.'

'Your sentiments do you credit, Watson. You think we should turn a blind eye.'

'I would not put it like that, Holmes, not in the least. What I am saying is that you have made a speciality of the detection of crime. Well, a crime has been committed. It was committed by S, and as a direct result of that crime he followed Miss Vincent to this spot, ran at her in an attempt to commit further criminal outrage on her person, missed his footing and slipped over the edge. The poor woman admitted to us that she had a motive for wishing him dead, but obviously in a court if she were found to have been here, then with such a motive she would be assumed to have pushed him. She does not need us to turn a blind eye, Holmes, she needs you to exert yourself on her behalf.'

'As to the manner of S's falling, we shall have to determine that, but why do you assume that Mr S followed Miss Vincent here? Might they not have come up here together?'

'I have a very strong mental picture of these events having occurred, of Miss Vincent walking up here, perhaps to get away from Vienna. Mr S follows her . . . he comes up upon her at this very spot, comes from behind. She hears his footsteps, turns, and he rushes at her as she stands with her back to this very rock.'

'I do not have your imagination, Watson. Now, if you are recovered from your recent exertions, I shall go down to the ledge again. I should like you then to allow this rucksack to roll over the edge of the path, just here, and I will see where it comes to rest. I will attach some twine to it. Please attach the other end to that piton, otherwise it may make its way entirely beyond our reach. It is not a very exact substitute for a human body, but it will give a rough indication. Then I will make a few more measurements, and then I think we may leave.'

A little while later, as we descended the mountain path, having completed our experiments with the rucksack and finding that when falling from the vicinity of the jutting rock the rucksack did indeed come to rest close to where the body was found, I said to my companion: 'What do you think of what I learnt last night at the Professor's meeting? Do you think my conclusions are right? Will you exert yourself on Miss Vincent's behalf?'

'My next step is to test whether the fountain pen with the two gold bands is the one with which Miss Vincent wrote the address on the envelope we acquired at B——,' said Holmes. 'What seems less than compelling to me is your surmise that Miss Vincent could not have been working with Mr S, and that she hated him. The evidence you present concerns her childhood. We know nothing definite about her relation to Mr S latterly.'

I knew I should have to content myself with this. Holmes was not be diverted when he had determined his course. We walked again in silence. After an interval, however, and as the terrain became less steep, my agitation would not subside, and I thought to approach Holmes from another direction. 'There are many ways, Holmes,' I said, 'in which the methods adopted by

Professor Freud are closely comparable to your own. He works by noticing small details, inconsistencies of speech and so on, and he identifies them as signs of mental events that the patient is unaware of, that are unconscious. I derived a very strong impression from the Professor's account that Miss Vincent in adulthood continued to be utterly repelled by Mr S, and would in no circumstances have associated with him if she had any choice in the matter.'

'Really, Watson? You interest me. You say this method, which is similar to my own, was used in his treatment of Miss Vincent?'

'Yes, I have been trying to explain that to you.'

'But you omitted telling me the most interesting part, the details of the method itself and how findings are derived from it.'

'I thought I had explained it. In any case, I have borrowed from the Professor the manuscript of his lecture. You may read it yourself when we get back, and you will see how he works. I need to read the last part myself, I was too tired to do so last night.'

'Very well, I shall read the Professor's lecture when we return.'

'I have also made an appointment to see the Professor again this evening, and hope you will come too.'

'So you have your way with me as you have wished?'

'Only, of course, if you agree to come. I cannot compel you, even though it is my medical recommendation that you see the Professor.'

'You have tempted me sufficiently now. This is what you have been keeping from me this last year, is it? I have a rival investigator, also observing the unconsidered aspects of people's behaviour, though to a different purpose than my own. Very well. I accept the invitation, on condition that on the train back to Vienna you explain these principles that he has developed. Start first with the general principles as you understand them from the reading you have done, then proceed to the particular case of Miss Vincent, describing what small clues she has let slip and what deductions the Professor has made from them.'

'I would be very happy to do that, as well as I can. I think it may indeed interest you.'

'First, though,' Holmes said as we made our way back through the village, 'at the station here we will ask whether anyone remembers Miss Vincent or Mr S coming here on the first Saturday in May, although I think the likelihood of us hearing anything useful at this distance in time is remote.'

As Holmes had surmised, we drew a blank at the village. In the train I started to explain the Professor's theories and methods. He interrupted me occasionally, with astute questions. After we had discoursed thus for an hour or so, he said, 'Pause for a while and let me think, will you, there's a good fellow.' I gazed from the window as the train drew into the station of Wiener Neustadt, which I supposed must not be too far from Vienna itself. As the train gathered speed again he said, 'What you have told me is uncommonly interesting. It seems, then, that according to this theory a person might act in some way but not consciously know what he was doing. Is that right?'

'Yes, Holmes, that is one of the main ideas, though the effect only occurs in certain persons.'

'So,' mused my companion, 'a person may commit an act that he desires and may indeed accomplish the end he desires, but although he is not conscious of having committed the act, he might nevertheless give himself away by small signs. I shall have to study the Professor's work carefully. It promises to add a challenging extra element to certain cases. Thank you, Watson, for your information on these matters. I shall contemplate this possibility with care.'

27

The Narrative of Sara and Emily
continued

Sara Takes the Initiative

On the second day of Sara's operations at the Hotel Imperial, her spy Lotte gathered the intelligence she was waiting for. Mr Holmes and Dr Watson have left for a visit to the mountains. No doubt they will go to that hateful spot where in a moment of time I did what could not be undone. They left the hotel bearing provisions and a rope. What will they find, I wonder?

The burglary was accomplished. Sara took the attaché case, still locked. She smuggled it out of the hotel, and went to a locksmith to have it unlocked, and removed those contents that were of interest to us. Then she returned the case to its place, unlocked so that she could return the papers and snap the lock shut later on.

Just as Sara had conjectured, Dr Watson was keeping a written account of Holmes's researches as they progressed. Sara has brought the manuscript back here. It is a set of loose pages in a folder. Beneath Dr Watson's manuscript there is another entitled 'Address to the Psychological Wednesday Society: A Case in Progress, by Professor Sigmund Freud'. Whatever is this? What is going on? Perhaps Dr Watson knows the Professor well. Could they have conversed about me? Had those sleuth-hounds found that I had received treatment from the Professor? I started to read the first paragraph of Freud's manuscript: he deployed his favourite simile, of his treatment being like an archaeological expedition. Sara interrupted my reading and said, 'You must not read that now. Read it later. This is more urgent. Read what Dr Watson has written. You read English more quickly than I. There are some matters to attend to in case we must leave,' and she left to bustle round the house.

I obeyed, and I read. I read quickly through Dr Watson's draft of the case. Their brief was to find out about the death of Mr S. It was as we feared. They not only suspect me, but towards the end it comes out that they have evidence that I had not considered. They have my fountain pen. It was found with Mr S's body. Yesterday evening Dr Watson attended a lecture by Professor Freud, and he has guessed that the pen is mine. It is the one Sara had given me, that I had lost. In the confusion of those days I had not known that it was lost on the mountain. I thought it had been lost when my things were carried to Sara's house, but Mr Holmes even now has my pen in his possession. He could take it to the school, and ask the teachers if they recognised it as mine. They would recognise it, and this would establish my guilt beyond doubt. That is exactly the way in which he works, but according to Dr Watson's account he had not done this yet, or has not told the doctor, who is often some way behind with the inventory of clues.

The doctor's story also made clear how a manuscript of Professor Freud's came to be with his own. The Professor's manuscript is about myself. I feel mortified, as if naked. Dr Watson had visited the Professor, heard him give a lecture about me and then borrowed the manuscript. I am deeply vexed with the Professor for doing this. He has betrayed my confidence.

When I told Sara of my conclusions, she responded immediately. 'Very well,' she said. 'We leave Vienna. I have everything arranged. A train leaves in one and a half hours.'

'We must return the manuscript,' I said. 'Perhaps we could also recover my pen, then they would not have the evidence.'

'We do not have time,' Sara replied. 'Besides, I made a survey of Herr Holmes's room. He had a quantity of the equipment that he uses, such as a folding microscope, a case of chemical agents and glass to make experiments, some surgical instruments and some watchmakers' tools, but I did not see your fountain pen. I would have recognised it. I think it better to depart. I wish to read these manuscripts myself. For now the most important thing is to leave. We have several hours before those two return. The plan of escape I have made.'

'And what is this plan?'

'It is to be seen to leave Vienna by train for Rome, and then into air we vanish,' Sara replied. As usual she was full of confidence, and happy in the course of doing something practical.

'But how?' I asked, lamely.

'You will observe.'

In little more than an hour we had arrived at the Sudbahnhof, with quantities of smart-looking luggage, including a very striking hatbox. Sara herself was wearing a hat that was yet more striking, and set off her handsome travelling outfit. She caused a considerable stir at the station, both because of her attire and by the way in which she fussed around, asking the coachman who had come to see us on to the train to do first one thing then another, and summoning a railway official to show us to our compartment.

We settled ourselves in a first-class compartment entirely to ourselves near the front of the train. I sat, taut as a bowstring, unable to refrain from imagining Holmes and Watson running on to the platform in our pursuit, even though I know that, if they had gone to visit the hateful spot, they could not possibly return for several hours. Sara would not allow me to keep watch on the platform, on the grounds that it is most unladylike. 'If they were as quick as they could possibly be,' she said, consulting a railway timetable, 'they will not be back in Vienna until four o'clock this afternoon. She tapped the timetable that she held in her hand. 'At their most rapid, after they have returned to the hotel and discovered that the manuscripts are missing, there is no train on which they could follow us until late tonight. More probably they are even now on some obscure mountainside in which we shall shortly have no interest. I estimate that it is most likely that we will be well on our way to the Italian border before the loss of the manuscripts is discovered.'

She sat, apparently unmoved by the danger that enveloped my whole being, and began to read Dr Watson's manuscript. 'Let me read this first. Why do you not read the Professor's lecture?' she asked, handing me the other document. 'It will make you less afraid.' She was right: it did make me less afraid. It rendered me alternately fascinated and furious.

At the appointed time, there was the usual huffing and puffing of the engine. We were leaving at last, and Sara looked up to smile at me. She placed her hand gently on mine. No policeman had come. The train was drawing slowly away, and I could not stop myself from rising to lean out of the window and look back along the platform. No running figures were seen jumping aboard at the last moment.

'First we will wait until we have crossed the Brenner Pass. For now we will have something to eat, and when we have descended on the other side of the Alps we will some rearrangements make,' Sara said as the train puffed laboriously to gather speed. We ate, and read, until we had both absorbed the two documents in our possession. Then we fell to discussing the Professor's treatment of my case. My anxiety had lessened with each hour that passed. We were deep in conversation when we realised that our train was climbing up the Pass, now on the direct line to Italy. As we left Bozen the ticket inpector began once more to make his rounds. By now we had become acquainted with this official, and Sara had ascertained that his duties ended for the day at Trient, the next station, where the train was to stop for twenty minutes before crossing the border to Verona. 'Good,' Sara said after she had learnt this information. 'I had thought from the twenty-minute wait at Trient that is advertised in the timetable that they must take on coal there, or some such thing. Now also we know that the men who work on the train change places here, which I had also thought but not known with certainty. We will make our rearrangements between Bozen and Trient.'

These rearrangements consisted in Sara opening one of the suitcases and withdrawing from it a suit of male attire, which she then put on. It was a shock, knowing her as well as I did, how much she looked the part. Then from the travelling trunk she withdrew two battered leather suitcases, one inside the other.

'Here,' she said. 'This is what we are going to take with us. Most of your things are already in the smaller of these cases. I will repack the things we need in the other one. Change what you have on. Here, I suggest this.' In a short time she had packed the hatbox inside a large smart suitcase that we had had conveyed to our compartment, and that inside the travelling trunk.

'We will take the trunk and this other case to the left-luggage office at Trient,' she announced.

At Trient Station the evening was approaching: a gentleman with a lady descended from the train. The gentleman was clad in a travelling coat while the lady wore an unremarkable green dress. A porter approached them and was asked by the gentleman to bring a trunk and a suitcase to the left-luggage office. At this office the lady paid off the porter, arranged the deposit and obtained a receipt. Following this she walked to the station restaurant, where she rejoined her male companion, now carrying two rather battered leather suitcases, and the couple took some light refreshment. When the departure of the train was announced for Roma, they did not board, but could have been seen some little time later boarding a train proceeding in the opposite direction, bound for Innsbruck.

'There,' Sara had announced. 'That is the first part completed without mistake. All we do now is to change trains at Innsbruck for the sleeper to Paris. On the Paris train we sleep. When you wake, you will put on the man's suit that I have brought for you. I hope it fits. I believe it will. Then in Paris, early in the morning, two gentlemen, one taller and one less tall, will descend from the train. Each will carry an old leather suitcase. They will take a cab. They will arrive at a café where they will take breakfast. Two ladies board the train in Vienna, and mysteriously disappear. Two gentlemen, also mysteriously, come alive in Paris. That should make some problems for the clever investigator, and at least occupy him for some little time. I calculate that even if Herr Holmes has an associate in Rome and wires ahead, by the time he finds we have not arrived there it will be too late for him to pick up our trail. From Dr Watson's manuscript we know that the matter for the British government a secret is, and this is to our advantage, since the police will not be called. Herr Holmes and Dr Watson must use their own resources.

'Then after the arrival of the two gentlemen in that great city, where it is easy to become lost, I believe one of the gentlemen will set forth and obtain a house or perhaps an apartment, perhaps on the Rive Gauche. Then a new life will begin. How do you think of that?'

28

The Viennese Affair

The Meeting of Holmes and Freud

It was a shock to discover, when we returned to the hotel later that afternoon, that my attaché case had been rifled, even though I had checked that it was firmly locked when I left. When I reported the loss of my own and the Professor's manuscripts to Holmes, he dissuaded me from taking the matter to the hotel Manager, on the grounds that the theft indicated a very selective interest in our possessions, and implied that we and our actions were under scrutiny. He thought he would be able to gain more information about the thief if the loss were not made public. 'I hope you have not written anything that would prejudice the case,' he said.

'Do you think that von Oldenburg has somehow got wind of us, Holmes, and that even now he is keeping some kind of watch on us?'

'It is one possibility. Another is that the women have the papers: if that turns out to be so, you will see why I have been reluctant to accept your idea that Miss Vincent is a simple girl to whom a wrong has been done, and that the case is nothing more than a *crime passionnel*. I also cannot say that I am surprised at the theft. I myself have taken the precaution of depositing objects that are irreplaceable in the hotel safe. I am going, indeed, this minute to collect from the safe the fountain pen with the gold bands so that I may examine it, and make comparisons with Miss Vincent's handwriting. I shall be occupied until dinner. Shall we dine at eight? Then we can make the visit to Professor Freud that you have arranged.'

I myself went out to walk round the city for a couple of hours, trying to distract myself from my chagrin at not having thought of using the facilities of the hotel safe for the document which I had promised faithfully to look after. When, after dinner, Holmes and I set off for our appointment, it was with a mixture of anticipation and trepidation on my part. As the cab rattled through the gathering twilight, knowing that I was uneasy about failing to return the manuscript I had borrowed, my friend assured me that we would certainly regain both this manuscript and my own. It would none the less be mortifying to inform a person whom one had so lately met, and who had granted so considerable a favour, that his manuscript had been stolen. I remembered that he had said he lent me a copy of his paper. I fervently hoped that he meant that he had retained another one.

Holmes sat in silence, and had I not known him better I should have said that he was mentally rehearsing what he might say to the Professor. When we reached Berggasse 19 at the hour appointed, although feeling the most extreme embarrassment at the loss of the Professor's manuscript, I was also keenly curious as to how these two would take to each other, both being in their different spheres investigators who sought out the small clues that go unconsidered by those whose thought processes are neither so subtle nor so penetrating as theirs.

The Professor welcomed us warmly: 'Ah, Dr Watson, this must be the friend of whom you spoke.'

'Yes, Professor,' I replied, 'I am sure you are acquainted with my companion's work. May I present Mr Sherlock Holmes. You have no doubt seen accounts in the newspapers of his remarkable feats of detection and his ceaseless fight against the most villainous of criminals. This,' I said to Holmes, 'is Professor Sigmund Freud, investigator of the mind.'

The Professor shook hands formally, and motioned us to chairs. 'You will have to excuse me,' he said. 'I see little of the English newspapers. Beyond what you stated in your letter and at our brief meeting on Wednesday, and beyond the evident fact that the two of you have a very close relationship, in which your admiration of your companion is matched only by his reluctance to allow you to discern his dependence upon it, I know nothing of Mr Holmes.'

At that moment I was thunderstruck, and I saw Holmes receive this extraordinary speech with a stony and silent formality. I think he had never been spoken to in this way. At first I thought I glimpsed the passage of anger across his brow, and I then feared that he might enter one of those fits of abstraction in which he becomes impervious to human discourse. Just as I was about to search for some words to try and extricate us from the awkwardness of an encounter that I myself had engineered, I became yet more astonished, as my companion burst forth.

'I'll be damned,' said Holmes. 'It is with words very similar to the ones you have used that I sometimes greet people who seek to employ my services. It keeps me alert to see what can be inferred from the small signs that they display inadvertently about themselves. Not infrequently they confess they are astonished at what I tell them, when to me they have revealed information about themselves quite openly. Now, sir, here are you using phrases such as I myself use, and if I am not much mistaken your observations derive from a comparable technique. Pray tell me what the basis is upon which you spoke as you did.'

'The tone with which your companion introduced you indicated to me that he admired you considerably. Then, as I observe you together, this impression is confirmed. Both the doctor's actions and the words he uses convey clearly that he holds you in the highest esteem. While you yourself, sir, if I may say so, although evidently comfortable in the doctor's presence, as if you have had a long and intimate acquaintance, hold yourself erect as if you are indifferent to every word he says about you. What else is one to infer but that you enjoy this praise, but wish to conceal its importance from your companion, and perhaps in part also from your own self?'

'I'll be damned,' said Holmes for the second time. 'You were right, Watson. We do use the same methods – I in the detection of crime, and,' he said turning towards the Professor, 'you, sir, in psychology. I am heartily glad that our fields of endeavour are substantially disparate. Otherwise I might have to regard you as a rival.'

'Well, gentlemen. Perhaps you will be so kind now as to tell me the real purpose of your visit. It was not, I am sure, purely to exchange pleasantries.'

'No,' I said. 'You are right. It was my idea. I have recently been making a study of psychopathology, partly because I have been concerned for some time about my friend's fits of morbid melancholia. After an acquaintance who had come across your work brought it to my attention, I thought it would be helpful if Mr Holmes could meet you. But first I must say something, so that we will not be on a wrong footing. I very much regret, sir, that the manuscript you lent me yesterday has been stolen from my hotel room. As it happens your manuscript was removed along with one of my own which I also value highly, since it contains a detailed record of an investigation on which Mr Holmes is engaged. You see, I write accounts of my friend's cases, and the account I had been keeping was of his present investigation. My companion believes that both manuscripts will be recovered soon. I have grown to trust his judgement on such matters implicitly, but in the meanwhile I have to say I am most abjectly sorry. I am covered in shame. I hope you will forgive me.'

'Please do not alarm yourself unduly, doctor. As I think I told you, the manuscript I lent you was a copy. My main concern is that it should not get into the wrong hands. I would be surprised if a thief who steals from hotel rooms would qualify as the wrong hands, though I would be very glad if Mr Holmes were right, and the manuscript were soon recovered.'

'You put my mind very considerably at ease, sir,' I said. 'You are most generous. I trust that my friend's prediction will be fulfilled in the very near future, so that your manuscript can be returned to you safely.'

'I look forward to that,' said the Professor. 'Now, as to the purpose of your visit, although I am flattered by receiving this interest from an English physician, since my work has attracted little attention from England, I fear I shall have to disappoint you in the possibilities of what may be done to help your friend. Though melancholia is a condition that interests me greatly, I am far from believing that the methods I have developed are as yet to be regarded as efficacious in its treatment, even if your friend would submit himself to my care, which we have not estab-lished.'

'Watson believes me to suffer considerably from melancholia,' said Holmes. 'He exaggerates. The condition is of very little moment. Merely I have the kind of mind that needs to be engaged in a problem. When there is none, I own I am a little flat.'

'Yes,' said the Professor. 'It is common to be unable to recall with any distinctness the despair of a melancholic mood when one is in a different state. Perhaps you would like to say how you occupy yourself in such moods?'

'I play the violin, and I wait. I believe that describes everything necessary. Invariably some event occurs, or I am charged with some commission, and then all is well. Watson makes too much of it. It is of no moment, of less than no importance. Let us speak of something else.'

'As you please.'

'I do not know, sir,' continued Holmes, 'whether it would be a breach of medical propriety, but I would very much value your opinion on a point in a case that I am investigating that concerns a woman who is your patient, Miss Emily Vincent. Dr Watson told me the general outlines of your investigations of this same person, as you reported them to your meeting last evening, though without of course divulging the medical details.'

'Indeed,' said the Professor. Now it was his turn to look taken aback.

'Yes,' said Holmes. 'I am investigating the disappearance of your patient's guardian, an official of the British Foreign Service, who was here on an engagement of some importance. He may have come to Vienna at least partly to see Miss Vincent. I interviewed her a couple of days ago, and she asserts that he came to her rooms on 6th May of this year, and implored her to elope with him.'

I was surprised to see how easily he spoke to the Professor, talking as one doctor requesting a second opinion from another.

'I am perturbed by what you say,' replied the Professor. 'You must understand that psychoanalysis is somewhat like the Catholics' confessional. I am like a priest whose ears hear things that other ears do not, and whose lips must, on some matters, remain forever closed. I can speak only in generalities. I believe it would be improper for me to be at all specific. The doctor will understand.'

'I understand the importance of medical confidentiality,' Holmes replied. 'I too am bound by confidentiality. What we are speaking of will go no further.'

I thought Holmes was not being entirely frank: if he could obtain some important piece of information in a manner that breached confidentiality then he would do so.

'I have evidence that Miss Vincent's guardian seduced her soon after she came into his care,' Holmes continued. 'Latterly she had tried to conceal her whereabouts, perhaps from her guardian or perhaps merely from his wife – she tried to cover her tracks by sending dutiful letters addressed to them via America to indicate that she was there, when in fact she was in Vienna.'

'I cannot pretend that this information is without interest for me,' said the Professor, evidently paying careful attention to Holmes's words. 'You say you have evidence of a seduction. Was this evidence derived from an interview with Miss Vincent?'

'Not solely: I also have evidence from an independent source.'

The Professor paused, as if contemplating something, and after an interval asked: 'If she covered her tracks, how then did you discover her here?'

'When I visited Miss Vincent's godmother, I happened to notice a letter from Miss Vincent, bearing an American postage stamp, sent from an American address, but the envelope could only have come from Vienna. Envelopes are distinctive, and the place of their manufacture can be determined by anyone who takes the trouble to study the subject.'

'So she made a small mistake in concealing her whereabouts,' said the Professor. 'That is what I call a *Fehlleistung*. "A faulty action" might be a good translation. In fact I have written a book about such little mistakes.'*

'Yes, Holmes,' I interjected. 'I don't know whether you saw it. I bought this very book the other day. I am sure you would be interested.'

---

*The Psychopathology of Everyday Life.

289

'I am sure that I would,' Holmes remarked.

'Tell me,' asked the Professor: 'did Miss Vincent inform you that her guardian came to visit her here in Vienna when you conducted your interview with her, or do you have any other indication that they met here?'

'She did tell me that he was here, but as it happens I also have a significant piece of scientific evidence implying that they met. A fountain pen was among Miss Vincent's guardian's possessions, and I now have this pen myself,' said Holmes. He was being careful not to give more away than was necessary. 'This pen is of Austrian manufacture. It is certainly not Miss Vincent's guardian's, but from Miss Vincent's handwriting on the envelope that I have already mentioned, we can infer that in all probability the pen does belong to her. One indication is a thinning of the line where her writing strokes attained their greatest velocity. This thinning is imperceptible to the naked eye, but is visible under a low-power microscope. The pen in question has a nib which had been used constantly by a single person for more than a year. The nib had been bent in a small accident and then straightened as carefully as possible, but without fully restoring the capillary channel along which the ink flows. Microscopically one can see that it had suffered its accident and been straightened some time ago, since there is an even pattern of wear across both parts of the nib, the edges of which are perfectly aligned. The effect of the accident was to produce just such a slight thinning of the line as I have described in Miss Vincent's writing. I have been able to reproduce exactly this effect using the pen myself, but the thinning does not occur with a pen of the same manufacture whose nib is undamaged. The type of ink, the width of the line and other features also match, so the implication is that Miss Vincent and her guardian did meet, and somehow her pen changed hands. I am however, missing the answer to a vital question,' Holmes concluded. 'Was Miss Vincent working with her guardian as part of the clandestine commission with which he had been charged, or was she, as she asserts, discovered here against her will by her guardian, independently of any political significance?'

'When you say working on a clandestine commission, Mr Holmes, do I understand you to mean spying?'

'That activity could be included in the commission.'

'Again, Mr Holmes, I doubt if I can help you. Even apart from confidentiality, I have no experience of the issues of which you speak. The clues from which I work come from the accounts my patients give me about themselves. I am prepared to say, though, that I have discovered nothing in what Miss Vincent has told me that would indicate that she was working as a spy.'

'You will forgive me, professor, if I put this to you? Dr Watson is of the opinion that Miss Vincent was much put upon, and that she must have attempted to repel the advances of her guardian when he visited her. He says she suffered a nervous collapse as a result of her guardian's visit, and that is why she was unable to give the speech that she was due to make at her school Founder's Day. I, on the other hand, believe we cannot exclude the possibility that she was otherwise occupied, and that is why she absented herself from her school duties. Would you, professor, as an expert in mental pathology, be at liberty to offer any opinions as to whether Miss Vincent was really suffering from nervous collapse, such as might have been brought on by the reappearance of a hated tormentor, or could it be that her collapse was a subterfuge?'

'What you say intrigues me considerably,' said the Professor, 'and some of what you have told me bears on theoretical questions over which I have been puzzling in this case. Your methods of investigation reveal a quite different aspect of the matter – quite different from my own diggings into the individual mind. The subject of my work has been that which people keep from themselves. I am not expert in the arena of spying or deliberate deception of others.'

'Nevertheless, professor, if you were able to say whether your conclusions are or are not consistent with a nervous collapse, that in itself would be most helpful to me.'

'Very well. I think the young lady's failure to perform her duties at her school, and the very profound anxiety that she manifested following the date that you mentioned, are consistent with her having been terrified at the reappearance of a man she despised and feared. You may wish to reflect that in my profession I would be predisposed to interpret what I notice in my patients as signs of psychological effects, rather than, for instance, as signs of deception such as a spy may inadvertently exhibit. Nevertheless, I offer the following for your consideration. I feel able to say this since Dr Watson has already communicated to you the main outlines of the case as it has appeared to me, and hence no further breach of confidentiality is entailed than that which has already occurred. Miss Vincent has suffered three periods of anorexia, a condition that she is not voluntarily able to control, and of which before my therapy she did not know the significance. This condition is a sign of profound anxiety, manifested in a disinclination to take nourishment. In her case, as I was able to demonstrate to her, it was precipitated by the contemplation of sexual activities. Her first episode of anorexia was associated with her original connection with her guardian when she lived under his care in England. The second occurred when she was in America when there was a possibility of becoming married, and she became afraid of the sexual activity that this implied. The third episode of anorexia began when you say her guardian visited her in Vienna.'

'So,' said Holmes, 'that would be consistent with the threat of recurrence of an unwelcome liaison rather than with a continuance of any co-operative clandestine association with her guardian.'

Professor Freud did not reply or elaborate the inference that Holmes drew, but sat as if pondering the issue. At length he said: 'I wish I could discuss these issues with you more fully, but I fear that if we were to talk in any detail about the case with which we are both concerned it would constitute a breach of confidentiality.'

'Thank you very much, professor,' said Holmes, 'Although I would dearly like to hear more about your methods as they touch this case, I fully understand your reticence. Watson, we should be on our way and leave this gentleman in peace.'

'Yes indeed,' I replied, having listened spellbound to this extraordinary discussion of the two men who had independently discovered the secrets of attending to unsuspected minutiae, and applied them, each within his own area of professional concern. 'Yes,' I repeated, 'yes, we must be going. My deepest thanks to you professor.'

'But you, doctor, are leaving without what you came for.'

'No, not at all. What you have said provides a piece in the puzzle of my friend's researches, and for me that is reward enough. Moreover, I am privileged to have met you, sir. I shall continue my study of your works, and if I can ever be of assistance to you in any way in England, please do not hesitate to let me know and I shall do everything in my power to assist you.'

'You are most kind,' the Professor replied.

Holmes and I stood up and made to leave. I noticed my companion indulging his usual proclivity to glean information – by perusing the Professor's bookcases. 'Ah, I see you have Morelli's book on how small and neglected details in paintings provide clues to the identity of the artist,'* he remarked. 'Morelli is one of the few authors whose work I have found helpful to my own methods of proceeding. His work on painters' unconsidered but idiosyncratic habits of depicting anatomical features prompted my own interest in ears as sufficiently distinctive in their patterning to allow unique identifications of individuals and the families to which they belong.'

'Morelli has been something of an inspiration to me also,' replied the Professor. 'I am pleased to find in you, sir, another admirer.'

I was gratified that a connection between Holmes's and Freud's methods, which I had recognised when I first came across the Professor's case of the Scottish governess, was here established. These two, the consulting detective and the psychologist, developing independently their methods of drawing inferences from trifles, had been subject to at least one common influence.

'I repeat, I do not believe that you have obtained what you came for, doctor,' the Professor persisted. 'Before you go I can perhaps make one small parting gift, bearing on the subject about which you intended to consult me.'

'A gift?' I asked.

---

*Holmes had no doubt noticed Giovanni Morelli's book *Della Pittura Italiana: Studii Storico Critici*, which Freud had in his library, probably purchased in 1898 on a visit to Milan. In his first paper on art criticism, 'The Moses of Michelangelo', Freud was later to acknowledge his indebtedness to Morelli, who had originally published under the pseudonym of Ivan Lermolieff. Influenced by Morelli also, Holmes published two articles in the *Anthropological Journal* on the shapes of ears: they are mentioned in 'The Adventure of the Cardboard Box', which Watson wrote up in 1892. In that case an innocent old lady had been sent two severed ears in the post. Holmes confirmed that this was not a bizarre practical joke when he noticed that the shape of the old lady's ear conformed closely to one of those in the box, and inferred that this severed ear belonged to the old lady's sister.

'Yes.' The Professor turned towards Holmes and said, 'Mr Holmes, I would need to spend much longer to assist you at all substantially with your outbreaks of melancholia, but I think I can say this. They are likely to be related to a very considerable yearning on your part to gain attention and respect. This you do by means of your work in detection which, from what I heard in the matter of the pen, is indeed remarkable. Dr Watson stands, as it were, both as the audience for your feats and, by means of his writing, as the gateway to a wider public. Possibly earlier in your life you sought to impress a parent, your father in all probability, with your acute observations. Your melancholia seems to indicate that except for your work, in which you believe yourself to approach perfection, performing better than anyone, you believe yourself unworthy of the respect you crave, so that when not engaged on a case you feel that you have nothing that will win that respect. The result is a morbid melancholia, in which you experience unspoken reproaches against yourself, and feel yourself to be the most lonely of men. This observation is very incomplete, but I hope it may help you in some way.'

The Professor said this in a tone that was even, and by no means unkind. Holmes was visibly shaken by what he said. I could see that it would be my business to complete the formalities of our departure. I did this, thanking the Professor again warmly, assuring him once more that my friend would do everything to recover his manuscript, and promising any future assistance that I might be able to offer.

As we walked back towards our hotel, Holmes said, 'Whatever did that fellow mean in speaking to me like that?'

'He works by offering people the means to understand themselves, Holmes,' I said. 'He believes that the mental torment in which people sometimes languish can be cured in that way, by obeying the Delphic Oracle: "Know thyself." Was nothing he said recognisable to you?'

'You will find this odd, Watson,' replied Holmes. 'It both does and it does not seem recognisable. In one way it does seem to describe something I recognise. In another way it seems the most damnable nonsense, which I profoundly resent. How can such speeches help me? I said before that you make too much of my fits of melancholia, as you call them. I need something challenging to occupy my mind. That is all. To the Devil with it! Pray let us speak no more of it.'

I was far from convinced by Holmes's protestation, which was made with some heat. I thought that in Professor Freud Holmes had met his match, and that the Professor had perhaps hit on something important that had touched my friend deeply. Here was someone whose intellect was equal to Holmes's own and who was able to see by small indications into his innermost being. I had not by any means absorbed all of what he had said about Holmes, but I resolved to continue my study of the Professor's works. I had thought when I started to read up on psychopathology that perhaps some simple remedy would lie at the end of the path. I now saw that the methods the Professor pursued were longer and more painstaking, a journey perhaps through arduous terrain, a mental equivalent of journeys on which I had sometimes accompanied Holmes in his cases. Perhaps, however, I had obtained a small glimpse of how I might be able to help my friend – it had never occurred to me that at the heart of Holmes's researches was a craving for respect, which he had perhaps been unable to win from his father. But this would explain the extreme reticence that he had always maintained about his boyhood and his family. By more study and careful application I thought I might be able to clarify the initial inklings I had received this evening, but the way would be long. I must learn to look out for these small indications before being able to help my friend in the way that I wished.

We had both been silent as we walked through the Innere

Stadt, our way illuminated only by the gaslights that cast flickering shadows as we passed. Then Holmes interrupted my thoughts. 'What do you think of our case now, Watson? It seems we are tending towards your theory of Miss Vincent.'

'Yes, Holmes, I believe we may be.' I was not able to elaborate my response. I did not know whether I was relieved or disappointed that my friend's thoughts had turned from himself back to the woman who had become the principal object of our researches. Though I sensed that the Professor had hit a raw nerve in Holmes, I must confess that what he had said about my admiration of my friend, and the role I played in his work, was strangely disconcerting to me also. I could not put my finger on why. It was as if this was not the proper way in which to think about such matters. It seemed in some respect less than decent.

This train of thought continued to occupy me. Then after an interval of silence Holmes spoke again: 'Despite his medical reticence the Professor gave us a piece of evidence that was helpful, his corroboration that Miss Vincent had suffered a nervous collapse. I think we may trust his professional judgement that the collapse was occasioned by the unwanted reappearance of Mr S. The case is not a satisfactory one, though, not satisfactory at all. I see little point in a further interview with Miss Vincent at this juncture. If we were to confront her with the facts, and let her know that we have in our possession her pen and the gold chain, recovered from close to the body, she would perhaps admit that she had been present when Mr S made his final descent. But we must not underestimate her, Watson. As we were saying on the train this afternoon, an aspect of the Professor's work is to show that people may be unconscious of what they do, and Miss Vincent may not know what she intended in the events that led to Mr S's death. It may merely be that finding herself pursued she acted to protect herself. Nor, despite being a woman, is she without a native cunning that has been sharpened by education, and she has furthermore recruited that other one to her side. So mere confrontation might fail to advance our case. We need objective evidence. An additional complication is that we may be unable to show whether or not any other person was in the vicinity of Miss Vincent and Mr S on the mountain that day. That trail has gone cold. Had we been able to investigate sooner, before the police, I have no doubt that I would have been able to solve the problem satisfactorily. I await, however, two further pieces of information. They will perhaps arrive tomorrow. We shall have to decide then what we must do.'

We had arrived at our hotel. 'Good-night, Watson,' said Holmes as we entered our rooms. 'I shall rise early. I have one or two errands, but I believe you are in need of the sleep that you missed last night. Why don't you lie in? We could take breakfast together at nine o'clock. That will not be too early for you, will it?'

29

The Viennese Affair

Breakfast at the Imperial

Next day the breakfast room was well populated when I came down. As well as a number of people I took to be Germans and native Austrians, others were there from further afield, including an English family who occupied a table by a large bay window. Holmes was already seated, reading a newspaper, and he had beside him on the white tablecloth two telegrams.

'Well Watson, how did you sleep? Soundly I trust. Why don't you have some of this excellent Viennese coffee? I ordered a large pot, so that we could drink it at our leisure. I believe we approach the end of the case of the death of Mr S.'

'I slept well, thank you,' said I, noticing Holmes's good spirits and wondering to what they might be attributed, since only last night he had been saying how frustrating the case had become. I was about to help myself to coffee when a waitress, a very presentable girl with a charming smile, had anticipated my movement and was pouring coffee for me: '*Danke, Fräulein.*' That is what service in a restaurant should be like, I thought as I ordered my breakfast.

'You said yesterday night that you thought the case lacked essential information,' I remarked to Holmes in a conversational tone as I unfolded the white damask napkin, 'so that it remains unsatisfactory.'

'That continues to be true,' replied my companion, 'but I have turned the matter over in my mind and come to certain conclusions. Moreover the information that has just reached me from Berlin leads me to conclude that I may safely make an unambiguous report to the Foreign Office.'

Holmes handed me a telegram. Sent from Berlin, it bore the following message:

G SAYS NO. INDEPENDENTLY UP TO 26 JAN EUROPE. 26 JAN TO 1 FEB BERLIN. 2 FEB LEIPZIG. 3, 4 FEB BERLIN. 5, 6 FEB HAMBURG. 7 FEB TO 26 BERLIN. 27 FEB TO 3 MAR DRESDEN. 4 MAR BERLIN. NO BREAKS. SINCE 5 FEB O AND STAFF CONCERNED AT XXI, EXCEPT NUMBER 4 ROVING.

'Well,' said Holmes. 'What do you think of that?'

'I can make nothing of it. It does not even bear the name of the sender.'

'Capital,' said he. 'That is the intended response of the casual observer. It is from Kydorf, my colleague in Berlin whom we visited last week. I arranged for him to send me this wire, and drew for him a rough map of Europe, with its countries numbered. XXI is that part of Russia which includes St Petersburg. It is a simple device. The disturbances in that area that have been occurring throughout the year evidently continue.' Holmes tapped the newspaper he had been reading. 'I deduce from Kydorf's information,' he continued, 'that the German government has sufficient interest in the commotions in that country, with which they have most curious relations, to have sent their team of agents there. *Ergo* they were not in Vienna, and hence not concerned with Mr S. All, that is, except for number four, whose presence we have already traced. Number four, on a list that Kydorf made for me, is von Oldenburg, whom we knew Mr S did meet here in Vienna.'

I was somewhat surprised as Holmes talked of governments

and commotions. He must have lately concerned himself with such matters. Until recently he had never taken an interest in political events or anything else outside the scientific detection of crime by individuals.

'All those dates in January and February,' I asked, 'what do they mean?'

'An even more flimsy subterfuge,' Holmes replied. 'I wanted merely to make my colleague's telegram inscrutable to a casual glance. A code-breaker would find it elementary. To such a person, however, neither the information in the telegram, nor the fact that I had received it, nor yet the identity and sympathies of the sender, would constitute information that could not be obtained elsewhere. I asked Kydorf to find out the movements of Herr G, the German government minister with whom Mr S was to make contact, between 26 April, when Mr S received his commission to meet with Herr G, and 10 June, a week before the discovery of Mr S's body. You will recall that the police said that carrion had been at the body, and that it had been there for several weeks. So I charged my colleague to discover where Herr G had been between 26 April and 10 June, and to make sure if possible that there were no breaks of more than twelve hours during which his movements were unaccounted for.'

'Ah, now I see. You have accounted for Herr G's movements and you wanted to know whether Mr S could have met him at any time or in any place.'

'You have it, Watson.'

'So this is what you meant by elimination, when I asked you how you were going to proceed?'

'Exactly. It is simplicity itself.'

'We know that Kydorf had the entry into the highest circles: would it not have been even simpler for him to come straight out with it, and ask this chap G, since they both had the same sympathies?'

'You are right, of course, except for one thing. Now we have entered the era of political subterfuge, Herr G would not necessarily have been truthful. It has become difficult to know whom one can trust.'

'I see.'

'None the less, I included that possibility, and that is the meaning of the the first sentence, "G says no." I know of S's movements since the day he was given this commission, now we also know G's movements. So we compare the two: G and S did not meet, and hence S could not have fulfilled his commission. It was a mere problem of elimination. As to the code: what could be simpler? January means April, February means May, and so on. When a simple means will suffice, one need not resort to anything more complex. I committed one oversight though. There may have been a difficulty if my colleague had occasion to report anything on the 30th of February. Do you see what I mean? He is an ingenious man. No doubt he would have found a form of words, but unlike the Roman numerals for European states and nations, which I have used before, I made up this scheme on the spur of the moment, without sufficient thought. It is not perfect. Perhaps my age creeps up on me, Watson. I believe that I used not to make such errors. I have, in any event, now mentally arranged a scheme of substituting months that would be foolproof should the occasion arise in the future, as I believe it may if my work as a consulting detective takes me more frequently into international matters, and I have to communicate with a network of colleagues. I shall have to overhaul my whole system of intelligence. The Baker Street Irregulars were once invaluable, but we have suffered the march of progress, Watson.'

Holmes looked at me, and a flicker of a smile played across his lips. He was becoming almost droll. I decided that he should be encouraged.

'You are very witty today, Holmes,' I remarked.

His countenance changed to one that was almost frosty, and I could see that I had said the wrong thing. Nevertheless he soon continued his narrative, as I ordered some more toast. 'I think we may sum up as follows. Point the first, as we have just agreed, Mr S did not complete the assignment given to him. He did not meet with Herr G. Point the second, he was probably not assassinated by those we might have expected would be behind an attempt on his life. Von Oldenburg, by the way, makes a great commotion wherever he goes, and it was not difficult to find the hotel in which he had stayed. It keeps a book for reservations on trains that it makes for its guests, and they had booked him aboard the Orient Express, bound for Istanbul on the 6th May. I shall return to considering von Oldenburg shortly. Point the third, I now accept that Miss Vincent had done what she could to avoid occasions for seeing S. Point the fourth, and this is the information the good Professor has supplied us with, she seems not to have acted as one would who was taking part in activities of a political kind. Point the fifth, we may deduce that Mr S pursued her to Vienna without her knowledge. Then, there are points the sixth, seventh, eighth, and so on. All these you know.'

As he finished these words, Holmes glanced around, and leant towards me to speak in a more confidential tone: 'It is very likely that Miss Vincent contributed to Mr S's death. We can presume there was a struggle, during which he lost his footing, carrying the pen and chain with him as he fell. Professor Freud did us another favour: as well as adding to the weight of evidence that Miss Vincent was not engaged in espionage, the Professor's information about her anorexia confirmed what you yourself had surmised, that she felt the deepest loathing for Mr S. Therefore at the moment when they confronted each other on the mountain path, although he was a determined man, she too was determined. She might have done anything, even if it seemed certain

303

to result in her own destruction. She may have arranged this event.

'The difficulty is this,' continued Holmes, now speaking more loudly. 'S was the subject of attention from the German contingent, and he could have been followed. By the way, Watson, would you like some more coffee?' He turned to the waitress and said, '*Danke, Fräulein*' as she leant over to pour coffee from the silver pot, into first Holmes's cup and then my own. 'We lack evidence about whether another person could have followed both parties, or seen what happened,' he continued. 'The drop to where S's body was found was not a large one. He might not have been killed by the fall, he could merely have been stunned or hurt, and another could have scrambled down to assist his demise. This is what makes the case so damnable. Do you remember what I used to say to you: that in the science of detection, when one has eliminated the impossible, whatever remains, however improbable, must be the truth?'

'Yes, I remember it well. I was always struck by this precept.'

'I think now that it was too simple. It is even misleading. It was a sign of a less than mature eagerness on my part to imagine that I could always, or very nearly always, ferret out the truth by sheer application of logic. I believe now that sometimes even the most exacting mind may miscarry in an inference, since there are some things one cannot discover. Sometimes evidence may be of uncertain reliability. Sometimes the significance of evidence remains ambiguous. It is highly regrettable, but there it is. The current case contains such lacunae, not least our inability to determine whether anyone other than Miss Vincent might have been involved.'

'You mean von Oldenburg, about whom you were going to say more?'

'He is a possibility. Again, on the information I have it is unlikely, but the easily followed trail he leaves wherever he goes would be the perfect screen for other actions that he performs more discreetly. He may have booked on the train to Istanbul but not taken it. I do not know, at least as yet.'

'Yes,' I said. 'I see what you mean.'

'What I was going to say on this subject is that Mycroft thinks S had persudaded von Oldenburg to work for us. I had wired to Mr Jones that I had discovered those slips of paper in S's writing case, and so eager was Mycroft to see them that he sent Jones over here immediately to collect these slips. I met him at the British Embassy. From there I also spoke to my brother on the telephone, and described to him what was written on these slips. He was most interested.'

'I did not know you had done that,' I said. I felt a little piqued at having been excluded from this development.

'This other telegram is from Jones. Its ostensible content is about prices on the London Stock Exchange, but this one really is in code, the code that Jones gave me when he first came to see us. It was sent after my brother had time to examine the slips of paper. It confirms that von Oldenburg was collaborating with S, and says the information on these slips, particularly those that were undated, had been of the utmost importance. These alone, Mycroft said, had made my work on the case invaluable.'

'You mean S had written them after discussions with von Oldenburg, who had turned traitor to his own country?' I was flabbergasted to learn that I had held in my own hand those flimsy scraps of paper, which were of national importance. I continued, 'So, each item on S's lists suggested some fact to your brother, and he discerned connections among them, and knew they were of importance to the German government? Is that what you mean?'

'Indeed so,' replied Holmes. 'That is his forte, the discernment of connections. In any event, there it is, a matter which in the end is only partly satisfactory.'

'Why is it unsatisfactory?' I asked. 'The points that you have discovered – which few others in the world, perhaps no person other than yourself, would have been able to discover – are compelling enough. Surely anyone would accept them. And that is apart from the worthwhile result that your brother described.'

'Any other person than myself might regard this conclusion as satisfactory,' replied Holmes. 'It irks me not to determine conclusively the event at the centre of a case. I rebel at lacunae, and yet we must close this case. I believe I shall be able to discharge adequately what I have undertaken for the Foreign Office. I shall tell them that Mr S died on Saturday the 7th of May, that he had not met Herr G between the 26th of April, when he was given the commission to conduct whatever negotiations he had been charged with, and the time of his death. I shall say that the reason he was in the mountains on that day was of a sexual nature, that his death was probably an accident, and that it is improbable that he died because of political action at the hand of any foreign agent. I think, Watson, that this is a fair rendition of events. What do you say? It does not deviate markedly from actuality in any regard which touches the concerns of the Foreign Office, but do you see what I mean about the intrusion of probability when one would wish for certainty?'

'So you are not going to pursue Miss Vincent?'

'I think not, Watson. Consider the possibilities. There was some kind of struggle during which Mr S detached Miss Vincent's pen and gold chain, and fell while grasping them. There is no other plausible explanation for their presence well off the path, and on the route of his fall, which, you remember, we have determined. Two questions remain. The first is this: Did she push him? I believe we could answer this by confronting Miss Vincent. But the second question is more serious. If S fell to the ledge where his body was found and was merely injured or stunned, was he dispatched by a third party? If von Oldenburg had come over to our side, who is to say that he was not suspected, and that some other person had not been keeping an eye on him and our man? Do you see how possibilities proliferate in a way that they do not with domestic crime? Miss Vincent would be unable to help us with this question. You remember that the ledge on which the body lay was invisible from the path, and that, unless one had gone further up the mountain to discover the ledge as it met the path, one would assume that Mr S had fallen a considerable distance. Miss Vincent would have assumed this, and she would not have scrambled down to find him. So although we could in all likelihood, by pursuing Miss Vincent, clear up the question of her involvement, we would be no further forward in repairing the ambiguity that remains in the case.'

Holmes paused, placed his napkin on the table and eyed me: 'Before you rose this morning I visited the house of Frau Rosenthal, and by questioning a servant I ascertained that the two of them left the house yesterday in the forenoon. It was not difficult to find out at the railway station where two young women with a quantity of luggage had been heading. They made for Rome. I wish them well.' I thought it odd that Holmes glanced round the room as he said this.

'You mean . . .'

'Yes, Watson,' he said, returning his gaze to me. 'I have come round to your point of view. I believe Miss Vincent was put upon, and that, despite the important work Mr S was evidently doing, he courted his own death. Miss Vincent had done what she could to escape him. He should certainly not have betrayed in such a grossly infamous way the trust placed in him by her parents. I do not believe that the interests of justice would be served by pursuing Miss Vincent.'

I found myself wondering what Holmes was about. He seemed to be acting oddly this morning, with his high spirits and his alterations between speaking normally and then in confidential tones. I wondered if he were not engaged in some ruse. 'I do not understand, Holmes,' I ventured. 'Yesterday we were in hot pursuit. You never desist in a chase. For your own closure of the case, why do you not wish to find what happened when Mr S came upon Miss Vincent?'

'I do not find it altogether easy to say, Watson. It may have been something that fellow Freud said to me. I have not been able to get it out of my mind. He said that in my work I believe that I approach perfection, and am better than any other.'

'Yes, Holmes, he did say that, and it is true.'

'I have been thinking, Watson, that this is not the motive that I thought impelled me in my work. Though I have thought that some of the chains of inference I have forged in my cases did have a certain elegance, I think too that in a world where much is haphazard, perfection cannot always be attained. Nor in this case do I wish to pit myself against that woman.'

'Against Miss Vincent?'

'No, Watson, against the other one, against Frau Rosenthal. She has become my real adversary in this case. Not since *the* woman, Irene Adler, have I encountered such a one.* Frau Rosenthal is a fitting adversary, but she is neither the criminal type, nor could she become the object of our search. If I discover the two of them, then outwit Frau Rosenthal, would my object be to have the other arrested? Your view is that this would not be an apt conclusion.'

'No, Holmes, it would not.' I felt puzzled by my friend, unable to guess what his intentions were, but I was uncertain how to frame a question. Were we going to determine whether some

*Irene Adler was Holmes's quarry in 'A Scandal in Bohemia', the first of *The Adventures of Sherlock Holmes*. Holmes always subsequently referred to her as '*the* woman'.

third person had been at the scene of S's death, or were we going still to pursue Miss Vincent?

As I tried to think of these alternatives, he said with an air of finality: 'Now I think we may prepare ourselves for departure. There is a very good train for London in about three hours. Would that suit you?'

'Yes,' I said, rather nonplussed. 'Yes, I think that would suit me very well.' Then, remembering my intention to continue my studies of Professor Freud's works, I thought of the books that I wanted to purchase and said, 'I will slip out for an hour, then I shall have time to pack and we can be on our way.'

'I shall see you in a couple of hours,' said he, returning to his newspaper, and motioning to the waitress who had been assiduously attending us to refill the coffee pot.

Not only was I confused about his intentions, still more so now he had said we would be returning to London, but I had been taken aback by my friend's rendition of events, and his saying that the case could be closed despite remaining uncertainties. Never had he willingly ceased his enquiries without bringing a convincing conclusion to a case. He was right of course that he was older now than when we first met, when I first accompanied him on his researches, and when I wrote my first account of his methods in *A Study in Scarlet*, nearly twenty years ago. Thinking back, I reflected that perhaps he had changed somewhat. Certainly, after all we had been through together, I knew him better than I had at first, when his character seemed most singular. What I could not fathom was whether his outlines had become, as it were, less hard, his view of the world less mechanical, his eccentric refusal to take part in the normal pleasantries of social intercourse less obdurate. Or was it, I wondered, that today in particular his mood was more sympathetic than usual? Could this in some way have resulted from our meeting with the Professor? Turning these matters over as I left

309

the hotel and walked towards the medical bookshop that I had located previously, I realised that today, and perhaps as a result of what the Professor had said, I myself saw Holmes as less godlike than in those first cases in which I became acquainted with him and his work. Perhaps, I mused, it was this change, by no means unpleasant, in my view of him that gave emphasis to his remarks at breakfast. Now he was countenancing traffic with the uncertainties of life, rather than the certainties of logical deduction which I had always thought he would maintain, while we more ordinary mortals would be consigned to grope in the dark. He used to compare himself, I well remember, to a geometer: he used to say that his conclusions were as infallible as so many propositions of Euclid. Now here he talked of probabilities, and the haphazardness of life. Perhaps a change had occurred, over the years, imperceptibly, and I had only just noticed it? Was this part of a tide of change that had been brought on by the turn of the century, in which many of the older certainties had been challenged?* Or had Holmes perhaps been cogitating on the remarkable developments that had recently occurred in science, and which rendered the world less rather than more comprehensible?† Or could it be, as he hinted, that he had been moved in some way by his meeting with Professor Freud? Had Freud's parting gift somehow affected him?

It was with such thoughts as these that I betook myself to the

---

*It is not clear to which developments Watson refers here when he speaks of older certainties being challenged. Perhaps it was the Boer War, which profoundly shook British confidence in the nation's military capabilities and in the stability of the Empire.

†As compared with the previous sentence it is even less clear to what Watson might be referring. He may have had in mind the biological challenges to the older certainties that were still occurring in the wake of Darwin's work on evolution, or he perhaps knew of the more recent discoveries in physics, of radioactivity by Rutherford and the Curies, which indicated instabilities in the supposedly solid building blocks of matter.

bookshop, determined to acquire, in addition to the book I had bought a few days ago,* whatever else had been written by the Professor. In the end I came away with only two further books. One was his book with Breuer, *Studien über Hysterie*, which I had already read but now wished to own, and the other was the book on dreams. I remembered having thought previously that this book was over-voluminous for so slight a subject, but now I knew that this was certainly an incorrect assessment.

Some time later, as our train rumbled northwards, I regarded my companion, who was lost in one of those fits of abstraction that are common to him. Until yesterday he seemed to be going full-tilt at gathering all possible evidence that would bear on whether Miss Vincent had killed Mr S. Although I had said that I thought her morally innocent, I had greatly feared Holmes would not heed me. He would be more concerned with his Euclid-like deductions. I tried to recall, without notable success, other occasions on which I had been able to bring him round to my view of one of his cases. Had such an event happened at last? Or perhaps a link in his chain of deduction had been added by this morning's telegrams, by which he had seen that the requirements of his commission from the Foreign Office had been met, and there were no more clues to follow that were strictly relevant to that commission.

At the border there was an opportunity to speak. 'Holmes,' I said, 'you had said that you were sure that we would get those manuscripts back. I am still most deucedly concerned about the one belonging to the Professor, and I would be pleased to have my own humble efforts back.'

'Do not concern yourself about them, my dear Watson,' he replied nonchalantly. 'I said that the manuscripts would be recovered. I may be uncertain about some aspects of the case of

The Psychopathology of Everyday Life.

311

Mr S, but that is not one of them. I am confident that I can reel in the line that connects us to the present possessors of those manuscripts, and that the documents will soon again be in the hands of their authors, Dr John Watson and Professor Sigmund Freud.'

Book 3   Obsession

Obsession. 1. The action of besieging; invest-
ment, siege. **2.** Actuation by the devil or an evil
spirit from without; the fact of being thus
actuated. **3.** The action of any influence, notion, or
'fixed idea', which persistently assails or vexes.

Shorter Oxford English Dictionary

30

The Narrative of Sara and Emily
continued

Arrival in Paris

Sara had booked a room in a small hotel, and I had been smuggled in without anybody seeing me. I was able to resume my normal attire. This was something of a relief, because although Sara managed to carry off the part of a man with conviction, I felt in a torment while I was dressed in that way. I was certain that I should be discovered and apprehended at any moment.

Sara went out for nearly an hour, to do I knew not what. I lay on the hotel bed, waiting for her to come back, turning over the events of our flight from Vienna, and listening distractedly to the street noises of the summer morning as they drifted upwards through the open window. Since Sara seemed comfortable to continue masquerading as man, we were to stay in the hotel together as a married couple, and we went about together in the same fashion. Arm in arm, we walked along the street until we found one of those delightful cafés with tables and chairs in the open air, under an awning. The air was warm, and for a moment I experienced a lightening of my mental turmoil, and imagined myself to be on holiday in Paris, a young woman with her new lover.

'Now we take *petit déjeuner*,' said Sara. We ordered *café au lait* and croissants. 'You did not sleep well on the train, but tonight you will sleep better, in our own *grand lit*,' she said. 'I think the end of this thing is near.'

'What can you mean? I am fleeing for my life. I agree we will have put them off for a while, but the indefatigable Holmes will get on our track again.'

'You do not think that my plan in its execution was masterful, and we fully escape?'

'It was of course a masterly plan, and I am sure it will have thrown him off the scent, at least for a few days, but you know what we have read in Watson's manuscript. He is setting up a network of associates. Perhaps he already has them in all the main cities. He will have discovered that we left for Rome, as you wished him to think. By now he will have telegraphed to some associate, who will have told him that we did not arrive in Rome as expected. He will deduce that we tried to elude him. He will infer that we had left the train, had changed trains. Then he will set out to follow us again.'

'Do not yourself alarm, dear one. I think the case towards conclusion comes. While you are in the hotel, I visit the Central Telegraph Office, and to there as arranged Ida and Lotte send a telegram. We too can have our associates in the main cities. Do you want to hear the latest report of intelligence?'

'Oh Sara, please do not tease me. For me this is not a game.'

Sara raised her eyebrows quizzically. 'You must allow a little levity. Here, I read.' And at this she produced a long telegram. 'I was just about to go into the telegraph office dressed as a man, and ask for a telegram for Frau Rosenthal,' she said. 'I had to retreat and rearrange myself. Here,' she continued, 'why do you not read it? Lotte's English is very good. You have taught her well, and she has worked hard.'

TO FRAU SARA ROSENTHAL

H AND W TOOK LONG BREAKFAST NOT HURRYING STOP. DISCUSSED TWO TELEGRAMS RECEIVED BY H STOP. TALKED MUCH OF DATES STOP. H FOUND TELEGRAMS MOST SATISFACTORY STOP. DESCRIBED

NUMBERED POINTS ONE TWO THREE ET CETERA STOP. CANNOT OVERHEAR ALL SOMEONE DIED ON MOUNTAIN STOP. FRÄULEIN EMILY THERE AND PERHAPS THIRD PERSON STOP. I HEAR DOCTOR ASK WILL THEY PURSUE WOMEN STOP. H SAY NO STOP. H SAYS WOMEN DEPARTED ROME BY TRAIN THURSDAY STOP. HE SAYS I WISH THEM WELL STOP. DOCTOR LEFT TO VISIT BOOKSHOP STOP. H ASKED HOTEL CLERK TO RESERVE SEATS LONDON TRAIN EARLY AFTERNOON STOP. LOTTE AND IDA.

'I asked that Lotte continue to wait at table during breakfast in the Hotel Imperial until certain guests depart. This is her breakfast intelligence report,' Sara said. 'I think from this they conclude that you are nothing to do with their main concern. They prepare to depart. That is how it seems to me. Of numbered points and of telegrams received they speak. I have sent another telegram to Ida and Lotte, asking them to clarify if they will not pursue us, and I ask if they think that Holmes guessed if they were overheard. Also to let us know if they leave on the London train this afternoon.'

'I cannot help suspecting a ruse. I mean a trick,' said I, seeing that Sara did not understand. 'Holmes is very cunning, and he never gives up.'

'Those are only the stories that the Dr Watson judges suitable to write,' replied Sara. 'Let me make agreement with you. I continue to have my spies watch on them. In return you assume, unless I say, that the chase is finished.'

'I don't know. Why should they just stop?'

'Promise. It affects me also.'

'Very well.' It was what I really wanted, just to trust Sara somehow to make everything all right, to repair the bad things I had done, to make it as if they had never happened. I thankfully gave way, hoping only that I could somehow keep my tormented thoughts at bay.

By the afternoon, Sara had succeeded in renting an apartment in the St-Germain district of the city. It has three bedrooms, and best of all a large sunny room with a huge bath in it. One bedroom we will convert as my study, one as Sara's, and one will be the bedroom we will share together, and it does indeed have a double bed. Then there is a large drawing room, and another smaller room, together with a kitchen with a huge stove, which as well as being good for cooking also heats water for the whole house. In the kitchen is a big wooden table at which it is easy to imagine eating the most delicious French meals together. Outside there is a small patio. We decided that we shall not have a servant, but look after ourselves. We will merely find a woman to come to clean and do our laundry for us two or three days a week.

'I think we are quite happy here,' announced Sara. I knew that she had the deepest misgivings about leaving Vienna and her life there. She was saying and doing these things entirely for me. Could it be that she loved me as much as that? Or was it merely pity, in the way she habitually took pity on unfortunates? What could I ever do to repay her? Nothing. At present I can scarcely prevent myself from covering everything around me with panic and fear. I cannot even do what she asks by avoiding thinking about the pursuit of Holmes and Watson.

'You ought not to be doing all this for me,' I said.

'Why not? It is what I wish to do. Perhaps also I do it for myself,' she said. 'Also, I do not want you to think these things. You have been quite ill, seeing a doctor for six weeks, every day. I want you to leave things to me, and to recover. Then we can discuss everything.

'In any case,' she said, 'I must visit again to the telegraph office. Do you wish to accompany?'

So we both went. There waiting for Sara was another telegram, this time in German. It confirmed that the first one really meant that H had been overheard definitely to say that he would not pursue me, and that he wished me well on my journey. Ida continued by saying that she had herself seen the two men board the train for London, and watched it leave the station. Though since our own subterfuge I could not feel that this evidence was very sure, I allowed myself to feel a certain amount of relief, and I think that perhaps we are no longer pursued, at least for a while. I realized how tightly I had been holding myself since our flight from Vienna had begun.

'Perhaps I will allow myself to feel relieved,' I said. 'I think I can believe that, at least for a little while.'

'I am glad,' replied Sara. 'I believe that Dr Watson persuades Mr Holmes that your are an innocent victim, even if they think you were on the mountain. Also I think this shows the doctor is of good sense, because this is what anyone will think who knows the facts. He will not allow you to be judged falsely.'

'What do you mean, he will not allow me to be judged falsely?' I asked. My fear had not abated: Sara's use of the future tense with the idea of my being judged, as in a court, made it rush to the surface again immediately.

'There is a word, I think, meaning to judge without evidence, or falsely.'

I had misunderstood her: 'Oh, I see what you mean,' I said. 'Yes, there is a word. Do you mean "prejudice"?'

'Exactly. Anyone without prejudice knows you are innocent, and to push away an evil attack is not to be blamed, but rather to be praised.'

If only I could believe that too.

31

The Viennese Affair

A Manuscript Returned

A week or so after our return from Vienna I called at Baker Street, and was relived to see my friend not down in the dumps but surrounded by reference books and papers. 'Good-morning, my dear fellow,' he cried. 'Observe this: it is a system of cross references that will allow me to keep track of certain events in the affairs of nations.' I saw that he had a box full of pasteboard cards, each perhaps three times the size of a playing card, on which he had written, in his exact script, details of persons and events.

'You will be interested to know, Watson, that I have now been retained by the Foreign Office to act for them in matters of the kind with which we have been dealing, international matters. My profession as consulting detective has been enlarged. The small byways of individual crime to which I have hitherto devoted my skills had of late started to bore me, as you know. They had become repetitive. I needed to have my mind stretched. I shall continue to maintain an interest in ordinary crime, but I have now fully decided. The commission we have just completed was the first of a series that I shall undertake. I believe that in this way I may be able to make some contribution to the welfare of our nation more generally than by assisting individuals. What I shall concern myself with may not always be so neat, but I am considering whether I may be able to add to the exact study of crime a new chapter that is less exact, on the study of clandestine actions with international significance.'

'You mean spying and that kind of thing?' Here, I thought, was the explanation for Holmes's good spirits. Even though the case of Mr S had not turned out in such a fully satisfactory manner as he had wished, he had decided that the wider horizons of this kind of work held an allure.

'Yes, Watson, that is what I mean, although it has many other dimensions in addition to spying. I have had two extensive discussions of the implications with Mycroft. I believe this new work may become thoroughly absorbing, and moreover that my gifts are such that I can indeed make a contribution. Indeed my talents and Mycroft's will complement each other nicely.'

'I am heartily glad. I believe that the first commission – shall we call it "The Viennese Affair"? – was just what was needed.'

'To prevent my lapsing into melancholia, as you call it?'

'Yes, that is what I meant,' I replied.

'Perhaps it was, perhaps it was. At any event, we have not yet concluded the case.' With this he slapped down on the table a sheaf of papers. It was my own lost manuscript, my account of this very case.

'Extraordinary, Holmes,' I expostulated. 'How in the world . . .'

'I expect you would like me to say, "Elementary, my dear Watson," would you not?' Holmes was certainly in a buoyant mood. I would never have anticipated that I would find him teasing me in this way.

I was astounded to see my lost manuscript lying before me on the table of 221B Baker Street. It was not really that I doubted my friend's assurance that we would regain it. It was rather that in the press of things I thought that the odd document or two would not figure largely among Holmes's concerns. I was distressed to see however that Professor Freud's manuscript was not with my own.

'Perhaps you will give me the credit for having predicted that we would recover this,' said Holmes.

'Yes, yes of course, my dear fellow,' I replied. 'Do you have Professor Freud's manuscript too?'

'Be patient, Watson. All in good time.'

'But how did you get this?'

'It required no more than a modicum of deduction and a dash of forward planning,' he replied. This was quite extraordinary. One teasing remark could have been a lapse, but now he seemed positively to be enjoying the joke.

'Let me into the secret, Holmes,' I pleaded. 'As usual, it is not at all elementary to me.'

'When the manuscripts went missing although the lock of your briefcase had not been forced, and when nothing else was stolen, I think I mentioned to you that it must have been the work of some person keeping us under surveillance. No doubt this person had known from your books your practice of recording my cases, and inferred that obtaining your notes would be an easy way of discovering what we knew. I own that at the time my mind had been turning on von Oldenburg, whose presence had seemed to give the case a sinister twist, but it occurred to me that Frau Rosenthal could also have been behind the theft. I continued enquiries about von Oldenburg – that was before we knew that S had recruited him to our side. But I also continued other enquiries: I questioned one of the kitchenmaids, who was not averse to some pin money. It turns out that Frau Rosenthal is well known as a philanthropist, or, I suppose one should say a philogynist, in Vienna. She runs an educational association for women, among whom are some who work in the hotels in the city. We can assume, therefore, that since you were kind enough to tell her the name of the hotel at which we were staying – you remember her asking this particularly? – she could have gained access to our rooms, removed your case, had it opened by a locksmith, purloined the manuscripts and then returned the case.

'My suspicions that it was her rather than von Oldenburg were confirmed when a further piece of information came to hand, from the manager who supervises the women at the hotel. Two new girls had started working there, supposedly filling in for ones who were absent. One of them, working as a chambermaid, answered to a description that corresponded exactly to that of Frau Rosenthal. Well, Watson, was that elementary or was it not? It was on the basis of the manuscripts having been removed by that woman that I felt confident that we would be able to regain them.'

'But you did nothing about this, Holmes – at the time, I mean.'

'On the contrary, Watson, I kept the women in the hotel under close scrutiny. Do you recall the waitress who attended us at breakfast during the last three days of our stay? She was in touch with Frau Rosenthal in Paris. She was not our waitress when we first arrived: she was the other person who started work the day after we interviewed Frau Rosenthal and Miss Vincent. Do you remember that she seemed uncommonly solicitous when attending us, do you recall that, Watson, enabling her to overhear our conversation?'

'We spoke in English, Holmes. A serving girl in Vienna would not have be able to understand us.'

'This is good, Watson, but your supposition is incorrect. I took the precaution of testing it. Before you came down to breakfast on that last day I had asked the head of that English family who sat by the window, do you remember them?, to address our waitress in English and to note the result. The girl spoke perfect English. I thought therefore that I should take care that she overheard that we had called off the chase. It was not a very direct method, but serviceable enough. When you went out to the bookshop before we left I was able to ascertain that this same waitress and another woman went to the telegraph office to transmit a telegram. The telegraph clerk could not be prevailed upon to tell me the contents of this message, but I was able, by dint of parting with a not insubstantial sum of money, to induce him to tell me where it was addressed – the Central Telegraph Office in Paris. They had started for Rome. So no doubt they had set us a difficult paper-chase across the railways of Austria, Germany and France, had we chosen to try and follow them after we discovered the theft of the manuscripts.'

Holmes paused, as if for effect. I could see now why he thought that Frau Rosenthal might have been a worthy adversary. 'I expect you would like to know how I effected the return of your manuscript?'

'Yes indeed, I was just about to ask.'

Holmes indicated to me an article in *The Times* of a few days previously. 'I arranged that a translation of this should appear also in the principal Paris papers,' he remarked.

SHERLOCK HOLMES SOLVES MYSTERY OF DIPLOMAT'S DEATH

The case of Mr Charles S, who lately died in Austria, having fallen from a steep mountain path, was resolved today by a famous detective. Everything pointed to Mr S's death having been an accident, except for one small detail. His widow had been surprised by her husband having been on a mountain path, since he had a severe aversion to heights of any kind. She had therefore asked Mr Holmes, of 221B Baker Street, London, to look into the matter. By following the minutest of clues, the nature of which cannot be disclosed here in order to avoid giving information to any of the criminal fraternity who might chance to read this, Mr Holmes was able to determine that Mr S had been lured to the mountains to make an assignation with a dealer in fine art, who had a painting which he wished to discuss with Mr S in secret. Suffice it to say that a photograph of this painting, very much faded from exposure to the elements, was found by Mr Holmes at the scene of Mr S's fall. Presumably unknown to Mr S, the dealer was a dishonest one, and had somehow persuaded Mr S to meet him in a place where they would not be disturbed. The painting has now been recovered, and the art dealer is in the custody of the Austrian police.

'Yes, Holmes, I had seen it already. It is a tissue of lies. I had assumed that this was the work of a newspaper correspondent who, having acquired an interview with Mrs S and discovered that you were on the case, had imagined the rest.'

'Not exactly, Watson. You are right, of course, it is an invention and you may think that I should be ashamed of myself for concocting it. I had Jones arrange with the police in Vienna that no exception would be taken to the publication of this. In fact the story serves not one but two purposes. One is that the Foreign Office is satisfied that the story will explain my involvement, which had become known to far too many people, by implying that I was working on a private not a government matter. This will ensure that future commissions will not be jeopardised. I shall have to be far more assiduous in keeping my involvement in such cases completely secret. The second purpose was to transmit a message to Miss Vincent and Frau Rosenthal in Paris, confirming the message they had received by telegram from the waitress. I expected that Miss Vincent and Frau Rosenthal would carefully attend to the newspapers in the hope of keeping abreast of information about ourselves or the case, which would tell them whether or not they were still being pursued. This article lets them know that they are not being pursued, and obligingly gives them my address in case they should wish to express their gratitude by returning anything they had borrowed. The Rosenthal woman is clever enough to realise that my address is out of place in such a newspaper report, and to infer that it is an invitation to write to me. The return of your manuscript is part of the result. Another part is this letter, which you may wish to see.'

I read with astonishment the following missive, which bore neither a date nor an address.

Dear Mr Holmes,

Today I have read in the newspaper that an art dealer met with my friend's guardian in the mountains, and that this dealer may have been implicated in the fatal fall. Naturally she is concerned that her guardian met his death in this way. If it is true, I am grateful if you confirm this conclusion, by a note to myself poste restante, Paris.

I wish you also to return the enclosed very entertaining piece of detective fiction to your friend Dr Watson. To Dr Watson, for borrowing this manuscript without permission, I apologise. Perhaps to make apology is not correct, since I cannot say that I take the manuscript by mistake. However, I am grateful if you convey to Dr Watson my thanks for the loan. Perhaps you construct some words better than I, suited for this unusual situation.

Also please to inform him that the paper by the Professor is being returned to its author. Until autumn the Professor takes holidays. Please if the doctor knows how letters may reach him while he takes his holiday, he can write to the Professor to say that the manuscript will await him when he returns.

With very sincere thanks, yours truly,

S. R.

'An interesting letter, is it not?' asked my companion. 'Your manuscript is returned, and the Professor's will be too. Moreover the writer requests, without giving away more than is absolutely necessary, that I personally confirm that they are no longer being pursued.'

'I am glad the Professor will get his manuscript back. Why did she not return it here? I should have liked to be the one to restore it to its owner, since I was the one who borrowed it.'

'I have no doubt that she thought that it might be too incriminating if both manuscripts together somehow fell into the wrong hands. It would be safer to return the documents separately.'

'She is an enterprising woman, do you not think, Holmes?'

'A clever and determined one, certainly. One who will stop at nothing in pursuit of her own ends. Nevertheless, I have acceded to her request.'

'So you have written to Frau Rosenthal, as she asks?'

'I have.' Holmes made as if to continue, and after a brief pause said, 'I hope you will forgive me, Watson. I may have presumed too much but in my letter I ventured the opinion that you yourself might be in touch with them in a week or so.'

I rather thought Holmes had presumed too much, since I had not entertained any such plan. I therefore did not answer directly, but said, 'I expect the young women will return to Vienna now this is all over. Perhaps Miss Vincent will continue her treatment with the Professor.'

'I would not be averse to seeing more of the Professor myself. He seems an interesting fellow.'

'I am glad at last you agree.'

At this point my friend hesitated once again. I had not often seen him embarrassed. I thought he was perhaps about to say something about the observations the Professor had made about himself, but I was mistaken. I was correct to diagnose embarrassment, but it was upon another matter: he returned to my account of the case.

'I am sorry to have to mention this again, Watson,' he said. 'It's about your manuscript that Frau Rosenthal has returned.'

'Yes,' I replied. 'What about it?'

'I think you continued with the story, did you not? I think I convinced you that I would get back the part that went missing, did I not, and that therefore your time would not be wasted if you wrote the conclusion?'

'Well, not exactly, Holmes. I did do a bit more on it, mostly in the form of notes. I wrote up our meeting with the Professor, since I thought that was too good to be allowed to slip away, but I have not completed the case. I have not written anything else since we got back to England, for instance. I was not able to continue with it since I could not bear to write more without the earlier part. I know you had tried to reassure me but, as someone who is not an author, you may not be able to understand how discouraging it is to contemplate writing all over again something that has been written already. In this case too it would have been especially difficult, since I had written the account with very careful attention to details as they happened. My manuscript was the only record, and without the exact details the case would have been much the poorer.'

'I knew you did not believe me. I could see how unhappy you remained about the whole matter.'

'I am sorry that I lost faith, Holmes. I should have known better.'

'Never mind that. I ask a favour, or rather two favours, perhaps three. First, I think that if you were to finish your account, then that would be very worthwhile. I myself would much appreciate a copy of the completed case. I would not ask you to make me a copy. I know a person of absolute discretion who could type it out, Watson.' He continued to look embarrassed as he said this.

'Secondly . . . secondly . . .' now Holmes hesitated again.

'Secondly, it would be a good gesture, do you not think, if you would send the completed story to Mrs Rosenthal?'

'You mean to Miss Vincent, Holmes: it is her case. Or do you mean to Frau Rosenthal?'

'Yes indeed, Watson, exactly: I meant Miss Vincent. In fact I would appreciate it very much if you would do that.'

I found myself, as so often in this case, perplexed about Holmes's motives. Was he at last indicating that he had been touched by Miss Vincent's predicament, and somehow wanted to express something of this to her, however obliquely, by having me send my story as a kind of peace offering? Had he, I wondered, been reflecting on the way in which the injustice of Miss Vincent's original misfortune had been multiplied beyond measure by what had befallen her? I wondered too whether the words said to him by the Professor had in some way been working within him, and that his embarrassment was because of the novelty of expressing something other than his usual austere views.

'Thirdly,' he continued, now seeming a trifle easier, though still tense, 'the largest favour of all. Mycroft has said to me that the minister would appreciate it if I do not in any way make my new position known. Nor, he says, must it be known even that Mycroft's department exists, or what kinds of relations they have with people abroad, or any of that kind of thing. Mycroft was somewhat disappointed that I had not been more circumspect. So if, Watson, you would not mind keeping this case back from general publication for a while, perhaps for a few years, perhaps permanently? I am afraid this will place a general stricture on your writing up cases of this kind we may undertake together. I hope, indeed I hope very much, that you will nevertheless feel able to accompany me, even without any prospect of pub-lication.' I was disturbed to see Holmes's eyes averted, as if ashamed at having to ask this of me, whilst at the same time requesting my continued companionship in his exploits. I had felt pleased about this new departure in his life, and had not realised that it would imply a prohibition of publication – but at the same time I found Holmes's appeal particularly affecting. I remained silent, uncertain how to respond.

Holmes resumed: 'I suppose I should not even suggest that you send the completed story of our present case to Frau Rosenthal and Miss Vincent, but since they have read the greater part it can do no further harm. You could, however, if you do send it, ask them to be especially discreet about it. Watson, I can trust your judgement, I know.'

This brings my story to a conclusion. It is a conclusion unlike any other I have written, since I am unable to explain in any satisfactory way why Holmes, seemingly in the last straight, has drawn back from determining exactly what the events were that stood at the centre of the case. Perhaps, as I like to believe, some inward change has taken place in my companion, who now seemingly is prepared to traffic with uncertainties, having been influenced by the meeting with the Professor that I had thought of arranging before we knew of Mr S and Miss Vincent. Even now, however, I find myself wondering about my friend's intentions. Also I have not settled on a title. My working title is 'The Viennese Affair'. In some ways I prefer 'The Case of the Fallen Diplomat', although the pun imparts a note of unseemly levity. In any event, here I bring my account to a conclusion. I dedicate the story to a person much put upon, in the hope that, in some small way, it may help her to a life that is less tormented than her previous one has been.

All that remains is to say that I have taken my friend's advice, and that although the story displays some of Sherlock Holmes's powers at their most subtle, I will not make this account available for general publication. On rereading it, moreover, I have decided that matters quite other than the strictures of the

Foreign Office make it unsuitable for my usual readership. I shall think, however, that the time I have devoted to writing this will have been well spent if I send the whole of this manuscript as it stands, the part that was returned together with the four further chapters, by registered post to Paris, to await collection from the Poste Restante Office.

32

The Narrative of Sara and Emily
continued

A Celebration

In a few days we had settled down to life in our new home. Sara would go on expeditions and return delighted with food from a market or with some useful household object, and from time to time vans would arrive and an item of furniture would be delivered. Sometimes we would both go out together, and I found that, apart from being still far from at ease with myself, Paris was just what I needed.

One day we had both gone together to the post office to see if there were letters for us. There were none for me, but several for Sara. She looked through them and said, 'Now here is the best present of all.' She handed me a letter.

221B Baker Street, London

Dear Frau Rosenthal,

I thank you for your communication, and confirm the inference you have made. The case is officially closed. I also confirm that Austrian police have concluded their investigations of the death of your friend's guardian. It has been recorded as an accident sustained while he was walking in the mountains, not an uncommon occurrence. The British Foreign Office has recorded the death as due to an accident, and for them too the file is closed.

With regard to the manuscript you asked me to pass on to Dr
Watson, I have done as you wished. He thanks you, and I believe
that you may expect a communication from the doctor himself in
a week or so.

I remain, madam, yours sincerely,

Sherlock Holmes

'The letter is formal, is it not?' Sara observed. 'I think you agree it
is conclusive.'

'Mr Holmes is a stiff sort of man. He dislikes women quite
strongly. You can read it between the lines in Dr Watson's
stories, but having met him one gets an even stronger impression.
He holds himself in check by being polite and formal, but to me
this makes him inhuman: I find him fearsome in the extreme. But
this letter does seem conclusive. The case is closed. It is a
relief . . .' and right there in the post office, in front of
everybody, I burst into an irrepressible flood of tears, which
seemed as if they would never stop.

In a cab on the way home I recovered myself somewhat, but
when we were indoors I ran up to the big bed, threw myself on it
and wept. Sara followed me and held my head in her lap, stroking
my hair. This somehow reminded me of my mother doing the
same thing, and my tears became yet more copious.

'Oh, Sara,' I said. 'Please hold me like that, and do not stop
. . . How I have wanted to be held, just like that, when that
hateful Mr S . . . started his wicked attentions. I longed to be
held like that. I longed for my mother to return, and take me
away, to tell me it was a bad dream . . . or somehow make it
better, just somehow, but really I was quite alone . . . I had to be
brave, and endure, and hold on tight, hold on tight, not let
anything touch me . . . Now he is dead – which I am glad of. See
how wicked I am, even to think that. I am glad, because it is
finished and can never happen again, never . . . At the same time

I have found you. You even understand, and accept me, although I have been so wicked.'

For what seemed like hours I wept wordlessly, as if the tears I could not shed when my parents died had been stored up and were now flooding out. Strangely, when I stopped I felt relief. Sara was still there. She had been holding me, not talking, still patient.

'I feel better for having wept like that,' I said. 'I don't know why. Somehow you have been able to make better the hateful disaster I have made of my life. This will sound most odd to you. I imagined when you were there, holding me, that you were my mother. Yourself at the same time, but also my mother. That seems strange to say . . .' As I said this, I noticed that Sara's eyes too had filled with tears. I was terrified lest what I had said had offended her. 'I'm sorry,' I said, 'was that a hurtful thing to say? I am sorry.'

'No,' she said. 'It is not hurtful at all. The opposite. I felt that after your life of so much holding in, and not trusting, now you trust me. I am crying because I feel very . . . I don't know how you say it. I feel honoured. No that's not right. I feel very close to you, and glad to be here, and to have in myself something to remember your mother whom you loved.' After an interval she said, 'Let me now make some dinner, and then after that we can go to bed properly. We have this bed to be together in now. I think we need a celebration. I shall go to do a little shopping, and then I come back directly. Is that agreeable?'

'Yes, perfectly.'

I lay on our bed in a kind of daze, just letting my thoughts drift, and knowing that to allow them to do this, without their heading for some fearful abyss into which they would plunge me, was a wonderful luxury. I thought of Sara walking along the road to the shops, with her long confident stride and her open expression that made people turn to see her. I thought just how extraordinary it was for us to be here, and to have discovered the things we have. I pictured her entering the *épicerie* and asking for provisions. I felt at one with her, as if connected by some magic thread, which soon I could tug upon gently so that she would be drawn back to me, to our home here. If only I can be good enough to make her happy, as she deserves. In this state I feel a kind of grace. My mind is filled with Sara, rather than myself. It is a kind of pure altruism. If only I could keep my mind in this state all the time. If only.

I do not know whether it had been a long time or a short one, or whether I had dozed off to sleep for a few moments or not, but I heard the door open, and Sara called out:

'Home!' That is what it is for us. Home. Or it could be.

'I'm coming,' I called back.

'We make a celebration of the end of the game,' she said. 'In the game of chess in motion that we played, the men have resigned, and therefore the women have won. You do not like me thinking it was a game, but that is not a bad way to think. I believe those men do not know that women could be a match for them. Therefore they were not prepared, which is good for us. Otherwise more difficult they will have been.'

'I suppose we could think of it like that.'

'You agree at least that we should celebrate?' She smiled.

'Yes, yes a thousand times. I felt, when you were holding me, that despite what has happened, everything may be all right again, without that awful threat in the back of my mind, waiting to burst out and flood over everything. It is you who have been able to make it all right.'

'Good. I like you to appreciate me. Now I make dinner. Very quick, very simple. I have bought an extra nice bottle of wine.' Sara produced a bottle of Moët. 'The patron of the café to which we go also gave me some ice. I must not forget to return this vessel. Here, we put the wine in here.'

Sara had bought a *baguette*, tomatoes, some Italian ham, some Brie and one of those tempting apple tarts that the French make. I laid the table, and Sara busied herself putting out the things she had bought, cutting tomatoes and sprinkling them with herbs.

'*Prosciutto?*' I asked. 'You know this is from pigs. Are you going to eat this?'

'Why not?' she answered. 'I have broken with tradition in many ways, why not in this one? I think we are now safe from dietary disaster of eating the pig. You can open the wine, when you think it is enough cold.'

We ate well, but did not drink more than half the bottle between us. I found I could not stop gazing at Sara as she spoke happily of how she liked living in this way, as Bohemians, she said. Perhaps nobody really needs servants, she continued. Then those people could be employed in other ways, perhaps in making things that would be useful. 'Although,' she added, 'perhaps there are already enough things. There seems no shortage of things in Paris.'

'I am so glad to have found you,' I said. 'I do not deserve you. It is as if my life, which started well, went into a long dark, cold tunnel, which seemed to be heading further and further away from everything worthwhile. Then suddenly, and unexpectedly, it has emerged into the light.'

'This is a good thing to say to me,' said Sara. 'I feel that to find you has been most good also.'

'Come,' I said, 'even though it is not late, shall we go to our bedroom, to our *grand lit*? I want to hold you close to me, not just to be held like a child. Quite close, and quite softly. Can that too be part of the celebration?'

So we did. Of all the confusing things, and all the turmoil of my life in the last weeks, nothing is so difficult to write about as this, my love for Sara. Not just love but our closeness. For me, for whom these matters had meant only a loathsome violation and a tight withholding of myself, what had occurred with Sara was a complete upturning of everything I knew. Could it have been that I could not contemplate marriage to Thornton because I was too much afraid that what we would have to do as man and wife would destroy what affection I had for him? No; although that thought occurred to me, it is too intellectual as usual. It had been deeper than that. I had recoiled from him involuntarily. I just simply could not make any move that would have led in that direction. Allowing him to think of me as someone he might marry was perhaps bad faith all along. Though perhaps not: I remember hoping that it would be all right, that my feelings would become properly ordered towards him, and that when he kissed me I would somehow feel the right thing, but it had not been so. I felt unclean, repelled. I could not help myself from holding back.

Then how, I wondered, has Sara managed to allow me to feel differently when what we did together, what we do together, is against everything that people are brought up to believe? With her I do not feel frightened, or intruded upon, or repelled. I do not feel that what we do is wicked. It is pure and lovely in every respect . . .

See: I just cannot write about it.

Let me try more carefully. My journal began with the horror and the effects of embraces that repelled me. I recorded that; and if I am to be truthful I must now be able to record its opposite, the embrace for which I long, and which has made me free. For that is how it feels.

After the relief of the pursuit having been called off, and our meal of celebration, we went up to our room. 'Now,' I had said, 'I am going to get you ready for bed. We do without servants, but this evening, I will be your lady of the bedchamber, and get you ready to go to bed, and then a little later your lover will appear.'

When I think about this, I am almost appalled at my

wantonness. From where did such thoughts spring? How did I have the courage to make such bold suggestions, to carry out such actions? With her it seemed, as one might say, natural. I felt taken over – no, that is not the right expression because it negates the action of my own will – I felt drawn towards expressing to her not just affection but also these activities of lovers. When I have read about them, and I have read about them frequently in classical texts and elsewhere, they have seemed to me alien, but now, in this state and in this mood, I cannot help myself being drawn to expressions of this same kind.

So, first, I took off Sara's outer garment. 'You are not to do a single thing for yourself,' I said, 'unless I ask you to. Now step out of your dress, and sit here in front of this mirror.' She did as I asked, and sat in her undergarments, while I brushed her thick hair, and while we could both see ourselves reflected in the small mirror with its simple wooden frame.

'Now you must just sit there for a minute, while I run your bath.'

When I returned Sara had sat as I asked. I stood beside her, with our eyes meeting in the mirror, and I unfastened her bodice. Then she sat with the upper part of her body quite bare. I believe I have never seen anyone so beautiful, and a tremor ran through my body as I gazed at her, and again the words of Sappho came back to me: 'a fine flame runs beneath my skin'.

'Now you must remove your other clothes,' I said, with complete calm, 'and when you have done so, come directly into the bathroom.'

I departed to supervise the running of the water into the deep enamelled bath. I added some perfumed oil, and in a moment of inspiration slipped quickly out of my own clothes too – which were not too many, because of the warmness of the weather.

Sara arrived in the doorway, modestly covering part of herself. I kissed her gently on the cheek, and led her to the bath. 'You can get in now.' She did so, and I soaped her all over, before climbing in at the other end where the big brass taps were. I sat and looked at her, happy at the expression on her face, which seemed contented, restful.

'Shall I wash you too?' she asked.

'No, certainly not, I said you must do only as I say.'

'Very well. I am quite obedient.'

'Only quite obedient?' I asked.

'What do you mean?'

'Nothing, it's just a peculiarity of expression. English is not a logical language. Sometimes "quite" means "very" and sometimes it means "not very".'

'In that case I meant what I say. I am quite obedient.'

'So you are.'

I washed myself quickly and then jumped out, leaving Sara resting back in the bath, with the top of her head just visible above the rim, as I dried myself and ran to our room to get my nightgown. 'You are just to remain there for a little while,' I said as I left. 'Are you comfortable? Has the water become too cold?'

'It is exactly right,' she said.

When I returned after turning down the covers of our bed, now wearing my nightdress and with my hair brushed, she was still in the same position. 'You may get out when you are ready,' I said.

'I am ready,' she replied, rising with the water running from her body, and with inches added to her height by the big bathtub.

'Step out and I will dry you.' We had bought some big towels, which were just right after one had taken a bath. I wrapped her in one, and gently rubbed her back and legs. 'You may finish drying yourself,' I said as I went to let the water out of the bath, 'and when you have done that,' I said as I left the bathroom again, 'you may come into the bedroom, and I shall meet you there.'

I ran into the bedroom, and suddenly could not think why I

339

was wearing my nightgown. I hurriedly took it off and put it under the pillow, and sat shamelessly on the bed, awaiting her.

She appeared in the doorway. She had left the towel in the bathroom. Now she was no longer screening herself. 'Come,' I said, laying my hand on the sheet beside me, and as she climbed on to the bed I put my arm around her shoulder and found her mouth as eager as my own. How can I describe it? I think perhaps I cannot. It is one of those things that cannot be described, only referred to, so that someone else who has known the same sensation, or felt the same way for another person, will recognise it. One could not describe it to someone who had never known that sense expressed in closeness and caresses. Such a person, like myself in former times when I would read about such things, would not understand the thousandth part of what was described.

'Must I still obey?' she asked.

'Oh, no. Now you have found your lover awaiting you, you may do as you please. In fact you must do as you please.'

'Then I will please again kiss,' she said.

We seemed to drift into a timeless state. I had the strongest impulse gently to stroke every last part of her – her ears, the nape of her neck where her hair began, her shoulders – all that soft warm skin, and much more which even in my shameless state I cannot say; though as I write and recall, I think of the poem that Marvell wrote, describing, like a voyage of exploration taken by a seafarer, each part of his loved one's body.* I cannot bring myself still to use his words, but how well, how well at last, I understand that feeling. Unlike Marvell, however, who complained about the coyness of his lover, I make no such complaint.

It is right, this thing that I had been thinking: however striking

* Andrew Marvell, 'To his coy mistress'.

340

the poem had been to me before, only now do I truly know that metaphor of exploration that the poet created. Sara was a new land to me. After torments, storms, tempests, a new land, of both body and spirit, entirely unexpected but at the same time a land one had secretly believed might exist in some time and some place.

Unlike any physical exploration, Sara let me know by a little movement here or a sigh there that this was not just me exploring, but we both were discovering something that is only possible together. A kind of expansion of the self into the other person, with new possibilities, and with a harmony of correspondence between wish and fulfilment.

'Here,' I said, 'I want you to sit like this.' I sat and leant back against several pillows at the head of the bed, and had Sara lean back against me. I felt her back pressing into me, and allowed myself to move a little, imagining what she might feel at her back. In that position I could not only nuzzle into Sara's neck, but my hands seemed ideally placed for yet further explorations, both above and below, heightened by a little assistance from Sara's own hands, urging me forward, which increased the trembling and tension that were running through my body.

When I found that secret place, Sara too was trembling, and this effect I was having on her seemed to me the most wonderful thing. It was as if I were able gently to touch her innermost being, which in response would quiver in unison with myself. The trembling increased until Sara's whole body seemed alive, and I imagined her like a bird taking wing and flying towards the sun. At the very top of her flight she sighed, such a sigh, hovering there in my arms. Me holding her: myself able for a moment to contain her, for that instant to care for her completely, in the way she had cared for me.

We stayed like that for some minutes, and I think she must have dozed for a moment, for her body had grown heavy on me. I

341

wanted just to hold her like that, but I felt one of my arms tingle and grow numb – and I was too excited to avoid longing that she would move, and I could spread myself out before her.

As she sat up, she placed my limbs just so, divining what had been in my mind. She then began to caress me gently, giving also a little kiss here and there, even in places that one might think she should not, though I had been longing for exactly that touch. Then too I started to feel that sensation, so sweetly that my body was trembling again. It was no longer my own but just hers. Then it was as if just precisely, exactly, that thing for which I longed began to occur. It was as if some telepathic link were formed so that, without my actions, my thoughts and desire were transmitted directly and wordlessly to her, and her actions then returned to me, and so perfect was this circle that when complete it made the whole world collapse into a single point, and then expand again, infinitely.

As I lay there, feeling the presence of Sara close by my side, thoughts came unbidden, of a stream beside a meadow, smelling of childhood and of happiness that had been regained. Images came, floating by, came from where I do not know. A tree, a house, a road winding up a gentle slope to a promontory with classical buildings and a temple. My mind in that state for a little while escaped from the confines of my own life, to some more universal place. It was as if in my life I had struggled through a dense thicket of thorns, not knowing my way, and I had now somehow come upon a wall in which there was a tiny, hidden, secret door, through which I passed into a garden of the most calm and peaceful kind. Whereas among the thorns my thoughts were constrained and controlled, and could only be directed to matters of escape, now here my thoughts could just run and expand, without let, without danger. As they did so they simply, exquisitely, turned themselves into a series of floating images, in each of which I was somehow a part.

33

The Narrative of Sara and Emily
continued

Letters to and from Paris

For several days after that day of tears in the post office, the day of the meal of celebration and the evening of infinitude, I would often just burst into floods of weeping, sometimes when Sara was there, sometimes when I was on my own. It was as if all my unshed tears had now to be let out. I was able to think calmly of my mother sometimes, and my father too.

Incidents in my life with Sara would set off a memory. Such memories of happiness had been too painful before, when everything associated with them was lost. Now, my emotions having been freed, I could think of things that had been previously unthinkable.

This had its bad side too: my anxious thoughts had not departed; they also became more acute. Though the imminence of discovery has receded, I still cannot keep from myself my own action in pushing Mr S away. Often that memory floods into my mind. Am I imagining that it is occuring more often again, now that I feel safer? I still have fits of cold terror seeing him coming up that mountain path after me, thrusting him away in fear as he grasped my dress, and watching helplessly as he lost his footing. Again like Raskolnikov, I find that my mind keeps returning to this moment, this fixed point to which my life led, and around which it turned. I cannot speak to Sara, since she has been so good, so generous. I am going mad, tortured by my own guilty conscience. Several times I have imagined giving myself up, taking the train back to Vienna and going to the police to announce: 'I am a murderess.' In this state I feel I do not deserve to live, that people who have murdered must be hanged. I have no right to exist.

One day, as just such a sequence of thoughts tightened its grip on me while I sat alone, Sara returned from an outing and said, 'Here we have a present from Dr Watson. I have just collected it from the post office. It is addressed to me, and enclosed is a letter to us both. It came by registered post.'

Sara handed me a bulky envelope, from which I drew the manuscript we had lately sent back to England. I read the letter that was on top of it.

Mes chères Mesdames,

I felt encouraged by your letter, and by the return of my manuscript, to complete the story enclosed. I have decided not to publish it in the normal way, for reasons that you may discern for yourselves.

I have decided instead that the story is for just three readers. Forgive me for its unpolished state, and also for my uncertainty about the title, for which I mention two possibilities at the end of the story, but I am not fully satisfied. Perhaps you could think of a title that would be preferable.

I would like to say that in writing this story I have been led to think more deeply than heretofore on the subject of the evils that can befall the fairer sex in ways that we men are never subject to. It is my opinion that the central character of this tale had been very grievously wronged. I can imagine all too clearly how the fearful scene on the mountainside must have taken place. As a humble doctor I thought I would jot down the following thought about the matter: No guilt, I believe, would attach to the central character in a story such as this, in the eyes either of the law or of

God. The doctor in this story may have helped persuade the detective to temper his pursuit of facts with understanding. If this meets with your approval then I would be pleased indeed.

I would be honoured if you would count me a friend and, if you ever need one at any time in the future, also a loyal ally.

Yours sincerely,

JHW

'What a very kind letter Dr Watson has written,' I said to Sara. 'He still seems concerned not to be too explicit, as if he thinks it would be dangerous for anyone to discover this. Of course the names he has given his characters are different from ours, another subterfuge. He seems to have completed the narrative especially for us. See here, there are four chapters we had not seen.'

I could scarcely wait to read the final chapters of his manuscript that Dr Watson had added. Then, as I read the whole story from beginning to end, I wondered if this tale of intrigue and detection had really concerned myself, or if it had happened to some person whom I only knew rather distantly. I marvelled at the minute and painstaking way that Sherlock Holmes had pursued his task. If he had not decided to call off his pursuit, perhaps persuaded by the gallant doctor, I knew what would have happened. There would have been but little hope of escape for me, though I could not help wondering in an abstract way whether in Sara's ingenious stratagems Holmes might have met his match. After all there was that other recorded case of his defeat, by Irene Adler.* Perhaps the detective had an Achilles heel, so that he was not as readily able to predict the workings of the female mind as that of the male.

*This is another reference to 'A Scandal in Bohemia' in *The Adventures of Sherlock Holmes*.

I composed a careful reply to the doctor, thanking him very kindly for so generously finishing his manuscript for us when he could have taken such a very different view of its loss. I thanked him even more for his consoling words. Both Sara and I assured him of our safekeeping of the manuscript, and of our complete secrecy over Sherlock Holmes's involvement. I also said that I had returned the manuscript of Professor Freud, to await his return from holiday, so he need no longer concern himself about it.

This last was an untruth: I was glad that I had not yet returned the Professor's manuscript before seeing the details of the meeting of Holmes and Freud in the doctor's story. In order to be almost truthful in my letter to Dr Watson, I re-read once more the manuscript of the Professor, and began a letter to him that I could post at the same time as my letter to Dr Watson.

Dear Professor Freud,

My main purpose in writing, apart from returning your manuscript, which I enclose, is to make a confession. I do not know whether you will have guessed it from the visit Sherlock Holmes made you, but I am a guilty woman. The reason I fell ill was that I pushed my guardian away from me on a mountain path where he had pursued me, and ever since have been tortured by the guilt of his death. Though Sherlock Holmes has called off his hunt, I feel in some way that I need to confess this to you. Is it perhaps because in all the time I was seeing you, though it was uppermost in my mind, I kept it from you, so that now I must make the amends of this admission to you at least? Is it because, as you yourself suggested, I had come to think of you in some way as like my father? I do not know. Neither do I know what I wish you to do about this awful fact. As each day passes, more and more I think that I should return to Vienna and hand myself over to the police . . .

I re-read this, and was appalled. Could this really be what I had written and was about to send through the public mails, when Dr Watson has taken such care to try and tell me I was not guilty? Is this what I wanted to say?

Yes. The truth is that I long to send some such letter to the Professor. Why do I have such a strong urge to confess to him, or to the police? Dr Watson says he does not condemn me. Sara does not condemn me. Why is this not enough?

I read somewhere, perhaps in one of the journals in which I was reading the Professor's papers, of a young man tortured by guilt of crimes that he did not commit, who was unable to restrain himself from visiting police stations in order to make confessions. How well I feel I can understand that young man. The difference, of course, is that I have committed a crime. Although to confess to the Professor or to the police would mean the end of my life, a life that is good now that I have found Sara, I may not be able to restrain myself from giving myself up.

It is all so illogical. When there was a danger that the Professor would cajole from me some unconsidered slip by which I would give myself away, or when Holmes and Watson were pursuing me, then it seemed natural to resist, to keep my secret and try to elude them. Both these dangers are past, but I am in greater danger than before – from myself. What can I do? I cannot tell Sara. She will be appalled and dreadfully hurt that I should even consider such an action as giving myself up. How would she think of it, except as meaning that I do not love her, since the action would destroy our life together?

I believe I do love her. Simply I am unable to untangle this knot. If I am guilty, then I ought not to live – at least not happily. Perhaps, after long years in prison, in thorough disgrace, having become known as a murderesss or manslaughterer or however I would be judged, then I could live in a despised and obscure way. The difficulty is that with Sara I am happy. Is that what makes this tormenting, because I swing from being more happy than I thought possible to this abject state, then back again?

Now here I am writing in this way again, self-concerned and private. This I cannot show Sara. What can I do? Have I truly become mad? I had not known that this was what madness was like. It is not seeing strange visions; it is thinking thoughts that completely contradict one another. On the one hand, I feel the most utter relief, and periods of intense happiness with Sara. On the other hand I long to give myself up. I can scarcely prevent myself from doing so, to be disgraced and hanged for a crime of which I am truly guilty, because I did kill Mr S. I had wished he were dead — so I had the motive, and I pushed him away in a place which was dangerous enough for him to be killed. That is all there is to it.

Some hours later I have read this over, together with the beginning of that unthinkable letter to the Professor. It will not do. Sara returned home. We have eaten dinner together. She has gone to see a friend she knew in Vienna who now lives here, and I said that I would stay home to write some letters. I do feel much better now, having been with Sara: I am a different person than this afternoon. Is that part of the madness too, feeling to be two different persons? Which one is myself? Which is the stronger?

While in my current mood I must write a proper letter to the Professor, and post it, so that then I will not send one of the other kind. Here is a more sensible letter.

Dear Professor Freud,

As you will see from this address, I have moved to Paris and my friend Sara Rosenthal has accompanied me.

I am returning the manuscript about my case, which had in a roundabout way come into my possession. I know you were concerned about it, since it was lost from Dr Watson's hotel room, and I hope therefore you will be pleased at its return. Apart from Dr Watson, and Sara and myself, it has not been seen by anyone else, so I hope you do not consider that ours were the wrong hands for your paper to have fallen into.

Be that as it may, I imagine that you had not directly anticipated that any medical case history you had written would be read by the patient whom it concerns, but I think you might none the less be interested in my reactions to it. In part, of course, as you may imagine, I felt pained by some of what you wrote, but in general I feel you have been accurate in your account of factual matters, and I also very much appreciate the strenuous application of thought that you have devoted to my case. If your method became widely adopted, only the most subtle and devoted thinkers could ever become doctors of your kind, who undertake analyses of people's inner lives.

First, of course, as you have every right to expect, I must make you an apology. As you will have learnt at your meeting with Mr Holmes and Dr Watson, the immediate cause of my falling ill was not any sexual event between myself and Sara, as you surmised, but the reappearance of my guardian. I am sorry I was not more candid about this. I hope you will forgive me. I felt I could not say anything to you about it. I think you believe that a patient's inability to speak candidly about matters which directly affect his case is part of the illness, and perhaps you are right. In any event, I hope you can accept my apology for withholding this material information.

About other parts of the case history let me say that that in many respects you have understood me very well – in some ways perhaps too well. Your understanding leaves me feeling almost as if I had appeared in public wearing only my undergarments. In the course of the analysis, however, I have come to understand aspects of my own life and character much better than previously, and I am heartily grateful for this.

Please do not think me impertinent if I say that, while I freely acknowledge that I have gained in understanding of what had been hidden in myself, there are parts of your case history, particularly your idea that the attentions of my guardian were merely a phantasy, that I cannot corroborate. What I told you about his attentions, their continuance, their effects on me and the nature of the actions involved was literally, regrettably, true. I believe that what Mr Holmes told you will have confirmed the fact of these attentions, if not the details. Perhaps if I had told you of the reappearance of my guardian at my rooms you would have believed me, but I am sure that now at least you will see that the part of my life between the age of fourteen and my departure for America had been for me an unspeakable nightmare, from which I am only now emerging. I repeat that I thank you for your part in assisting that emergence, but at the same time I believe that your researches on myself took an incorrect turn with your conclusion that I was merely engaging in virulent adolescent phantasies.

Please do not imagine I am reproaching you for thinking I might have entertained phantasies of seduction by my guardian. I should tell you that as well as your dream book, and *The Psychopathology of Everyday Life*, I have also read the book on hysteria which you published with Dr Breuer, and also some other papers of yours published in medical journals, and I have begun to understand from your works that people suffering from hysteria may have symptoms that are very strange. So for you to think that I too suffered from strange symptoms, and that you had come to doubt the stories of seductions told to you by women suffering from hysteria, is easily comprehensible to me. If your inferences were not correct in my case, I was to blame, because I kept from you an important fact: that my assailant had returned with protestations and blandishments – a fact so appalling to me that it devastated my life in Vienna. So please regard me as responsible for misleading you in this way. The representation I make to you now is that, from your manuscript, you seem *too* eager to accept this other conclusion, the conclusion that my sickness had been caused by phantasy, and try as I may I am unable to see the compelling reasons for your conclusion. I say this with great respect for your powers of inference. I hope I am not merely being self-justificatory when I say that I beg you to consider that the situation in which I found myself, of being unwillingly subjected to unwelcome embraces, may be common, as you yourself once believed.

Other than that, I would of course like to discuss with you this point or that, and perhaps even argue with you about some things, but I would have no serious contradictions to offer.

I would like finally to say something, however, about the last part of your manuscript; even though, as you say yourself, you feel uncertain about parts of what you say there.

I am even sure you know what I shall say. I do not feel that my love for Sara, though technically called 'homosexual', is perverse. On the contrary it feels good and true. There is too much of gratitude and dependency on my part, and not enough that I give her. All the same it is not perverse, as I understand the term. As perhaps you can imagine, I have thought long about this, wondered if it were perverse, or sinful, or wicked. I would however like to say to you that I now do not believe it is so. If human love has anything of good in it, then the love that is possible between two women is just as worthy as that between a man and a woman.

I do not know quite how best to think about this theoretically, and I do not imagine that anything I say from my own experience would convince you. I also think that your idea that sexuality develops over stages, and that in order to explain how each of us can as children love both our father and our mother requires that we are each fundamentally bisexual, is a wonderfully imaginative theory. Instead of your idea of attraction to someone of one's own sex being due to fixation at a certain point during development, however, why could it not be that, with a bisexual nature, one can come to love either someone of one's own or of the opposite sex, as a matter of upbringing and what we are led to expect? I am sure you know that homosexuality was common in classical Greece, and thinking over this I am rather attracted to Plato's idea that love is like finding the lost half of ourselves.* For some this half is the other sex, and for some the same sex. No doubt the fairy tale on which Plato bases this is childish. At the same time is there anything, other than the need for some other member of our species to reproduce, that decrees that the only love that is not perverse must be for the opposite sex? According to your own doctrines, love is based more on experience with parents than on biology.

I am not sure about any of this, and as I sit and write it I feel my words are dreadfully inadequate. I would like so much to be able to come and talk these things over with you. I did very much appreciate the help you gave me, and I still think often of your offer for me to continue, after the summer holidays, the treatment which I started. Though we are in Paris now, I do not know whether we may return to Vienna. If we do, I shall come and discuss the possibility with you, otherwise I shall write.

So here, duly returned, is the case of Miss Emily V. May I ask a favour? If you have, as you said to Dr Watson, another copy, and if you have no objection, I would very much appreciate it if you would send this one back to me – the whole of it, including the last part, without changing it at all, please, even if you rewrite it later in the light of the additional information you now have. I long to keep it as a memento of yourself that I can treasure. I can then re-read it, and think it over as many times as I like. As I am sure you know, I still have many things that I do not fully understand about myself. Your manuscript would be a gift of something of yourself that I would value very much. It would help me to contemplate those matters that I am sure I still am unwilling to acknowledge about myself.

I will let you know if my address changes.

Yours with thanks, and yet more apologies,

Emily Vincent

*In the *Symposium*.

I made a fair copy of the letter and addressed it to the Professor's house at Berggasse 19, and labelled it 'Private and Confidential: To await return from holidays'. I had enough postage stamps, and I went out into the summer night to find a posting box straight away, so as not to give myself any chance of changing my mind.

I inserted the letter to Dr Watson into the box. Then I put in my package to Professor Freud: the moment I heard it drop, an anxious feeling overcame me. Had I been honest? Had I said the right thing to the Professor? Under the guise of a careful letter, I had been evasive about the most central thing. My machinations had taken hold of me. Even in confession I was false. I should have sent the other letter, saying what I had done. My crime would find me out. I walked through the streets, retracing recent events, now including the arrival in Paris of Watson's story, and my reading of it.

All at once something struck me: it was Sherlock Holmes who had wanted Watson to complete the story, and send it to us. Why had he done that? He is a man of infinite wiles, who regularly employs deception. I tried to recall his letter. He said the case was officially closed. But he was anything but official in his methods. I had been alerted by Professor Freud's ideas to wonder about discrepancies and about motives: the last chapters of the doctor's manuscript had large discrepancies, and a lack of closure – Holmes talked of the case being closed, but also that it irked him to leave it unfinished. He thought me capable of some cunning, and he talked about reeling in the line that still connected us to him. When Lotte was overhearing their conversation at breakfast in the Hotel Imperial, Holmes had by no means given up. Unknown to Sara, he was keeping careful watch. The idea of getting Watson to send the story could be a ruse, to let us think that the case had finished. Watson several times says that Holmes never gives up, and at the end of his story he pronounced himself puzzled at Holmes's intentions.

Then it crashed in on me. Sara had been too trusting. This very correspondence would make it simple for Holmes to trace me. Perhaps even the postmark of the letter that I had let drop into the posting box, now already irretrievable, would indicate the district in which it had been posted. Moreover, we had been trotting backwards and forwards to the Poste Restante Office. That would be it: Holmes could pay someone to have it watched. Sara was all too easy to recognise, being nearly six foot tall. Or Holmes could have devised some way of getting the post office to notice when the packet was picked up, because it was registered and Sara would have to sign for it. In either case Sara could be followed, and so with very little difficulty I might be discovered. Holmes might reappear at any moment. He still had in his possession the evidence that would surely convict me in a court of law, and perhaps his hatred of women, which comes over so clearly in the story, is such that he would want to see me brought to justice. In a frenzy I wondered whether I should return home, or whether I should communicate to Sara that our house was no longer safe, that it was even now being watched. I thought of finding some paper – it was too late to buy any – and giving some money to someone to deliver a note to Sara.

After another hour of pacing the dark streets, turning these burning thoughts over and over, the idea no longer seemed so compelling. Instead the reassuring tone of the doctor's letter came uppermost in my mind, with the idea that he would be our ally. My sense from meeting him was of kindliness, while that other one had the quality of cruel implacability that I knew all too well. Why the thought of the doctor had now come uppermost, I cannot say. Perhaps the thought was prompted by my ever-present urge to make confession. Now it seemed that he really would be my ally as he had offered. I could confess, and the doctor would make sure that I was not handed over. If they both appeared here on our doorstep, the doctor would prevail upon his friend and intercede on my behalf.

So, my panic subsided and, furtively circling round our house, unable to detect any lurking watchers in the gloom, I returned home.

34

The Narrative of Sara and Emily continued

A Decision

'Soon we must decide,' announced Sara one day.

'Decide what?' I asked, interrupting a train of thought that began with an image of opening the door to the gaunt figure of Sherlock Holmes on the doorstep, and continued with the question of whether I should go to the largest office of the *gendarmerie* in Paris so that they would be able to telegraph or telephone to Vienna and discover that there had indeed been some suspicion about the death of Mr S. I imagined instructing the officer in charge about what questions exactly he should ask of me.

'I mean we must come to a decision about what we will do. Will we stay in Paris, or return to Vienna?'

'Oh Sara, I find that so difficult to think about. What would you like?'

'I have thought much on the subject,' said Sara. 'Very much, and I must discuss it with you. First, there is nothing now to stop us returning to Vienna. You are not in danger there. Even it would have the advantage that you can finish treatment with Dr Freud, since I believe you are still not quite well. You have quite bad moods, I think you are sometimes happy, but sometimes very quiet and keeping yourself away from me. I find it disturbing.'

I was shocked at this from Sara. I did not know my moods had been so obvious to her. 'I am sorry I am moody,' I said. 'I have tried to get over it, but you are right, of course. I still sometimes feel very fearful, and withdraw into myself. I am sorry. Please bear with me a little longer.'

'I do not reproach you. Of consequences for us of possible actions I wish to think. If we will remain here then I must finally give up my post at the school, also the Educational Association, also give up seeing often my mother and father, my friends, my house in Vienna. Perhaps still this will be best. I have thought that here in Paris I can start an institute for women's education. All women could come, and they could learn whatever they liked, languages, science, how to run a shop; even how to make things perhaps, like men do, all kinds of things. As well as learning, some will have skills to teach. I can use some of my money to buy a building, and we can arrange the rooms for different functions, for large lectures, for small talks, a laboratory, a library of books especially for women, rooms for a few people to discuss, or just to sit and read. I think my new occupation can be as the administrator of such an institute. I will do that well I think. Perhaps also to teach some subjects, such as science. If we do that you can have a job also, without problems of a letter from your previous employer. That way, we can both use our skills, and I can carry on what I have learnt in running our educational association in Vienna . . .'

Sara talked on in this way for some time, thinking now of this aspect of her plan and then that one, airing first one idea about such an institute, then another. Finally she said: 'What do you think? Why do you not say something?'

'I do not know. It seems a good idea.'

'Is that all you say? That it is a good idea? This is our life together that we discuss, and you only say it is a good idea. What is wrong?'

'Nothing is wrong. It is a good idea. Truly it is. I just do not know what to say.'

'You have nothing to say, no suggestions, nothing about your part in this, and you say nothing is wrong! I think of a plan that means changing my life, for us, and for you, and you have nothing to say. You have become very self-concerned.'

'Sara, I am sorry, I did not mean it like that, I merely meant that what you have suggested seemed a good idea, an excellent idea. I am sorry I did not add anything. I am sorry. I did not mean . . .'

'I know what you meant. We will not discuss this.' With that Sara marched out of the room, and a few seconds later I heard a door slam as she left the house.

It has come to this, I thought. We are quarrelling. The reason is me. It is that I have become too much absorbed in my guilt that I can no longer even take part in a conversation, when Sara has done everything for me and is now talking about rearranging her whole life for me. She has every right to be angry. I am not worthy of her. I have not only been corrupt, and then committed the most wicked of all deeds possible for human beings, but I cannot even be grateful, or give my share to the friendship. I only take from her, just take everything. Now I think she hates me.

I sobbed tears of self-pity – not the healing tears that I had wept before, but bitter tears of dejection and reproach for my life and my situation. Sara did not return, and hence did not observe me weeping. I found, on thinking about it, that I had wanted her to return and find me in tears. At length I stopped.

She is right, of course, to be angry. She should just leave and go back to Vienna. She should go now, and leave me to myself. Perhaps I will live here on my own, or perhaps I will hand myself over to the police and accept my punishment. If Sara has gone, that will be best. I will wait for a few days, and then do it. I will not have to involve her at all. That will be best.

That set of thoughts did not sustain itself. It was replaced by others, and by an action that they prompted. I left the house, to return thirty minutes later with a large bunch of flowers. Sara had still not returned. In fact she did not do so for another hour.

When she did return, I rushed over to her, threw my arms round her and said, 'I am sorry, I am truly sorry. I have become unbearably self-centred. You have every right to hate me. I need to continue my treatment with Professor Freud. I believe I have gone mad. Please forgive me. Look, I have bought these for you.'

'Flowers!'

'Yes, they are for you. To say I am sorry, and to hope that you will forgive me. I will make myself better, and become a better person.'

'But why . . .? What is all this about? I had almost decided, when I was out, to leave you here and to go back to Vienna on my own. I have a life there. If you do not want to, if you are so unhappy with me, as sometimes I think you are when you do not speak for many hours, we need not make life here together.'

'No, it is not that. I am not unhappy with you. It is that I feel I do not deserve to be happy, so that when you talk about starting an institute in which we could both work, and do some good in, and make our life together . . . I feel I could not do it.'

'Why ever not?'

'I have been worrying terribly that Mr Holmes may come here, may have tracked us from our visits to the Poste Restante Office, and will come and find me. Then sometimes . . . quite often, I feel I might just give myself up to the police. I think I may not be able to stop myself. Such thoughts come into my mind, and though I try to oppose them, to argue them away, I cannot prevent them coming. I don't have these thoughts all the time, but when I do have them, it seems as if I will not be able to resist the urge to act always as a guilty fugitive, or else to give myself up. Either course would destroy everything. So, except for imagining myself to be in prison, I have not been able to think much about the future.'

'Why have you not said this to me? You are the most secretive person alive. You promise that you will not keep secrets like that any more. I knew there was something wrong, but I did not know what, or what to say. I thought you were unhappy with me. I began to lose confidence in us. I thought you felt badly about me, or our love, that it was unnatural.'

'No, it was none of those things. I could not tell you.'

'Why ever not?' Sara had not ceased being angry.

'Because if I had, you would have been most awfully hurt, that I was thinking of giving myself up rather than thinking of being with you.'

'You think that hurts more than withdrawing your mind, so that in truth you are not with me?'

'Oh Sara, you have every right to be angry. I am not myself. I believe I have gone mad. I will go to a doctor here. There are doctors with whom the Professor worked in Paris. I will explain everything; my guilt, everything.'

'You will do no such thing. Have you written to Professor Freud about your part in Mr S's death?'

'No, I wanted to, but I stopped myself.'

'Good. We shall need to think of this carefully.'

'You are not angry with me any more?'

'I am still angry that you did not tell me. I am angry that you keep these thoughts private, because you promised me that of this kind you would hold no more secrets. I felt confused by you, and your silence. I may forgive you, but perhaps not for some time.'

We did then manage to make it up – but only by my promising that if I had any more mad thoughts I would tell her.

'Your secretiveness leads to the madness,' Sara said. 'The secretiveness is the madness. Because if you tell me these thoughts, then you will not find yourself in such impossible position. Your secretiveness says that me you do not trust. In your case I can understand that you have little trust, even though it hurts me. Do you not see that by being untrusting you drive me away, so that then you truly could not trust me. You yourself create the loss of trust.'

She is right. She points right to the centre of it. She has been nothing but loyal and trustworthy.

Next day I again raised the subject of the institute for women's education. 'I am sorry I could not talk about it before,' I said. 'When you described your idea, it made me terrified, and I had those feelings of panic, I think because I thought you were doing it for me, and that I might let you down if I could not prevent myself from giving myself up to the authorities. Today I do not feel like that. I can talk about it properly. I think it is a wonderful idea, and if you would really like to do it, for yourself I mean, as well as for me or for us, then I think it would be just wonderful. I think perhaps Mr Holmes has really given up the pursuit, and if I can master this impulse to give myself up, my guilt will fade. I could really throw myself into an institute like that. It would be so worthwhile, and I could perhaps help other women to be independent. Perhaps I could do all the menial things, to help make up, just a little, for my wickedness.'

'I am glad you feel positive about it,' said Sara, 'but I do not wish to talk with you about this while you still keep secret thoughts. I do not want to risk starting something believing one thing, while in truth you are thinking some other thing. So, before we do anything more, or discuss our plans any further, there is a step that I think we should take, if you agree, to help arrest your desire to punish yourself, and to torture the one who loves you.'

'I do not mean to torture you.'

'Good. Then we shall see if you can stop it.'

'Yes.'

'You must do exactly as I say. This is about your trusting me. I cannot promise that this will be effective, but it may be. Do you promise?'

'I do, truly I do.'

'As punishment that will allow me to forgive you, you must trust me enough to ask no questions whatever, but just to do exactly as I say?'

I was not sure if she were teasing me, or serious. I decided the latter, and feeling abjectly repentant for almost driving away the one person who had been able to transform my life into something that could be good, I consented. I said, 'That seems a proper punishment for my secretiveness. I agree.'

'Very well then, I will expect the promise to be perfect.'

'Yes.'

'So, you must prepare for a journey. Perhaps in two weeks' time.'

'A journey?' I was bursting to ask where, and why, but of course I could not.

'No questions,' Sara reminded me.

'No questions,' I replied.

35

The Narrative of Sara and Emily continued

A Journey

Strangely, the next day, and the ones following, my mood of dejection and guilt did not press upon me. I felt able to be affectionate to Sara, in that proper way, the way in which I know I should be, not self-absorbed. I found myself wanting to do everything I could for her, I suppose to reassure her. If I could have a long interval when this mood predominated, what a tremendous relief it would be, and perhaps that other would just fade.

'This is very pleasant,' she said laughingly. 'I can see I shall have to set you more penance – is that how Catholics say? – then you are cheerful, and I am well cared for.'

Was I just a simple person, like that? Happy and affectionate if I were doing a penance, being constrained, like a child? No, not a child, worse: it made me think I was like a kind of machine, with a lever that, once pulled, set it going in a particular way; but I felt too relieved of my guilty and self-accusing mood to rebel against the idea. I felt also that my mood of love for Sara was somehow the right one. It was more really myself.

Sara was adamant that she would not discuss her institute with me. 'I do not want you to say something that hurts me about it. We may discuss it when we return,' she said. 'I believe you have what Professor Freud calls a conflict. Two wishes equally strong fight for your soul. One part of you does love me, I believe, and I am happy in this, because it means to me very much. The other part is punishing, and quite cruel. This is too important to me to risk that I discuss plans with the wrong one, with the wrong part of you.'

That Sara could talk to me like this took my breath away. I felt that I must have wounded her deeply. Or perhaps she had understood better than me the principles of Professor Freud's theories, and could see how they applied to me, where I could not.

I kept my resolve, though, and did not ask questions. I wondered about our journey. I cooked meals for Sara, and enjoyed being with her, just as in the days when we had first discovered our love for each other.

'May we read a book together?' I asked, a week or so after Sara had spoken of the journey. 'I would like to be able to read out loud, and discuss what we read, as we go along on our journey, perhaps.'

'I would like that. Shall we read in German or English, and what shall we read?'

'I have a suggestion. We will each choose books alternately.'

'Very well.'

'What about that book those American women we met last week were discussing? Did you not find their enthusiasm exciting?'

'Yes, I enjoyed very much meeting them. But which book do you mean?'

'*The Awakening*.* It is by an American, of the same age as ourselves.'

*A novel by Kate Chopin, published in 1899. It has a surprisingly modern theme: its central character Edna Pontellier is awakened from a stultifying marriage by falling in love.

Sara smiled. 'The title sounds, how do you say . . . suggestive?'

'Is there anything wrong with that?'

'No, not at all. The opposite.'

'Then I shall see if I can buy it, if I can obtain it here, otherwise I shall borrow it, and you must go and buy a German book, or any book you want really. You do not need to read aloud, I will do that. I would like to do something for you.'

I could not find the book by Kate Chopin at first, so we read Charlotte Brontë's *Villette*, about a woman teacher living away from her native land, and then *Tonio Kröger* by the new German writer Thomas Mann, about a character who was a kind of emotional orphan longing for love, who was divided in himself and became an author. Sara would sit in a comfortable chair, and I would read aloud. After each chapter we would discuss – anything: the writing, the ideas, the characterisation, whether we felt close to each character, what we thought this person or that ought to do. I was glad I had thought of the idea. It was something, however small at present, that I could do to build our friendship and to keep me from dwelling on myself.

Two weeks after our argument Sara said we would set off. She told me to pack enough for a week's travel, and to take clothes suitable for late summer, and also some things in case the weather should become cool and wet. A cab took us to the Gare du Nord, and we boarded the Flèche d'Or, bound for Calais and London. Well, now I knew our destination, but for what reason? It was with difficulty, as our train rumbled out of the city, that I maintained my promise and did not ask her.

'Are you wondering where we are going?' Sara asked.

'I am, rather.'

'We are going to London.'

Sara had forgiven me at last, and was making gentle fun of me.

'But I am not allowed to ask where, exactly, or why?'

'You may ask where, but not why,' she said.

'Very well then, tell me where.'

'We stay at the Grosvenor Hotel.'

'In one room, or two?'

'I think the question is improper, and I decline to answer, but you may read to me from *The Awakening*. I am quite desperate to know what happens next, and when I want to know something in that way, I cannot stop my curiosity.' Of course, I deserved this, but I did not mind. I had got hold of a copy of the book at last, and in it the author was exploring, in the lazy atmosphere of Louisiana, the theme I knew so well, of the awful predicament of a woman. Society prescribes only that she becomes a dutiful wife and mother, submits to the male will, gives up aspirations of her own. The woman in the book had made the choice expected of her, had submitted, but mere submission is not enough. One has to give one's will to it. Perhaps, I thought, even without Mr S, I would not have been able to do that, and would have been doomed to unhappiness. I too had become curious as to what would happen to Edna now that she had met the alluring Robert. But would that not end the same way, or even worse? It seems so unlikely that it could end well.

The Grosvenor is a very large hotel, next to Victoria Station, so that if one opened a window one could hear the engines of the trains. We had one room, though unfortunately with two beds. After the porter had left, I found myself wanting to hug Sara – and I did. How extraordinary this is, being with her, and how extraordinary that she has transformed what had been the hateful topic of what Freud calls 'sexuality' into . . . into what? I still do not know. Is it a need? Because my desire seems to grow the more it is satisfied. I feel I should not bother her, but then I find that she too desires me. What could be better? Is it right to do this so often? I do not know.

'Tomorrow,' she said, 'I would like my English friend to show me the English capital. Whatever you like, whatever you think I would like. We may proceed however you wish, by cab, by walking, by the underground railway or in any other way. We are perfectly free. We have no appointments.'

So I had two tasks: to think of what Sara would like and to wonder why we have come here. The first was quite easy, though I did not know London very well, since I have not been here as an adult at all, but I could remember the new Museums of Natural History and of Science. They were quite distinctive and Sara would like them, I thought. In the afternoon I thought we could walk through the park of Kensington Gardens, if the weather remained fine, and take tea perhaps in a restaurant in Piccadilly, then come back to the hotel here, and do again what I longed for, what I seemed obsessed by. Then in the evening we can dress up, and go to the theatre.

Why are we here at all? Sara has obviously made an appointment, but with whom? Most likely, I thought, it is with Dr Watson. She must have written to him. She will shepherd me to meet him, and he will say something fatherly and reassuring, to try and relieve my mind of guilt. This is the most obvious explanation. Possibly she has arranged an appointment with Holmes. Has she been in direct communication with him? Has Holmes discovered a mysterious third person present in the mountains? Did an agent of the German state see what had happened? When I left did this person go to find Mr S, stunned by his fall, and then kill him by a blow with a rock? I was daydreaming again. Then I had to suppress the thought that Holmes was tricking her, had succeeded in luring us to England so that he could catch me without himself so much as leaving London. I did not dare dwell on this idea, for Sara would see me become quiet and taciturn, and now I feared her anger more even than Holmes. Keeping my promise to her had a magical quality. If I thought of her command and my promise, then her will somehow prevailed, and these other thoughts lost some of their power. This was part of the trust in her that she had said I did not have. So I put the idea of a trick by Holmes aside to think about later, when I was on my own, perhaps when Sara was asleep. I countered it with the thought of Dr Watson as my ally. We would visit Dr Watson and Holmes would be quite elsewhere, working on his new career of espionage for the government. Or perhaps we would meet someone I did not know, perhaps the woman in black in Watson's story. Sara could have got her address by writing to Dr Watson. We were going to see her, so that she could tell me that Mr S had wronged me and I was not to blame. Or maybe Mr Mycroft Holmes, the detective's brother, with his penetrating mind, might know some extraordinary fact that would put my own mind at rest.

Only the idea that Sara had arranged that the good, kind, gallant Dr Watson would be able to say some comforting word is at all likely. Could anything he would say really help? How empty it seems. But I must stay in this mood that Sara has somehow inaugurated by announcing our journey. Strangely, because of the mystery of our journey, my generally good spirits have not been interrupted more than briefly, and only then in the small hours of the morning, when I found myself wide awake and lying there not daring to move for fear of waking Sara. Perhaps I could make myself choose between these two selves, the happy affectionate one and the fearful, persecuted, guilty one whom Sara has called 'cruel'. When I started to think of it in this way it emphasised again that I am mad, like some Dr Jeckyll and Mr Hyde.* Which self would make the choice? Either one would

*The Strange Case of Dr Jeckyll and Mr Hyde, by R. L. Stevenson.

naturally choose itself. I have only limited influence over the matter, perhaps no influence at all.

Our day together in London came and went. Sara enjoyed the museums very much but not tea in the expensive restaurant. 'This is a side of the English I do not like,' she said. 'To say the truth, it reminds me of the worst side of Vienna. It is full of contempt for others such as foreigners or Jews, for any who do not properly understand the correct customs. At such places one sees these people gathered together, talking loudly in their voices of superiority. Otherwise they do not speak at all, because they do not want to be with the person with whom they take refreshment.'

The next day she said, 'This afternoon we have an appointment. First I have an errand, so this morning you are free to do as you please. I meet you in the restaurant of the hotel for lunch at one o'clock, and then we leave for the appointment.'

'But with whom?' I asked. 'And what is this errand?' I think my voice must have sounded a note of panic.

'No questions,' she replied, and kissed me reassuringly. 'Perhaps you should take a walk in one of the parks.' She advised me what to wear for the appointment that afternoon, and at half-past nine she left the hotel. I thought of following her, and then of her suggestion of going for a walk, but instead I lay on my bed, with the sounds of steam engines faintly audible in the background and with the huge din of my thoughts drumming within. What was this errand? Whom were we going to see? In England here we could fall into Holmes's trap. I tried to calm myself, and somehow reached a state of suspension, waiting only for Sara to return. Then I hit upon a plan. I would wait in the entrance hall of the hotel, reading a newspaper, to await Sara's return. Then I could see if she had been followed. So that is what I did. I descended. I ordered a copy of *The Times* and some coffee.

And there, in an unobtrusive corner, I sat observing the comings and goings. Perhaps this was part of my madness, this fearful, watchful activity that occupied my mind. It was after half-past eleven when she returned. I let her go up to our room without telling her I was there, and then looked round. I waited. Nobody followed her, and out on the street there was nothing suspicious. I went up to our room.

'So you did go out,' she said. 'I have only just returned.' She seemed in good spirits. 'My errand is made. You wish the result to hear?'

'Sara, please do not tease me,' I begged. 'I have been waiting in a paroxysm, thinking the most terrible things.'

'Perhaps this will calm you. I to Mr Holmes and Dr Watson have been, at the rooms at Baker Street.'

'But he could have followed you, and have me arrested.'

'I had previously obtained a promise that he would do no such thing, and in any case I was careful. I do not believe I was followed. The Underground Railway is useful in this way. I make sure I am the last person to board the train, just before it leaves the station. Please be calm. What I found is reassuring.'

'Please tell me.'

'When you believed that Mr Holmes had persuaded the doctor to send his manuscript as a trick to allay our suspicions, to Dr Watson I wrote. I believed the doctor to be sincere, and asked him if he would keep his promise to assist us. In an exchange of letters, I made the arrangement to meet them both at Baker Street this morning. I had said to Dr Watson that I wished to reassure myself from Mr Holmes directly that he did not intend to pursue you. In return, and if Mr Holmes were able to reassure me, I would undertake to clear up any details for his own private satisfaction, so that he might regard the case as truly closed.'

'Oh, Sara. How could you? What did you tell him?'

'There is nothing material I could say that Holmes does not already know.'

'What happened? Tell me.' I could scarcely imagine that Sara had done anything so dangerous, venturing into Holmes's own den.

'Mr Holmes is proud of his work. I thought he would wish to tell me any details that Dr Watson had not included in his manuscript, so I asked what he had deduced of the final meeting between Mr S and yourself on the mountain. Mr Holmes explained that he knew that you had not arranged the meeting, that Mr S had followed you covertly, and so what happened had not been premeditated by yourself. They are very strange, those two men, let me see if I can imitate them for you.

'But Holmes,' Sara had lowered the pitch of her voice to imitate the English accent of Dr Watson, 'you had said we did not know whether Mr S had followed Miss Vincent. Would not you have to exclude the possibility that even if Mr S had arrived to Vienna without Miss Vincent's knowledge, they might have arranged to meet and go together to the mountains?'

Sara now turned her head to imitate the supercilious expression that Holmes affected: 'The evidence is not as complete as I would like, but you would be wrong to assume that I gathered no information on the matter. One of my errands before breakfast on our last morning in Vienna was to question the night porter at the Stadt London. He says Mr S left the hotel that Saturday morning at five o'clock without so much as a cup of coffee. Was this the action of someone who had an appointment at a place that cannot be reached except by train, the earliest of which leaves from Vienna at seven a.m. on Saturdays? Or was it the action of one who keeps watch on a person he wishes to follow unobtrusively, making sure she does not slip away unseen from her residence?'

'By Jove, Holmes. You never cease to astonish me.' Sara imitated the doctor's bluff manner.

'It is scarcely very remarkable, Watson.'

Sara laughed. 'Do you think I am a good actor?'

'So that is how Mr S followed me. I'm glad Mr Holmes does not think I premeditated the event,' I replied. 'I did not. I only wanted to escape.'

'Then Mr Holmes asked me what I could add,' said Sara. 'I told him I only had the account you had given me, but this would not satisfy him, because I could not add any outward evidence, only inner evidence. I said to Mr Holmes that he should not think of the matter as guilt and innocence, as in a court of law. I said that I thought this was not correct in this case, as I doubted whether you yourself knew whether you were guilty or not. A person can be divided in themselves. I said you had told me that Mr S rushed at you, as Dr Watson had guessed. He tried to grasp you, and I told him my theory about the reflex act of fear, of pushing away the feared object. At the same time, I said, you loathed Mr S. Despite yourself you had wished him dead. In that moment the wish for his death may have come uppermost. "Does that make you wish to condemn Miss Vincent?" I asked.'

I sat and listened, horror-struck that Sara could be discussing the matter so coolly with my pursuer. I had a sense of numbness, but I did not interrupt.

'Mr Holmes said this was not the issue,' Sara continued. 'He said that if we had ourselves observed the scene, it would be quite different if Mr S had run at you and in a struggle lost his footing, than if you ran at him to topple him from the cliff. "It is the actual events that my methods discover," he said. "I reason backwards from effects such as the traces that are left from an incident to the events that caused them."

' "Very well," I said. "Consider this. When you and Professor Moriarty confronted each other twelve or fifteen years ago, at the Reichenbach Falls,* if I had been there what would I have seen? According to your own account, as related by Dr Watson, Moriarty rushed at you. You evaded his grasp, using your knowledge of a Japanese art of wrestling, and you sent him towards his destruction. Imagine yourself in court, charged with the murder of Professor Moriarty; imagine Colonel James Moriarty defending the good name of his brother the professor. Suppose evidence of Moriarty's wrongs were not fully accepted, we might know only that you wished the man destroyed, and that such destruction was accomplished. Look into your heart, Mr Holmes; was it not a battle of your wits and strength against his at that moment? It was not the pursuit of justice. Did you not wish him dead, and for your own reasons?"

'I believed I had made my point, because Mr Holmes sat still and did not speak for several minutes, during which the atmosphere in the room became most tense. Finally he spoke. "Very well, Frau Rosenthal. I admit that I had hoped that Watson's manuscripts might draw you and your friend out, and indeed your presence here indicates that I had partly succeeded. I had also conceived a plan of questioning Miss Vincent on certain details, to satisfy myself. What I had said about giving up the pursuit for official purposes was true, but you and she were correct in thinking that as far as I was concerned the case had not yet reached its conclusion. I believe, however, that in what you now say you are right: we may not know what happened

*'The Final Problem' is the last story in *The Memoirs of Sherlock Holmes*, which Sara mentions having finished reading in Chapter 24. In this story Watson recounted how Holmes and Professor Moriarty, the 'Napoleon of crime', had met at the Reichenbach Falls in 1891 and had apparently both fallen to their deaths. In 'The Adventure of the Empty Room', the first story of *The Return of Sherlock Holmes*, Holmes reappeared and told Watson that he had slipped through Moriarty's grasp when they struggled together and that Moriarty alone had fallen into the chasm. What Sara says to Holmes indicates that she must have read this latter story also.

between Miss Vincent and Mr S on that fateful day. The crucial event left no signs. We are not in a position to judge."

' "The events have left signs, Mr Holmes, but they are invisible signs; you may not be able to observe them from the outside." I told him this, and I believe he understood me. Then I asked: "I would like to know that you do not condemn Miss Vincent, any more than you condemn yourself over the matter of Professor Moriarty; is that right, Mr Holmes? I would like to hear it from your own mouth." '

Sara turned to me and said, 'Do you know, I think that the inflexible Mr Holmes became more soft. He said, "Please reassure Miss Vincent that I believe her innocent in the matter of Mr S's death. Should she ever need my services, she need merely ask. I am grateful to her – the case was an interesting one for me, and as well as marking a turning point in my career."

'He and the doctor thanked me for coming to visit them, and said they wished us both well. They were both kind. What do you think of this?'

'Oh Sara, you do so much on my behalf. What can I say? I have been so stupid. I see spectres everywhere. But you see, I was right: even though it seems that he might not have had me arrested, he was still enacting his schemes. I knew it. I am relieved that now he has desisted. I must go to thank him.'

'No, you need not do that. He does not expect it. We have other matters to attend to. You may write him a note. That will be best.'

'Yes, you are right, that would be best. Do you think now my fears will subside? Those men cannot allay them, since for the most part they are my own accusations, not theirs. I know I should not have done it, whatever they say. Whatever the provocation, it is not right. I should not have hated him.' I found myself once again in tears. But mysteriously they were short-lived, and I looked through them to see Sara gazing at me.

'Remember we have an appointment,' she said. 'Before that we can take lunch. And you remember too that you have put yourself in my hands.'

I did remember, and felt contained by her, like a child trusting in a parent. When I had dried my eyes the two of us went to the restaurant, and for all the world became like two people on holiday.

36

The Narrative of Sara and Emily
continued

A Conversation Long Postponed

After we had taken lunch in the restaurant of the hotel we set off in a cab. I had not overheard Sara's instruction to the driver, and I still had not the least idea of whom our appointment might be with. For a moment I thought, as the cab turned up Park Lane, that we might perhaps be going to Clifton Gardens to visit the woman in black, who had come to know so much about Mr S and his ways, but I could not see the point of such a visit. Holmes and Watson were now ruled out: I believed Sara when she said that Holmes had at last desisted, and this was in truth a relief. But I did not know whether Sara knew the worst part. I have deceived her about its seriousness – that I myself am the principal danger to our life together, that I myself cannot be trusted to avoid brooding, or even to avoid rushing into a police station one day to confess my guilt. Neither the woman in black nor any other person can help to resolve my dreadful struggle, of me with myself.

I gazed out of the window, at the people walking in twos and threes in the park, seemingly as if they were without pressing concerns, and I wondered how many of them had dark secrets that they kept hidden. It was after we had passed the Marble Arch, and rattled along some side streets, that the cab pulled into the forecourt of a railway station. At that moment suddenly I knew.

'We are going to visit Mrs S,' I said.

'No questions,' she replied. 'Perhaps you could read to me as we journey on the train.'

Why, I thought, are we going to visit her? Instantly, my panicky state was with me, at its very worst. It was with difficulty that I accompanied Sara into the station, and when we entered the train, I was glad we had a compartment to ourselves. I felt drenched in perspiration, and felt nauseated, as if at any moment I should be sick.

'You look pale,' Sara said. 'Perhaps I will read to you. Or would you like to talk? We talk now. The interval without questions ends.'

'Why are we going to B——? We are going to see my godmother. Why? I killed her husband. Why do I have to see her? How can I face her?'

'I have exchanged letters with her,' Sara said. 'My letter to her was the most difficult I have ever written. I had to say that you were in a state of despair, and that it seemed possible that it had something to do with her late husband, though of course without being specific. I hoped to hint that it concerned what she already knew about Mr S's seduction of you, and that she might be able to help your mind to be calm. Here, you may read her reply.'

My dear Mrs Rosenthal,

It was with very mixed emotions that I received your letter. I am most distressed to hear that Emily is not well. Please convey my regards to her. At the same time, as you may imagine, the events at which you hint took place a long time ago now and it is painful for me to have to recall them.

You seem to know Emily very well, and to have her welfare closely to heart. It seems that she has told you a great deal. If therefore you believe that there is anything I can say to her, or do, that will relieve her mind in any way, please come and visit me. I shall remain at B— now until November, so please make your visit at any time. I am often out in the morning, but almost every afternoon I am at home.

I have the warmest regard for Emily, and felt her to be like a daughter to me, though I fear that because of my own sorrows at the time I may have failed to convey my affection to her. I shall be very glad indeed to see her again.

Yours very truly,

Catherine S

I read this with astonishment. I did not know what to say. At length I said, 'It is a very friendly letter. I am touched that she feels so warmly towards me. I did not know she felt me to be like a daughter.'

'I think it is not difficult to love you Emily,' she replied. 'You have an affectionate nature.'

I looked away, out through the windows at the passing of the green countryside, with its cows grazing, its hedgerows and trees. Was that the cause? I asked myself silently. Was Mr S attracted to me because it was easy to love me, because I was affectionate? Obscurely, I felt the sting of an accusation in what Sara had said. It had been my fault to attract his attention, but I knew she had not meant it in that way.

'You are very silent,' she said. 'You need not say anything to Mrs S that you do not wish, but I believe if you do wish to say anything about what happened, it might cut the terrible knot.'

'I should say that I killed her husband?'

'You could talk about how he followed you, and you struggled, and he fell.'

'Why are you making me do this, Sara?'

'I do not make you do it. If you wish you may merely exchange greetings with Mrs S. Why do we not see how the meeting goes?

378

I know it is difficult. I bring you here because it is distressing to you, distressing to me, damaging to us both, that you are tormented by guilt.'

She squeezed my hand, affectionately. Again I had an overwhelming sense of how unfair I had been to her: by torturing myself, I tortured her. Instead of leading a new life, a more generous life, I was even unable to requite the love of the person I cared most about. 'I will try,' I said. 'I know I have not been good to you. I will try.'

'Yes,' she said. 'Just try.'

My mind became blank. A void enveloped me. I stared through the window without seeing. My mind held a readiness for I knew not what. It was a kind of calmness that lasted minutes or hours. I could not have said.

'Here we are,' Sara said as our train drew into the station at B—. In this same mood of suspense we began to drive through the town which I had not visited for so long, which I thought was far behind me. As we did so my mood changed. I began to notice familiar buildings and sights, and began to reflect on this journey into my past. Suddenly I understood that behind Sara's plan was some idea she had borrowed from the Professor, but of course, being herself, she had not just borrowed, she had transformed the idea and made it her own. She had made it practical. We should not just remember the past, but revisit it. That is the kind of way in which she would put it. Why had she always said I was cleverer than she? It is not true. I have never met anyone with more practical intelligence than Sara. It made me profoundly grateful simply to know her. She also has a centre of calm, so that I know that when I am with her nothing truly bad can happen.

What was that thought? Why was I thinking that now? Why did I not feel that all the time? Why, if this were true as I am sure it is, had I let these other thoughts pursue me and torment me?

'Look,' I said. 'This is the main square, with the Town Hall. It is a typically English town. All these shops . . . there is the draper's and haberdasher's. I used to visit that shop with Mrs S. I wonder if the same people still work there. It looks the same.'

Was it the reassuring thought of Sara? Whatever it was, my spirits, inexplicably, had changed from the panic of realisation that we were coming here to that mood which I value – of being with Sara. Before long, on the other side of the town, we reached the house. It too was familiar, and I could not suppress a wave of terror as I glanced towards that ground-floor room where his study had been. Sara pulled the handle to ring the bell.

'You must be Miss Emily, and Mrs Rosenthal.' A maid I did not know had answered the door. 'Mrs S is expecting you.'

Before we could go any further, Mrs S had come to greet us herself. She reached for my hand, and kissed me warmly on both cheeks. 'Emily,' she said, 'come in. Mrs Rosenthal, how do you do. I am very pleased to meet you.'

The maid took our things and the three of us entered the drawing room, still like a picture gallery with its bright and vibrant paintings on the walls.

'You are keeping all these paintings?' I asked. 'I thought you had not liked them much.'

'I don't know,' Mrs S replied. 'In some ways I have grown used to them, but I expect I shall move from here. There is no especial reason for me to be near London now. I can as well do parish work in other places as here. Though I should miss this garden. Perhaps I shall remove to Wells. My sister is there. I have not fully considered yet.'

The maid knocked and entered with a tray of refreshments. Evidently the kettle had been set to boil ready for our arrival. 'Will you take tea, Mrs Rosenthal?' my godmother asked.

'Yes please.'

'And you, my dear?' she said, turning to me.

'Yes. Thank you, very much.'

'I think your friend is right,' she said, after we were all served, and sat facing one another. 'We should talk. We should have talked before today. I wish I had been able to do so.' After a pause which I knew not how to break, she turned to Sara and said: 'I gather from your letter that you know what had passed between my husband and Emily.' My godmother looking meaningfully at Sara. 'So I need not feel reserve towards you.'

'I would be grateful if you have no reserve,' replied Sara. She was not at ease in this situation, and was sitting very erect, striving no doubt to be proper in this British ritual of drinking tea together.

'Before you left for America, I did not know how to speak to you properly,' my godmother continued, glancing briefly towards me. 'I was too much distressed, I think, and only wanted to end the possibility of you and my husband being thrown together. I had wondered that summer if my husband had become attracted to you, but until that afternoon when I had returned home unexpectedly I had not known, or known that there was more than that. I confronted him, and he confessed.

'Forgive me,' she continued. 'This is painful for me. The truth is that I should have known better, and should have been able to protect you. You see, my husband was a damaged man. This kind of thing had happened before. When we had been posted to America my husband had become involved with an awful couple, and under the cover of their gallery – they bought and sold paintings – they introduced men to young women, very young women, who were artists' models or girls who worked in the choruses of operas there. That is where my husband acquired his taste for paintings of this kind, and perhaps also for the women portrayed in them. I had not believed, though, that he would abuse his trust at home.'

'Why do you say he was damaged?' I asked.

'His family had lived close to that of my cousin, and when we

381

were both young I had met him at some functions. We were not exactly thrown together, but on several occasions I found myself in conversation with him. I could see that he was a very nervous and withdrawn soul. I think I felt sorry for him. He had a very polite and apparently assured exterior, but behind it there was someone very lonely, and I believe this touched me. I was able to tempt him out of his shell, and I suppose what drew me to him is that as I did this he began to come alive, to unbend, and I knew this was my influence. I thought I would be able to make him happy. He began to confess to me too, that he suffered from thoughts that he could not stop or escape from. He spent a great deal of time thinking about a particular problem. It was whether we are all like pieces of clockwork, or machines, which seem to have feelings for one another but do not. He felt he had to solve this problem, of whether people are really alone in themselves, just machines, or whether it is possible to understand anyone or to love them. He said such thoughts just forced their way in on him. He said he simply could not stop them.'

'I believe I can understand what that is like,' I said.

'Then there were ceremonies he had to perform to get through each day,' she continued. 'He liked things in threes, and he explained to me how in any of his daily actions, for instance walking towards a doorway, he would need to take three steps from a certain point to arrive at the threshold exactly, and if it went wrong he would have to go back and repeat it. Patterns would occupy a great deal of time, and he would fight against them. Sometimes he would succeed. Sometimes a pattern he had been compelled by would just die away. Sometimes he would be able to stop one by starting some alternative pattern.

'I am telling you this to try and help explain. You see, my husband was a driven man. It is confusing, because he always wanted things to be under his own control, but at the same time he was unable to control himself. With me, when we got married, his ceremonies all but disappeared, and we could laugh about them. I suppose I felt pleased to have rescued him – and I loved him. Yes, I did. We were happy. That was when we knew your mother and father. We were in the same embassy together, in Paris, and we saw a great deal of them socially. We could not have children, but you were small, and I became extremely fond of you. It was natural, therefore, that your father should have thought of my husband as guardian for you in case of any accident.'

'I have often wondered why Mr S had been chosen as my guardian.'

'Yes, that was the reason. When they came to know us well, I think your parents thought that we were a normal family, and felt that we would be people they could trust to take care of you. I felt so too. As years passed, I suppose they did not think that anything fundamental had changed, and saw no reason to alter the arrangement. I, however, knew that things had changed.

'We were posted apart. We did not lose touch, exactly, but our intimacy was lost. I don't know whether we could have maintained it even if we had been nearer, because little by little my husband's rituals began to take over once more. My influence waned. I do not know why. I have racked my brains for a reason, and I tried everything I could think of. It was as if something had possession of him. For a while I had won the battle – and he had won the battle – to be free of it. Then insidiously it crept back. The ruminations on insoluble philosophical questions, the habits, the making of patterns and the counting: they all grew to take him over again. Had he not explained it to me previously I would not have been able to recognise what was going on, but, knowing, I saw the signs. It was in America that I realised that it was not just daily things, but now there was another thing too; I do not know whether it was part of the same disease or separate.'

She stopped. 'I am sorry,' she said, 'I have never spoken of this before. It has been a private grief. I want to try to explain to you, but I do not know how.'

Again there was a pause. 'I will not tell you how I discovered. It is too, too sordid, but he had lost all passionate interest in me. I had merely thought I had lost to this occupying demon. What I found out, though, was that he had become, as he put it, drawn to seeking young women. I was wounded more that I can say. Looking back I realise I was beside myself with jealousy. I pleaded with him, talked of the way in which his compulsions had taken him over again, and that he was no longer himself. In the end he said he thought he could repent if he could make a full confession to me. I agreed, and heard a catalogue of doings that made me feel desperately ashamed, for him and for myself. Briefly, then, for a few months, his interest in me was renewed. I do not know how I mastered my bitterness, but I did, thinking that this was our only chance of happiness. For these few months I thought we might win through, until with horror I realised that the patterns were again taking hold, and occupying more and more of the time. When I tried to speak about it he rounded upon me angrily, saying I did not understand, that I never had understood, and that I was to leave him strictly alone and not to interfere.'

My godmother stopped speaking again, and stared at the floor. At length she resumed: 'I do not know whether he had calculated this to be the most cruel thing that he could ever have said to me, but I received it in that way.'

My godmother paused again for a little while, and I had an overwhelming sense of the sadness of her life, and the bravery with which she had persevered. 'I did try several times more,' she continued, now turning to gaze steadfastly through the window into the greenness of her garden, 'but by then he was gone, lost for ever. I thought too, at my most bitter, that he had never loved me, but that I had merely provided an interlude in his onward path. I do not think that now. I think that I – both of us – were battling with something larger than we knew, something like a devil that could possess one. It was a kind of sickness of the spirit, I believe, which has no remedy. So, you see,' she turned to me, 'when I realised that you had become an interest, I had to get him away, and get you away as soon as possible, but I did not know what to say to you.'

'I thought that what you said was the most tactful and gentle thing I could have imagined,' I said. 'You let me know that you knew, but did not condemn me. I have always been grateful to you. I only wish that I could have known to talk about it earlier.'

'Earlier?' she asked. 'You mean that it had been going on for some time?'

'Some little time,' I replied, not wishing to wound her more than she had already been wounded. I changed the subject: 'I was mortally frightened, you see,' I went on. 'I had not known how to keep him away, but also I had not known how to speak to you. I thought too that you would be angry with me, and blame me or hate me. It was horrible. I felt so ashamed. I did not know what to do.'

'You poor dear.' She looked at me compassionately. 'I wish you had been able to speak.'

'One thing I have always wanted to ask you, ever since, that I have never been able to resolve within myself,' I continued, 'is if I ever did anything to encourage the attentions of Mr S to myself. Was I coquettish in any way? Did I use feminine wiles? I am very naïve about such things, but I feel I must have done something.'

'You were very sweet,' she replied. 'When you came to us you were a waif, distraught and withdrawn. You buried yourself in your books. As you grew older you started to become the attractive woman you are today. You were not a coquette in any way whatever. You must not blame yourself. As I said, my husband was under the influence of things he could not control.'

'You do not blame me?'

'No, my dear, I have never blamed you. You were just a young girl. I blame myself for not having stopped him, for not having been able to draw him back from the brink when we were in America, for many things. Perhaps I was too cold to him then. I felt bitterness and betrayal, which I found it hard to bear. Most of all I blamed him.'

'Did he not express remorse at your pain, at that time, Mrs S?' Sara asked.

My godmother looked across at her, somewhat surprised, and said, 'Yes, he did. He too said it was something he had to struggle to control.'

'I am sorry that I interrupt,' Sara said.

'No,' my godmother said. 'You do not interrupt. As I had said, I think he was a tormented man, somehow damaged, I believe. When I think about it calmly, I think that he could not be saved, or not without some miracle. Not by me, certainly.'

'So you had grown apart?' I asked.

'We had become very far apart,' she replied. 'Further than you can imagine. After I had overcome my grief when we were in America, if ever I did overcome it, I decided that we would just live in the way that you saw when you came to live with us, observing the outward forms alone. I no longer tried to interfere. I was glad when you came, I admit. I thought I would have someone to care about. You were all alone, so I do not know what else could have been done. It must sound improbable given what I have told you, but I simply did not realise the danger. I am so, so sorry.'

'Please,' I said. 'Please do not be sorry. I was always grateful for your presence. I am glad I now understand it all better. I have not been able to make sense of it myself.'

There was silence for a long interval, with only a clock ticking and the occasional sounds of birds singing in the garden.

'How did you two come to be friends?' my godmother asked.

I do not know what prompted her to ask this. Was it merely that, having got the more difficult part of our interview over, as she had thought, she was now changing the subject? Was it a simple expression of interest in me? Or had she some inkling of something else? She had travelled widely in Europe, perhaps she even recognised Sara's accent as not German but from the city her husband had last visited. I do not know why she asked, but one thing is plain to me. Had she not asked this question, I would not have found the courage to speak of what tormented me.

'I am afraid I deceived you,' I replied. 'I lived in fear of Mr S. I could never bear his attentions, and I wanted him to believe I was still in America. I had a friend forward my letters from there, but in fact I was in Vienna. Sara and I taught at the same school for two years. We met there.'

Again a pause. 'My husband, on his visit to America earlier this year, must have discovered you were not at your address in Philadelphia, and had found out that you were in Vienna.' Mrs S pronounced this with an air of inevitability. 'I knew he had been in Philadelphia,' she said. 'Despite our leading separate lives, my husband had ways of confronting me with the unwelcome. In this case it was a train ticket from New York to Philadelphia, which the maid removed from his pocket when his suit was to be cleaned, and said to me: "Do you want these things, madam?" '

'Yes. I am afraid he did go to Philadelphia, and there found my address in Vienna.'

'I did not realise that the obsession with you had lasted so. He would never allow himself to be thwarted in anything he wanted. He had not given up.'

'No, I think that is right.'

'He came and pleaded with you, or something of that kind?'

'Yes. I tried to dissuade him from his course, but the only way I could get him to leave my rooms was to promise to consider what he asked. Early next day I left by train to walk in the mountains, to escape, and to try and think what to do.'

'Ah,' said my godmother, as if she had made some connection, 'and he followed you?'

'I did not know that he had followed me. I went to escape. He came at me, in a deserted place. We struggled, and I tried to push him away. I did push him away. He fell.'

For some reason, I was able to say this clearly, without weeping. My godmother listened gravely, merely nodding her head as if all this were understandable.

'I wanted to ask your forgiveness,' I said, appalled as I heard myself speaking at how crassly foolish this sounded. What could I be thinking, telling a woman that I had murdered her husband, and was now asking her forgiveness?

'My dear,' she said. 'You have had to live with a terrible burden. If my forgiveness helps you bear it, I give it freely. It is your forgiveness I should ask. In truth I have nothing to forgive. Please do not grieve on my behalf. I mourned my husband's death many years ago, before you came to live with us. He had died for me and, sadly, I think also for himself. He was no longer himself. He was besieged, and had lost the battle. He was a country that had been invaded by an enemy. The occupation is lifted at last.'

Again a long silence.

'So that is how it happened,' she said. 'The mountains that he feared.'

Then she asked: 'You decided not to go to the police in case they might not understand, or the court might not believe you?'

'I persuaded her this is the best way,' said Sara. 'It was difficult to decide, but for many reasons I think correct, and I adopt responsibility for this. I believe Emily will not receive justice if she will go to the police, but perhaps I was too angry with your husband for what had taken place before. I thought this earlier part, the part that had happened before when Emily lived here, would not be considered by the court. Only they would consider what happened on the mountain, or perhaps believe Emily was not telling the truth and was an aggrieved lover, or some such. Even if they had believed it, they might then have said, "There, you see, she hated him, and this was her revenge."'

'I am sure you are right. What happened earlier might not have been given weight in a court, or it might have been given the wrong weight,' my godmother replied. 'Though I would have spoken for you.'

'I still think very often of giving myself up,' I said. 'I think I needed to hear you say that you forgive me. No, I do not mean that. It would not be fair to ask you that.'

I started to speak again, but nothing less foolish came from my lips. I said to her, 'When I was telling you what happened, I was thinking, Now she is having to listen to yet another paining confession. But I found I wanted to tell you.'

'I do not mind hearing your confession. Forgive me, for the moment I hardly know what to say.' Then, after an interval she said, 'I believe you should not think yourself guilty. You were not guilty. If anyone was, it was I, for not seeing what might happen.'

'No, no,' I cried, rising and going over to take her hands and to kneel by her chair. 'Please do not say that. That is not why I came, to pass my guilt over to you. I should not have come.'

We stayed thus, in silence, for many minutes.

She said: 'Do not regret it. I believe it is for the best that you came. At last we can bury this together, the three of us.

'Come,' she said, raising me and taking me by the arm, 'let me show you my garden. Perhaps when we have had time to get used to this, we can meet and talk of more ordinary things. I would like still to be your godmother. That is perhaps too much to ask? Perhaps I could come and visit you in Paris.'

'I would like that very much. I do think of you as my

389

godmother, my closest relative, and I would like you to come and see us.' I looked over towards Sara to make sure she approved. She did.

'And our letters need not now take so long.'

'Not nearly so long.'

'Your godmother is a good woman,' remarked Sara as we sat in the train once more, clattering back towards London.

'Yes, she is. A kind person, and very sad in her life.'

'Will that be part of your penance, to be for her a daughter?'

'Yes, I think it will, but not so much a penance. I feel I could love her properly now. I did not understand her before at all.' I thought for a while. 'In part I feel I should not have said what I did, because I shifted part of my burden of guilt on to her. She said she felt it was her fault, but at the same time she seemed not be to cast down by it, as if the worst had already happened, a long time ago, and whatever part she had played would now not alter this . . . and she wanted me to be a daughter again to her.'

'Your godmother is a wise woman. Perhaps she knows that we all have our burden, but that in the end it is not good if we only face towards the past.'

'I think it was good to come,' I said. 'I believe I shall be able to escape the influence now. Perhaps also I shall be able to stop thinking of Mr S as just some incarnation of evil, who had put that evil inside me. Those triangles he used to trace on my body, he was counting in threes. And then there was that Greek E by which he referred to me, and that Mr Holmes found on his wretched lists. Again it is a three in reverse. It makes me shudder to think of it. He had a kind of sickness.'

'Yes. I believe he died from this sickness. When your godmother was speaking I thought how sometimes, with the wrong kind of liaison, people can catch a disease – I think it is called a disease of sexual meeting or something like that. In your case you were infected, but it was a mental disease. Mr S passed on to you something like an obsession, like a plague of the mind.'

'I think it was something of the kind. Now my godmother has told me about it, I think I understand more about the cure.'

37

The Narrative of Sara and Emily
concluded
Looking Forward

Ten years after that summer when the events recounted here took place, developments that Sherlock Holmes's brother had foreseen came to horrifying fruition. Now, two years later still, Europe is in the grip of a seemingly endless war. I have wondered, in my guilty thoughts which still sometimes occur, whether my part in the death of my guardian had quickened the pace of those ominous processes that even then were taking place. I do not know whether the British government was able to parley with the Germans on the subject that my guardian had been charged to broach. On other occasions, when I am not beset by this universalised guilt, perhaps more rationally, I assume that the British government must have tried other means to reach some agreement with the Germans, and I can believe that those distant events in which I was involved were no more than drops contributing to the huge tides of conflict that have now rolled over us all.

I have been rereading my journal and our narrative, and have been correcting the punctuation. There is an interest in memoirs in our circle of friends, and I am wondering whether any part of it could be published. That year of my own turmoil and confusion now seems distant. It was the time also of Sara and I discovering our love for each other. That has lasted and grown, while the inner turmoil has finally subsided. Not entirely. Still I can feel panicky, reminded by an incident or a thought, or sometimes for no reason. There are some things one never really gets over. I know I am not as other people, but now that knowledge is not like a brand within my brain. Perhaps too it helps me understand others, rather than dragging me downwards as it did. Now sufferings, infinitely worse than the evils that befell a few people in the narrative I have written, have overtaken everything we know. One small crumb of comfort for my still occasionally obsessing self is that others too live, like me, with the burden of having killed another person. No one is untouched by this dreadful war. Sara finds herself separated, and on a different side, from her own family and friends in Vienna.

We decided to live here in Paris. Sara bought a house, not far from the place we had rented. Before the war began she spent much time in Vienna too, and I missed her painfully when she travelled, but this now has come to be our home, and yes, we did start the Institut des Femmes here. It has been quite a success, enabling women to become educated in many subjects, and enabling me also to earn my living so that I am independent.

There has been something of a gathering here in Paris, of women like us, and I think perhaps, during our first few months here, it was this that decided us to stay. Our life is sometimes intense. Many people here care, as I do, for books and writing. One friend opened a lovely bookshop, quite nearby, in the rue de l'Odéon.* Some of the women we know are writers. Some write poetry, or stories, or even undertake experiments with language parallel to the experiments in form that painters have achieved.†

---

*No doubt Adrienne Monnier, who opened her bookshop, La Librairie A. Monnier, in 1915. Her shop later became the famous Maison des amis des livres.
†It seems likely that Emily's mention of 'experiments' is a reference to Gertrude Stein, a friend of Picasso, who thought about her work as parallel to his.

Some of the women live as Sara and I do, together, and this has made our state seem not so odd, not so much as if society would frown upon us.

Some of the women here have even celebrated this state in their writings. Some speak loudly and rather often about returning to the Sapphic isle, or of building Mitylene here in the Paris streets, or in some such way. They seek to celebrate Sappho, not only as one of the world's greatest poets, with which I am inclined to agree, but also as a forerunner of a new kind of world in which all women can be as she was, or as they imagine her to have been.

One of these women, herself an American writer who makes a great splash wherever she goes, even tried for several weeks to seduce Sara, since free love was supposed, by her at least, to be part of this recreated state.* I was tormented with jealousy, though it was of my own making, since Sara did not give me cause.

Although there is a taste here for poetry, plays and novels, I have stuck to translation except for 'The Narrative of Sara and Emily'. It seems to be my *métier*. I am not bold enough to send anything I might write to stand on its own, in public. Perhaps, as Professor Freud once remarked, this shows I have no real creative talent.

The Professor was kind enough to let me have a copy of the manuscript I had returned to him, with a note that I still have.

1:ix:04

PROF. DR. FREUD   WIEN, IX. BERGGASSE 19.

Dear Miss Vincent,

Thank you for sending my manuscript. Mr Holmes had given

---

*This may well have been Natalie Barney.

assurances that it would be returned, but I had not guessed how it would arrive. It was a shock to find that it had fallen into your hands, and I can scarcely imagine how this happened, but I was gratified to see from your letter that you have appreciated its main proposals, though not agreeing with everything.

It is with some reluctance that I pass this copy of my manuscript back to you, because on rereading it I find that it is much more unfinished than I would like. May I enjoin you to keep it solely for your own use?

I would be very glad to discuss with you the outstanding matters that you mention in your letter, preferably by your resuming your consultations with me in the ordinary way.

I look forward to receiving a communication from you should you wish to become a patient once more.

Yours truly,

Sigm. Freud

I believe he sent me his manuscript as I asked partly because he wanted me to return to treatment. I had not realised when I asked him, but I can see that he may have thought that if he did not grant my request I would be less likely to return.

In his letter he did not acknowledge the events about which Holmes told him, of my seduction and of Mr S's appearance at my door. I can only suppose that he did not know what to say about them. I think my case was not a very satisfactory one for him.

I replied to his letter, and about two years later I went to see him once more. By then he was becoming quite well-known, and by now of course he is well-known indeed. I continued to read his works avidly, and was especially struck by the case of Dora, which was in some ways so like my own.* I had also read his

*Fragment of an Analysis of a Case of Hysteria ('Dora'). Published in 1905.

essays on sexuality.* I was eager to discuss them when I visited him, though in the event I did not.

I was glad to see him again, but our meeting was strange: uncomfortable, with a sense of unsaid things. In some ways it was rather formal, as if what had originally brought us together had passed, and could not be recaptured. Perhaps it seemed flat because by then I was so much better. This, of course, I was delighted to be able to tell him, as I thanked him in person for the help he had given, but from his point of view I suppose I must have been one of his unsatisfactory cases, not someone of whom a clear account could be written of a recovery deriving from the insights gained in the analysis.

Since the meeting, I have continued to read the Professor's works as they become available. His description of a case of obsessional neurosis had a special interest for me.† In my readings I admit to a certain disappointment that our meetings together, and the evidence with which the Professor had been confronted in my case, seemed not to have influenced him much. He seemed, since seeing Dora and myself, to have lost all interest in the idea that seduction in early life can leave a hidden scar. He came instead to concentrate entirely on his other idea, of the conflict of inner desires. He was such an independent thinker that perhaps he rebelled against the idea that I might have been more correct than he about the effects of Mr S in my case. Or perhaps he saw, in his meeting with Holmes, that his method of listening and making sense of what came into his patients' minds was inadequate to discovering what had really occurred in a person's past, and that he had better concentrate on his patients' inner worlds as they emerged in their associations.

As to Sherlock Holmes and Dr Watson, I never saw them

*Freud's *Three Essays on the Theory of Sexuality* were published in 1905.
†*Notes on a Case of Obsessional Neurosis ('The Rat Man')*, published in 1909.

again, though I did write to Mr Holmes, thanking him for being reassuring when Sara went to see him – and this, I thought, was a sign of my recovery: I wrote giving our proper address in Paris, and received a reply to our apartment there, which, though brief, seemed less frosty than his previous letter. I am glad that Sara went on her own to see Mr Holmes when we made our journey to England. I would have found an interview with him terrifying. It frightens me still, as I reread these pages, to see how I had crossed the border of madness, and how Mr Holmes had become one of my terrifying persecutors. This sense has still not entirely left me: only a few days ago, when I started to work on these papers, I had a frightening nightmare – by no means the first of its kind – in which I was being pursued by my guardian, who then turned into Mr Holmes. In the caricature from which I cannot escape, of Mr Holmes as unrelentingly cruel and Dr Watson as paternal, I know I am still caught in the residue of my fear of those days, and that this is unjust to Mr Holmes. More rationally I can see, reading the end of Dr Watson's story, that Mr Holmes too was quite ambivalent, and this explains the oddness of the way in which he had left the case unfinished before Sara went to see him. I am sure he did want to reel in the line which had me at the other end – I knew he had not relinquished his pursuit. At the same time Dr Watson's text implies that, had he wound in his reel, he would have been at a loss to know what to do with me. The doctor had indeed prevailed upon him, at least to some extent.

Though I started looking through my papers to see if there was anything I could write about that experience, I now think there is not. I wrote what seemed to force itself upon me at the time. Now I do not know whether any of it would be suitable for publication, even if greatly transformed. In the confusion of these times, moreover, it hardly seems appropriate.

'Whatever are you doing?' Sara had asked. 'Are you rummaging through all that stuff to remind yourself of when you were so miserable, or to remind yourself that twelve years ago you fell in love with the most wonderful person you can imagine?'

'Perhaps both,' I said. Even after these years I knew she still loved me, even though I had not been always easy for her, and her sense of fun had not left her. Indeed it sustained us both.

'I hope you are not going to start dwelling on the past again,' she remarked, 'because if you do, it may return to haunt you.'

'I was thinking more about the future, and wondering where we will be, and what we will be like, twelve years from now,' I said.

'There, you see what I mean: you have started becoming morbid again already.'

'I am serious, Sara. One disadvantage of living as we do is that although we can pass things on to the people we teach, we have no children to pass things on to.'

'We could adopt someone, perhaps a child whose parents have been killed in this unspeakable war,' she suggested.

'I have been thinking the same. Perhaps if there were a little girl who was too small to know her parents, we could adopt her. What would we call her?'

'I have already wondered about this,' she replied. 'Perhaps "Judith" would be good. She was a heroine who was not overawed by men. "Hannah" is also a good name: it means "grace". Or, best of all, maybe we should call her after your godmother: "Catherine".'

Postscript

by Dr Ellen Berger

I have been asked to write briefly on these newly discovered manuscripts, and to comment upon this case. I am glad to do so, and am only sorry that this work was not available to me when I was preparing my recent book *Women Patients and Patient Women: An Analysis of Freud's Relations with the Opposite Sex*. I will not recapitulate here the arguments of that book, preferring to await an opportunity that I hope may be offered for a second edition, where I may deal with the case of Emily more fully. I will instead use this opportunity to point out a number of features of interest to the general reader touching on these newly found manuscripts.

Freud wrote up his case of Emily V in 1904, as he went along rather than in retrospect. The case that comes closest in time and theme is that of Dora, written in January 1901, immediately after Dora left treatment.* Because of his own ambivalence Freud did not publish it until the fall of 1905. Dora and Emily had many differences in their lives, not least in their educational opportunities. It is, however, striking that in some ways their lives were

---

*S. Freud, *Fragment of an Analysis of a Case of Hysteria ('Dora')*, cf also note on p. 395. Two recent books, both of which can be highly recommended, are C. Bernheimer & C. Kahane, *In Dora's Case* (an anthology of the large literature on the case), and H. Dekker, *Freud, Dora and Vienna, 1900* (a historical work).

similar, in that both had to cope with the attentions of insistent and intrusive male suitors at the age of fourteen. In Emily's case we know that she had to submit to full sexual penetration, and these intrusions were to continue for four years. One might argue that, in the very narrowest sexual sense, Dora's abuse had not been not so severe, having been confined, at least according to the evidence of Freud's text, to having a bulge in Herr K's trousers pressed against her during an attempted embrace.

Many of the issues Freud raises are similar in the two cases, including his desire to present his analyses of dreams in hysteria. It may be therefore that, having decided at first against publishing Dora's case, he was considering making similar points by means of the case of Emily. Perhaps too, it was when he was unable to bring Emily's case to any satisfactory conclusion that he decided at last to publish his case of Dora. What is striking is that in Emily's case Freud is less insistent than he is in Dora's case, although in both he wishes to make similar interpretations. One that fascinated him in both cases was that one side of his patient's inner conflict was her own sexual desire. Perhaps Dora's abrupt departure from treatment warned him of being too insistent and enabled him to await the patient arriving at her own conclusions. Emily was therefore not subjected to a symbolic repetition of her earlier experience of male intrusion, as Dora had been, by Freud ramming his ideas into her. Emily's case, moreover, points forward to themes that Freud articulated later, in his essays on sexuality, in his writings on the aetiology of hysteria and in his case of female homosexuality.

When I first read the manuscript of the book that is now in your hands, I thought it must be a fabrication. It is a story of a woman forced to kill the seducing man who had come to occupy the place of a loved parent. The woman had both to bear the guilt of this act, for which she is barely to blame, and to make her own life independently of the patronage of men. I thought there could

400

scarcely be a more apt allegory for women of our century. Having perused the text closely, having cross-checked many details and having questioned certain people who knew about Freud's Wednesday meetings, I have concluded that the case is genuine; so it is simultaneously allegorical and authentic.

The publishers have asked me to comment on some other works which are relevant – one is by Mr Nicholas Meyer, *The Seven Per-Cent Solution*, about an imagined meeting of Freud and Holmes. In the best traditions of fiction of this kind, the book ends with a chase across the Continent. As fiction, of course, it would be wrong to cavil at small inaccuracies of detail regarding Freud's life. Mr Meyer's idea for a story is an excellent one, and entertaining in execution. One can even say that if the two great men had not met, then it would be necessary to invent their meeting! This is what Mr Meyer did. Were the present work also one of fiction, it would be necessary to acknowledge with all generosity that it was Mr Meyer who first conceived the idea of such a meeting. As readers have seen, the meeting was different from the one that was imagined, and this, of course, is what we might expect – life does not always imitate art.

A second work on which I have been asked to comment is not so felicitous – it is by Dr Michael Shepherd, a professor of psychiatry. It is a pamphlet called *Sherlock Holmes and the Case of Dr Freud*. In it the author asserts that Freud's work as a whole is merely a form of fiction and is therefore not to be taken seriously. He does not say, as some have, that Freud and Holmes did not meet. He says that they do meet on the shelves of detective fiction. I cannot speak warmly of this booklet, which seems to me as tendentious in its arguments as it is superficial in its appreciation of the works to which it makes reference, many of them via secondary sources. All I shall say is that it does little for any of us with a commitment to intellectual matters to find that one who gives himself the title of 'scientist' should sneer at fiction, as if science alone were the arbiter of truth, or as if its solutions were either complete or comprehensive.

The third work to mention, one of the best academic articles on the relation of Freud and Holmes, is by Carlo Ginzburg, 'Clues: Morelli, Freud and Sherlock Holmes', published in a collection edited by Umberto Eco and Jean Sebeok entitled *The Sign of Three*. Ginzburg discusses the history of the important idea that knowledge can be derived from insignificant clues. It was Holmes who gave the best definition: 'reasoning backward from effects to causes'.* Ginzburg points out that although the method itself is ancient and widespread, embodied for instance in both the tracking of animals and in medical diagnosis, its significance as a distinctive mode of inference emerged only towards the end of the nineteenth century: for instance in the writings of C. S. Peirce, the founder of semiotics and pragmatism (who called this process of reasoning backwards 'abduction' or 'retroduction'); in the cases of Sherlock Holmes; and in the psychoanalytic work of Freud. Both the importance of this idea and the history of its emergence are still insufficiently appreciated. Ginzburg traces the first explicit discussions of it as a deliberate method, to an Italian physician, Giovanni Morelli, who wrote between 1874 and 1876 a series of articles describing how to authenticate paintings by examining unconsidered aspects – the minor details of an ear, or fingers, or toes – rather than the larger impression of the work as a whole. Morelli made attributions, both positive and negative, to many works in the galleries of Europe, for instance identifying a painting in Dresden Art Gallery believed to be a copy by Sassoferrato of a Titian, as one of the few definitive works by Giorgione. It was Morelli's

*In 'The Adventure of the Cardboard Box', in *His Last Bow*.

book that Holmes noticed on Freud's bookshelf as he and Watson were about to leave after their meeting with Freud.

A fourth work on which I have been asked to comment in relation to this case is the book by Jeffrey Masson, *The Assault on Truth: Freud's Suppression of the Seduction Theory*. Both Mr Masson and his book have caused some considerable perturbation in analytic circles. Masson's proposal was that Freud lacked moral courage and intellectual honesty, in that, although early in his work he came across evidence of women having been sexually abused in childhood, he progressively downplayed the importance of externally imposed traumata in favour of the hypothesis that neurosis is due to inner conflicts, and that memories of sexual molestation are more likely to be due to fantasy than reality. Here, of course, the narrative of Emily is among the most valuable that could be imagined, since in this case Freud writes more explicitly on this issue than elsewhere, and at a time when the question of whether hysteria was caused by actual molestation must have been most acute for him. It is significant for assessing the later development of his ideas that we now know that Freud came into possession of evidence of an external and independent kind, brought via Holmes, that Emily had been sexually abused in a highly damaging way.

If we were simply to side with Masson, we could offer the discovery of these manuscripts as showing that Freud had been confronted directly with this evidence of one of his patients having been subjected to childhood seduction, and agree that Freud had taken a wrong turning by not emphasising the importance of early sexual traumata. In some ways I am attracted to this interpretation of events. The case of Emily makes Masson's argument against Freud seem damning. Rereading some of Freud's later work in the light of Emily's case has, however, given me pause. The influence of Emily's case on the

Three Essays on the Theory of Sexuality* is clear enough, but from then on, the lesson that Freud learnt from Emily seems to have been progressively forgotten, and this cannot but be cause for regret.

I think, however, that there is another interpretation, which in the end is the one I prefer. Though one cannot say for sure, I think what must have happened is that, as Emily herself suggests, the encounter with Holmes made clear to Freud that his patients themselves could only ever bring to him reliable evidence of a particular kind, of their own inner worlds. Evidence from the outer world, for instance of what really happened in childhood or indeed at any other time, was simply not available to him while pursuing the methods of the couch. The outer world is the world of detection and forensic science, the science to which Holmes contributed. This world even coincides with the world of detailed empirical research in social science. With the method of free association which Freud had by then developed, such a world would never be open to him. So if Freud had a contribution to make it had to concern just the inner worlds of his patients, and the interactions of patient and analyst in the consulting room. This world is one of wishes and perhaps of fantasies. So, on reflection, and although I much regret that Freud was not more influenced by his meeting with Holmes, and more particularly by his work with Emily herself, I believe that by continuing to explore this inner world Freud made the contribution that he was cut out to make. Without his explorations the twentieth century would be much the poorer.

Finally we turn to Emily's journal and narrative. Some readers may think that, written in 1904, these have a surprising directness. Emily herself says that twelve years after the events

*Published in 1905, the same year as the case of Dora, and a year after seeing Emily.

404

she corrected the punctuation of her narrative. The manuscript of Emily's part of this account is carefully written as a fair copy. So knowing Emily's somewhat obsessional character I think we can infer that in 1916 or 1917 she went carefully through her original journal entries and narrative, probably making alterations of both style and content, to produce the fair copy that has survived. Possibly she thought that with a fair copy she would then be in a position to see whether she could abstract parts of it, or perhaps even transform it substantially for publication in some form.

In its liveliness and directness, Emily's writing shows the influence of her turn-of-the-century American education and of contemporary writing of that time, for instance of William James. By the time of her revision she would also have been subjected to, and taken part in, the literary debates and influences of the intellectual community of which she was part in Paris – for instance she refers obliquely to Gertrude Stein, and no doubt there were others. We know that in that community there was a great deal of debate about style, and we may suppose that this was a subject of interest to Emily herself. Because of her reluctance to publish on her own behalf, she did not become part of the modernist movement in literature, in which this same Paris environment was an influential centre. Her directness of style, the explicitness of the sexual parts of her writing, and her concern with inwardness would have been expressions of new developments that women were making on the Paris Left Bank at the time.

Emily herself was an early feminist, having been educated at Bryn Mawr, one of the first universitites to award degrees to women. No doubt Freud was challenged by this fact. One would like to think that this too would have influenced his later work, though I have to say that it is regrettable that this influence was not more substantial. I suppose this should not surprise us. The unconscious thoughts of male prejudice are rooted in society and are no more easy to challenge and divert than those of individual neuroses.

In some of her reflections, particularly of her separation of the biological from the social significance of the male organ, Emily strikingly anticipates Lacan.* It is sad that with such incisive thinking occurring at such an early date Emily should not have written books of more directly feminist and literary influence instead of confining herself to translating the classics as she did. Sara also was a remarkable woman, and though she is remembered in Paris for her work in women's education, few will have heard of her further afield. In therapy too she made a contribution: her plan of reuniting Emily with her godmother very strikingly anticipates a procedure that became current sixty years later with the advent of family therapy.

It is sad that neither Emily nor Sara made any contribution to published psychological thinking at the time. This failure of the woman's voice to be heard at the beginning of the century was, as we all know, very common. What is significant about this book is that despite impediments we see a female discourse growing up alongside two distinctively male discourses, those of Freud and Watson.

At first this female discourse, speaking as it does of fear and confusion, then of love, runs alongside the male ones of the scientific investigation of inner and outer worlds. Finally the male discourses in this story fade, and we are left with a narrative of courage to endure the uncertainty of possible guilt. Most of the interactions between the male and female elements occur in the first two books of this volume, where, unusually, male and female voices are heard in counterpoint. How different these

*E.g. in 'The Signification of the Phallus', translated into English by A. Sheridan in J. Lacan, *Ecrits: A Selection*.

voices are. Freud thinks Emily hysterical, while she sees herself as having had to struggle from an unprepossessing start in an alien world, overtaken by an evil she does not understand. Holmes is predisposed to find someone guilty, and his gaze comes to rest upon her, whereas she, having grown up with the same social mores, also sees herself as guilty, but hopes to exonerate herself in some way.

From our own perspective, I think the issues remain problematic for each of us, however we view those events that occurred at the beginning of the century in which we live.